LOVE ME DO TO LOVE ME DON'T

The Beatles on Record

Spencer Leigh

McNIDDER & GRACE

Published by McNidder & Grace
16A Bridge Street
Carmarthen
SA31 3JS
www.mcnidderandgrace.co.uk

First published in 2016
©Spencer Leigh
www.spencerleigh.co.uk

Every effort has been made to obtain necessary permission with reference
to copyright material. The publisher apologises if, inadvertently, any sources
remain unacknowledged and will be glad to make the necessary arrangements at
the earliest opportunity.

A catalogue record for this work is available from the British Library.
ISBN: 9780857161345

Designed by Obsidian Design

Printed and bound in the United Kingdom by
Short Run Press, Exeter, UK

ABOUT THE AUTHOR

The journalist, author and BBC broadcaster Spencer Leigh was born in Liverpool, England, and is an acknowledged authority on the Beatles. He has been broadcasting his weekly show, *On the Beat*, on BBC Radio Merseyside for 30 years and over that time has conducted more interviews about the band – all captured on tape – than anyone in the world. He has written over twenty-five books, hundreds of album sleeve notes and he has written obituaries of musicians for the *Independent* and the *Oxford Dictionary of National Biography*. He is an Honoured Friend at the Liverpool Institute of Performing Arts (LIPA), co-founded by Sir Paul McCartney, and he has a Gold Badge of Merit from the British Academy of Songwriters, Composers and Authors. Spencer will always live on Merseyside.

Spencer Leigh is also the author of:
Best of the Beatles: The Sacking of Pete Best
The Cavern Club: Rise of the Beatles and Merseybeat
Frank Sinatra: An Extraordinary Life
Simon & Garfunkel: Together Alone

ACKNOWLEDGMENTS

Some years ago a member of staff at BBC Radio Merseyside was showing some visitors around and when she got to me, she said, "This is Spencer Leigh: he interviews the Searchers." I thought it a very amusing remark and quite possibly, some people think that my passion for interviewing beat group musicians is a full-time job.

And in a way it is.

In the 1980s, I wrote a book about Merseybeat, *Let's Go Down the Cavern*, which was packed with first-hand quotes from 200 musicians, promoters and fans and based on a series of the same name for BBC Radio Merseyside. It was unique for its time and very well reviewed but looking at it now, I think I believed anything that anyone told me. I didn't realise that Pinocchio was alive and well and living on Merseyside. Now I hope I can separate the fact from the fiction.

In the 1990s, I was again using my interviews for *Speaking Words of Wisdom; Reflections on the Beatles*, which was published by Cavern City Tours. It did okay but it is long out of print and, in 2010, it was expanded into *Tomorrow Never Knows: The Beatles on Record*, which was published by a Southport company, Nirvana Books. It was marketed around Merseyside, and McNidder and Grace, which has published several of my books in recent years, thought it deserved a much wider circulation. This, with some changes, updates and expansions, has become *Love Me Do to Love Me Don't: The Beatles on Record*.

The sub-title is *The Beatles on Record* as I wanted to tie the book in with the remastering of the Beatles' catalogue in 2009. Since then, the Beatles' catalogue has, after long negotiations, appeared on iTunes, but is not available on Spotify and YouTube. The Beatles created their music 50 years ago but they are determined that you are not going to hear it for free. You can purchase the Beatles' individual tracks for 99p each and maybe the lot for £125, and yet in this curious new world we live in, you will have nothing physical to show for your purchase.

My thanks to everyone I have spoken to for this book and to Ron Ellis, Bill Heckle, Dave Jones, Billy Butler, John Firminger, Mick O'Toole and Mick Ord. I am very pleased to count the Beatles' historian Mark Lewisohn as one of my friends, not least because we can swop phone numbers of people we have traced. I am especially grateful to Andy Peden Smith of McNidder & Grace for his belief in this book.

How time flies. At the time of writing the original book, I did not know that Jimmy Savile and Rolf Harris were such reprehensible characters. I had spoken to them about their connections with the Beatles and I think that what they say is valid and should remain in the text.

You can read this book either quickly or slowly. I would recommend the latter and that you read it with your Beatles collection to hand – vinyl, CD or digital. It is easier to appreciate the observations of some contributors when you can hear the music as well.

Bear in mind that some negative opinions come not from a jaded Albert Goldman-style outlook but from noted musicians, people who can justifiably comment on the Beatles' abilities and, perhaps, limitations. Mind you, I'm used to hearing negative comments about the Beatles every day: my wife Anne is completely Beatled out.

Spencer Leigh
Liverpool, July 2016

CONTENTS

INTRODUCTION

The heading on the press release said that the Beatles' entire original recorded catalogue had been remastered by Apple Corps Ltd and EMI Music for worldwide release on 9 September 2009.

In 2010 the UK retail price for the box set containing the stereo mixes was around £200 usually discounted to £170: still a high price for fourteen albums spread over sixteen CDs. It was roughly 80p, a track, the same price as downloads had they been available. The price was similar in the rest of the world but by the end of the month I knew the recession was over as 2.25 million copies had been sold. In addition, there were huge sales from the specialist box set of mono mixes (ten albums over twelve CDs) and priced, despite fewer tracks, at £240, discounted to £200. In addition, the individual stereo albums were sold separately and clocked up spectacular sales with *Abbey Road* being the top seller. All this for a group that had disbanded around 45 years earlier. Close to a billion pounds had been spent on the Beatles.

More than anything else, these gigantic sale figures were a triumph of marketing over content: we were being sold what we already had at inflated prices. In most instances, the purchasers would spot few differences. My preference, anyway, is for the tracks the raw and rough way I first heard them on cheap equipment in the 60s. Their youthful enthusiasm shone through and did the Beatles, of all groups, now need increased brightness?

In 1954, when Elvis Presley started recording for Sun, the LP was in its infancy. Record companies started packaging old singles by Frank Sinatra, Bing Crosby and Glenn Miller on albums, but they were not promoted heavily. They considered that there was only a limited market for old records – confined perhaps to diehard fans – and thus concentrated on promoting the new. Now, reissuing and often expanding the contents is a fact of life: Penguin Books bought the Beatrix Potter franchise and went through a similar exercise. Jack Kerouac's original manuscript for *On the Road* has been published and has added greatly to our knowledge of the writer.

On 9 September in 2010, I went into an HMV store in Liverpool just to see if folk were buying the remasters. They certainly were and to reach the counter, were walking past box sets of Abba remasters – the complete Abba collection, spread over nine CDs and only £15 per set.

Despite the media blitz, there was not that much extra on offer. We were told that the Beatles catalogue had been digitally remastered for the first time. This was an exercise in semantics. They had been digitally mastered for CD in 1987 and now they were being remastered. Listening at home, I couldn't detect much difference. Then I played 'Hey Bulldog' on a radio programme and felt it was pulsating with excitement. It sounded so new and vibrant over the station's speakers that I wondered if other listeners had the same reaction.

The CDs were reissued with their original art work, much reduced in size but with expanded booklets and brief video documentaries about each album, directed by Bob Smeaton and only viewable on computers. The documentaries were available for a limited period: why so parsimonious? To reinforce the message, "Buy now – don't even wait for Christmas."

By 2009, the CD was losing its popularity to downloads but the Beatles resisted that technology for as long as they could. In the same way, those first Beatle CDs hadn't appeared until 1987: definitely a late entry in the field. It was difficult to see the Beatles' reasoning for lagging behind other acts in the technology stakes: was it to build up demand? Okay, they ignored younger fans (for a while at least) who only wanted downloads but commercially speaking, hadn't their strategy been right? They had built up the demand for their product.

Nevertheless, the indications suggested that the Beatles did want younger fans. On 9 September 2009, the well-received video game *The Beatles: Rock Band* hit the shops, the first time that the Beatles had released a product that I didn't want. As Apple approved it, I suppose it must be a good example of the genre. However, there is no assessment in this book: life's too short to play video games (especially at my age) and, besides, real life is exciting enough for me, thank you very much.

However, I am aware *The Beatles: Rock Band* has one intriguing spin-off feature: it isolates the contributions of the individual Beatles for many of the key tracks.

In 1995, the world had been awash with the Beatles at the time of their TV series, *Anthology*. Over the next couple of years, three double CDs were issued under the *Anthology* title: over six hours of alternate takes, live versions and a few unreleased songs. The first volume sold 13 million copies. It was churlish not to include these performances on the remasters, but heck, they can be used in a few years' time, perhaps for another marketing hype. The remastered *Live at the BBC* anybody? Whatever happened to that vinyl album *The Beatles at the Hollywood Bowl* recorded in August 1964, but not issued until 1977? Why aren't their Christmas singles for the fan club on CD? If we are into digital remastering what about a whizz-bang-super reworking of those tapes from the Star-Club, Hamburg from December 1962? That really would be a challenge. More bites from the Apple are likely. Not maybe. Definitely. I can't even see the issue of the complete *Complete Beatles* taking place in my lifetime.

Although I'm sounding sceptical, I'm not really. I'm all for anything that gets new audiences to appreciate this music. After all, the Beatles are the keystone of modern culture. However, Apple and the otherwise troubled EMI could have shown more generosity and provided better value for money. Look at the monumental first volume of Neil Young's archives. This is a truly creative package, made with the full assistance of the performer. The trouble here is the artist himself: it's hard to listen to Neil Young for several hours at a time.

And what will happen next? Can we claim our money back on the original CDs under false claims as to their quality? I'm being flippant but Led Zeppelin fans would have a strong case as the band members themselves have complained about poor mastering on their original CDs. Of course you can't get your money back but a trade-in allowance on your old CDs would have been a fantastic marketing ploy, if an administrative nightmare.

What do purchasers do with their old albums? Maybe the first issues of the Beatles' CDs will be flooding charity shops but I doubt it. There are, after all, relatively few vinyl albums by the Beatles in their racks. These racks are still full of the more mundane and ephemeral artists and it suggests that purchasers hang on to their Beatle records. The Beatles are a special case, but you know that.

How did the Beatles manage it? And what makes them so special? How did they get so far ahead of the pack? This is what this book is about and you don't have to take my word for it as the book is packed with extracts from my interviews with their fellow musicians. I have always been careful not to lead the witness and all the quotes accurately reflect, I believe, what the interviewees think.

In the 60s the Beatles were certainly the top group, but they were not *that* far ahead of the competition – the Rolling Stones, the Beach Boys, the Who and the Kinks always rivalled them at some aspect of their work: live performance, record production, street cred or carefully crafted material.

The Beatles were still on top when they broke up although the public were tiring of 'johnandyoko' and disputes within the band. Their bitter comments reflected the end of a marriage. In the 70s, there was a backlash against the Beatles as they were regarded as 'pop' rather than 'rock'. At the same time, though, ELO were fashioning a career from 'A Day in the Life'. The punk groups denied the Beatles and, indeed, everyone else but this was largely affectation and was out of a desire to start, as it were, at Year Zero. Glen Matlock of the Sex Pistols has since told me that he loved the music of the Small Faces, the Who and the Beatles.

Things have changed again: Oasis owed a huge debt to the Beatles and so do many other bands, sometimes less obviously. The Beatles, unlike the neophytes, were writing the rule book and most acts have followed that. They have defined a huge amount of popular culture, from the way that music is written, played and produced, down to the way we dress.

Here's proof of their versatility. If a writer is said to be Pinteresque, we know what that means: he is copying the menace and foreboding, often with chilling silences, that occur throughout Harold Pinter's plays. If we say a band is Beatlesque, what do we mean? ELO and Oasis are both Beatlesque but they don't sound the same. Are 'From Me to You', 'Penny Lane' and 'Hey Jude' all Beatlesque?

I come from Liverpool and oddly, there seems to be more criticism of the Beatles here than anywhere else. People often say, "What did they do for Liverpool?" There is a long answer to that, given in this book, but the short answer is "They were born here, la, that's enough."

Author's Note
Roughly speaking, the exchange rate during the main period the book covers was $3 to £1. The British currency was pounds (£), shillings (s) and pence (d). There were 20 shillings to a pound and 12 pennies to a shilling and the population was much better at mental arithmetic.

CHAPTER 1

Somewhere Boys

I don't say we're the chosen race but there is a feeling of being special if you were born in Liverpool and this can irritate outsiders. Liverpool poet Roger McGough: "If you were asked to choose somewhere to be brought up, you would pick somewhere else, but I was told I was lucky. You're lucky to be born in Liverpool; you're lucky to be born a Catholic; you're lucky to be born short-sighted; and you're lucky to be born during the Blitz."

Even Raul Malo of the Mavericks has picked up on the special vibe of Liverpool. "Before I came to England, people were telling me how reserved the English were. Then I came to Liverpool and found the Scousers were fantastic. They remind me of the mid-west: good hard working people who love to be entertained and love music and want to have fun. Anyone who says the English are reserved hasn't been to Liverpool."

Liverpool comic Ken Dodd: "Liverpool exports more entertainers than any other city in the world and, whatever else Liverpool entertainers do, it's always done with tremendous enthusiasm. People in Liverpool live their lives in a higher gear than most people. We're very enthusiastic, and the Beatles were four young men with a tremendous desire for life and with the typical Liverpool trait of not caring what they said. They ad-libbed everything and they personified life and brought a lot of credit to Liverpool."

Liverpool is often said to be the fifth Beatle, but it was so important that it could almost be the first Beatle. Dr Ian Biddle, lecturer in music at Newcastle University: "Being a port city, Liverpool had an influence on the Beatles. There was a constant inflow and outflow of people from all over the world, and it was an outward looking city. There were lots of venues and a large young population with growing amounts of disposable income. Large port cities always inspire creativity and the Beatles' natural Scouse ingenuity enabled them to draw on influences from everywhere leading to a mishmash of musical styles. Hamburg, being a similar sort of city, naturally went crazy for the Beatles."

To answer why Liverpool is so special would merit a book in itself. Frankie Vaughan, talking to me in 1998, summed it up. He was raised in poor housing just outside the city centre but it didn't bother him. "I consider Liverpool to be the great melting pot. People from all walks of life with different faiths and different colours have settled here. In Liverpool, you were accepted as long as you were a kindly, reasonable person. I really understand Liverpool, with its wonderful people and its great sense of humour. We took a bashing during the war and then were promised that the city would be rebuilt and yet I am still looking at bombsites. The heart of Liverpool is something very, very special. We don't want much out of life, just a break occasionally and a chance to make a reasonable living. The sooner we get the people back into the city itself the better as that is where the heart is." Though Frankie Vaughan died the following year, the regeneration he wanted is now taking place.

The rebuilding of the city centre with the Liverpool One development is very impressive, yet you only have to walk a quarter of a mile to see neglect and dereliction. Despite the recession, Liverpool is, for the most part, thriving. Tourists flock to the city and many feature films are made here. The opening sequence of *Nowhere Boy* shows John Lennon running amidst the columns of St George's Hall. The city looks magnificent, but this is the Liverpool of today. Fifty-odd years earlier, in the chronology of the film, the building was black and grimy and being law courts back then, it is unlikely that anyone would have run across the front. On the other hand, the scene can be accepted as a dream sequence.

Nowhere Boy is the story of the adolescent John Lennon and how his group, the Quarry Men, developed into the Beatles. A director's main concern is usually to tell a good story and as a result, historical accuracy often falls by the wayside. Although I would quibble over details with any film that covers 18 years of life in an hour and a half, *Nowhere Boy* has been exceptionally well made and is a superb reflection of growing up in Liverpool in the 1950s.

The tug of war between John Lennon's mother, Julia, and his aunt, Mimi, does not concern this book, except inasmuch as John's character was shaped by his relationships with them. John did poorly at school, not for lack of intelligence but because he couldn't apply his mind to studying. Mimi's attempts to bring him into line failed, largely because John's interests lay elsewhere.

Late in 1954, rock'n'roll came to the UK with Bill Haley and his Comets' 'Shake, Rattle And Roll', to be followed in the new year by the battle-cry of the new music, 'Rock Around The Clock'. To outsiders, rock'n'roll appeared to be a short-lived novelty music, but then, in May 1956, came the evidence that this music was here to stay – Elvis Presley's 'Heartbreak Hotel', which climbed to No.2. It was a very different sound to 'Rock Around The Clock' – Albert Goldman called it a 'psychodrama' – and it shows that critics who said rock'n'roll sounded the same were talking nonsense. Rock'n'roll was to split the generations. At the time, I never met anyone over 30 with a good word for it, but we know John Lennon's mother, Julia, loved Elvis.

It was so hard to hear the new music as the BBC was very restrictive about what it played. I was too young to hear 'Heartbreak Hotel' in a record shop listening booth, and I eventually heard it in the *Five To Ten* slot on the BBC Light Programme, where it was being denounced by a minister as an example of delinquency. I had no interest in fairground rides but I liked to go to Pleasureland in Southport and soak in the rock'n'roll music being played over the loudspeakers on the rides. Rock'n'roll always sounded great in that context, one reason why the David Essex film, *That'll Be The Day*, was so evocative.

Steve Turner, author of *The Gospel According to the Beatles*: "It was as difficult to hear music then as it is to get away from it now. It made rock'n'roll even more exciting and when you bought a single, you couldn't play it in the living room because your parents didn't want to hear it. You had to go to your bedroom and it was a special experience, it wasn't like walking around with an iPod. When you played the single in your bedroom, you couldn't play it too loud and anyway, record players didn't have a lot of volume. Even jukeboxes weren't that loud. A fairground was the only place where you could hear rock'n'roll at full volume. A generation growing up today wouldn't understand what the music meant to us at the time, what kind of impact it had. Seeing somebody with long hair in the 50s was staggering: you'd stand and stare at them. Now you can have your hair cut any way you want. To be a Teddy Boy was making a really big statement."

Up until that time, the popular music of the day had been safe, well-sung ballads and cheerful, often novelty, songs, but the hipper youngsters, especially university students, preferred jazz. Chris

Barber's banjo player, Lonnie Donegan, encouraged Barber to include American folk songs in their performance such as Huddie Ledbetter's 'Rock Island Line'. Redeploying an American word for house party music, it became known as skiffle and although Donegan recorded 'Rock Island Line' for the album *New Orleans Joys* in 1954, it wasn't a hit single until January 1956, just a few months before 'Heartbreak Hotel'. Although Donegan was forever knocking rock'n'roll, the two forms of music had much in common. Donegan largely ignored the skiffle trademarks of washboard and tea-chest bass, preferring professional instrumentation.

With a cheap, mail order acoustic guitar, John Lennon formed the Quarry Men, largely with schoolfriends, and on Saturday 6 July 1957, they played a fête at St Peter's Parish Church, close to his home in Woolton. The tapes surviving from this period indicate that the Quarry Men in *Nowhere Boy* were more accomplished, but then they had to keep the audience in the cinema.

Paul Du Noyer, author of a history of Liverpool music, aptly called *Wondrous Place*: "It's tempting to say that I can see the seeds of genius in the Quarry Men but of course I can't. 'That'll Be The Day' is a bunch of lads singing a hesitant version of a Buddy Holly song. The Beatles came to life when Lennon and McCartney began to ignite as a songwriting partnership. Prior to that, they were a very accomplished band with terrific power; they were a storming rock band at the club stage, and they didn't have much competition in terms of live rock'n'roll at the time. It wasn't until they began to write original songs that something truly magical took place."

During that afternoon at St Peter's, John Lennon met Paul McCartney: in the film, John seems old for his years and Paul too young and gawky, but maybe that's the way it was. The meeting is skilfully handled and, in cultural terms, is as significant as Stanley greeting Livingstone. The date is significant too – just go forward two weeks. The aftermath of the war brought further hardships and rationing but on 20 July 1957, the Conservative Prime Minister, Harold Macmillan announced, "Most of our people have never had it so good."

Owned by a dockland doctor's son, Alan Sytner, the Cavern club opened in the basement of a warehouse building in Mathew Street, close to Liverpool's city centre, on 16 January 1957. Its policy was to "put Liverpool on the map as the leading jazz cellar in the country outside London". At the time, you were more likely to find jazz and dance bands in the city centre, but the new beat and skiffle music was being played in the suburbs. Because of the connection to Leadbelly and Josh White, skiffle groups were tolerated at the Cavern and the Quarry Men with John Lennon as leader and lead vocalist played there on 7 August 1957, Paul McCartney being at scout camp in the Lake District.

Colin Hanton was the Quarry Men's drummer: "We did some skiffle numbers to start off with at the Cavern but we also did rock'n'roll. John Lennon was passed a note and he said to the audience, 'We've had a request'. He opened it up and it was Alan Sytner saying, 'Cut out the bloody rock'n'roll.'"

Alan Sytner: "Skiffle was a breeding ground for musicians - one or two of them became jazz musicians, but more ended up doing rock'n'roll. I knew John Lennon quite well as we lived in the same area: he lived 400 yards up the road from me. He was 16 and arrogant and hadn't got a clue, but that was John Lennon."

John Lennon's childhood friend, Pete Shotton: "I'd known John since he was seven years old. The fame, the money, the status he achieved, never affected the fundamental person that he was. He was a classic example of what Kirk Douglas said, 'Success doesn't change you: it changes the people around you.' A lot of people do change and become full of their own self-importance but that never happened to John, maybe because he felt pretty self-important from the time I met him. He always had enormous confidence in himself."

By 1958, John and Paul were writing together. Although usually one would have the main idea and structure, they would complete the song together. Most of their early songs are forgotten now, but several did emerge in the 60s. Although they didn't know it, they had written several hit songs before they signed their EMI contract in 1962. Not always in their finished state, they included 'Love Me Do' (written in 1958), 'Hello Little Girl', 'Love Of The Loved', 'A World Without Love', 'Like Dreamers Do' and even 'When I'm Sixty-Four'. Sometime during the summer of 1958, they made a private recording at Percy Phillips' small studio at 38 Kensington, Liverpool: John sang lead on both the Crickets' 'That'll Be the Day' and a rare Paul McCartney and George Harrison composition, 'In Spite of All the Danger'. Today there's a plaque above the doorway.

When we think of the individual members of the Beatles, we recite John, Paul, George and Ringo. It doesn't sound right in any other order and it is the correct hierarchy as well as historically noting when they joined. John Lennon formed the group and Paul McCartney came second. Although John was the leader (dominantly so in the early years), Paul recommended George Harrison and so, early on, he was capable of getting his way. The drummer Pete Best joined them for club dates in Hamburg in 1960 and he was replaced by Ringo Starr in 1962.

Laurence Juber, session guitarist and member of Wings, says, "When I worked with George Harrison, he told me that when he was 13, he had some jazz guitar lessons from someone on the boats who was familiar with Django Reinhardt. Those diminished chords that George uses came from Django, so he was a very sophisticated guitar player." For proof, listen to George and Pete Ham from Badfinger play 'Here Comes the Sun' on acoustic guitars during the 1971 *Concert for Bangladesh*.

With a new owner, Ray McFall, the Cavern succumbed to beat music and the Beatles were to play there around 280 times. There were many other venues for beat music in the area including the Jacaranda (owned by Allan Williams), the Casbah (run by Pete Best's mother Mona and opened by the Quarry Men in August 1959), the Iron Door, the Mardi Gras, the Grafton Rooms, Blair Hall, Lathom Hall, Wilson Hall Aintree Institute, the Orrell Park Ballroom and, over in Birkenhead, the Majestic Ballroom. By 1962, the Cavern was one of the UK's leading beat venues.

The 1960 Scottish tour on which the fledgling Beatles backed Larry Parnes' protégé, Johnny Gentle (born John Askew), also from Liverpool, had not led to regular work from the London impresario. As Parnes was a shrewd businessman, this suggests that their own spot was not as good as some reports suggest. John Lennon helped Gentle to complete 'I've Just Fallen for Someone', which he released under a second pseudonym, Darren Young, in 1962. We've only Gentle's word for this but I believe him, chiefly because Lennon's contribution, the middle eight, is clearly derived from one of his favourite records, 'Money (That's What I Want)' by Barrett Strong, released in 1959. It is the first example of John Lennon's songwriting, albeit uncredited, on record.

Pete Frame, famed for his *Rock Family Trees*, remarks: "When all the bands were starting in Liverpool, the records they were playing and getting excited about were by Jerry Lee Lewis, Chuck Berry, the Everly Brothers and Elvis Presley. They were records made for the white American teenage market or the mixed American market as it was becoming clear that you couldn't segregate the airwaves. These records sounded so much more exciting than the English ones, which at the time were very tinny. Americans think it is bad that they had to put up with Pat Boone and the Crew Cuts, but we had to put up with *The Billy Cotton Band Show* and Ray Pilgrim with the David Ede Orchestra: absolutely rubbish versions which murdered the original records. We idolised American records, as indeed we idolised everything American. Their sports were more exotic, and we thought that they had better coffee and better candy and better architecture. They had the skyscrapers, the cars, the girls, the mountains, the rivers, the Grand Canyon, the cowboys, the gangsters and the movies. Everything about America was better than England. All our parents had had it really bad in the war but we were liberated from that and we just wanted to enjoy ourselves and have a great time."

The standard group format emerged of four white teenagers playing lead guitar, rhythm guitar, bass guitar (the electric bass was then a new instrument) and drums: that is, the same as the Shadows and the eventual line-up of the Beatles. There were variations such as Les Maguire playing keyboards with the Pacemakers or Brian Jones on saxophone with the Undertakers. There was the occasional female vocalist – Beryl Marsden, in particular, gigged far more than Cilla Black – and some black performers: Derry Wilkie and the Chants vocal group.

The 300-plus groups drew their inspiration from American rock'n'roll and obscure rhythm and blues. It is often said that the Liverpool sailors going to New York on the liners – the so-called Cunard Yanks – brought a lot of these records back to Liverpool. Although this happened with jazz and country, I am less convinced about beat music. How did the Cunard Yanks know which records to buy? Moreover, this theory ignores the fact that the original version of every one of the 300-odd covers recorded by Liverpool beat bands was released in the UK at the time on such labels as Oriole, London American (for the Decca group), Stateside (EMI) and Pye International.

The most likely source for their repertoire was Brian Epstein's record shop NEMS in Whitechapel, some 400 yards from the Cavern. Epstein had the enlightened policy of stocking every record that was released in the UK and potential customers could sample the records in listening booths.

Pete Best: "We were very friendly with the girls behind the counter at NEMS, which worked in our favour. We would go into the listening-booths and they would play us the new releases. If there was one we liked, we'd hear it a couple of times, write down the chords – there was nothing very complicated in those days – and then disappear very quickly to rehearse it before we forgot what it sounded like. We owe those girls a debt of gratitude but Brian didn't approve. He'd glare at us when we came in. We were taking up his valuable selling space."

Billy Bragg: "If the Beatles had grown up only listening to English music, how boring would they have been? They would have been awful. They grew up listening to the music of black America. Conversely, that inspired them to write the most English music of the latter half of the twentieth century. What that says about the process of writing the music of your country is very interesting. We shouldn't overlook this: it is an example of the diversity and multiculturalism that has enriched English culture."

A key reason for the multiplicity of beat groups in Liverpool and indeed around the country was the abolition of National Service. Pete Frame: "Our generation was very lucky – it was the first generation not to be called up. When they did abandon National Service, a lot of youths, instead of going into the army for two years, went into a group for two years. Then they got married and settled down, and their wives cut their guitar strings!"

Playing in Hamburg for hard German club managers was no piece of cake. Horst Fascher, the tough-minded manager of the Star-Club, admits: "Some English military bands played swing and we had some jazz and rhythm and blues in Hamburg, but no rock'n'roll. The very first group we had was led by Tony Sheridan. It was a surprise to see rock'n'roll music live on stage. He was wild and he'd sweat all over. Within five minutes he looked as though he'd come out of the baths and we liked him very much. He did *mach schau*. You see, to have a band on stage, standing there and only singing and playing, was not enough. You have to *mach schau*, do a show, put on a show. That was what I wanted and I liked the Beatles doing funny things on stage, although I had to be strong with them. Sometimes they got heavily into drink and I would say that work is work and drink is drink. When they were too pissed, I had to kick them in the arse."

Tony Sheridan, a disruptive rock'n'roller from Norwich who had worked for Larry Parnes, found himself at home in Hamburg. "When

I got to Hamburg, I found that there was no German musical scene as the war had left a void. We shocked everybody and they all flocked in. You could get killed in Hamburg but the musicians were blessed. All the gangsters, all the pimps and all the prostitutes loved us."

Pete Best: "There are lots of anecdotes and funny stories about the things we did in Hamburg. If you compare them with today's standards of living, they seem tame, but, going back to when it happened, we were wild. We wrecked places; we'd fall about drunk and act the goat on stage. Women in Hamburg were no bother – they were ours for the taking – we were healthy young lads and we enjoyed ourselves."

Gruelling nights in Hamburg developed both the groups' repertoires and their stamina, although Tony Sheridan was equally influential. John Lennon's famous stance was copied from Sheridan as well as Gerry Marsden placing his guitar high on the chest.

Johnny Hutchinson, drummer with the Big Three: "It was as though the Beatles had gone to Hamburg with an old banger and had come back with a Rolls-Royce. The Beatles owe everything to Tony Sheridan because they copied him to a T. They copied his style on guitar. Sheridan was a fantastic guitarist, the governor."

Tony Jackson of the Searchers: "Tony Sheridan was a tremendous guitar player with a wonderful sense of feeling and a great image on stage. He had a magnetic personality and you couldn't take your eyes off him. Every Liverpool guitarist picked something up from Sheridan's way of playing. Instead of just playing major chords, he would make it into a 7th to give it more of a bluesy feel."

Paul McCartney founded the Liverpool Institute for Performing Arts (LIPA), but he has acknowledged that the courses might not have been suitable for the Beatles. Music writer Paul Du Noyer: "Very few bands get the kind of intensive apprenticeship that the Beatles got in Hamburg. They played several sets a night, day in and day out, and it must have helped them in forming an affinity with each other. Lennon and McCartney could read each other's mind on stage and it stood them in good stead when they became a songwriting team. It toughened them up as people and as musicians."

The Beatles' appearance at Litherland Town Hall on 27 December 1960, for which they were billed as 'Direct from Germany', was the turning-point. From then on, they wanted to sound distinctive and look different from their rivals, although, of course, many bands were to copy them. They set new standards in scruffiness, although they were uniform in their untidiness, i.e. "Leather jackets tonight, chaps."

Tony Sanders of Billy J. Kramer's first group, the Coasters: "A friend of mine told me about the fabulous group he'd seen at Litherland Town Hall. He said 'They're all German. They wear cowboy boots and they stamp on the stage.' A few weeks later we were coming off stage at Aintree Institute and these guys were coming on next. Lennon wore a leather jacket and McCartney had a jacket that looked as though he'd been sleeping in it for months, but when they kicked off it was unbelievable. They were all smoking cigarettes and that tickled us because it went right against convention. They were so cheeky with it. Instead of trying to look good, they didn't give a damn. They played 'Wooden Heart' with Pete Best on bass drum and hi-hat. He was only using one hand and he was smoking with the other. We thought this was tremendous. We were all smoking next time we went on stage, but it didn't go with our short haircuts and boy-next-door image."

John McNally of the Searchers: "They had just come back from Hamburg and they appeared at St John's, Bootle with us – Johnny Sandon and the Searchers. They went on before us and they made 'Roll Over Beethoven' last for ten minutes because they put three guitar solos in it. Most of the bands were playing very controlled, rhythmic bass drum patterns but Bestie was playing straight fours. It was thump, thump, thump all of the time, which was really unusual at the time."

Don Andrew from the ultra-slick Remo Four: "We were shocked that they commanded such a following when they looked so dirty and made such a horrible, deafening row. We were intent on making our guitars sound as nice as possible, and Colin Manley changed his strings religiously. He got the real Fender sound out of his guitar and they came along with big amplifiers and a big throbbing noise."

Unlike other Liverpool beat groups, the Beatles were professionals, i.e. no day jobs, which gave them time to discover obscure American songs and so develop a large repertoire. It enabled John and Paul to work on their writing partnership although those songs only emerged gradually in their performances. Supremely confident in their ability, they thought nothing of switching from menacing rhythm and blues to 'Over the Rainbow' or Wilfred Pickles' 'Have a go, Joe' theme. Late at night they might slip into straight blues.

No one had been surprised when the Beatles' then bass player, Stu Sutcliffe, left the Beatles in April 1961 to remain in Hamburg and develop his artistic talents, although his death a year later shocked the Beatles. Stu was close to John Lennon and his death added to the complexity of Lennon's psyche. Mike Evans, author of *The Art of the Beatles*: "The Beatles had been a fairly *ad hoc* band, thrown together, an electric skiffle group if you like, and they grew better by hard practice which occurred mainly in Germany. Stu Sutcliffe didn't leave the group for conspicuous musical reasons such as not being good enough. He simply wanted to get back to painting."

Pete Frame: "Most of the musicians who went to art school did it because it was a good lig and you could get by with doing very little work. You could get your posters done for nothing and you could rehearse. Very few musicians who went to art school produced anything in the way of real art. Stuart Sutcliffe was an exception, perhaps *the* exception. You could tell by the sheer number of paintings that he produced that he was intensely interested, and from what one reads, he wasn't concerned about pursuing a musical career at all. The others – Eric Clapton, Ray Davies, Pete Townshend, right through to the Belle Stars, the Clash and Wreckless Eric – used art school as a lig so that they could practise."

In 1961, Tony Sheridan and the Beatles (John, Paul, George and Pete) recorded a session for the German bandleader and record producer, Bert Kaempfert, at the Friedrich Ebert Halle in Hamburg, which was a school assembly hall.

Tony Sheridan: "Bert Kaempfert came into the Top Ten club with his entourage and he bought us all drinks. He told us that he would like to record myself and the Beatles. When we did the session in June 1961, we went to bed at five and got up at eight to record. We took uppers to keep awake. Bert told us to record something that the Germans would understand. They knew 'My Bonnie' because it was taught in English lessons. 'My Bonnie' is public domain, so I would have expected to get the royalties for arranging it. However, the guy who wrote the German introduction got it instead. It wasn't a bad record. The guitar was all right."

Five songs were recorded with Sheridan as well as John Lennon working through Gene Vincent's arrangement of 'Ain't She Sweet' and John and George's instrumental, 'Cry for a Shadow'. That title is deliberate: they had been trying to convince Rory Storm that this tune was the Shadows' new single. In 1964, 'Cry for a Shadow' became a hit in Australia.

By far the best track, 'My Bonnie', was issued as a single in Germany,

11

credited to Tony Sheridan and the Beat Brothers and becoming the Beatles' first-ever chart entry. This exuberant track is underrated today. It is among the best examples of British rock'n'roll (albeit recorded in Germany): not quite up there with 'Move It!' (Cliff Richard), 'Shakin' All Over' (Johnny Kidd and the Pirates) and 'Wondrous Place' (Billy Fury) but close.

Bonnie Raitt: "I was 13 when the Beatles were on *The Ed Sullivan Show* in 1964 and it was not lost on me that their first single was 'My Bonnie', I know it wasn't their first hit but it was the first thing that they recorded. I love all their stuff and the fact that the *Sgt. Pepper* and the *Abbey Road* era are so different from what they were doing at the beginning. I loved all their R&B covers. They really nailed 'Twist and Shout'. John had a brilliant vocal on that and it certainly won my heart. He was the one I had a crush on."

A request for 'My Bonnie' became the catalyst for Brian Epstein's interest. At lunchtime on 9 November 1961, he walked from his record store, NEMS, up an alleyway, round the corner into Mathew Street and down the steps into the Cavern. By then, the Beatles were the most accomplished group on Merseyside and he became their manager.

One of Epstein's friends was the painter and club owner, Yankel Feather. Although homosexuality was against the law, Yankel Feather was as openly gay as Epstein was furtive. "Brian had problems with being queer. Being gay has never been a problem for me: it's been a blessing in many ways. As there were no places for homosexuals to meet, it was inevitable that if you hung around pubs and clubs, you were going to meet low life. One day I went into NEMS, I was buying records and he wasn't looking at me and I said, 'Look Brian, I wish you'd look at me,' and he said, 'I'm just looking at that young man in the corner.' 'What are you looking at him for?' 'Well, he's the man who attacked me and he's just come out of prison.' I said, 'You'd better ring the police' and he replied, 'Oh no, I'm taking him to lunch.'"

Brian Epstein arranged a recording test with Decca on New Year's Day, 1962. The Beatles had to travel overnight to London in appalling weather and they were tired. The recordings are still okay (this is, after all, the Beatles) but they didn't do themselves justice and Decca turned them down. The fifteen songs replicate their stage act and it's good to hear them having fun with the Coasters' novelty, 'Three Cool Cats', while John Lennon offers a plaintive 'To Know Her is to Love Her', written by Phil Spector.

The Decca tapes include such oddities as George Harrison singing 'The Sheik of Araby'. Many critics cite this as the Beatles' worst performance but it is an engaging oddity. Joe Brown performed 'The Sheik of Araby' and, as we now know, George Harrison was working his way through Joe's repertoire. In November 2002 Joe Brown ended the *Concert for George* at the Royal Albert Hall with 'I'll See You in My Dreams', a standard associated with Django Reinhardt, and there are these wheels within wheels throughout the Beatles' story.

Recording engineer Mike Smith: "Someone at Decca had to show some interest in the Beatles because Brian Epstein ran NEMS, which was an important account for the sales people. I thought the Beatles were absolutely wonderful on stage and, in retrospect, I should have trusted my instincts. They weren't very good in the studio and really we got to the Beatles too early. I've nothing against Pete Best, but Ringo wasn't in the band and they hadn't developed their songwriting. Had I picked up on them six months later, there was no way I would have missed the quality of their songs. I think they were overawed by the situation and their personalities didn't come across. I took the tape to Decca House and I was told that they sounded like the Shadows. I had recorded two bands and I could take one and not the other. I went with Brian Poole and the Tremeloes because they had been the better band. So much in this industry depends upon being in the right place at the right time and whether I did the right thing or not, I'll never know. In fairness, I don't think I could have worked with them the way George Martin did – I would have got involved in their bad habits and not encouraged the good ones. When I met them later on, they gave me a two-fingered salute."

Billy Kinsley, later with the Merseybeats, saw the band for the first time in January 1962, at the Cavern. "They opened with 'Memphis Tennessee' with John hunched at the microphone: he had his Rickenbacker held really high. I know now that he had got that stance from Tony Sheridan in Hamburg. I could see that Paul's bass was a Hofner but I hadn't seen a violin bass before, although it had the same control panel as any other Hofner instrument. At least I thought I hadn't but it turns out that Little Richard's bass player in those rock'n'roll movies like *The Girl Can't Help It* had one, and maybe that's why Paul chose it. Actually, John and Paul's instruments were so dirty that you couldn't see the names on the headstock. I had seen a lot of rock'n'roll stars at the Empire and so I knew how to compare them, and I thought right from that moment that the Beatles stood out.

Albeit reluctantly, the Beatles followed Brian Epstein's suggestions, wearing stage suits for the first time in March 1962 at Barnston's Women's Institute on the Wirral, a prestige gig if ever there was one. Paul Du Noyer: "Brian Epstein put them into suits – they hated that but it was the next stage commercially. It helped to get them a record deal and it got them to EMI and George Martin. That's when history really moves forward for the Beatles." Du Noyer may be right: when Johnny Kidd signed with EMI, he was told, "You'll have to change your clothes. We've already got one scruff here with Adam Faith and we don't want another."

When the Beatles conformed, they usually did it unwillingly, adding their own touches. The high-buttoned jackets and tight trousers were an integral part of Beatlewear, but note how John often had his top shirt button undone. The Beatle mop came from Jürgen Vollmer: "When I came into the club in Hamburg, I had this brushed forward hairstyle and they thought it was funny. I moved to Paris in late 1961 and John and Paul visited me and they wanted to change their clothes. I took them to the flea market and they dressed in the style that I had: corduroy trousers and turtle-neck sweaters. They wanted my haircut and that is when I cut their hair. I had been forced to cut my own hair as the German barbers always cut hair too short. It was inspired by the French bohemians on the Left Bank. I was influenced by that style ever since I first went to Paris and I did want to look like Marlon Brando in *Julius Caesar*." A less flattering comparison would be Moe from the Three Stooges.

Mike Evans, author of *The Art of the Beatles*: "Stu Sutcliffe and his girlfriend Astrid Kirchherr foisted the flat, mop top haircuts and the leather jacket look upon the Beatles, but, more interesting and more subtly, Stu influenced John in artistic concepts such as surrealism and Dada. John was very much a primitive – you can either do it or you can't – whereas Stu was academic and articulate. Arthur Ballard, who taught them both in college, says that, before he knew Stuart, John didn't know a Dada from a donkey and his reading matter didn't get much further than *The Beano*. John was a very primitive, intuitive person, which came out in rock'n'roll 'cause he did that off the top of his head."

Klaus Voormann saw the Beatles playing several hours a night in Hamburg: "The Beatles had an amazing repertoire, the biggest of all the bands I've ever heard. They would pick up songs really quickly and when they were not playing them on stage, they were rehearsing. People were asking them all the time to play this song or that song and so they might repeat themselves because people wanted to hear them, but they could have played different songs all night. I especially liked to hear 'Please Mr. Postman' and 'Twist and Shout'."

Mike Gregory of the Escorts: "I love the sound of the bass with the Beatles. Paul McCartney had a big cabinet that Adrian Barber had made. It had an 18 inch speaker and the sound would hit you in the chest. It was really driving stuff and I loved them doing 'Besame Mucho' and 'Dizzy Miss Lizzy'. They also did the Crickets' 'Don't Ever Change', but I preferred that by Gerry and the Pacemakers as they had a pianist and it sounded better. The trend had been to have a singer with a band like Cliff Richard and the Shadows, and the Beatles changed all that."

Billy Kinsley of the Merseybeats: "I remember feeling the pangs of Beatlemania at a lunchtime session at the Cavern when Pete Best was still there and they were finishing the session with 'Money'. I felt my whole body reacting to it. It was getting more extreme and more exciting as it went along. Only the Beatles did that for me."

Chris Curtis, drummer with the Searchers: "You could ask Pete Best to play for 19 hours and he'd put his head down and do it. He'd drum like a dream with real style and stamina all night long and that really was the Beatles' sound – forget the guitars and forget the faces – you couldn't avoid that insistent whack, whack, whack! The rhythm guitar went along with it and the bass chucked in the two and four beats and George was wonderful on the guitar. His little legs would kick out to the side when he did his own tunes. He'd go all posh and say, 'I'd like to do a tune now from Carl Perkins, 'Everybody's Trying to Be My Baby', and it's in A.' Who wanted to know what key it was in? But he always said that."

Back to Billy Kinsley: "The Beatles sang 'A Shot of Rhythm and Blues' in unison and then broke into a little harmony with some backing vocals from George. 'Some Other Guy' was also in unison and it became a Liverpool thing to sing in unison. George had a monotone Scouse accent and he sang like that when doing harmonies, which was the perfect way to do it. You wanted that in there because John and Paul were so melodic. That was good luck – they thought, 'Doesn't it sound great?' and did it. It was the same with Badfinger: they had two incredible singers with Tommy Evans and Pete Ham, and then Joey Molland came in, a bit like George Harrison. He was the perfect guy for them."

Cynthia Powell, who became Cynthia Lennon: "When they were in Hamburg, we would write to each other every day. John was always asking me for the words of songs. I remember slowing down Ketty Lester's 'Love Letters' on my little record player and so if he got the words wrong, it was down to me."

In 1992, there was a unique CD release for its time, *Under the Influence*, on Sequel Records, which featured the original versions of twenty-four songs that the Beatles covered. There was *Pre Fab!* on Connoisseur in 1999, and five years later, EMI released a 2CD set, *John Lennon's Jukebox*, which featured forty-one tracks that were listed on a portable jukebox that John Lennon carried around with him (or rather someone else did). This project was a little nebulous as I couldn't come across anyone who had seen the jukebox in action. I suspect that John put the collection together one day, played with it for a couple of weeks and then forgot about it. In 2010, Rhythm and Blues Records released three albums in the series, *Beatles Beginnings*, which featured original versions of songs performed by the Quarry Men and the Silver Beatles. More volumes would follow.

Stu Slater, lead singer of the Mojos: "The Beatles played a much wider spectrum of music than most groups. Paul McCartney sang ballads like 'Til There Was You' and 'Over the Rainbow'; John Lennon did the more abrasive stuff; and George Harrison was singing Joe Brown's songs. They were fantastic and like the Big Three and the Undertakers, they had real musical power. Gerry and the Pacemakers never did it for me as they were of the show business generation."

Tony Crane, who formed the Merseybeats: "I went down to the Cavern when I was 15 to see Peter Jay and the Jaywalkers who impersonated the Shadows, and I thought they were marvellous. After they had been on, I stayed around to see this scruffy band from Liverpool called the Beatles, who would drink soup on stage and wore leather jackets and old jeans. Paul jumped into the audience singing 'What'd I Say' and 'Long Tall Sally' and screaming his head off. Lennon would lie on the floor and play guitar solos. It was marvellous and such a contrast to the smarmy, smiling balladeers we heard on the radio, like Bobby Vee and Bobby Rydell. The Beatles were playing rock'n'roll, raw and alive, just as it should be played."

CHAPTER 2

Love, Love Me Do (1962)

The Sunday Times introduces the first colour supplement – Telstar satellite launched – Death of Marilyn Monroe – Macmillan sacks seven ministers and Harold Wilson calls him 'Mac The Knife' – US discovers Soviet missile bases in Cuba and imposes a naval blockade – James Hanratty executed – Anthony Burgess writes A Clockwork Orange *and first James Bond film,* Doctor No *is released.*

Straight up, Parlophone was a joke label. Its big-selling albums included *At the Drop of a Hat* (1957), *Songs for Swingin' Sellers* (1959) and *Beyond the Fringe* (1961) and its artists included Charlie Drake, Spike Milligan and Bernard Cribbins. The label manager was George Martin, who says, "You've no idea of the enormous trouble we had in finding the right material. Good comedy songs are so hard to come by."

By June 1962, the label was the weakest link in EMI's chain and the popularity of its biggest act, Adam Faith, was dwindling. Meanwhile, Brian Epstein was desperately looking for a national label to sign his band, the Beatles. They had already been rejected by the EMI labels, Columbia and HMV, but now, some months later, George Martin was asked to consider them.

Paul Du Noyer: "There are so many enormous strokes of luck, or fate, in the Beatles story. One stroke of good fortune was in meeting George Martin, who was known for comedy records. He had this incredible intuition about the Beatles and they produced sounds, the quality of which had never been heard before in a British recording studio. They pioneered lots of the advances that came about as well."

George Martin: "I was pretty desperate for anything, and I envied Columbia who had so many hits with Cliff Richard and the Shadows. I saw Brian Epstein and heard his tapes of the Beatles. They weren't very impressive but there was something peculiar about the way they sounded that I thought should be looked into. I asked Brian to bring them down from Liverpool so that I could have a look at them. I was immediately impressed by them as people, not particularly as musicians, but I did think that they sang in a very unusual and engaging style. I put them under contract, knowing that I couldn't lose very much."

EMI recording engineer, Harry Moss: "The Beatles came here in 1962 for an artist test and that was the first time I met them. Before anybody was given a contract, they did a test first and I attended hundreds of these tests. I was blasé because of every hundred that you had to sit through and suffer, there would only be one that was any good. Frankly, I wasn't impressed by the Beatles at that time."

Fortunately, it wasn't up to Harry Moss to make the decision. The signing of the Beatles was somewhat unusual. The EMI publishing company, Ardmore and Beechwood, had heard Lennon and McCartney's original songs on the Decca tapes, liked them and wanted EMI to sign them. Although their first studio appearance would normally have been a test, it would appear that George Martin was obliged to take them.

On 6 June 1962, the Beatles (John, Paul, George and drummer Pete Best) came to the EMI studios at Abbey Road to make their first record. Ron Richards, George Martin's assistant, proceeded to record them for a potential single, with George Martin joining them partway through. They played a stage favourite, 'Besame Mucho' (taken from the Coasters' repertoire) and three songs written by John and Paul, 'Love Me Do', 'P.S. I Love You' and 'Ask Me Why'. In 1995, when this version of 'Love Me Do' was included on *Anthology 1*, we could hear what George Martin heard.

While he was visiting Liverpool, I played the session to Garry Tamlyn, an Australian academic whose area of expertise is drumming technique. Commenting on this slow version of 'Love Me Do', he said, "The cymbals are only audible in the breaks and the middle eights. The first time round Pete plays a shuffle rhythm all the way through, and the second time he reverts to an even quaver rhythm on cymbals with a syncopated snare drum rhythm – a Latin beat, really. He has some tempo variations, particularly in the second break. Even his quaver rhythms on cymbals are uneven. On this showing, it doesn't surprise me that George Martin was critical of his drumming. To be fair though, Pete plays a similar snare rhythm in 'Besame Mucho' and that is very tight drumming, which goes against my comments on 'Love Me Do'. Maybe he hadn't had enough time to rehearse that song."

To put it more directly, Pete Best sounds as though he's banging bin-lids on 'Love Me Do' and his drumming goes AWOL in the middle eight. Possibly he went to pieces when George Martin entered the studio. Martin recognised the group's potential, but if this was all he heard of Pete Best, is it surprising that he was sacked?

George Martin: "I thought Pete was an essential part of the Beatles because of his image. There was a moody James Dean look about him, but I didn't like his drumming. I didn't think it held the Beatles together as it should and I was determined that the Beatles weren't going to suffer because of it. I told Brian that I was going to use a session drummer when we made records. I didn't realise that the other boys had been thinking of getting rid of Pete anyway and that my decision was the last straw that broke the camel's back. So Pete was given the boot, poor chap. It was hard luck on him, but it was inevitable."

Pete Best felt that he had played okay: "George Martin liked us and said, 'Fine, rehearse 'Love Me Do' a little more and come back and we will add the finishing touches.' At some time between that session and the next, I got kicked out."

The repercussion over the percussion was more dramatic and longer lasting than the remaining Beatles would have wished and, even today, Paul McCartney sidesteps questions about the dismissal.

The Beatles' take of 'Love Me Do' featured John Lennon's harmonica, which was to be more prominent on the hit recording. Although John had been playing the harmonica for some time, its use had been inspired by the hit record. 'Hey! Baby' by the American, Bruce Channel.

In June 1962, Channel was on a UK tour with his harmonica player, Delbert McClinton, and they played the Tower Ballroom, New Brighton with the Beatles in support. Bruce Channel reflected, "There were lots of kids there, a whole sea of people, and I said to Delbert, 'They can't all have come to see us' and we soon found out that the Beatles were popular. Delbert was in the dressing-room with John Lennon who was interested in his harp. Delbert played something for him and evidently John kept the idea and used it for the sound on 'Love Me Do'. We had heard harmonica on blues records by Jimmy Reed and people like that, and that influenced 'Hey! Baby'. It's a great thrill to know that our record influenced the Beatles, that our music was appreciated by someone of that stature."

Bobby Graham played drums on Joe Brown's biggest hit, 'A Picture of You' and in July 1962, Joe and his Bruvvers also played the Tower Ballroom: Bobby Graham: "The Beatles had Pete Best with them and Brian Epstein sounded me out about taking his place. He said that Pete's mum was causing problems and they needed a change. I said, 'No thanks' as the Beatles hadn't had any hits and anyway, I had a wife and family in London. I don't think he had even discussed it with the Beatles as they surely would have wanted someone from Liverpool."

Rick Wakeman: "When you know what the future is, it's easy to criticise the past. Nobody could have foreseen what would happen to the Beatles, and Pete Best was just unlucky. Who knows why some people leave some groups? It can be something that doesn't have a verbal explanation, something intangible, you know. It just didn't feel right and no-one knows why."

Paul Du Noyer: "The sacking of Pete Best is one of the great enigmas of musical history. You can say with hindsight that Ringo Starr fundamentally affected the chemistry of the group. Lots of things about the Beatles seem slightly magical, not quite explicable in ordinary terms, and one of those magical things is the interaction of those four personalities. The presence of Ringo acted as a subtle counterbalance to the personalities of the other three. It was all part and parcel of what made the Beatles happen. Had they stuck with Pete, they might have not have taken off to the same extent. They might not have captured the subconscious of the population."

George Melly: "I think they were right in getting rid of Pete Best and recruiting Ringo Starr. Pete Best was tremendously popular in Liverpool and undoubtedly it was a great tragedy for him to be sacked at the very moment when they were breaking out but, whoever it was, be it Brian Epstein, George Martin or the Beatles, saw that Ringo's personality was the perfect foil. He was plain, whereas the others were all rather good-looking. He was thick whereas the others were rather bright. He was working class whereas the others were basically suburban. Ringo completed the Beatles and made them more effective, not just musically, but as personalities."

Mike Gregory from the Liverpool band, the Escorts: "I was at the Cavern for Ringo's first gig there with the Beatles and the crowd was throwing tomatoes. It was a lunchtime session and they were shouting 'Pete Forever, Ringo Never'." (The Cavern was in the midst of fruit and vegetable warehouses so the punters picked up tomatoes on the way in.)

Granada TV producer, Johnnie Hamp: "I first saw the Beatles

when I was with Granada Theatres and I was booking acts for the thirty theatres where they also had stage shows. I saw the Beatles first at the Star-Club and I was very impressed. When I became a television producer, they made their first appearance at the Cavern doing 'Some Other Guy' and it was one of the first times that Ringo had worked with them and you can hear the crowd shouting, 'We want Pete' at the end if you listen carefully."

Oddly, the footage was not screened at the time. As a contrast, Granada shot the Brighouse and Rastrick Brass Band and the film was never shown. Hamp continues, "The Beatles film was too grainy but another, more important reason was that the brass band wanted union rates for their members. There were fifty of them so the idea was dropped. I had met Brian Epstein in Hamburg and he rang me and asked me to bring some pressure to bear on showing the film. Instead, I brought them in to do 'Love Me Do' on *Scene at 6.30*. The grainy quality of that film doesn't matter now. If you had a piece of film of the sinking of the Titanic, it wouldn't matter that you couldn't hear the band. It is history."

Billy Kinsley wrote a song for a Liverpool Express album, 'Best Years of My Life'. It's a nostalgic song about growing up in Liverpool and he describes a cobbled street (Mathew Street) where he hears the Beatles. "I put 'Ask Me Why' in the last verse because when Ringo joined the Beatles, we had just done a lunchtime session We were gigging that night somewhere else and I decided to help our roadie when he returned. The Beatles and me were in the Cavern together and they were teaching Ringo an early Lennon and McCartney composition, 'Ask Me Why'. They had done the song before with Pete. I watched them going over that song for about two hours, doing the harmonies and learning it. They were working out all the little breaks and the tempo so that they would be ready to record it. They worked out a three part harmony, which was superb."

George Martin had reservations about the commerciality of Lennon and McCartney's songwriting and he wanted the Beatles to record a new song, 'How Do You Do It', written by a Denmark Street writer, Mitch Murray. The song had originally been submitted to Adam Faith, who, allegedly, turned it down. Adam denied this when I asked him, so it was probably rejected on his behalf. 'How Do You Do It' was a cheeky pop singalong: highly commercial, ideal for Bobby Vee, say, but the Beatles preferred material with a harder edge.

The Beatles returned to Merseyside and their second visit to Abbey Road was on 4 September 1962. By this time, Ringo Starr from Rory Storm and the Hurricanes was the new drummer and they recorded 'Love Me Do' and 'How Do You Do It'.

Mitch Murray: "I was doing all right as a songwriter. I had written some B-sides for Shirley Bassey and I had the B-side of Mark Wynter's 'Go Away Little Girl', 'That Kinda Talk'. I wrote 'How Do You Do It', but Adam Faith's management had not taken it up. The music publisher Dick James had heard 'How Do You Do It' along with a comedy number, 'The Beetroot Song', and he said, 'I think 'The Beetroot Song' will be a very, very big hit.' A singer called Johnny Angel was going to record 'How Do You Do It' but he changed his mind and recorded another song of mine, 'Better Luck Next Time', so better luck next time, Johnny Angel. The next thing I heard was that a new group from Liverpool was going to record 'How Do You Do It' and I said, 'I'd prefer a big artist, but let's see how it goes.' The Beatles recorded 'How Do You Do It' and I hated it. I felt that something had been screwed up, perhaps deliberately, although it now sounds very evocative of the early Beatles. I can't blame them because they were songwriters themselves and didn't want to do it, but it was a waste of a good song. I thought it was terrible and fortunately, Dick James agreed with me. He told George Martin that the Beatles had made a very good demo record. George Martin took it very well and said that he was planning to do it again with the Beatles."

Bob Stanley from Saint Etienne and music critic of *The Times*: "Even early on, when they did 'How Do You Do It', they loused it up so it didn't come out. If they hadn't done that, you wonder where their career would have gone. That was the one time that they were forced into doing something that they didn't want to do and they managed to get out of it."

George Martin: "The Beatles didn't like 'How Do You Do It' very much, but in those days they had no option but to do what the boss told them. They recorded it but they came to me afterwards and said, 'Look, this really isn't our scene. We'd much rather have our own material.' I told them that they'd have to come up with something as good as that."

Mitch Murray: "It makes me cringe to think that George Martin told the Beatles to come up with a song as good as mine, but he knew that I was a professional songwriter and he liked the song. Brian Epstein then suggested that Gerry and the Pacemakers should do the song and he told me that Gerry was a Liverpool Bobby Darin. George Martin asked me to come and hear Gerry at the Cavern but I said, 'I don't care what he sounds like, it's the record that counts.' Arrogant little sod, wasn't I? They made the record, I loved it and it delighted me when it got to No.1."

Fred Marsden, drummer with the Pacemakers: "The 1963 winter was a bad one and we drove down from Liverpool overnight, and we sat in the back of a van for ten hours in the worst weather you could imagine. We reached London about half-past one and we were recording at two o'clock. The road manager fell asleep in the studio while we were recording as he was so shattered. We heard the Beatles' demo, but we decided to put a heavier beat on it. The Beatles would have been better off releasing 'How Do You Do It' as a single rather than 'Love Me Do' as it's the better song and they, not us, would have been the first act to have No.1s with their first three records."

A week after that session with 'How Do You Do It', the Beatles were back at EMI, recording 'Love Me Do', 'P.S. I Love You' and an early version of 'Please Please Me' performed like a Roy Orbison ballad. George Martin recognised the potential of 'Please Please Me' but wanted a faster arrangement and strong harmonies. Being unsure about Ringo Starr on 4 September, he brought in a session drummer Andy White, thereby reducing Ringo Starr to tambourine for 'Love Me Do' and maracas for 'P.S. I Love You'. White, who sometimes played with the Vic Lewis Orchestra, was married to Lyn Cornell from another Liverpool act, the Vernons Girls.

Aside from denting Ringo's confidence, Andy White's presence made little difference and the two versions of 'Love Me Do' are similar: you can spot the difference by listening for the dull thud of a tambourine. Their first single combined the 4 September take of 'Love Me Do' with 'P.S. I Love You', but that take was quickly replaced by the Andy White version. White's version made the *Please Please Me* LP. Both versions were included on the 12-inch single issued in 1982. In 2009 Andy White played drums on a new version of 'P.S. I Love You' by the Smithereens. Let's hope he got more than £7.10s this time.

Liverpool club owner and painter, Yankel Feather: "One day I came into the club early and I was surprised to see that Brian Epstein was the first customer. He said, 'I am so happy.' He had come back from London and he had the first pressings of the Beatles' first single, 'Love Me Do'. Well, after listening to people like Sacha Distel, who was making good jazz records you could dance to, and the soprano,

Adèle Leigh, this was a shock to my system and it sounded like an Arabic dirge. It sounded miserable and I said that they would never get anywhere with that. He looked disconcerted and I don't think he ever forgave me for that. I regret that I didn't enjoy them from the beginning because songs like 'Eleanor Rigby' and 'Yesterday' are absolutely bloody marvellous."

The Epsteins' next door neighbour was the solicitor, Rex Makin: "I knew Brian because he used to try and sell me LPs and other items from the shop. We did buy a dishwasher and a washing machine from him. He told me that he had discovered a group that would sweep the world and I thought it was pie-in-the-sky stuff. I was wrong and he was right. I had heard his enthusiasms for various things, and I knew his temperament was volatile but I never dreamt that he would be involved in pop music as he loved the classics. It was a strange departure from his normal path."

Brian Epstein was telling everyone that the Beatles would be bigger than Elvis. Paul Trynka, who edited *Mojo*'s coffee-table book on the Beatles: "Who knows how much of that was bravado and how much was naïve enthusiasm. Brian Epstein wasn't schooled in rock'n'roll and so from his point of view, he had picked on something that was very fresh for him. Probably the fact that they were very good looking guys who were very sexy had something to do with it. There is a tradition of gay managers in pop and rock'n'roll and they often pick the winners."

Press officer Tony Barrow: "Brian Epstein met me in London when he was looking for contacts. From the very start, he was telling not just the media, but also those around him that the Beatles were going to be as big as Elvis. I liked the Beatles immensely and saw that there was a great deal more to them than their music – they were much more than just four guys in a group – but I didn't class them alongside Elvis, and I took what he was saying with one gigantic piece of salt. I wrote the Beatles' first press release but I printed Andrew Loog Oldham's telephone number instead of mine as I worked for Decca and I couldn't use theirs. When I told my parents that I was going to leave Decca to work as a full-time press officer for NEMS, they said, 'Listen, lad, do you know what you're doing? You're leaving a reputable company for someone with a record shop and a group.' They said the same thing in 1968 when I left NEMS to set up my own PR company, 'Do you know what you're doing, lad, leaving a reputable company like that?' Brian Epstein was good to work for but he had a violent temper as have a lot of artistic people. He fired people all of the time, including group members, but he would rehire them ten minutes later. Notwithstanding the Pete Best incident, he was unable to get rid of people and he asked others to do it for him."

Brian's brother, Clive Epstein: "Even before 'Love Me Do' came out, Brian was saying that the Beatles would be bigger than Elvis. When he first played me the acetate of 'Love Me Do', he said that the Beatles would become a legend. I don't believe he had the evidence at that time but he was absolutely right. He sensed that John and Paul had a songwriting talent that was far beyond anyone else's, and he also felt that Gerry and the Pacemakers and Billy J. Kramer would become important acts."

Ray Coleman, then with *Melody Maker* and later Epstein's biographer: "Brian Epstein did believe that the Beatles would be bigger than Elvis. He saw something chemical about them that was even bigger than the music. He also became hooked on the minefield of talent in Liverpool and he enjoyed their company. It was much more than just another job to him. He already had money and, unlike a married man, he didn't have other priorities. Although his homosexuality is important in understanding him, the crucial factor is that he was available for work 24 hours a day. He made the Beatles very famous very quickly and, if there were mistakes later on, it was the fault of others. He was given bad advice over merchandising, which became very hard to control."

Music writer Johnny Rogan: "There was a degree of hyperbole about his statement that the Beatles would be bigger than Elvis. If he really believed it, he's an even bigger visionary than we give him credit for. I see him as a businessman. He knew that Liverpool was a happening place for beat groups, he knew that it was going to take off, and so he signed up as many groups as he could. He was an excellent manager and he's only been criticised from the money aspect – he should have made more money from the Beatles. He had integrity as he didn't get involved with tax avoidance schemes, although admittedly, there was some trouble with *Help!* There are so many different functions which a manager has to perform and many of the qualities are mutually exclusive – some pamper their artists and others have them like frightened schoolchildren. Being a good manager is about getting success for your artist to accord with your personality, and that's what he did."

One indication that Brian Epstein thought so highly of the Beatles' talent is his attitude towards John's fellow art student, Cynthia Powell.

When she became pregnant, John married her in August 1962 and they had a son, Julian, in April 1963. Brian Epstein, in keeping with the times, told John to keep the marriage secret as fans liked to believe that their heroes were available. A ridiculous concept, and I can't think of anyone whose career had been wrecked by being married, but there you are. Well, Jerry Lee Lewis of course, but that's an extreme example.

Cynthia Lennon: "John and I were only like children in those days, 21 or 22, that's all. We were used to being told what to do and what not to do, so it wasn't an effort to keep the marriage quiet. Pop stars weren't supposed to be married. It was no strain for me because I had my man and we loved each other and we were having a baby. Whatever anybody else thought didn't matter to me."

British rock'n'roll star, Marty Wilde: "I played the Liverpool Empire about four times in one year and every time this journalist would be there, saying, 'Have you heard the Beatles? They're fantastic.' People in Chester were even telling me about the Beatles, and this was well prior to their records. I don't think that rock'n'roll could have gone on the way it was for much longer. The songs weren't coming through and there wasn't the surprise anymore. It had lost its newness and its buzz. Elvis Presley had been tamed and with Frankie Avalon, the music was getting tamer and tamer. When Eddie Cochran came over in 1960, I hardly heard him mention rock'n'roll. It was all Ray Charles, country music and the blues. He was ready to move on. When the Beatles made the charts, I felt a jump ahead of the public as I had already heard of them."

Frank Ifield: "I had had two No.1s and before I started my tour, I was doing a week at the Liverpool Empire and when I was there, the doorman said there was someone who wanted to speak to me. He looked important and was wearing a suit and carrying a briefcase. It was Brian Epstein and he told me that he had taken on the Beatles and things were starting to happen for them in Liverpool but they hadn't done a tour. Would I consider using them? I said that the bill for my tour was already booked but he could contact the promoter Arthur Howes. As it happens, they played on the bill when we went to Peterborough."

October 1962 – Love Me Do/ P.S. I Love You (Parlophone R 4949, UK No.17, US No.1) (B-side also made No.10 in US. The single reached No.4 in the UK on reissue in 1982.)

The single, 'Love Me Do', was released on Friday 5 October 1962 and the Beatles celebrated by signing copies in local record stores. On 7 October, they played the Cavern, supported by the Swinging Blue Jeans. Ray Ennis of the Blue Jeans: "That was the first time that I had heard them perform 'Love Me Do'. It wasn't rock'n'roll, and it sounded more skiffley to me. I know that EMI had wanted Paul to play a string bass on it because he had had a word with Les Braid about that. Paul said, 'How do you do it because there are no frets on a string bass?' Les showed him how to get the octave with his left hand, and I can picture the two of them around the bass together. The Beatles did try it with a double bass but they preferred it with the electric."

The American rock'n'roll stars, Little Richard and Sam Cooke were touring the UK, and Brian Epstein was the local promoter for the final night of the tour, October 28, at Liverpool Empire. However, Sam Cooke was unavailable as the promoter Don Arden was billing him with Sophie Tucker at Palace Theatre, Manchester. Epstein added the Beatles to the bill and Arden brought in Craig Douglas to replace Cooke. Douglas' version of Cooke's 'Only Sixteen' had been a UK No.1, so at least the audience was still sure of hearing 'Only Sixteen'.

Craig Douglas: "I was deputising for Sam Cooke at the Liverpool Empire and I went there with my pianist. Brian Epstein came to my dressing-room and said 'Are you ready for a rehearsal, Mr Douglas?' The Beatles had been hired as my backing group and although they couldn't read music, we bashed through the songs for a couple of hours and they did a very good job. I was closing the first half. They finished their spot with 'Love Me Do', which brought the place down, and I had to follow that, which was very difficult but great fun."

Leo Sayer: "I was not a great Beatles fan at the time. I preferred the Stones, but I loved their first record 'Love Me Do'. It turned me on to the harmonica John Lennon was playing it in a completely different way, picking out that riff almost like a trumpet, and it was great."

Allan Clarke of the Hollies: "I still think that my favourite Beatles record is the first one they ever made, 'Love Me Do'. It took me ages to learn the harmonica part, but I learnt it. It's a great song and it's a great record, especially with the B-side being 'P.S. I Love You.'"

George Martin: "I had reluctantly agreed to release 'Love Me Do' as the first single. I thought it was the best of the bunch and John's harmonica was very appealing. It got to No.17 and I never thought it would do much better because I didn't think the song had much to offer."

Tony Barrow, who became the Beatles' press officer: "I do not believe the story about Brian Epstein buying huge quantities of 'Love Me Do' to get it into the charts. I know for a fact that the record sold enormous quantities on Merseyside as soon as it was released. I was writing the Disker column for the *Liverpool Echo*, and either my wife or I would ring the various wholesalers in the city to find out what had been selling. This wasn't ringing NEMS, but the wholesalers to find out what retailers were ordering. As far as the wholesalers were concerned, 'Love Me Do' was the No.1 best-selling record, and that had nothing to do with Brian Epstein directly buying, or not buying, a quantity of records. All those who were involved with the Beatles, including the Beatles themselves, got a greater thrill out of seeing 'Love Me Do' creep into the charts and make No.17, than all the records that went to No.1 later on. Then the questions were, 'Will it outsell the last one, and how many weeks will it be No.1?' It was a forgone conclusion that it would go straight to No.1, so the nail-biting, white knuckle ride as far as the Beatles were concerned has to be 'Love Me Do' at the very beginning."

Liverpool star Frankie Vaughan: "The Beatles made their first television appearance on my show from Birmingham. They sang their first hit and their manager, Brian Epstein, wanted them to work with my office. My manager didn't like them at all, he didn't like their long hair and he didn't like the way they were dressed, and it was very embarrassing to say no to them, although we did use them on shows that my office put on in Blackpool. They worked for us for £75 a night and then it went up to £125 a night and then my manager thought they were charging too much."

Music historian Charlie Gillett: "I was at a bonfire party in November 1962 in a big tent and this fantastic record came on, and I had never heard anything like it. I asked the DJ what it was and he said, 'The Beatles.' It was a corny name, a bad pun, but now you forget that was how it first seemed. I would have bought it except I never bought records full price in those days. I would look in second-hand shops and get them for 2/6d instead of 6/8d and I got it very soon afterwards. I loved it, and I loved everything that they did after that."

In November 1962, the American hitmaker Bobby Vee was touring the UK with the Crickets. "I was on tour with my producer Snuff Garrett in the north-west when someone played me 'Love Me Do'. We loved it and thought it sounded like a Crickets' record. Snuffy got very excited and wanted to buy the rights for America, but EMI wanted

$25,000 which at the time was too much money. It seemed outrageous – RCA only paid $35,000 for Elvis and this was a new group. We could tell that they were going to be popular and I started to learn their tunes. I also wrote six or seven tunes such as 'She's Sorry' in that fashion. It was done with the kindest of intentions, a proclamation that there was this new sound in England. It never entered my mind that I was ripping them off, although it may look like that now."

Snuff Garrett: "We were opening the Liberty label in England through EMI, which was a big deal for us. My British publisher Dick James and I had lunch together and he told me that the Beatles were big fans of Bobby's work. They wanted to meet me. They were also doing *Sunday Night at the London Palladium* and he picked me up and we went backstage after the show, and two of them were in the shower and two of them had just come out and were in towels. They said, 'This is our favourite Bobby Vee record', and they put their hands in front of each other's face and went (sings) 'Shaving you, shaving you, shaving you'. When I came back to America, I told the guy that ran the west coast pages in *Cash Box* that this group in England was going to tear the heads off our shoulders. He put it in the California column, and I was right, but there was no question about that. They were so innovative and so inventive and so funny."

Rory Storm's sister, Iris Caldwell: "I dated Paul McCartney for sometime on and off as everybody dated everyone in Liverpool – there was nothing in it – and one night he said to me, 'Do you want to hear the song we've written?' and he sang the first verse of 'Please Please Me' with all those 'Come ons'. I burst out laughing and said, 'That's not a song, don't be silly.' I was also dating Frank Ifield and I told him about the Beatles and sang 'Please Please Me' to him, and he said, 'Well, I don't have to worry about that.'"

The Beatles appeared with Frank Ifield at the Embassy Cinema, Peterborough on 2 December 1962. Frank Ifield: "We did two shows and they had to do it for no money and had to provide their own transport. I wanted to see them as I had heard so much about them. They sounded bloody loud and I thought we were going to get complaints from the management. Their amps were on stage and I thought that was why it was loud. I was at the side of the stage and they were very good, but the audience hated them. I don't know why the audience didn't like them – perhaps they weren't ready for it. Perhaps they thought, 'Who are these upstarts?' Perhaps they were just too loud. The write-up in the paper wasn't too hot either."

'Love Me Do' and 'P.S. I Love You' were published by Ardmore and Beechwood. EMI historian, Brian Southall: "Lennon and McCartney hadn't got a publishing contract when they started so a deal was done. It was an EMI company, and the person who had tipped off George Martin to the Beatles ran Ardmore and Beechwood. 'Love Me Do' made the Top 20 but Brian Epstein was disappointed and blamed Ardmore and Beechwood. He thought that their pluggers hadn't worked hard enough, and he vowed not to give them any more songs." Still, Ardmore and Beechwood did issue sheet music for both titles and the cover for 'P.S. I Love You' shows Paul and Ringo looking one way, and John and George the other. Flash forward a decade or so and you have an Abba LP.

Peter Noone, Herman of Herman's Hermits: "Most of us didn't take playing in bands too seriously, we listened to our parents who said 'Put that guitar down and do a job with your hands'. We did it half-heartedly but the Beatles wanted to make a career out of it right from the beginning. Their attitude was, 'We're not messing about up here. We take ourselves seriously.' That attitude rubbed off on a lot of bands including ours."

Jimmy Tushingham replaced Ringo in Rory Storm and the Hurricanes: "When Ringo made it with the Beatles, he had to declare everything he'd been doing in the past to the Revenue, and so we got hit for an income tax bill. Ringo sent a cheque to Rory saying that he was very sorry about what had happened and to put this money towards it, which was very nice of him."

On 15 December 1962, the Beatles took part in the *Mersey Beat* poll awards show from the Majestic Ballroom, Birkenhead. They won the poll, but Lee Curtis and the All-Stars (with drummer Pete Best) were second. Billy J. Kramer remembers it well: "The Beatles did 'Please Please Me' and I told George Harrison that they should record it. It was the first time I'd heard them perform an original number. Brian Epstein said in his book *A Cellarful of Noise* that the first time he heard the Beatles he knew that they were going to be as big as Elvis. Well, the first time I saw them at Litherland Town Hall I thought that, and my friends thought I was crazy. When I heard them do 'Please Please Me', I knew it."

Aaron Williams of the Merseybeats: "The first time that I realised that the Beatles were special was when we were on with them at the Majestic Ballroom in Birkenhead. They opened up with 'Please Please

Me' and had a really good sound. The intro was great although I can see now that it is almost note for note the same as the Shirelles' 'It's Love That Really Counts', but played faster. It's in the same key too! All their middle eights were good. In a lot of songs, the middle eights don't really benefit the song but their middle eights were songs in themselves." This is feasible as McCartney has said that 'P.S. I Love You' was an attempt to write a song like the Shirelles' 'Soldier Boy', and there are two Shirelles' songs on the Beatles' first LP, 'Boys' and 'Baby It's You'.

Adam Faith was working with his band, the Roulettes. "I remember doing pantomime in Bournemouth and one of the Roulettes came in with the first Beatles' single 'Love Me Do'. He said 'Listen to this, Adam, this is what is going to happen in the future.' I was very struck by it and we were influenced by what the Beatles did from that moment on. We made records like 'The First Time' that were more aggressive than what I was doing before. To be honest, it was the Roulettes' doing as I was already thinking that I should stop singing."

Very reluctantly, the Beatles returned to Hamburg for the fifth time in the final weeks of December 1962. Two weeks at the Star-Club was wasting time when things were going well in the UK. Their final evening, on New Year's Eve, was taped on a domestic recorder and has been released, much against the Beatles' wishes, in various forms. Hopefully, an officially authorised, technically enhanced and annotated version will be issued one day. The set is intriguing as it includes Buddy Holly's 'Reminiscing', Marlene Dietrich's 'Falling in Love Again' and Fats Waller's 'Your Feet's Too Big'.

Frank Allen from Cliff Bennett and the Rebel Rousers: "I met the Beatles for the first time in the Star-Club on 30 December 1962. We were at Hamburg for a stint and they were on their final shows and I was seriously impressed, and what's more Cliff Bennett was seriously impressed. Usually, nobody impressed him because he was such a fantastic singer!"

So, 1962 ended with the Beatles playing in a seedy area of Hamburg. Their one single, "Love Me Do', had only briefly made the Top 20, but it was a start and nothing would be the same again.

CHAPTER 3
Everything That You Want (1963)

BBC withdraws ban on mentioning sex, religion, politics and royalty in comedy programmes – Profumo resigns – President Kennedy visits Berlin – Philby discovered in Moscow – Martin Luther King's "I have a dream" speech – Great Train Robbery – Alec Douglas-Home becomes PM – de Gaulle says 'Non' to UK entry into Common Market – Khrushchev toppled in coup by Brezhnev – President Kennedy assassinated.

No one, especially the Beatles themselves, could have predicted what would happen to them in 1963. They saw in the New Year at the Star-Club in Hamburg and then flew to London. They planned to continue to Edinburgh to start a short Scottish tour but the first appearance had to be cancelled because of bad weather. Not a good start to the year.

January 1963 – Please Please Me/ Ask Me Why (Parlophone R 4983, 1/63, UK No.2, US No.3)
On 26 November 1962, the Beatles had recorded their second single, 'Please Please Me' and 'Ask Me Why', two Lennon and McCartney songs. George Martin was delighted with the way that they had reshaped 'Please Please Me'; it was now faster, sharper and full of tight harmonies: "I flipped over that. I thought it was a great song and after we'd finished, I told them that they'd got their first No.1."

Mark Lewisohn: "The Beatles were working so hard most days and nights in the early years that they didn't have time to record over several days. They tended to record on off-days during the tours – *With the Beatles* and *Beatles for Sale* are like that. They didn't have the time to be fussy and the beauty of their early recordings is that they made mistakes. In the last verse of 'Please Please Me', when they should be singing the same words, they go off on different paths and come back together. John gives a little chuckle and they carry on."

On 10 January 1963, the Beatles played at the Grafton Rooms in West Derby Road with Gerry and the Pacemakers and Sonny Webb and the Cascades. They hadn't played Liverpool for a month and since then, 'Love Me Do' had made the Top 20. The fans were hearing their instantly catchy 'Please Please Me' for the first time. Although the ballroom was on his doorstep, Billy Kinsley couldn't attend as he had a gig with the Merseybeats at the Cavern. He recalls coming home and experiencing what was really the start of Beatlemania: "Most people still went on buses to gigs. It was 11.30 p.m. There were hundreds of fans waiting for buses in West Derby Road singing 'Please Please Me'. Everybody was happy and there was no trouble. It was an incredible atmosphere and I knew something special had been happening."

Steve Turner, author of a book about the Beatles' songwriting, *A Hard Day's Write*: "With 'Please Please Me', John had this idea of using the word 'please' twice in a song. He got the idea from a song that Bing Crosby sang which was written by Leo Robin and Ralph Rainger and was called 'Please'. It plays with the word 'please' against the word 'pleas', 'Please lend your little ear to your pleas,' John liked that play on words. I was with Roy Orbison the week before he died and he didn't know that until fairly late on that it had been written in his style originally. I was saying to him 'It would be great to hear you do a version of it.'" Possibly John Lennon was throwing us off the scent: the premise of 'Please Please Me' is identical to Cliff Richard and the Shadows' 'Please Don't Tease', a 1960 chart-topper.

Maybe it's my dirty mind, but it does seem to be an early example of John Lennon's cunning. Listen to the lyric again and this could easily be a song about oral sex. He, perhaps encouraged by Paul, probably thought that no one really listened to pop lyrics, not even George Martin, and anyway, if they were caught, John could simply say, "Really? That's just your dirty mind. I don't mean that at all." Having slipped through this innuendo, John did it again with the "tit-tit-tit" in 'Girl'; the "fish and finger pie" in 'Penny Lane' and, naturally, the punning title of 'Come Together'. Just what is Ringo feeling when he turns off the light? He can't tell us, but he knows it's his. Having said that, we do have, in complete contrast, the innocence of 'I Want to Hold Your Hand'. Not that the Brill Building songs were so innocent: "the magic of your sighs" in 'Will You Love Me Tomorrow' is a poetic way of saying something rather intimate. I'd better stop this: after all, I'm writing a book on the Beatles and not the sexual codes of popular songs. It would be an interesting subject, though.

Although Billy Kinsley appreciated the Beatles' originality, he could also see their influences. "John used to sing 'Please Please Me' on his own at the Cavern, but they changed it and Paul added some harmony. What they did could have been influenced by the Everly Brothers' 'Maybe Tomorrow' or 'Cathy's Clown', Don Everly sang lead, while Phil kept his harmony on one note and that was total magic. Nobody else was doing that, and that is exactly what Paul did on 'Please Please Me', and it was great."

George Martin told Brian Epstein about his friend, Dick James, whom he had produced for many years as a singer for Parlophone, resulting in a hit with 'Robin Hood'. Brian took Dick James the new single, 'Please Please Me'. Dick James picked up the phone, telephoned the producer of *Thank Your Lucky Stars*, played it down the line and secured a booking for three weeks hence. Brian Epstein said, "Dick, you've got the publishing." Already, Dick James had done more for the Beatles than Ardmore and Beechwood.

'Please Please Me' was released on 11 January 1963 and the Beatles promoted it on ITV's *Thank Your Lucky Stars* and Radio Luxembourg's *Friday Spectacular* with Muriel Young. They also played live sessions on the Light Programme.

John Lennon's half-sister, Julia Baird: "We knew that Jimmy Savile was going to play 'Please Please Me' for the first time on Radio Luxembourg. We were all huddled around the radio upstairs because there was better reception. Jimmy Savile played 'Please Please Me' and then said, 'Well I hope it pleases someone. It's a terrible noise.'"

Notwithstanding Savile's assessment, the Beatles were on a fast track to fame. Tony Barrow: "Muriel Young introduced a series of programmes for Radio Luxembourg and the Beatles were there to promote their second single, 'Please Please Me'. She introduced them by saying 'And when I tell you that their names are John, Paul, George and Ringo...' and the crowd in the studio went mad. They were much more interested in the Beatles than they would be in the average pop group who'd had one hit record."

Andrew Loog Oldham: "I was in Birmingham as Mark Wynter's press agent. The Beatles were about to do 'Please Please Me' on *Thank Your Lucky Stars* and looked really interesting. They had an aura of been there, done that about them and now we know how long they'd been playing, it's apparent that they had. I asked John who managed them and he pointed to a gent in an overcoat and Paisley scarf, Brian Epstein. I worked on that single and a couple more. At the time, long distance calls were usually only made to announce births and deaths and therefore phoning from Liverpool to London was as unlikely as phoning from Inverness to Sydney. It was normal to hire a young chap like me to do the press in London as Brian Epstein wouldn't be picking up the phone in Liverpool and getting things done from there."

1950s singer Joan Regan: "When the Beatles started, I was doing a television show with them and they said, 'Do you mind if we stand with you and get our picture taken, so we'll get our photo in the *New Musical Express?*' There is the picture of me with the boys and it is in the *NME.*"

Norman Jopling of *Record Mirror*: "I had seen bits and pieces written about them when they were doing well in Liverpool and I read *Mersey Beat* and liked its art school look. 'Love Me Do' came out which was a moderately okay record but I was convinced that it would go further. Andrew Loog Oldham was doing their publicity. Paul McCartney came up to the office with Brian Epstein who sat there blushing furiously. We were talking about Motown and R&B. Over the next couple of months, I would do a couple of articles about the tours but as they got huge, I had less to do with them as they moved out of my orbit. The editors wanted to interview them instead. I wasn't that interested in them artistically at the time as they were a band for the girls."

Ray Coleman of *Melody Maker*: "John Lennon used to hate *Melody Maker*, 'Those damn jazz people', he used to call us. He thought the publication was a closed shop for jazz artists but he thought it was an achievement to get in there because we knew about music. The British pop music of the previous years – Frankie Vaughan, Ronnie Carroll and Cliff Richard – had little inventiveness, and *Melody Maker* was into the creative music of the day, which happened to be jazz. As the jazz audience was getting older and dying on us, I argued that we should investigate this new, curious pop music from Liverpool. I was lucky enough to become the Beatles' reporter and went round the world with them. We were polarised in the office: some preferred the Stones, but I was very loyal to the Beatles."

Ray Coleman continues, "The Beatles brought articulacy to pop music interviews. Cliff Richard, Frank Ifield and Helen Shapiro never expressed any interesting opinions. It was, 'Who wrote your last record?', 'When are you going on tour?', 'Do you live with your mum and dad?', 'Do you play an instrument?' and 'What did you have for breakfast?' It was very elementary, and it was a dramatic change when the Beatles came along. They wrote their own songs, and had a lot to say for themselves."

Joe Brown: "John Lennon once said to someone, 'You're asking me about yesterday, so why don't you ask me what I'm doing tomorrow?' The bloke said 'Okay, what are you doing tomorrow?', and John said 'I'm not going to tell you.'"

Cynthia Lennon, John's wife: "John was a natural leader. He could say things in a few words that most people would say in long sentences. Paul would go on and on because he was much more of a social creature than John. He was also very much into PR and John would just let him get on with it. Without each other, I don't think it would ever have been so wonderful. John wanted love, he needed love, and I think when the Beatles split and when we split, he lost a lot of love, from the people, from the fans, from everybody."

'Please Please Me' entered the Top 20 at the beginning of February and by the end of the month, it was No.1 on the *New Musical Express* chart, at first sharing the top spot with Frank Ifield's 'The Wayward Wind' and then being the sole chart-topper. When the Cavern's compère and disc-jockey Bob Wooler announced that the Beatles had gone to No.1 with 'Please Please Me', a hush fell upon the Cavern dwellers. They were glad for the Beatles but they had lost their local heroes.

Rod Argent of the Zombies: "There have been two or three times in my life where I have felt completely turned around by music. I was in a choir initially and I only liked classical music until I was 11 and then I heard 'Hound Dog' and didn't want to hear anything for six months but the rawest rock'n'roll. There was another time when I first heard Miles Davis and as a result, I sold all my Elvis records, which I later wished I hadn't, but I had to find the money to buy a couple of Miles Davis albums. The third epiphany was hearing the Beatles, but not 'Love Me Do'. I thought that was good but it was hearing 'Please Please Me' on Radio Luxembourg that did it. I remember staying awake all night trying to hear it again. It was fantastic and from then on, I was totally in love with everything they did. They were very original and they had huge creative energy. I adored it all. I love the early stuff like 'From Me To You': I love the later stuff like 'Strawberry Fields Forever',

'Hey Jude' and 'Across The Universe'. Not only were they magical but they were also a very good example of the sum being much greater than the parts. Lennon and McCartney were brilliant on their own, but together, they were unmatchable."

Mojo writer and Beatles expert, Paul Trynka: "The Beatles were competitive and wanted to be the No.1 band in Liverpool but so did some of the others, so their advances were fired by rivalry. A lot of their subsequent advances were fired by rivalries between Paul and John: it was that competitiveness that made them such a good band."

Cynthia Lennon: "The songs poured out of them. Paul would come round for a visit and they would sit at the piano and knock out a song. John always had paper and pen by the bedside and he would wake up at odd times and write down lyrics."

Tony Bramwell, who followed the Beatles on Merseyside and worked with them as a factotum throughout the 60s: "John and Paul always fancied themselves as budding Brill Building writers. They even liked the idea of sitting in a room, tinkling the piano while somebody asked them to write a song for Cliff Richard. They thought that was what they would be doing after the beat bubble burst."

Pete Maclaine of the Dakotas: "I remember asking John what drink he wanted and it was brown ale. I asked him if he wanted a glass and he said yes and put the bottle in the glass and drank it that way. The Beatles were a pleasure to be with and had a real energy field around them. Paul knew that we did 'A Taste of Honey' and one night he asked me if we would mind if they did it, which was nice of him."

'A Taste of Honey' was a modern day standard, a US hit for Lenny Welch, albeit given a folky arrangement by the Beatles. Billy Kinsley: "We played a gig at Liverpool University with the Beatles and it was the first time they'd sung 'A Taste of Honey'. Paul had chosen the song, and the others didn't like it. Paul came up to me and said, 'What did you think of 'A Taste of Honey'?' and I said, 'I was knocked out by it. Superb.' Paul grabbed hold of me and said, 'Go and tell the others that.' He took me into their dressing room and John said, 'Go on then. What do you think?' I was 15 years old and very nervous because there was Big JL asking me what I thought of a song he didn't like. I told him that I thought 'A Taste of Honey' was great. Paul said, 'Ha, ha, John, told you so.' They decided that night to put it on their first album."

Alexei Sayle had an unusual upbringing in Liverpool. "I was dragged along to see the Red Army Ensemble which was a group of thuggish soldiers with beautiful voices. While other people were seeing the Beatles, I was watching the 9th Armoured Mechanised Corps of the Bialystock Rifles singing 'Roll Out the Barrel'. Pop music wasn't particularly valued in our house, and I have a lifelong dislike of folk music from all those Aldermaston marches. My wife who is two years older than me saw the Beatles at the Cavern and I missed out on that altogether."

During February 1963, the Beatles appeared on their first package tour, which starred 16-year-old Helen Shapiro and Kenny Lynch. Helen Shapiro: "The Beatles were the second act on although, by the end of the tour, they were closing the first half. I had heard 'Love Me Do' before I met them and straightaway I thought, 'Yes, it's good, gutsy, bluesy music and they're bringing it back.' I was pleased that I was going on tour with them and we got on like a house on fire. They were very raw because, although they'd done a fair bit, it had been in clubs and ballrooms rather than theatres and concert halls. I watched them adapt themselves and polish up their act, not too much polish though – I was glad that they kept some rawness. As the tour went on, they released 'Please Please Me' and I could see how they were developing a following of their own."

Another touring package featured Brian Hyland with Little Eva. Brian Hyland: "I played in Liverpool when the Beatles had 'Please Please Me' out and it sounded great. It was clear from listening to it that they sang and played their own instruments and were involved with the whole process of making records. This contrasted with a lot of American performers who made records with session guys they didn't know. I did an American tour with Bobby Vee in 1963 and I remember us sitting in the dressing-room on the opening night singing 'Love Me Do' and 'Please Please Me' together. The others on the tour were amazed. They'd never heard the songs before and they thought they were great."

The first Beatles' single to be issued in the US was 'Please Please Me' on 25 February 1963. Bob Gaudio from the Four Seasons: "We played the Hammersmith Odeon and two of the Beatles were there, but I didn't meet them. I had heard 'Please Please Me' which was No.1 in England. We took it back with us and I told Frankie Valli that we should cover it for the US. It would have been fun to do but we had 'Walk Like a Man' ready and we went with that. We could have cut a really good version of 'Please Please Me'. Vee Jay liked their record and they were the first label to issue Beatle records in the States. They didn't have a lot of their tracks and when the Beatles made it big they tried tricks like the LP, *The Beatles Vs the Four Seasons* and everybody sued them over that! We had our own problems with Vee Jay and there was litigation. They went bankrupt and we couldn't record for six months."

In 1964, the Vee-Jay label proved themselves expert at conning the public. They were to milk the handful of tracks licensed to them and one release was *Jolly What! The Beatles and Frank Ifield on Stage*, only they weren't. They were studio recordings but the sleeve note, with a brilliant Freudian slip, hopes you will enjoy this "copulation".

March 1963 – Please Please Me LP (Parlophone PMC 1202, 3/63)
Produced by George Martin, 14 tracks – 32m 45s
Side 1: I Saw Her Standing There/ Misery/ Anna (Go To Him)/ Chains/
Boys/ Ask Me Why/ Please Please Me
Side 2: Love Me Do (Andy White version)/ P.S. I Love You/ Baby It's You/
Do You Want To Know A Secret/ A Taste Of Honey/ There's A Place/
Twist And Shout
On a day off from their tour with Helen Shapiro, on 11 February 1963, the Beatles spent their time at EMI, recording ten tracks for their first album, *Please Please Me,* to which would be added their two singles. The day might have started off badly as the *Daily Express* had reported that they had been ejected from a dance in Carlisle for creating a nuisance. It was the Beatles' first front page story in a national newspaper.

Helen Shapiro: "It was a hotel called the Crown and Mitre in Carlisle. The Beatles, Kenny Lynch and me were having a drink: I was having a cup of tea as I was too young for alcohol. After the show, this guy kept begging us to come into the dance they were holding in the ballroom and we said, 'No, no thank you.' The guys were in leather jackets and I was in slacks and Kenny was in wellington boots and we didn't want to go in. Finally, to appease this guy we went in and had something from the buffet and started to dance. Some other chap was very irate, very blustery and very red in the face and said we had to leave because we weren't invited. We got thrown out. It got blown out of proportion in the press. I never did find out who told them but it was probably the Beatles' press officer as it was a good story. I was mortified as I thought I was in terrible trouble."

George Martin: "There wasn't a lot of money at Parlophone. I was working to an annual budget of £55,000. I could spend it however I wished but I had to produce a certain number of records per year. I wanted to get the Beatles' first album out quickly and we recorded it in a day. We started out at 10 in the morning and finished it about 11 at night. It was recorded in mono only. We had a quick cover done and we were out in a few weeks."

The opening cut on the *Please Please Me* album was 'I Saw Her Standing There'. Iris Caldwell: "One night at the Tower Ballroom in New Brighton, I was asked to demonstrate the twist. The twist had just come out and the Beatles were playing for me. That is when I first met Paul McCartney and as I was 17, it could be that 'I Saw Her Standing There' is about me. I did date Paul for sometime on and off."

Billy Kinsley: "Paul McCartney nicked the bass line from Chuck Berry's 'I'm Talkin' About You' for 'I Saw Her Standing There'. I can say that without fear of contradiction as it is so obvious. It was a dream bass line and it suited the song so well."

US reporter Larry Kane: "In 1964, 'I Saw Her Standing There' was one of the great breakthrough songs for the Beatles in the States and I felt it was because it was the ultimate song about instant love."

Beatles biographer Mark Lewisohn: "The *Please Please Me* album starts with Paul counting '1, 2, 3, 4.' They would count in a song and John always did it in a fantastic way, sometimes in German or as '4,3,2,1.' They included the count on the record for 'I Saw Her Standing There' because it captured the excitement and it was ideal for the opening track. Paul originally wrote, 'She was just 17, she had never been a beauty queen'. John said it was naff and they changed it to 'She was just 17, you know what I mean', which has no meaning but adds a sexual inference." True, but it is only a variant of Little Richard's "I've got a girl named Sue, She knows just what to do" in 'Long Tall Sally'.

Although presented as a cheerful rocker, 'There's a Place' gives us an early insight into John Lennon's mind. If things go wrong, he has the ability to withdraw inside himself. It is not the best song on the album but it may well have prompted Brian Wilson to write the highly perceptive 'In My Room', which was released in October 1963.

John Lennon was at his best singing Arthur Alexander's 'Anna (Go to Him)'. Rock writer Michael Gray: "Arthur Alexander said 'girl' instead of 'baby' and the Beatles took that up. He had a very distinctive voice and there is a lovely understatement in his records as most performers did the opposite. There is great scrupulousness in his work and some lovely songs about eternal triangles and struggles between lovers and friends. He was full of delicacy of feeling."

Billy Kinsley of the Merseybeats says, "I can remember standing right next to the curtain at Queen's Hall, Widnes when John Lennon was singing 'Anna' and the emotion that was coming out of his body was unbelievable. It was a wonderful song and we did have a go at it but it became too associated with the Beatles and we dropped it."

Although the Beatles performed Arthur Alexander's 'You Better Move On' on stage, no recording has surfaced. They did, however, perform his 'Soldier of Love' and 'A Shot of Rhythm and Blues' on the Light Programme in 1963. Nashville songwriter Buzz Cason recalls: "We had an opportunity to write for Arthur Alexander and 'Soldier Of Love' is probably the only R&B song written in Belle Meade as that is a ritzy, all-white neighbourhood. Arthur cut it on the other side of 'Where Have You Been', but it became a cult song. It has been recorded by Marshall Crenshaw and the Beatles. I remember my songwriting partner Tony Moon calling me about 1980 and saying, 'Listen to this' and he had a recording of the Beatles doing our song on the BBC. I still get blown away when I hear their version."

Beatles' press officer Tony Barrow: "I heard John doing 'Stand by Me' a number of times. He'd sing snatches of it in the dressing room when everybody was messing around with their instruments before going on stage. They'd limber up vocally by just doing a few lines from something and it could be 'Stand by Me'. I can remember way back, must be 63/64 where John would be going into a crazy version of 'Stand by Me' in dressing rooms. It was the way Reeves and Mortimer did their nightclub skit."

The Beatles showed their love of New York girl groups with the Cookies' 'Chains' and the Shirelles' "Baby It's You' and 'Boys'. The harmonica at the start of 'Chains' reminds us of 'Love Me Do' and by making the backing vocals as loud as the lead vocal, this becomes very lively. The desperation in John Lennon's voice on 'Baby It's You' makes the track as strong as the Shirelles', but I'm less sure of Ringo's vocal on 'Boys'. It could be argued that no Beatles album is perfect because John, Paul or George could have recorded a better vocal than Ringo's. On the other hand, having all four contributing to the LP is part and parcel of them being the Beatles, so on the whole, I give Ringo the benefit of the doubt. Also, you can sense that the other Beatles know that this is their weakest vocalist by the way they liven 'Boys' with rebel yells.

Shirley Alston Reeves from the Shirelles: "We were very pleased that the Beatles said that we were their favourite vocal group and we loved them doing 'Baby It's You'. When we did 'Will You Love Me Tomorrow', we didn't think much about the B-side, 'Boys'. It was a fun song, rather like 'What'd I Say'. We were surprised when we heard Ringo's version because it was a girl's song but he did it well. I still sing 'Boys' because it's a nice rock'n'roll number and the band can have fun with it."

BBC presenter Paul Gambaccini: "You liked the Beatles so much that you didn't mind their covers even if some weren't that great. Ringo Starr singing 'Boys' is not one of the world's greatest achievements, but it's fun and it sounds good. The only ones I would rather not hear are 'Please Mr. Postman' because I love the Marvelettes so much and 'You Really Got a Hold on Me' because I love Smokey Robinson and the Miracles, but even then they are very decent covers."

John had been reluctant to record 'Twist and Shout' for the first LP as he felt his voice was going and he had been sucking Zubes most of the day. It could have been a disaster but the result was stupendous. Well, Ronald Isley, the raucous lead singer of the Isley Brothers, wouldn't agree. He said that on a scale of one to ten, the Beatles' version merited a seven. Cyril Neville of the Neville Brothers was more generous: "The first tracks that I heard by the Beatles were Smokey Robinson and Larry Williams covers, and it was cool that some white cats were doing our music and doing it well. I especially liked 'Twist and Shout'. They didn't want to stand in one spot and were innovative. They knew how to take snippets of this and snippets of that and mix it up and make it their own thing."

How about this for an embryo Mr Bean? Rowan Atkinson: "When I was at primary school, we used to do a school concert at the parish church hall. Someone had the idea of playing 'Twist and Shout' and sending me on the stage to jive around to it all by myself, and I remember raising laughter. My mother couldn't stand the sight or sound of the Beatles and she scolded me afterwards for doing such a ridiculous thing on stage, even though I was only seven at the time."

Joe Elliott of Def Leppard: "The Beatles were masters of melody and they had great attitude in their performances. If they were singing something sad, it had a sad tinge to it, and if they were singing something aggressive, oh boy! When Lennon sings 'Twist and Shout', you almost get a headache listening to it. It's in a head exploding register."

The *Please Please Me* album had a cover photograph from theatre photographer, Angus McBean, taken on the balcony at EMI House. McBean was a society photographer, known for his portraits of Marlene Dietrich and Audrey Hepburn. The photograph works fine – perhaps because the Beatles look so young, but George Martin had favoured a shoot at London Zoo. Just as well the idea was dropped as the Beach Boys' *Pet Sounds* has a mundane cover for a groundbreaking LP. Ringo has not yet got a Beatle haircut, which makes nonsense of the claim that Pete Best was sacked for just that.

The sleeve note was written by Tony Barrow. "The very first album was recorded in a day and it took them a shorter time to make the recording than it took me to write the sleeve notes. I had been Britain's only full-time sleeve-note writer, employed by Decca to write for their artists, from Gracie Fields to Duke Ellington and Anthony Newley. Because I liked editorial stuff on the sleeves, it was natural that I should write descriptive pieces about the Beatles and we talked through the tracks on the album. The main thing was to make sure that the listeners knew who was doing what. A copy of the *Please Please Me* album was used to answer press questions about the group and was kept near the switchboard."

John and Paul shared composing credit on their compositions. Songs would be listed "Lennon/ McCartney" even if it was completely Lennon ('Help!') or completely Paul ('Yesterday'). Although it was a cause of friction in later years, Tony Barrow thinks it was the right decision: "Lennon and McCartney shared composer credits equally. This ensured that they derived an equal financial share from everything they wrote. They did collaborate with each other on songs but, creatively, it was never a 50/50 split. It could be 75/25 or even 90/10. One would have a pretty solid idea and the other would add the rest." The phrase "Lennon/ McCartney" sounded much better than "McCartney/ Lennon", though probably not to Paul McCartney.

Paul Du Noyer: "The great strength of their songwriting partnership is that they were exactly equal talents. They were individually great songwriters and each man acted as the quality controller for the other and raised each other's position."

Recognising the potential of the Lennon and McCartney partnership, Dick James established the Beatles' own music publishing company, Northern Songs. EMI historian Brian Southall: "'Please Please Me' was published by Dick James Music and when Northern Songs was founded in 1963 and Dick was reassigning the songs from DJM, Brian told him not to bother as 'You never know what is going to happen.' It was a thank you to Dick James. It was kept by the family who sold it to Polygram which is now Universal. Dick was an old-fashioned music publisher, who took the view that he had contributed an awful lot to the success of the Beatles, and I would agree with him. They needed a music publisher who knew what he was doing. Records are easy: you make a record, EMI sells it and then gives you some money. Publishing is different. You have a song and you need someone to publish it. The publisher is responsible for getting it covered and for collecting the royalties from the record and the sheet music as well as overseeing its publication and sales overseas. Dick James ploughed his efforts into making Lennon and McCartney hugely successful. It was one of the best deals that Brian Epstein ever did. Later on, the Beatles questioned the integrity of the deal: they thought it was a bit of fix as George, Dick and Brian had all known each other."

We don't know how George Harrison felt about the Lennon and McCartney partnership: George had co-written 'In Spite Of All The Danger' and 'Cry For A Shadow' and he might have wanted to be included. But he wasn't. Cynthia Lennon: "I think that had to do with George being younger than they were. It took time for him to evolve as a songwriter, but he was a great guitarist all along. He became a really wonderful writer in the later years."

April 1963 – From Me To You/ Thank You Girl (Parlophone R 5015, 4/63, UK No.1) (The US single only made No.41 - curious.)
Early in March 1963, the Beatles returned to Abbey Road to record their next single, 'From Me to You' and 'Thank You Girl'. They also put down 'One After 909', but they weren't happy with it. 'One After 909' was shelved, but a new version was recorded during the *Let It Be* sessions in 1969. Their third Parlophone single was released on 12 April 1963 and was No.1 on all the charts within a fortnight. There was now a feeling that we were witnessing something special – already, the Beatles had the same level of fame as Cliff Richard, Lonnie Donegan and Billy Fury.

Singer and songwriter Charlie Dore: "The Beatles were completely instrumental in me loving music. I feel so lucky that I was at school while they were recording their singles. I was seven years old and I was excited that a new single was coming out. I would ask if we could buy it and then there was the real excitement of getting it. I wanted to marry

Paul McCartney and I was terribly jealous when he was with Jane Asher and then when he married Linda Eastman. Kids like Beatles music today but it was really something to have been there when those singles were being released."

Helen Shapiro: "I enjoyed 'Please Please Me'. I thought it was very unusual for those days, very different. 'Love Me Do' was very gutsy, very earthy, and 'Please Please Me' was more sophisticated, certainly compared to the little poppy things I used to do. During the tour, John and Paul came and said, 'Would you come over and listen to this song? We've written two songs and we can't decide which one we want to be the A-side. Well, we think we know, but we're not sure.' Paul played the piano and they both sang these two songs to me, one of which was 'From Me to You' and the other 'Thank You Girl'. I did prefer 'From Me to You', so it was nice to be asked."

Gilbert O'Sullivan: "I come from the McCartney school as I was always more into melody. John Lennon wrote great melodies too but his lyrics had more effect on me than his melodies. There are great lyrical ideas in McCartney too. I loved some of the B-sides, 'Thank You Girl', 'I'll Get You', great stuff. You can hear the collaborative effect better on some of those tracks. They were great and they weren't played all the time like the A-sides."

Mick Box of Uriah Heep: "I'm an East End boy and I can remember walking down Walthamstow High Street and hearing 'Love Me Do' and 'From Me to You' coming from the stalls. I thought they were fantastic records with beautiful harmonies. All the 60s harmonies were quite sweet and enhanced the melody or chorus line or backed it up with an 'aaah' but we were to use harmonies as another instrument. What is wonderful about the Beatles is that they captured every genre – there is folk, rock, soul and country in there and they were absolutely brilliant. The guitar sounds that George Harrison got were stunning."

The Merseybeats made their TV debut on *ABC At Large*. Billy Kinsley: "It was filmed in Droylsden and I was violently sick when we heard we would appearing live. I was that scared. We met Brian Epstein downstairs in the Blue Angel and we told him that we were going to do the Beatles' song 'Misery' the next day and he was so pleased about that. He took us upstairs to speak to John and Paul and it may have been the first time that somebody else was singing a Lennon and McCartney song on television. We went on and did the live programme and it was not frightening at all, just a great experience. The programme was a joke as the viewers had to identify which of two bands was the Liverpool band. As we were called the Merseybeats, it rather gave the game away! Still, the Mersey starts in Stockport so it was possible that we came from Manchester. The other band was Deke Rivers and the Big Sound."

John and Paul were prolific and usually wrote quality songs. Their B-sides – 'Thank You Girl', 'I'll Get You', 'This Boy' and many more – would have been A-sides for lesser groups. No wonder that other acts were looking to Lennon and McCartney for their singles. Album cuts such as 'Misery', 'I Saw Her Standing There', 'Do You Want to Know a Secret' and 'There's a Place' were recorded by Kenny Lynch, Duffy Power, Billy J. Kramer and the Kestrels respectively.

Kenny Lynch: "We were all swapping songs on the coach. I wrote one and gave it to Johnny Tillotson. I later had a hit with it myself – 'You Can Never Stop Me Loving You'. The Beatles offered 'Misery' to Helen Shapiro who said, 'I don't want to do it. I don't like the title.' She was only a kid, so I said, 'I like the song. I'll do it.' They said, 'Great' but John Lennon gave me the greatest rucking in the world because I had Bert Weedon on it. He'd been booked for the session and I'd been told that he was very good. I played the record to John in Dick James' office and he said, 'Who's that on guitar?' and I said, 'It's Bert Weedon.' He said, 'Why didn't you tell me? I'd have done it for you.' I said, 'What can I do? Do you like the record or don't you?' He said, 'Well, I quite like it.' He didn't pin any medals on me but it was the first song recorded by someone else from that great catalogue. It sold about 10,000, but it didn't get anywhere near the charts."

Helen Shapiro: "I had been away in America, it happened when I was on tour, I was doing *The Ed Sullivan Show* and I came back and started the tour and they told me 'We offered you this song 'Misery' but Norrie Paramor turned it down.' So I never knew about it till it was a done deal unfortunately."

Duffy Power: "I got to record for the producer, Ron Richards, at EMI. He told me that the Beatles said I was the best R&B singer in England and they had a song for me, 'I Saw Her Standing There'. I did it with the Graham Bond Quartet who were very avant-garde with their sense of rhythm. John McLaughlin was on guitar, but that first session was not thought successful because I didn't stick to the tune. I had silly ideas in those days and this was a rock'n'roll song with a very definite melody. I had to do it again. John McLaughlin was ill for the second session and we had Big Jim Sullivan instead."

Maggie Bell recorded the song on *Suicide Sal* in 1975: "I loved 'I Saw Her Standing There' from the moment I first heard it. It's a great song and Paul McCartney has one of the best rock voices in the business. The arrangement that we had on our version was very good. Pete Wingfield was playing piano and it was incredible. Just listen to the speed of it. I couldn't sing it at that speed every night – it would kill me. I've got to be careful with that gospel ending too as I don't want to end up laughing."

On 9 March 1963, the Beatles joined another package tour, this time with the American hit-makers, Chris Montez ('Let's Dance') and Tommy Roe ('Sheila'). Chris Montez: "I had been on tour with Sam Cooke. He had taught me a lot of things and I had a positive attitude about performing. I liked the way that Sam Cooke sang to the ladies. He was real stylish and I tried to be the same. Jerry Butler and Smokey Robinson charmed the ladies too and they were screaming for me as well as the Beatles."

But maybe not screaming as much. Chris Montez: "The Beatles were booked to get the show going and they had such energy and power. They played me their album, *Please Please Me,* before it was released and I was knocked out. I couldn't stop singing 'I Saw Her Standing There'. It was such a great song. I had hit records and was topping the bill but when we got to Liverpool, I said, 'This is your town, you close the show. I'm not the headliner here.' They were amazed that I should say that."

Tommy Roe: "I am very proud to be a part of the history of the Beatles and my memories of our tour are all great. They were getting hot in England and it was tough following them. We turned the whole thing around and they ended up closing the show. I was so impressed that I started doing their songs and tried to get them a deal in the States. My record company turned them down and I think now that they should have seen them. Their records weren't too impressive in the beginning – they were doing their take on 50s music – and you really had to see the image alongside the music. Once the Beatles started getting publicity in America, it was bound to happen. I was so influenced by what I heard in this country that I wrote 'Everybody' on the way home. I tried to get that same sound. We recorded it in Muscle Shoals and it was a big record."

Chris Montez changed the Ritchie Valens song, 'In a Turkish Town' to 'In an English Town'. "I had such a wonderful time when I came over here that I thought I would sing about an English town and an English girl. I had a coat with a round collar and a belt that was made in England but bought in America. People wanted to buy the jacket from me, which used to amaze me. The Beatles took me to their tailor and he made a couple of suits for me. On the last day of the tour, they said, 'We hope you don't mind but we're having jackets made like yours.' No problem, I was impressed."

Gordon Millings worked for his father, Dougie, a tailor to the stars: "Brian Epstein and my father came up with the round neck, collarless jackets for the Beatles. We made that kind of coat before the war for the stewards on the big liners, so it was nothing new. Then there was the Chesterfield look – single-breasted suits with velvet collars and cuffs and, after that, the military style with epaulettes and brass buttons."

In March 1963, Gerry and the Pacemakers released their version of the song the Beatles rejected, Mitch Murray's 'How Do You Do It'. It was followed by another of his compositions, 'I Like It'. Mitch Murray: "When you have a No.1, you think, 'Phew, at last.' It's not bottles of champagne but relief. Then you think, 'Maybe it's a fluke' and you spend your whole career trying to prove yourself. I wrote 'I Like It' for Gerry's follow-up but John Lennon had given him 'Hello Little Girl'. John threatened to thump me if I got the follow-up and I thought it was worth a thump. 'I Like It' had the same cheekiness and innuendo and it also went to No.1. I didn't get a thump."

Gerry and the Pacemakers' third No.1 was with 'You'll Never Walk Alone' from *Carousel*. This was taken up by the Kop Choir, which coincided with the rise of both Merseybeat and Liverpool FC.

Gerry and the Pacemakers did demo Lennon and McCartney's 'Hello Little Girl', but didn't take it any further. Gerry was treating it just as the Beatles had treated 'How Do You Do It'. "I don't think that Gerry ever wanted to do Lennon and McCartney songs," said the Pacemakers' drummer and Gerry's brother, Fred Marsden, "At NEMS Enterprises, it was always the Beatles No.1 and Gerry No.2, and Gerry was competitive."

Instead, 'Hello Little Girl' went to another of Epstein's groups, the Fourmost. Brian O'Hara recalled, "We had nothing original to offer George Martin for a single. I asked John Lennon for a song and I've still got the tape he gave me. He says, 'I wrote this one while I was sitting on the toilet.'" Brian died in 1999 and I don't know where the tape went.

The Fourmost followed 'Hello Little Girl' with the romantic

'I'm In Love'. Billy Hatton: "As opposed to the Beatles doing new songs on an album and people saying 'Can we have this one?' or 'Can we have that one?' before they're released, 'I'm In Love' was written by Lennon and McCartney for the Fourmost. That was a big NEMS Enterprises operation." The Fourmost also considered, but did not record, 'It Won't Be Long'.

A feature of many pre-war songs from Tin Pan Alley and Hollywood was an introductory verse which led you into the song itself, the most famous example being 'Stardust'. These were not used very often in rock'n'roll and teenage pop but examples include Dion's 'Runaround Sue', Bobby Vee's 'Take Good Care of My Baby' (both 1961) and the Beatles' 'Do You Want to Know a Secret'. This has a lead vocal from George who doesn't sound as Scouse as usual, perhaps because of the echo on the voice, and certainly not in comparison to Billy J. Kramer.

Outside the Beatles' themselves, Billy J. Kramer wasn't the first choice for John and Paul's 'Do You Want to Know a Secret'. The song was offered to Nottingham's Shane Fenton and the Fentones. They had had hits with 'I'm A Moody Guy' (1961) and 'Cindy's Birthday' (1962). Shane Fenton became Alvin Stardust. "Brian Epstein came up to me at a Sunday concert somewhere and said he had a number called 'Do You Want to Know a Secret'. He thought it would be perfect for me but I told him that I already had a manager and that I'd have to pass on it. Maybe if I'd gone and done it, I'd have done the things that Billy J.Kramer did but you can never say what would have happened if you'd done something else."

Kenny Johnson, then Sonny Webb of the Liverpool country band, Sonny Webb and the Cascades: "I signed for Eppy after we'd been on the Queen's Hall in Widnes. He came to my house in Speke and he gave me three songs and told me to rehearse them. The first one was 'Do You Want to Know a Secret' and then he said he was giving it to Billy J. I said 'Billy who?' because we just knew him as Billy Kramer. He said, 'Never mind, you can do 'Misery'' but then Brian sent me a note saying, 'Kenny Lynch is doing 'Misery', try 'Tip of My Tongue'. I said, 'I've had enough of this. I'm signing with Les Ackerley.'"

Billy J. Kramer recalls, "We'd had 'Do You Want to Know a Secret' on tape from John Lennon. It was just John on acoustic guitar and he'd recorded it in the loo because it was the only place where he could get peace and quiet. We did it every night at the Star-Club in Hamburg and it didn't do anything. I came back and we did a test for EMI and two weeks later Brian said, 'EMI are going to release 'Do You Want to Know a Secret'.' I was a bit sick because the Beatles had had hits and Gerry had just had a No.1 and I said, 'Does that mean that I've finally got a recording contract?' He said yes and I said, 'Well, let's find a good number because I don't think that song's strong enough. 'Love Me Do' and 'Please Please Me' were great but I can't see this happening.' Brian said that EMI were happy with it. The success of 'Do You Want to Know a Secret?' was the biggest surprise of my life."

In April 1963 the Beatles recorded BBC radio appearances in *Side By Side*, and the success led to their series *Pop Go the Beatles* in May. They also appeared on *Easy Beat* and *Saturday Club* and the double CD, *Live at the BBC*, released in 1994 included many of their one-off recordings. The cover versions, often not recorded for EMI, indicate what they had been doing at the Cavern and because they were largely doing short sets on package tours by then, they were not often performing them in public.

British country singer Lorne Gibson: "*Saturday Club* got 150 requests a week for Cliff, 100 for some of the other stars, and the odd one for me. Suddenly, huge sacks of mail began to appear and they were full of requests for the Beatles. The Beatles came on my radio show *Side by Side* and then I was a guest on *Pop Go the Beatles*. It was very refreshing because they had their own ideas of where they wanted to go and they didn't want to be stereotyped. They tried thirty times to do 'Pop Goes the Weasel' as 'Pop Go the Beatles'. Eventually, Diz Disley and my guitarist and bass player did it for them. Paul liked country and he sat in on some of our songs, just as we did odd bits in theirs. It was great. Eppy wanted to sign me but I was working for Tommy Sanderson who'd already lost a few artists. I thought, 'No, I like little Tommy. I'll stick with him.'"

Frank Ifield: "I loved the banter between the Beatles and envied it to some degree as they were together as a group and I was a loner. I could have a different band every night and I only had a close rapport with my manager. A group is facing something together and I didn't have that. When I was at the London Palladium, the boys came to see the show and when they came backstage, there weren't any seats left. John and Ringo were sitting on the floor and John said to Ringo, 'Well, if we never make it anywhere else, we can say we made it to the London Palladium dressing rooms.' They were so funny."

In April 1963 Frank Allen of the Rebel Rousers went with Cliff

Bennett to see the Beatles at Kilburn. "I went to the Gaumont State Ballroom. They were becoming a big deal and the girls were screaming but you could still get close to them. They were playing on a stage that was only a couple of feet higher than the audience. They did two half-hour sets and we saw them in the dressing room between sets. I was with some friends who supported the Rebel Rousers around the Middlesex area. They didn't care for the Beatles at all. They wanted to leave at the interval and go to a Wimpey bar. We had to leave and I never saw the second set."

Pete Frame, noted for his *Rock Family Trees*, lived in Luton: "The Beatles had the most extraordinary influence, absolutely everywhere, and Luton was no exception. The Beatles came down and played, and overnight a dozen pop groups sprung up who wanted to be the Beatles. Pretty soon it was a hundred or so, it was like the Gold Rush."

The Beatles didn't make an impact in America until 1964 and so the visiting American stars coming to the UK in 1963 were witnessing a phenomenon they knew nothing about. Pat Boone: "I was gathering songs from all around the world that I might record and I brought an English song home – (sings) 'If there's anything that you want, If there's anything I can do.' I tried my best to get Randy Wood to let me record the song but he said, 'No, that'll never be a hit'."

The American star, Del Shannon did record "From Me To You", thus becoming the first person to take a Lennon and McCartney song into the US Top 100. Del Shannon was with the Beatles as part of *Swinging Sound 63* at the Royal Albert Hall in April. "'From Me to You' was a big hit in England and I told John Lennon that I was going to do it. He said, 'That'll be all right', but then, just as he was going on stage at the Royal Albert Hall, he turned to me and said, 'Don't do that.' Brian Epstein had told him that he didn't want any Americans covering their songs. The Beatles were going to invade America by themselves." Del Shannon did it anyway.

I thought that Del's 1965 hit, 'Keep Searchin'' owed something to the Mersey sound but he disagreed: "That song is the same as 'Runaway' and that was before Merseybeat. I strum hard, double."

Three days after *Swinging Sound 63*, the Beatles were playing to 10,000 pop fans at the *NME Pollwinners Concert* at the Empire Pool, Wembley. They received a remarkable reception for a group which hadn't won a poll and had just three records out. John Stewart from the Kingston Trio: "I was playing the London Palladium and the opening of the London Hilton with the Kingston Trio. We were big fans of the Springfields and we went to see them get an award at some big concert. The Beatles did 'Twist and Shout' and some of their own songs. Nick Reynolds and I both said, 'That's it. When this hits America, it's over for us.' Within a few months, 'I Want to Hold Your Hand' had come out, they had done *The Ed Sullivan Show* and we never had another Top 40 record."

At the end of April 1963, the four Beatles took a short break, John going to Spain with Brian Epstein. Considering that John's son Julian had just been born, this was a bizarre and insensitive decision, even by John Lennon's standards. Possibly John Lennon seized the opportunity to assert his role as leader of the Beatles to Brian Epstein.

Beatles' biographer, Steven Gaines: "The fact that Brian was gay has everything to do with the Beatles' story. One reason that they happened the way they did was because of Brian's deep affection for John Lennon. It was the reason for Brian's great vision of the Beatles and the reason why he changed the look of rock'n'roll. He was a very driven and obsessive man and it's important to understand that when discussing the Beatles phenomenon."

Colin Middlebrough, drummer with the Liverpool band, the Kansas City Five: "When I saw the Beatles, I would be waiting in great anticipation for 'Please Mr. Postman'. Lennon had bent knees and he would be looking down his nose as he sang it. Lennon didn't have much time for people and he totally ignored me most of the time. Paul McCartney, on the other hand, was very much in your face. I remember Mike Millward of the Fourmost bringing a cake down for Paul's 21st birthday one lunchtime and he was so pleased that he was jumping about."

Paul McCartney's 21st party was held at his Auntie Gin's house in Huyton. Bob Wooler made a disparaging remark about John Lennon's holiday and was beaten up for his wisecrack. Following a tip-off from Allan Williams, the story made the *Daily Mirror* and led to an out-of-court settlement.

In May 1963, the Beatles were touring the UK with Roy Orbison. The bill also featured Gerry and the Pacemakers and Erkey Grant and the Earwigs (What a ridiculous name – whoever thought that an insect's name could lead to success?) Duane Eddy: "I was supposed to tour with the Beatles in 1963 but my manager messed that up and Roy Orbison went instead. That was one of the greatest things that ever happened to Roy. It rejuvenated his career and he had several more hit records. He was very thankful to me for not going on that tour!"

Promoter Tito Burns: "The deal with Roy Orbison was that he closed the show. By the time he got here, the Beatles were flourishing but Orbison said, in his quiet voice, 'I'll stay where I am.' The first show was at the Adelphi Cinema, Slough with 3,000 seats. The Beatles came on and you could only see their lips moving. You couldn't hear them. When Roy went on, everyone was still screaming. Roy went into 'Only the Lonely' and they quietened down. He did his act and got six encores. I wouldn't have believed that he could have followed the Beatles by just standing there, but he did. He did it every night of the tour and it didn't seem to worry him. He was incredible."

Roy Orbison had no sooner arrived than he was confronted by Brian Epstein and John Lennon: "Brian said, 'Who should close the show?', and John said, 'You're getting all the money, so why don't we close it?' I don't know whether that was true or not, whether I was getting that much more than they were. I certainly wasn't getting that much – and the tour had sold out in one afternoon."

On 26 May 1963 I caught the tour at the Liverpool Empire, where the Beatles topped the bill. I remember the cries for the Beatles as Orbison stepped out on the stage. I wondered how he could cope with it but he simply whispered "A candy-coloured clown they call the Sandman" and he was away. The audience loved him and forgot the Beatles for thirty minutes. Roy Orbison: "I remember Paul and John grabbing me by my arms and not letting me go back to take my curtain call. The audience was yelling, 'We want Roy, we want Roy,' and there I was, being held captive by the Beatles who were saying, 'Yankee, go home.' We had a great time."

Peter Noone, aka Herman: "The Beatles were really nice to all the lads who were coming up. When you got on a show with them, they came to the dressing room and said, 'Welcome to the tour, lads. We're happy to have you on the show.' They had got it from Roy Orbison. He went around all the dressing rooms and thanked everybody. It was a great thing to do and I did it myself later on."

In June 1963, the Beatles starred in the first, all-Merseyside edition of ABC-TV's *Thank Your Lucky Stars*. It was especially encouraging for the Searchers, a non-NEMS act, who then topped the charts with 'Sweets for My Sweet'.

July 1963 – Twist and Shout EP (Parlophone GEP 8882, 7/63)
Neither George Martin nor the Beatles wanted to lift singles off albums and so 'Twist and Shout' became the lead track on a huge-selling, four track EP. The Beatles dominated the EP chart as much as the singles and LP charts. The US single by the Isley Brothers made the UK charts as well as another British version from Brian Poole and the Tremeloes. Writing the liner notes on that EP was Tony Barrow: "I didn't feel there were enough best-selling EPs to qualify for an EP chart. They were the same size as singles and played at the same speed and I felt that they should be included in the singles chart. The *Twist and Shout* EP competed very successfully with the singles of the day."

Some years later, Tony Barrow was asked to repeat his liner notes: "They say that copying is a form of flattery and, in the case of the Genesis *3x3* record, it is self copying. Phil Collins wanted a record that would be packaged in the same way as the *Twist and Shout* EP. I found it very difficult to copy my own style."

Brian Poole: "I thought that the Isley Brothers' version of 'Twist and Shout' was the greatest record I'd ever heard and I can remember buying it with the earnings from our first gig. We were doing 'Twist and Shout' on stage before we knew that anybody else was doing it and we felt that we could have a hit with it. Unfortunately, we had it in the can for about a year before Decca decided to release it as a single. We received a telegram saying that 'Twist and Shout' had sold 40,000 in a few hours and was going to be a hit. We didn't know that the Beatles had also recorded it and suddenly there was a massive fight up the charts because the Beatles' EP was shown on some singles charts. Our managements agreed that we would say whatever we liked about each other as it would generate publicity and help both versions. Our version was totally different from the Beatles'. You can hear the Buddy Holly influence on mine and I didn't sing with that gruff, John Lennon voice."

August 1963 – She Loves You/ I'll Get You (Parlophone R 5055, 8/63, UK No.1, US No.1) (Both English and German language versions made No.7 in Germany, one following the other.)
Sean O'Mahony (aka Johnny Dean), a publisher of fan magazines, suggested to Brian Epstein that the Beatles should have their own monthly magazine, somewhat ridiculously to be called *The Beatles Book*. Sean joined the inner circle and was at Abbey Road on 1 July 1963. "I got to Studio 2 in Abbey Road and Brian Epstein, George

Martin and Dick James were hanging around waiting for the Beatles. I learned that the boys were completing a song on the way to the studio. They walked in and they sang it with acoustic guitars and with everyone cocking an ear to hear what it was like. It was 'She Loves You' and it didn't sound very impressive. The song when I first heard it and the song when they'd finished it sounded completely different. What they did in between was the Beatles' magic."

And George Martin's. It was his suggestion that the record should go straight into the chorus, which is one reason why the track is so vibrant.

John Lennon acknowledged that the 'woo woo' in 'She Loves You' was taken from the Isley Brothers' 'Twist and Shout' and the 'yeah yeah' from Elvis Presley's 'All Shook Up'. When the musical *Laughter in the Rain* came to the Liverpool Empire in 2010, Wayne Smith as Neil Sedaka said, "The Beatles weren't that original. I did the 'yeah yeah yeah' first in 'Little Devil'." The audience booed him like a pantomime devil and someone shouted, good naturedly, "I dispute that."

Kenny Lynch recalls, "I was on a coach with the Beatles and they played me a song which included 'woo woo'. I said, 'You can't do that. It's horrible and you sound like a bunch of fairies.'" But they did do that, and 'She Loves You' with its 'yeah, yeah, yeah' catchphrase sold a million copies in Britain alone.

Freddie Starr, then a Liverpool beat musician: "At first I didn't think the Beatles would last. I remember Bob Wooler playing me one of the Beatles' records before it was released. It was 'She Loves You' and I said, 'It's terrible. It'll never get anywhere.' I've never really been into the Beatles' material. I liked Paul McCartney's music much more after he left the Beatles and I also prefer John's solo work. I think they tried really hard to establish themselves in their own right."

Charlie Dore: "I loved the melodies and also the simplicity of not over-adorning something. They knew instinctively how to make emotional chord changes that speak to you straight away. I'm a sucker for harmonies and I loved the way that their voices sounded together, with Paul's rather sweet voice, John's harder edge and George with that magic in the background."

Rolling Stone writer Dave Marsh: "'Strawberry Fields Forever' is great, but it's not a question as to how great they became because they were great from the beginning. Their hard rock years were as good as their psychedelic years and that point is continually lost. They were a rock band who could swing and they sang with heart and soul. Listen to 'She Loves You' and you'll discover a very dangerous message – 'She loves you and if you're too big a fool to respect that, I'm going after her.' That's what the song really is about. It's John Lennon at his slyest."

George Martin: "The talent was always there but they hadn't had the opportunity before. They responded to the challenge. The 'yeah, yeah, yeah' in 'She Loves You' was a curious singing chord. It was a major sixth with George Harrison doing the sixth and the other two, the third and fifth. It was just the way Glenn Miller wrote for the saxophone."

Bandleader Syd Lawrence who promoted the legacy of Glenn Miller: "Put it down to my age, if you like, but I was brought up in the big band era and I could not grasp that four guys could go on stage with three guitars and a set of drums and thrill me. I was brought up with an array of musical instruments – trombones, trumpets, clarinets, saxophones – and there was no way that three guitars and drums could replace that. It made me very sad because it wasn't educating the boys and girls as to what real sounds could do – symphony orchestras, light orchestras, big bands and the like."

Cabaret entertainer Earl Okin: "What makes their songs special are the interesting chord sequences. They played very simple chords as they weren't great musicians technically but they kept playing those simple chords in the wrong order and they changed keys and went weird places and that dragged their melodies around strange corners. That's how to write good songs. You use notes as pivots and you change key on that so that you have the same note harmonised by different chords so it goes sideways. They did it naturally. As they got more involved, they had a better idea of what they were doing. Irving Berlin is another example. He wasn't a great musician."

Beatles biographer, Steve Turner: "Younger people today assume that the groups will write their own songs, but this was completely novel at the time. In Cliff and the Shadows, some songs were written by Bruce Welch and Hank Marvin but that's about it. You were expected to get songwriters from Tin Pan Alley to do the work for you. The Beatles were the first of a breed of better educated musicians and they'd had a taste of further education and they knew a bit about Chaucer and a bit about Shakespeare, and a bit about Picasso and that's the huge difference between the Cliff and Elvis and Billy Fury generation and this new generation. They knew a bit about artists, a bit about writing and they could imagine themselves, not only as Elvis or Billy Fury on stage, they could also imagine themselves as writers like Shakespeare or Chaucer. Lennon sometimes compared himself to Van Gogh. They related to artists in a way that previous generations hadn't."

Barbara Dickson: "The 50s was the start of the modern age, but at the start of the 60s, you had the bomb, equality for women and the pill, which all fired the writers. They were also very educated, and that's the key. They were well taught with a good command of English and knew about literature. Look at Paul Simon – he had a very college-educated approach to music and it was wonderful. The pop charts were still toe-curling a lot of the time and some very bad records were alongside the very good."

Richard Barnes was part of the Quiet Five, which made the charts with Paul Simon's 'Homeward Bound': "We did a short tour with the Beatles and the song I remember best is 'She Loves You'. I never saw it from the front of the house but I saw it from the side and there was something special about the way their heads all shook to the 'oohs'. After one gig in London, I remember standing next to John Lennon in a toilet. A guy stood in the toilet stall and he kept looking over and down to see what John Lennon was made of. John kept winking at me and he thought it was so funny. The guy turned out to be a great fan."

George Harrison had said in an interview that he liked jelly babies. An innocuous remark, but it led to fans throwing jelly babies on stage. Geoff Nugent of the Undertakers supported the Beatles at the Grafton Room in August 1963: "George Harrison had said that he liked jelly babies, and so the audiences started throwing them onto the stage. Our sax player, Brian, thought it was great fun to try and catch them in the bell of his sax. The heat was so great that they congealed and melted in the bottom of the horn. He had about a pound and a half of jelly in the bell of his sax."

Paddy Delaney, the doorman at the Cavern: "The last time the Beatles appeared in the Cavern was in August 1963 and it was for £20. The booking had been arranged months before. In the meantime, they had risen to the top. They were making thousands of pounds. The crowds outside were going mad. By the time John Lennon had got through a cordon of girls, his mohair jacket had lost a sleeve. I grabbed it to stop the girl getting away with a souvenir. John immediately stitched the sleeve back on. They may have altered their style elsewhere but they didn't for the Cavern. They were the same old Beatles, with

John saying, 'Okay, tatty-head, we're gonna play that number for you.' There was never anything elaborate about his introductions."

Chas McDevitt, famed for 'Freight Train': "We were doing a Sunday show with the Beatles in Blackpool and we stayed behind to watch them from the side of the stage. We wanted to leave at the end of the show but we couldn't get out of the theatre until one o'clock in the morning. The streets were packed solid. Somehow they'd spirited the Beatles away off the roof, but we were stuck in the theatre because the kids thought they were still there. I remember George Harrison telling me that they'd been offered a contract to go back to Hamburg. 'We're not going,' he said, 'We're not bloody soft.'"

Barbara Dickson, then 15 years old, saw the Beatles on 6 October 1963. "I was a great Beatles fan and they were coming to play at the Carlton Theatre in Kirkcaldy 15 miles from where I lived. They had to fulfil some small gigs in Scotland and this was at the back end of Fife in Kirkcaldy, which is not a big town. I cycled from my home to get tickets and I found out when I got there that tickets were to be applied for by post. I had to cycle home and write a letter but I did get the tickets and I did see the Beatles."

And was it worth it? Barbara Dickson: "We were little girls in the same room as our fantasy heroes. They were musicians and they must have thought it absurd that they couldn't be heard over the screaming. That was fundamental as to why they stopped performing. They hated it. They could have sung 'Three Blind Mice' and nobody would have known. I was probably doing some shouting and standing up myself but I was never a good screamer. They didn't play for long in those days. It wasn't Bruce Springsteen with a three hour set: you were lucky to get six or seven songs. You never felt short-changed as you had been there and seen them in the flesh."

Ray Coleman of *Melody Maker*: "Live, the Beatles weren't that wonderful. You couldn't hear them because the screams were so overpowering. It was an event to go to but, musically, I never saw them give a fantastically good concert. John Lennon felt that four waxwork dummies could do the job. They couldn't hear him so he took to singing nonsense words and taking the mickey out of his performance. He was very cynical about it all."

Allan Clarke, lead singer of the Hollies: "The screaming was the same for everybody. It was the same for the Dave Clark Five, the Rolling Stones or the Hollies. It wasn't really the music as such on stage: it was the happening of being there to see your idols. I'd be singing but very often I couldn't even hear the group behind me."

Tony Palmer: "Back in Cambridge in October 1963 the Beatles came to town and there was a press conference and I went representing *Varsity*, the university newspaper. It was a ridiculous affair and we had a cup of tea after the press conference and John Lennon said, 'Why didn't you ask any questions?' and I said, 'I thought it was pretty silly.' I told him that I was studying Moral Sciences, and he said, 'That's silly too.' He asked me to show him round the university, and I said, 'No, we would be mobbed and that's not my idea of fun.' He said, 'How about it if I come in disguise?' I turned up at the hotel to pick him up and he was in a long brown raincoat and a fedora with a huge great beard. It was too ridiculous for words, so we got rid of it and I got him into the Wren Library and King's Chapel and showed him some of the sights. He was very grateful and he gave me tickets for the concert and he said, 'This is my number, if you come to London, give me a call.'"

On 13 October 1963, the Beatles appeared live on *Sunday Night at the London Palladium*. Comedian and sometime *Palladium* host Norman Vaughan: "A lot of the first pop groups didn't want to play *Sunday Night at the London Palladium*. They wouldn't let you mime because it was a live show and the groups thought that the sound wouldn't be good enough. A lot of these groups had created wonderful sounds in the studio but they couldn't do it as competently live, so it was very risky."

Maybe but the Beatles were so successful that the term "Beatlemania" was coined by the *Daily Mirror*. The Beatles undertook their first tour outside the UK with some dates in Sweden. The mayhem on their return to London was noticed by the American TV host, Ed Sullivan, who realised that they would be ideal for his show.

In November 1963, the Beatles were invited to appear on the Royal Variety Performance at the Prince of Wales Theatre in London. American jazz singer Buddy Greco was on the bill: "When I got to rehearsals, there were thousands of people outside the Prince of Wales Theatre and I had no idea who they wanted to see. I didn't think it was me and I didn't think it was Marlene Dietrich, who, incidentally, had a young piano player called Burt Bacharach. Young men were walking around with crazy haircuts that looked like the Three Stooges, and all the magazines and newspapers had the Beatles on the front page. When I saw them at rehearsal and they did a couple of songs, I thought they were just a nice little rock'n'roll band. *Melody Maker* wanted my opinion of the Beatles and I said very bluntly, 'If I know my business, the Beatles will be out of fashion in about a year.' Little did I realise that they would turn out to be geniuses who wrote wonderful songs."

Buddy Greco also witnessed John Lennon's eccentricity: "I knew John Lennon was a little nuts because while we were talking upstairs, he was putting water in balloons and throwing them into the street. When he said that line about the jewellery, I was backstage and I fell on the floor laughing. It was a great line." Indeed it was. The funniest remark that people recall from a Royal Variety Performance is John Lennon telling the aristocracy to rattle their jewellery and it wasn't even made by a comedian.

Tommy Steele was with the West End cast of *Half a Sixpence* on that bill: "Everybody goes around petrified on those shows. You've only got a couple of minutes and you don't want to mess it up. To be honest, I was too wrapped up in what I was doing to pay much attention to the Beatles. There is the rehearsal, the run-through and then the dress rehearsal so it is exhausting. The television critics would review it the next day as though it was the opening of a show. It was always said that if you failed on a Command Performance, it was better not to get mentioned at all. That year of course the papers were full of John's line about rattling your jewellery, which was a chancy remark – that joke could have gone either way."

Cynthia Lennon: "John's comments were always off the cuff, but that's Liverpool for you – everybody here is a comedian. I was so proud of him that night, still am if I see it again on television. He knew he was slightly stepping out of line but it was just something that he had to do, that's the way he was."

That November, the Beatles starred in their own package tour, supported by the Brook Brothers, the Kestrels and Peter Jay and the Jaywalkers. The cost of police protection for the Beatles was raised in Parliament.

When the Rolling Stones had been stuck for a commercial follow-up to 'Come On', their producer, Andrew Loog Oldham, asked John and Paul for something suitable. They had the half-completed 'I Wanna Be Your Man', which they played to the Stones. They liked it so John and Paul retreated to another room to finish it. The next day the Beatles recorded the song with Ringo on lead vocal. The Stones' single was released in October. It had a superb driving guitar break from Brian

Jones and it became the Stones' first Top 20 single. The Beatles' version, released on *With the Beatles,* can't complete with the Stones but it does have John Lennon on Hammond organ and entertaining sound effects.

Billy J. Kramer had further hits with Lennon and McCartney's 'Bad to Me' and 'I'll Keep You Satisfied'. 'I'll Keep You Satisfied' was one of Lennon and McCartney's best songs and a potential No.1 but Billy, appearing on *Sunday Night at the London Palladium,* went to pieces and the record dived down the chart. Another Brian Epstein signing, Tommy Quickly, recorded Paul McCartney's 'Tip of My Tongue' but McCartney, like anyone else, is entitled to an off day. I once heard John Gorman of Scaffold parody this as 'Tip of My Thingy'.

Songwriter Mitch Murray: "I loved the stuff that John and Paul wrote for Billy J. Kramer. I thought 'Bad to Me' was better than the songs they were writing for themselves. There's so much colour in their songs, 'Maxwell's Silver Hammer', 'Michelle' and 'Yesterday', and there still is. I love the one Paul McCartney made with the Frog chorus 'We All Stand Together'." Now there's an unexpected view for you, although it's unfair that McCartney is savaged for 'We All Stand Together'. It was made as a children's record and it served its purpose.

Wayne Fontana: "So many people were after their songs that you had to be very lucky to get one. I nearly did that one that Cilla Black did, 'Love of the Loved', but Brian wanted Cilla to do it instead. George Harrison had given it to me as a demo and I was already practising it. I'd have been happy to record anything – their songs were all fabulous. These days everybody does Beatle medleys and, if I'm ever stuck, I go into 'I Saw Her Standing There' and everybody will be dancing."

In October 1963 Cilla Black started her recording career with a Top 40 hit, 'Love of the Loved'. Cilla Black: "Paul McCartney wrote it and I'd heard the Beatles do it many times in the Cavern. I wanted to do a group arrangement and I was ever so disappointed when I got to the studio and there was brass and everything. Les Reed did the arrangement. He was playing piano and Peter Lee Stirling was on lead guitar. It was very jazzy and I didn't think it would be a hit." The song made the Top 40 and paved the way for her No.1 early in 1964, Burt Bacharach and Hal David's 'Anyone Who Had a Heart'.

November 1963 – With the Beatles LP (Parlophone PMC 1206, 11/63)
Produced by George Martin, 14 tracks – 32 minutes 24 seconds
Side 1: It Won't Be Long/ All I've Got to Do/ All My Loving/ Don't

Bother Me/ Little Child/ Till There Was You/ Please Mister Postman
Side 2: Roll Over Beethoven/ Hold Me Tight/ You Really Got a Hold
On Me/ I Wanna Be Your Man/ Devil in Her Heart/ Not a Second Time/
Money (That's What I Want)

The Beatles' second album, *With the Beatles*, had advance orders of 300,000, and their first album, *Please Please Me*, was still top of the LP charts. Although it did not affect the sales, *With the Beatles* was released on the day that Kennedy was assassinated, 22 November 1963.

The cover of *Please Please Me* had been traditional, the four Beatles leaning over a balcony, but for *With the Beatles* it was an atmospheric, black and white photograph of their four heads with their polo necks fading into the background. It showed off their moptops and Ringo now had one as well. Their unsmiling pose was copied by other bands including the Rolling Stones, the Kinks and Them (and Van Morrison has continued in the same vein ever since). The photograph by Robert Freeman was influenced by Astrid Kirchherr's photographs in Hamburg.

"I knew Robert Freeman and he adored Astrid's photos," says Klaus Voormann, "The Beatles asked him to do a picture like Astrid with the light from the side and that is why he did it. It was great and why should Astrid be the only one who can do that?"

Rock writer Jon Savage adds, "You can't do better than that *With the Beatles* look. If somebody did that today for the first time, it would look extraordinary."

Actress Sue Johnston: "I was working in NEMS and it was all hands on deck when *With the Beatles* was released. The advance orders were so huge that we took practically every other LP off the shelves and it was just *With the Beatles*. We were working day and night to reload stock and we were selling them as quick as they could press them at EMI. If I'd been given a percentage for every one I sold, I'd be very rich today."

'It Won't Be Long' is a good, throaty opener but it's familiar territory as John is attempting a similar play on words to 'Please Please Me' with "It won't be long 'til you belong to me." Originally considered for their first LP, 'Hold Me Tight' is a good, catchy song and Paul has admitted that he was trying to write for the Shirelles. Some of the other Lennon and McCartney compositions on the album, 'All I've Got To Do', 'Little Child' and 'Not A Second Time' are all good but not great. They work fine as album cuts but wouldn't have got far as singles.

The best moments come with the cover versions. John's power-packed 'Please Mister Postman' is excellent, all the more for his voice being double-tracked, and the Beatles' cover of the Donays' 'Devil in Her Heart' is often overlooked.

Wanting to emulate 'Twist and Shout', the album concluded with another raucous John Lennon vocal, this time a cover of Barrett Strong's 'Money', and like 'Please Mister Postman', a Motown song. The stereo version has the standard four seconds between 'Not a Second Time' and 'Money' but the mono has 10 and that makes the outburst of sound even more exciting. The powerful backing is superbly brought out on the remasters – just listen to the drums and the backing vocals. The fact that another Liverpool band, the Undertakers, had already released 'Money' as a single didn't bother the Beatles.

Written on the bus while touring with Roy Orbison, 'All My Loving' was Paul's attempt at a middle of the road standard with good country guitar playing from George Harrison, clearly inspired by Chet Atkins. The lyrics are good but not especially distinctive but the melody is instantly memorable.

Mark Lewisohn: "'All My Loving' is a complex song from Paul McCartney, who was just twenty-one at the time. The harmonies are very complex and John Lennon plays some beautiful, very fast triplets on rhythm guitar. For most songwriters, it would have been the best thing of their career, but it was so early in Paul McCartney's time. 'Love Me Do' and P.S. I Love You' are lovely songs, but they are simple and naïve, and yet, less than one year later, Paul McCartney came up with something utterly different in 'All My Loving'."

Yes, but play 'Kathy's Waltz' from the Dave Brubeck Quartet on their *Time Out* album. If you hear it now, you might think that a modern jazz group was improvising around 'All My Loving': however, 'Kathy's Waltz' was recorded in 1959. To add to the problem, Ronald Binge, who was Mantovani's orchestrator, wrote and recorded 'When You Are Young' early in 1963. This was made available for radio and TV productions and if McCartney heard it, it would have been as part of a play or documentary. Nevertheless, a similar melody to 'All My Loving' is in there.

Country musician Peter Rowan: "If you go through these songs of the past, you will hear where the Beatle songs came from. They came from the music of their parents' generation. These chord changes were taken up by the Beatles. Rock'n'roll was three chords until the Beatles but Roy Orbison was probably the first one to influence writers into the vast possibilities of the pop song. The Beatles opened up their hearts to their own tradition."

With the Beatles contained the first George Harrison song, the sulky and self-protective 'Don't Bother Me'. Lionel Bart: "George Gershwin lived in Catfish Row when he wrote *Porgy and Bess* and so I thought I would live in Liverpool to get some local colour for *Maggie May*. I got to know Liverpool and the Cavern and the Beatles became close friends of mine. I talked George Harrison into writing his own songs. At first he said, 'I don't want to write any songs. I've got two guys who do that all right.'"

Bill Harry, the editor of *Mersey Beat*: "When everyone was going on about the Lennon-McCartney partnership, I felt that the others should come to the fore in some creative way. I kept on at George Harrison by saying, 'Look, the first original number the Beatles ever recorded was one of yours, 'Cry for a Shadow' in Hamburg, so why don't you write some more?' He would say, 'I can't be bothered.' That led to him writing 'Don't Bother Me' 'cause I was always on his back. When I met him after its release, he said, 'Thanks very much. I've already made £7,000 in royalties.'"

George's sister, Louise Harrison: "When I got the albums, I never played George's songs first. I always took the album as it came, and I never thought of George as being better than the others. Their strength came from them as a group – the blend of personalities was so magical and no other group managed to create the same magic. The old expression about the sum being greater than the parts applies to them."

Paul sang a modern show tune, 'Til There Was You' from *The Music Man*, which had been recorded by Peggy Lee. It's a warm, soft sound with Ringo on bongos, but what a suspect lyric. "There were birds in the sky, but I never saw them winging"?

Paul Du Noyer: "It is always said that when white artists cover black songs, they clean them up. People are generally thinking of the difference between Little Richard and Pat Boone. If you compare John Lennon's treatment of Smokey Robinson's 'You Really Got a Hold on Me', you will find that Lennon's delivery is far more aggressive and rough. Smokey is a subtle and refined singer. John is not so refined and so it is more belligerent."

Jazz guitarist Barney Kessel: "The Beatles handled their career very well and they used some brilliant recording techniques but I find that, both individually and collectively, their music is very ordinary.

It has very little to offer people except young children and people who like to hear white boys play black man's music. It's like being given the carbon copy instead of the original. I applaud their success and I think it's wonderful to have made so many people happy, but even if they were playing across the street, I'd have no desire to go and see them."

Experimental musician Robert Wyatt: "The first beat group that I liked was Van Morrison's Them but to me English pop music was karaoke rhythm and blues, boy next door stuff, and I didn't take it seriously. I preferred the originals they were taking it from. I've never been able to appreciate the Beatles: it's guitar based and the guitar has always been a marginal instrument for me. I have always been more interested in the instruments used in jazz."

Film director Mike Figgis, who made a film about the blues in the UK: "It is all about tangents. Lennon said that he became American the first time he heard Elvis Presley. If you are turned on by Elvis, you are turned on by the blues as Elvis comes out of a blues tradition. It doesn't really matter if you go to the source or the second generation. I would say that any musician coming out of that early 60s movement will, sooner or later, because of the whole phenomenon of listening to records and sharing them with others, become very, very interested in sources and origins. Musicians in Liverpool were touring and so they would have met Eric Burdon say at the Club A Go Go and they would have talked about sources. Lennon made tons of references to the blues when he was talking. It was the cult of 'If you don't know about this, you aren't very cool'."

Ralph McTell: "I wasn't impressed when the Beatles were launched because they had been cleaned up by Epstein and they were wearing silly, little jackets and had daft haircuts. *Melody Maker* had told us that the Beatles were a great, raving R&B band, but they definitely weren't playing R&B, which was gigantic in London at the time. The Rolling Stones were shooting off in Chicago style and there was also the Cyril Davies All Stars, Alexis Korner and the Yardbirds. I suppose, too, that Londoners like to think they're the first, so there's a resistance to music from anywhere else in Britain."

By now, Andrew Loog Oldham had moved away from working with the Beatles to managing the blues-based Rolling Stones and deliberately creating a rivalry between them. "That rivalry comes from being a fan and knowing the Cliff Richard vs Billy Fury or Tommy Steele vs Cliff Richard debates; even James Dean vs Anthony Perkins. Whatever you pick as your passion you are telling your parents or your girlfriend, something about who you are. The groups themselves were friendly – the Beatles and the Stones were very good friends, but then everybody wished everybody well in those days. You know, 'I've got a job and my friend can have a job too.'"

George Melly: "The Stones came from the Thames Valley cottonfields and they had their roots in earlier music. Their drummer, Charlie Watts, had been a jazz drummer, even played trad, whereas the Beatles had no truck with any of that. They sprang from skiffle to the black blues of the electronic age, the post-war age, whereas the Stones were influenced by the classic primitive blues, the field blues. Mostly, however, I think it was the difference between Liverpool and London, between the provinces and the capital. The Beatles had a cheekiness that was ingratiating, whereas the Stones came on as monsters. Later on, the Beatles lurched some way towards provoking people but, at the beginning, under Epstein's surveillance, they were eager to please. The Stones, on the other hand, were eager to offend."

The Beatles were show-biz whereas the Stones were defiantly not. They would not step on the roundabout at the end of *Sunday Night at the London Palladium*; they would not swap wisecracks on regional TV with Ken Dodd; nor participate in a sketch with Morecambe and Wise.

Johnnie Hamp, a director at Granada TV: "When *Scene at 6.30* was running, we had the boys lined up to appear with Ken Dodd. Brian Epstein thought that they were too big for the programme and wanted to pull them out at the last minute. If he had, Gay Byrne would have said on air that the Beatles would meet the same people on the way up as on the way down. Just before air time, we got a message from NEMS to say that they would do the show after all. Ken Dodd was supposed to talk to them for a couple of minutes, but it stretched to 22. We had filmed every stage of the Beatles at the studio, thinking that we might not get the chance again, so it's a valuable piece of film."

November 1963 – I Want to Hold Your Hand/ This Boy (Parlophone R 5084, 11/63, UK No.1, US No.1) (US B-side, I Saw Her Standing There, made No.14: German language version of 'I Want to Hold Your Hand' made No.5 in Germany.)
On 29 November 1963, the Beatles released their best-known single, 'I Want to Hold Your Hand'. The single had advance orders of over a million and went straight into the charts at No.1, which was highly unusual in 1963.

British rock'n'roll singer Mike Berry: "I remember listening to 'I Want to Hold Your Hand' in the car and turning the radio up until it wouldn't go any louder. I went bananas over it and yet I was a hardened pro and the feelings they generated got to me. If they hadn't happened, God knows what would have happened to the music over here."

Tony Hicks of the Hollies: "I have so many favourites by the Beatles but, if it's a single, I would say 'I Want to Hold Your Hand'. That was very meaty. George has some very good guitar going on there; it probably was a Gretsch going through a Vox amplifier."

Guitarist Laurence Juber, later with Wings: "I started playing guitar the week that 'I Want to Hold Your Hand' was released. It was very clear to me what I wanted to do and when I asked around, I found that you could make a good living as a session player and I set my sights on that. Along the way, my parents were insistent that I got a real education, and so I went to London University and got a music degree."

Hereward K from the Flying Pickets: "I don't think that anybody has done middle eights like the Beatles. You get verse, chorus, verse, chorus, and then twenty glorious seconds of middle eight. My favourite one of all is in 'This Boy', the B-side of 'I Want to Hold Your Hand', 'Oh, and this boy would be happy just to love you...' and all that stuff. Another great middle eight is in 'And Your Bird Can Sing'. They sum up the naivety, the directness and the innocence of the early Beatles."

November 1963 – The Beatles No.1 EP (Parlophone GEP 8883, 11/63)
This EP repackaged another four tracks from the *Please Please Me* LP. It's an odd title as there was no No.2, but it may simply mean that the Beatles were No.1.

December 1963 – The Beatles Christmas Record Flexidisc (Fan club, 12/63)
By December 1963, the Beatles' fan club had 25,000 members and was rising fast. They recorded a Christmas flexidisc for members and did this throughout their existence. During its playing-time of six minutes, the Beatles gave individual Christmas messages and larked around with 'Good King Wenceslas', 'God Save The Queen' and 'Rudolph The Red-Nosed Ringo' on which they sound very like Dr. Hook.

On 7 December 1963 the Beatles formed the panel for a special edition of *Juke Box Jury* from the Liverpool Empire and then moved to the Odeon for a concert for their fans that was televised as *It's The Beatles*.

David Jacobs: "We broadcast *Juke Box Jury* from the Liverpool Empire. I spoke to the audience first and as you can imagine, they were very excited, and I knew that if I wasn't able to control them, they would run riot. When I introduced each of the Beatles on stage, the cheer was so great that it sounded like the entire jet fleet of British Airways taking off. Once they'd settled down, the boys were tremendous and it was a great programme. We had our highest-ever viewing figure, something like twenty-four million people watching it that night."

The Beatles had been featuring Chan Romero's 'Hippy Hippy Shake' in their stage act. When they appeared on *Juke Box Jury*, they criticised the Swinging Blue Jeans for taking their song. As it wasn't their song, they could hardly complain and it was probably because they were so surprised to hear the Blue Jeans doing raucous rock'n'roll. Ray Ennis from the Blue Jeans says, "We had to fight like hell with EMI to get 'Hippy Hippy Shake' released. They said, 'No, this'll never make it.' We felt so strongly about it, four little humble lads from Liverpool, that we said, 'If you don't release it, we won't make any more records.' They released it, and Wally Ridley, the A&R man, apologised afterwards. 'Hippy Hippy Shake' sold three million worldwide."

And a similar story: when Roy Barber of Dave Berry and the Cruisers told John Lennon that they were about to release 'Memphis Tennessee' as a single, John Lennon, "Shit, we wanted that one out."

Eddie Amoo: "I was in the Chants and we were guesting on one of the Beatles' shows at Colston Hall in Bristol. Wherever they played, the dignitaries wanted to meet them. We had done our rehearsal in the afternoon and as the Beatles had been reviewing our record on *Juke Box Jury*, we went to their dressing-room to chat about it. The Mayor and Mayoress came in and John Lennon was sitting there with toilet paper stuffed up his nose. He kept his face dead straight as though it was perfectly normal for him to be sitting with toilet paper up his nose. We were trying to keep straight faces. It was hilarious."

On 21 December 1963, the Beatles starred in the second all-Merseyside *Thank Your Lucky Stars* and were presented with gold discs during the show. They recorded a Christmas radio show for the BBC, *From Us to You*.

Over the seasonal period, the Beatles starred in *The Beatles Christmas Show* at the Astoria in Finsbury Park. It featured Rolf Harris, the Barron Knights and several NEMS' stablemates – Cilla Black, Billy J. Kramer, Tommy Quickly and the Fourmost.

Rolf Harris: "I was the compère on their Christmas show at the Finsbury Park Empire. I did my own spot just before them and I was the only bloke that the audience listened to. I used to say, 'Please don't scream or you won't hear anything. Here they are – the Beatles!' And wooo, they never heard a word they sang. I lost my temper with John one night. He had a microphone off stage and he was mucking about, making comments during my act and wrecking it. After the show I stormed into his dressing room and said, 'If you want to mess around with everybody else's acts, okay, but don't mess mine up again.' He was shocked that anyone would shout at him like that but I was so livid. He left me alone after that."

Toni Avern, manager of the Barron Knights: "The Beatles used to start their act by standing on a blacked-out stage and a pin-spot used to pick out each one's head in turn and the crowd would go wild. One night a couple of the Barron Knights held John in the wings so that he couldn't take his place on the stand. John was the last one to be lit up and when the light came on, he wasn't there."

Butch Baker of the Barron Knights: "We did *The Beatles' Christmas Show* when they were at the peak of their excitement in England. When we looked out of the dressing room windows, the streets were crammed with people as far as the eye could see. It was a very exciting time for us although we were near the bottom of the bill. I think our names were under the printers."

Colin Manley of the Remo Four: "We went on with Tommy Quickly for a short spot just before the Beatles. John Lennon let me use his 12-string Rickenbacker for the introduction on 'The Wild Side of Life'. When we finished our spot, we'd come off and I'd give it back to John. I could tell by the look on his face that it was all too much for him. I don't think they had any interest in what they were doing. No one could hear what they were playing. It was like being in the bird house of a zoo, greatly amplified. They threw their guitars on the floor when they'd finished. Police appeared from the back and they fled as fast as they could into limousines to get away. They weren't enjoying that."

On 27 December 1963, William Mann wrote the first of several favourable critiques of the Beatles for *The Times* but the technical terms baffled Lennon and McCartney. He compared "Not a Second Time" to Mahler, but John Lennon commented, "They were just chords like any other chords. It was the first intellectual bullshit written about us."

Tony Barrow: "Most of the songs the Beatles wrote were either good fun or romantic but critics started to look for hidden meanings in their songs. It was fruitless and pointless and these critics were far more interested in the depths of these songs than the Beatles themselves. I don't recall them wanting to do something that was deeply intellectual or meaningful and those who looked for such messages were a source of amusement to them. They'd fall about laughing at some of the things that were written and say, 'Oh, really? Is that what we're doing?'"

Rick Wakeman: "The Beatles broke the rules because they didn't know any better. I was at grammar school in Ealing when the Beatles broke big, and I couldn't understand their success when they could neither write music nor play something that was put in front of them. I couldn't appreciate what people can do when they work together. They weren't the greatest musicians in the world but they produced a sound that made them the best in the world. It's like a football team – you can put eleven great individual players together but it doesn't mean that they'll win matches. There's no doubt that the chemistry that the Beatles had between them was very special."

Mike Smith from the Dave Clark Five: "I was still working in an office and the Beatles had 'I Want to Hold Your Hand' at No.1 for Christmas 1963. We were at No.2 with 'Glad All Over'. We did manage to knock them off the top but it had to sell a million to do it. The press loved it as all the other big groups were from the north and so they got a North vs South with us. We were said to have the Tottenham sound, which was a load of rubbish but it was good copy."

Jon Savage: "From late on in 1963, the Beatles weren't really a Liverpool group. They had become a metropolitan group although they often mined their Liverpool past for their records. The thing about the Beatles is that they made changes. They made so many changes and that is what is exciting about them."

The NME's final Top 20 for 1963 included 'I Want to Hold Your Hand' (No.1), 'She Loves You' (hanging on at No.4), two Lennon-McCartney covers ('I Wanna Be Your Man' and 'I'll Keep You Satisfied'), and Dora Bryan's novelty, 'All I Want for Christmas Is a Beatle' (No.16) as well as two Beatle EPs and an LP. Gerry and the Pacemakers, Freddie and the Dreamers, the Dave Clark Five and the Hollies were there, whilst the most successful non-British performer was the Singing Nun from Belgium (No.3). Pride in British beat music was such that only two

American artists, Elvis Presley and Roy Orbison, had No.1 hits during 1963 and 1964.

Steve Harley: "I remember being in hospital when I was twelve and 'I Want to Hold Your Hand' was No.1 that Christmas. I was in hospital a lot from the ages of three to sixteen, about three or four years in total. Dylan came along about the same time and he was really saying, 'You can have pop music and proper words too.'"

Good point, Steve. 1963 was the Year of the Beatles, but it was also a year when any songwriter faced incredible competition. 1963 could have been the Songwriting Year of the Century. Try these: 'Blowin' In The Wind', 'Lord Of The Dance', 'Blue Bayou', 'In Dreams', 'Anyone Who Had A Heart', 'Close To You', 'Then He Kissed Me', 'Surfer Girl' and 'If I Ruled The World'. The record that kept 'I Want to Hold Your Hand' from No.1 in France was Charles Aznavour's 'La Mamma'; here recorded as 'For Mama' by Matt Monro. In addition, there were some extraordinary productions such as 'Fingertips' from Little Stevie Wonder and 'Deep Purple' from Nino Tempo and April Stevens.

Writing this chapter has made me realise how busy the Beatles were in 1963. They performed two hundred concerts, made scores of media appearances, did hundreds of interviews, created new fashions and made, and often wrote, a succession of excellent recordings which had topped the singles, EP and LP charts.

What has also surprised me is how short records were back then: 'Please Please Me' and 'From Me to You' don't even make two minutes. By the end of 1963, the Beatles had yet to record a track which was over three minutes long. With the lower attention span experienced today, you would expect records to be much shorter today.

It is hard to appreciate the controversy over the Beatles' hairstyle. Even the Rolling Stones don't look unkempt today. It wasn't long since the end of conscription where the short, regulation haircut was the norm. Many people kept their hair the same way after they left the forces and, indeed, barbers were reluctant to offer much else. Hence, the Beatles hair did look long. Also, this was a generation that was starting to rebel against its parents and the cheapest and simplest way to rebel was to grow your hair.

George Martin referred to the Beatles' "endless curiosity" and no matter how busy they were, they were always willing to try something new. Despite all that they had done in 1963, they couldn't have guessed what was to happen the following year.

CHAPTER 4
All I Got To Do Is Act Naturally (1964)

Cassius Clay (Muhammad Ali) becomes world heavyweight champion
– Dr Beeching closes railways – Radio Caroline starts broadcasting –
Nelson Mandela starts prison sentence – Harold Wilson becomes
Prime Minister – Mods and rockers clash at Brighton – UK abolishes
capital punishment – Films include A Fistful Of Dollars *and*
Mary Poppins *– The Moog Synthesiser goes on sale – Lenny Bruce*
convicted for obscenity.

In January 1964, the Beatles went to France for concerts at the Paris
Olympia. Whilst there, they taped German-language versions of 'I Want
to Hold Your Hand' ('Komm, Gib Mir Deine Hand') and 'She Loves
You' ('Sie Liebt Dich') as well as their next single, 'Can't Buy Me Love'.
These were the only studio recordings that the Beatles made outside
the UK, although the Stones, the Animals, the Yardbirds and several
other British acts recorded in America. The Beatles must have wanted
to record at Chess Records or Sun, so why didn't they? Perhaps they
were being loyal to George Martin: if he wasn't there, they wouldn't
record – as simple as that.

George Martin: "When the time came for them to record 'She
Loves You' and 'I Want to Hold Your Hand' in German, there was no
sign of them. I rang up their hotel and spoke to their road manager. He
told me that they weren't coming, that they didn't want to do it after
all. I was absolutely livid because I'd gone to a lot of trouble setting up
the session and someone had come from Germany to coach them. We
hopped into a cab and burst in on them. They fled to all corners of the
room, pretending to hide behind cushions and laughing. I told them
that they owed this man an apology as he'd travelled so far to come
and help them. They in turn said, 'Sorry, Otto, sorry.' After that, they

came and did the record. Of course, they still didn't like doing it. This sort of thing didn't happen often and it was the very first time that I had a row with them."

George Martin never asked them again to record in a foreign language. Gene Pitney, who did it regularly, recalls, "The Beatles changed a lot of things that were law in the music business, and not just the music. Before the Beatles, you automatically recorded your singles in foreign languages but the Beatles refused to do that. Their popularity was so immense throughout the world that the fans had to buy the English versions and accept them as they were. The French charts pre-Beatles were 80% French and 20% English but the Beatles changed that, and a lot of people learnt English through their records. In some countries, you had to sing in English or you wouldn't chart at all. I was relieved when the market changed and records in English were acceptable everywhere, and I have the Beatles to thank for that. I did a show in Italy and I'd worked hard to do the whole show in Italian. I found out later that I'd been wasting my time as they didn't want me to do that! They wanted to hear the majority of the show in English."

By the time the Beatles had finished in Paris, 'I Want to Hold Your Hand' was the No.1 single in America and they were to appear on *The Ed Sullivan Show*. After the explosion of rock'n'roll in the 50s, the US music scene in 1963 had become staid. Robert Reynolds of the Mavericks: "It was a special time in which popular music was still proving itself. There were people who thought it should just go away and that it was a passing fad. Just before the Beatles, rock was getting very lightweight with the Italian New York or Philadelphian boy singers. They weren't very original and they didn't have the talent anyway, although there were some good songs."

José Feliciano: "I don't know how it was in Britain but in America our music was getting stale and we had suffered the Kennedy assassination, so the Beatles were a breath of fresh air. The whole world owes them a great debt as they brought happiness to all of us. They put Britain on the map as not too many English acts were making it in the States. I can remember Laurie London and Russ Hamilton having success before the Beatles. 'We Will Make Love' was a very good record."

Feliciano's knowledge is impressive. Up until then, no British chart acts had amounted to much in America. There had been occasional one-off hits for the likes of Lonnie Donegan, Russ Hamilton (also from Liverpool) and the Tornadoes. Major British chart names, including Billy Fury and Marty Wilde, counted for nothing. Cliff Richard's American tour had not established him, so the odds were against the Beatles. With good reason, Brian Epstein might have shrugged his shoulders and said, "Forget America."

Before the Beatles conquered America in 1964, there were signs of their impending popularity. Songwriter P.F. Sloan: "I was working for a publishing company in 1963 and I heard 'Love Me Do', 'Please Please Me' and 'From Me to You'. They were fantastic, like putting your fingers into an electric socket. I went to the head of the company and said, 'These guys are going to be bigger than Elvis', and the record company called up Brian Epstein and said, 'There's a kid here who says this group is going to be bigger than Elvis.' Brian said, 'I've been saying the same thing myself.' Capitol worked out a deal and the Beatles came out on Vee Jay. They bombed terribly until 'I Want to Hold Your Hand' and suddenly they were everywhere."

Singer/songwriter Rodney Crowell, who was born in 1950: "I had heard of the Beatles about a year before *Ed Sullivan*. There was a radio station in Houston, Texas that had got hold of 'Please Please Me' and I heard it every morning on the school bus. The record slayed me but I couldn't buy it. When the Beatles released their album, *Introducing the Beatles*, I saw it in the shops and I knew it was the music I was hearing on the radio"

Introducing the Beatles was issued by Vee Jay as early as July 1963. It featured twelve of the tracks from their first UK album. For a variety of reasons, usually idiotic, the US Beatle releases had different packaging to the British ones. As it happens, Vee Jay hadn't paid any royalties for the tracks they had licensed. Prior to 1964, they hadn't sold much but they did owe Capitol/EMI $700. They reissued the album in January 1964, knowing that Capitol might take legal action. They did but following challenges, the ban was dropped and then reinstated. To complicate matters, Vee Jay put out a new version of the album with two changes in the listing but the same catalogue number. Mad and, of course, all this could have been avoided if they had paid Capitol the $700 it was owed.

Walter Becker of Steely Dan: "When I started becoming aware of music on the radio, it was already a pretty eclectic mix of Elvis, rockabilly, black New Orleans music and other kinds of rhythm and blues records. There was some very poppy, fluffy stuff that was going on in the 50s and early 60s before the Beatles. When the Beatles came along, it was the perfect moment to rock the pop world because there was nothing very substantial around. Ray Charles did that country record and redefined the genre, so there was interesting stuff that didn't fit and some strange novelty records." You're not kidding: 'Dinner with Drac', 'Hello Muddah, Hello Fadduh' and 'Alley-Oop', for starters.

Andrew Gold: "My father had a friend in England who told him about this new group who were making a big scene like Elvis. I saw an import of *With the Beatles* in a store and I thought that they looked so weird. They looked like beatniks with those turtle-neck pullovers. Then they did *The Ed Sullivan Show* and it was an epiphany. They looked great and they were exuberant and funny and cute and yet tough at the same time. I don't know how they managed that. The girls wanted to rip their clothes off and they were making tons of money and I thought, 'I want that job.' From then on, I was a pop wannabe."

The Ed Sullivan Show was not screened in the UK and watching it now, it is hard to believe that such a wooden personality could host the most popular show in America. UK theatrical agent Peter Prichard: "We had great variety shows here and the cost of buying that American show would have been more expensive than staging *Sunday Night at the London Palladium,* which was a similar type of show. Ed had seized the opportunity. When television came along, all the major studios barred their artists from appearing on TV. They thought it would take away from the magic of the motion pictures. Ed became the only one they would trust and he said, 'Look, it'll gain publicity for your movies.' They tried it with Jimmy Stewart and John Wayne, who were big stars and to see them on TV was extraordinary. It worked well and the rules were relaxed."

Paul Gambaccini: "Ed Sullivan is a key figure in American television history, although he was stiff. The guy had formaldehyde in the veins. Nowadays, they would not employ someone who is as physically unattractive and vocally as wooden as Ed Sullivan, but it is people like that who are distinctive. Look at Patrick Moore. If Patrick Moore was new, they wouldn't have him on, but he became famous in the days when they didn't have experienced television presenters who were also astronomers. He has personality and uniqueness and Ed Sullivan was the same. The whole myth of Elvis being too sexy to be shot from the waist down was just Ed Sullivan's way of getting ratings.

In late 1963 he arrived in London amidst all these screaming girls, who were waiting for the Beatles. He didn't know the Beatles from Adam but he was so impressed by the reaction that he signed them up for three shows. With stroke upon stroke of good luck, 'I Want to Hold Your Hand' came out, entered the American chart in January and went to No.1. The Beatles' first visit to the United States was for Ed Sullivan and, in terms of popular music, it became the single most important TV show for my generation. So many artists cite that as being the most influential show, the one that inspired them to go into music. It had the largest rating in television history at its time and, even now, it is the most requested broadcast at the Museum of Television and Art in New York City. It has passed into history."

The UK agent Peter Prichard would recommend British talent to Ed Sullivan. "I suggested that we use the Beatles on *The Ed Sullivan Show* as they were the first long-haired young men to appear before the Queen and perform rock'n'roll music. Their manager Brian Epstein was in New York at the time and I rang him and told him that Ed was interested, and he was very pleased. I did the deal, which was for three shows at scale, $750 for each show and not $750 for each person."

Capitol Records was losing ground in the contemporary market and their rock'n'roll star Gene Vincent had a tendency to self-destruct. In 1962 their managing executive Alan Livingston approved the signing of a young California band, the Beach Boys, who sang about teenage lifestyles. Despite their success, the Beach Boys presented Livingston with several problems not least their uncompromising manager, Murry Wilson, the father of three of them and an uncle to a fourth.

EMI was the majority shareholder in Capitol but Capitol executives were impervious to the British owner, believing they knew better. They considered that British records were non-starters in America and, in 1961, allowed Matt Monro's 'My Kind Of Girl' to be licensed to Warwick, where it became a US hit. They were similarly disinterested in the Beatles. Swan Records of Philadelphia released 'She Loves You' in September 1963 and had an option on their next single.

Even though Beatlemania was rampant in Britain and the group was to be launched in America early in 1964 on *The Ed Sullivan Show,* the Capitol executive Dave Dexter Jr still had no plans to release Beatle product, and Brian Epstein, dismayed with his attitude, phoned Livingston direct. Realising that Epstein had EMI's support, Livingston felt boxed in and rather reluctantly, overruled Dexter and persuaded Swan Records to drop their option. Livingston agreed to release 'I Want to Hold Your Hand' on Capitol and spend $40,000 on promotion, the campaign focussing largely on the length of the Beatles' hair, which was insignificant by today's standards.

Charlie Gillett, author of *The Sound of the City*: "The Beatles were very lucky to have Brian Epstein, no question of that, and he was very resourceful. Persuading Capitol Records in America to take his band seriously was a huge achievement. They had ignored everybody from Britain before that time and the first singles had been licensed to Vee Jay, Swan and Tollie. For any other label but Capitol, having Beatle hits was to be the kiss of death – what a strange story that is."

Meet the Beatles! the first Capitol album, was released in January 1964, mostly comprising of tracks from *With the Beatles*. With such a title, they were simply causing more confusion with *Introducing the Beatles*. Tommy James, leader of the Shondells: "I was 15 years old and I worked in a record shop in Niles, Michigan when the Beatles came out and Capitol Records had a brilliant plan for introducing the group. Kennedy had been assassinated, which was a horrible feeling for everyone, and the Beatles was the only thing that made life palatable. In December 1963, that is before they appeared on *The Ed Sullivan Show*, they put displays in American record stores with the four of them turned around with their backs to you. Each week, the record distributor would come in with a new picture, it would fit in a tripod on the counter and little by little the group would turn around. The last one showed you their album cover, *Meet the Beatles!* It was a brilliant strategy and things were at fever pitch by the time 'I Want to Hold Your Hand' came out. Soon, I was in a cover band with patent leather shoes and we wore Beatle wigs for our third set and the girls were screaming."

Dennis Locorriere, Dr. Hook's lead singer, was born in 1949: "Before *Ed Sullivan*, there was a little clip on *The Jack Paar Show*, which he regarded as an oddity, you know, 'Wow, look at this freaky thing from across the ocean.' It was like he had discovered aliens. It was a pretty dark clip from some club. I first really noticed them when I heard 'I Want to Hold Your Hand' on the radio. It jumped off the radio; the cymbals were so bright and vibrant. It made me want to play something, bang on a box with spoons I suppose, but it got me going." Good memory – Jack Paar had footage of the Beatles at the Winter Gardens, Bournemouth in November 1963.

Beatles' biographer Steven Stark: "They changed the music of the day which changed the culture which changed us. Feminist gender bending was a feature of their music and a big part of their cultural impact. On and just before the first visit, the American press said very little about the music – it was all about their hair and how they looked like girls. Jack Paar broadcast a clip of them doing 'She Loves You' and all the talk was about the girls screaming and their haircuts. It was a real shock as the crew-cut was the big thing in the US and anything more was a big deal."

Paul Gambaccini: "The first Beatle song I heard was 'I Want to Hold Your Hand'. I was on the couch on the porch of our house in Westport, Connecticut. I was listening to Stan Z. Burns on WINS, New York and he introduced this song. I was impressed by it but I had no idea that it was going to be as huge as it was. I have my own theory on this, which Paul McCartney doesn't agree with, but he needs an American perspective to judge. The country had been in deep mourning over the assassination of John F. Kennedy – deep, deep mourning and it really needed an up. It was such mourning that the Singing Nun was No.1 – this was like penance. Everyone wanted to be happy again and the Beatles with 'I Want to Hold Your Hand' was the first positive thing to come along. They had been very unsuccessful at first, so much so that their previous records had been with different labels. 'Love Me Do' was with Tollie, 'She Loves You' was with Swan and the *Please Please Me* album and single were with Vee Jay. They were all reissued and promoted, so the Beatles had the whole Top 5 that famous week in April 1964. No one had ever done that and yet that was just the beginning of the whole thing."

In my view, the Kennedy factor is significant, but not crucially so. The Beatles would have made it anyway. Richie Havens: "My radio was on top of the refrigerator and I remember walking into the kitchen and the music stopped me stone dead. I thought, 'Thank God for something new'. It turned out to be 'I Want to Hold Your Hand' and they had changed music forever. There was a clarity in their music that we in America didn't have. It was the same kind of love that we sang about but it was more sophisticated and much better linguistically – the Queen's English, I suppose! Their music had depth and we just had hooks."

There was a remarkable welcome for the Beatles at the airport in New York, both by the media and the fans, and then they were besieged at the Plaza Hotel. The DJ Murray the K was tagging along with them and calling himself the Fifth Beatle. Impresario David Stein: "Murray the K was impish and he knew a good thing. His radio station, 1010 WINS, sent him out, whereas the other stations had sent out newsmen. Murray didn't understand why they sent him but he soon latched onto what was happening. He had his own language, Meusurray, where every word had an extra vowel or consonant. It was like Ebonics. It was like the language of the black people but much hipper. He butted in and took over their press conference. He was pretty much on 24 hours a day, but he was a very lovable man."

The Beatles' first appearance on *The Ed Sullivan Show* on 9 February was watched by 73 million people. Even the evangelist Billy Graham, who campaigned against television on Sundays, tuned in. Graham said that the Beatles' performance displayed "all the symptoms of the uncertainty of the times and the confusion about us." Smart of him to pick up on that.

Blues rocker George Thorogood, who was born in 1950: "Ed Sullivan said, 'Here they are, these four lads from Liverpool, the Beatles.' Paul McCartney stepped to the mic and sang 'Close your eyes...' and the world exploded. The President had been assassinated a few months before and so the Beatles couldn't have hit at a better time. They didn't sound or look like anything we had heard or seen before. On Monday in school I was in the cafeteria eating lunch and the guy next to me was screaming in my ear about them. Everybody – the cooks, the janitors, the teachers, the police, every kid in school – was talking about the Beatles and talking at the top of their lungs. I've never seen anything like it, though the comparison would be the day that Kennedy was shot. In April, I remember being in English class at about two o'clock and it was the first day in two months that I hadn't heard anybody talk about the Beatles. Two months!"

Scott McCarl of the Raspberries: "I listened to Elvis and Buddy Holly and the Beach Boys who started before the Beatles. Then it all spun around when we heard the Beatles for the first time, what a strange wonderful sound that was. It was so different from the records they were emulating. They may have thought that they were sounding like other people but they were so different. The records jumped out of the radio. I was thirteen and it was all there was to talk about."

Rock guitarist Jennifer Batten, who has worked with Michael Jackson and Jeff Beck: "I was with my parents watching *The Ed*

Sullivan Show when the Beatles were announced. I remember the excitement and I loved their sound and their looks. Everything about them was so different and so great – the Beatle boots and the haircuts. It was delightful and dig this, man, I asked my mother if I could join the Beatles fan club as there was a kid selling memberships door-to-door. She said no and I stole the money from her purse. I felt so guilty about this and I never stole anything ever again. When the stuff started coming in the mail, I think she forgot that she had said no. I remember being in a friend's bedroom and on the wall he had all these cards that he had collected from chewing gum. I was envious of them but I wondered how much gum do you have to chew to get all of that?"

Rosanne Cash was rather more enterprising: "I was president of my local Beatles fan club when I was 10 years old. I loved the Beatles so much and my dad got that. He understood what that felt like. My dad got me the Beatles' autographs from Candlestick Park. I can't remember if he was at the concert but they certainly hung out together. My husband John and I are always getting outtakes and buying the books. As a songwriter, I find that they provide a template for how to construct great, simple songs, ones that can resonate to anyone and have universal appeal. The songs are so refined and yet so accessible. Even today I refer back to them. You know, what would they have done with the middle eight? What a trick that is, to make the middle eight just as good as the verses. We all strive to that."

Rodney Crowell: "I missed them on the first *Ed Sullivan Show*. The next day the kids were talking about nothing else. The Beatles were really smart as they were on it three times in quick succession. I was cued in front of the television for the second appearance and I was mesmerised by so much inspiration and energy from people so close to my own age."

Emmylou Harris: "I remember being as infected by the Beatles as everyone else but I was a very serious young woman and I didn't really want to let on to anybody that I really liked them as much as I did."

Boz Scaggs: "It's funny the way we first perceive things. Being a musician and more or less their age, I was somewhat sceptical about them and their talent. I was jealous of this raving success that they were having. After I got over my own pettiness and really listened to them, I realised that they were one of the great musical events of my life. They put out one genius work after another. I had a little weekend band at one point and we did some Beatle songs that were just irresistible.

I love 'Yes It Is'. I heard it again the other day and I thought it was one of the most exotic things I've ever heard."

TV commentator Loyd Grossman: "We hadn't seen anything like that *Ed Sullivan Show* since Elvis Presley made his appearance. It was remarkable and it changed the lives of lots of people. In terms of innovation and energy, they compared very favourably with Elvis and both came along when they were so energetic and so more much creative than anything else around. It was mind-blowing and of course John Lennon became a person of great, great significance."

Loudon Wainwright: "I remember seeing the Beatles on *The Ed Sullivan Show* which was our big variety show in the States. The hype was already there, of course, but they were great on the show and they generated so much excitement. Like millions of other people, I was blown away and became a big fan. Although I wrote a song about John Lennon and his assassination, my favourite Beatle was Paul, great singer and great guitar-player too."

Billy Bob Thornton: "Taken just as pure pop, forgetting anything deep or meaningful, 'I Want to Hold Your Hand' is a great song. It was the first 45 I ever bought. I worshipped Lennon as many people did. If he'd recited the phone book, I'd have listened. They got me through my childhood. It was the world I disappeared into. When the Beatles came out, I was like, 'Okay, it's time to rebel against dad. I'm going to be in a band.'"

Singer and songwriter Jeff Alan Ross: "When I saw the Beatles on *Ed Sullivan*, I realised that something different was going on here and I wanted to start learning guitar. I learnt those songs when I was ten or eleven. I know them inside and out. They are indelibly printed on my brain matter, however that works. It is always great to play those songs as they are so much fun. What they did with harmony is fantastic. 'This Boy' is sung really well. They do 'This Boy' round one mike on *Ed Sullivan* and it is spot on. Nowadays you can correct pitch and overdub and get it right, but that's what they sounded like. Millions of people were watching them live but they had an attitude and they were young enough to do it. They had guts."

Beatle biographer Stu Shea: "Ed Sullivan knew everyone. He had a direct line to every angle of showbiz and he could pick up the phone and have the biggest acts come on his show. Sixty per cent of the viewing public watched the Beatles on that first show and the crime rate that night in New York was the lowest for 40 years. It was a cataclysmic cultural explosion. It was the first time that the record industry, radio and TV had all come together."

Roger McGuinn of the Byrds: "The very first Beatle song that caught my attention was 'I Want to Hold Your Hand'. I loved the bridge – the chords and the harmonies are just so amazing. The middle eight was a pop music invention but the chords in that bridge are like folk music chords. People often pick *Rubber Soul* or *Sgt. Pepper* as their favourite but I would go for some of the first tracks they came out with: they are just incredible."

Back to George Thorogood: "The Beatles were on *The Ed Sullivan Show* on 9 February and from the next day, anybody who walked into a recording studio – whether it be Frank Sinatra, the Rolling Stones, Bob Dylan or us – was influenced by them. Ten per cent of everything we earn should go right into the Beatles' pockets. They put us all on the map."

Max Bygraves: "I got on very well with the Beatles at the *Royal Variety Performance* from the Prince of Wales – they wanted my autograph for their aunties and the like. When I went to New York, I was going to stay at the same hotel as the Beatles but the clerk had let my room go. I phoned up Brian Epstein, whom I knew was upstairs. He wouldn't even talk to me. It was a sad blow: I felt that I was close to them and that we were all Britons in America. I had to leave the hotel and find another room elsewhere."

As well as appearing on *The Ed Sullivan Show*, the Beatles gave concerts in Washington and New York. Promoter Sid Bernstein: "We did Carnegie Hall in 1964 and I was told that I could have sold 200,000 more tickets. Hearing that, I offered Brian Epstein Madison Square Garden but he said, 'Let's wait; let's save it.'"

George's sister, Louise Harrison: "I was living in the States when the boys came over for *The Ed Sullivan Show*. George had been out to see me in Illinois in 1963 and he had loved being able to walk around like a normal person for the first time that year. He wanted to come back while in the States but with the outbreak of Beatlemania, they could not cross the country. They couldn't even cross the street. I had to go to New York to spend time with him. Their appearance on *The Ed Sullivan Show* was great – what you could hear of it. Cynthia Lennon was with me and a couple of nights later they were on at Carnegie Hall. Normally, we travelled in the same car as they did but we had our own little limo that night. The entourage had seats at the back of the stage.

At the end of the night we found that someone had commandeered our limo. We had no idea that we were so close to the hotel so we took a taxi. Neither of us had any money so we had to persuade the driver to take us to the hotel and then we went upstairs to get the money."

In the late 70s Marshall Crenshaw got his break playing John Lennon in a Broadway revue. "As part of our training for *Beatlemania!* we had to watch a film of the Beatles' first American concert in Washington DC. I can still get off on that. It was the one and only moment when they thought they were going to have to work to make it in America. It turned out that they didn't. They just showed up and everybody went 'Aaaaah!' They were working hard in Washington and they were really pouring it out. Ringo had so much energy. They owed a lot of their early fame to him because he drove the band."

Pat Boone: "I have never seen anything like the audience reaction for the Beatles. The fans would shriek from the moment they came on until long after they'd gone and you couldn't hear them perform. It was somewhat like that with Elvis and somewhat like that with me, but with us the screaming was at the beginning, at the start of a song they'd recognise, then they'd go quiet because they wanted to hear it and go crazy at the end."

Bobby Vinton: "I had the No.1 record in America with a sentimental ballad 'There! I've Said It Again' and it was a historic moment when the Beatles replaced me with 'I Want to Hold Your Hand'. I was still No.1 on a radio station in Philadelphia and the Beatles were No.2, but the Beatles had such hardcore fans that they were threatening the DJ. They said they would break his car window or flatten his tyres. He said, 'Bobby, I'm sorry. You're outselling the Beatles here but I'll have to drop you to No.2.'"

Bobby Vee: "There was such an influx of British records after the Beatles made it that anyone with an English accent was in demand. It was absolutely essential that the disc-jockeys should be Beatle crazy and English mad. It made a major dent in the careers of so many American pop singers." His own single, 'She's Sorry', was advertised in *Billboard* on 1 February 1964 as 'Bobby Vee with that new hit sound'.

February 1964 – All My Loving EP (Parlophone GEP 8891)
The first release of 1964 was more repackaging: two tracks from *With the Beatles* and two B-sides. This mini-collection was on the EP charts for the best part of a year and topped it for 8 weeks, but it could have

made as big an impact as the *Twist and Shout* EP if they had chosen 'Money' as the lead track and released it earlier to compete with the Decca single from Bern Elliott and the Fenmen. But this was minor league compared to what was happening in America.

'I Want to Hold Your Hand' had a seismic impact, immediately changing the direction of the American record industry. Capitol became the biggest and most renowned US record company of the period but the label still spurned many British hits, several of which were released on other labels when Capitol, still somewhat unreceptive and superior, could have had the rights for free. Capitol took Cilla Black and Peter and Gordon but sidelined the Animals, the Hollies, Manfred Mann, the Dave Clark Five and Gerry and the Pacemakers. What's more, the Beatles' success affected Capitol's roster of American artists.

Frankie Laine: "I left Columbia in '63 and after spending some time considering other record offers, I signed with Capitol. We spent two months getting the material together for an album but before it came out, Capitol received the masters of some group from Liverpool. That was the Beatles. They started selling like crazy and I was ignored. After all, Capitol hardly had the capacity to cope with the phenomenal demand for Beatle records, let alone anybody else's. Consequently, I sat there for two years. I looked around for songs I'd like to record once I'd left the label."

Debby Delmore, the daughter of Alton from the Delmore Brothers, a famed old-time country act: "When I was eleven, I saw the Beatles on *The Ed Sullivan Show* and thought this was the greatest group I had seen. I was buying their music and I had an album before my dad found out. He said, 'Debby, I'm going to listen to this album and if I don't like it, I won't let you keep it.' I thought, 'Oh no, there goes my album.' One day I was at my friend's house and he called me and said, 'I'm coming to get you and we're going shopping.' That was kinda strange but when he picked me up, he said, 'We're going to the record store.' He gave me some money and said, 'You go in there and get some more of those Beatle records.' That was the greatest compliment that he could give to anybody. He realised how much talent they had and he was truly impressed."

Mike Brumm of Ohio Express: "I got my start by listening to the British Invasion which inspired me to learn the guitar when I was about thirteen. There had been the Beach Boys before that but it didn't really click until I heard the Beatles. That got me interested in the American stars that had influenced the Beatles like Buddy Holly. I didn't know 'Words of Love' until I heard the Beatles do it. We were talking about them all the time, on the bus to school, in the classes and at lunchtime. Nobody talked about anything but watching the Beatles. They were bigger than Christmas. Ed Sullivan was very staid like an undertaker and these guys came across on the screen so vibrant, so that was a great juxtaposition which helped them. They looked so different with their hairstyle, the clothing and the boots: they could have dropped in from Mars."

Nils Lofgren: "I was about eleven and my friends had been playing rock'n'roll to me and I didn't get it. I guess it was too simple and I was too young to understand the emotion behind it. Adding another year or two of age and the Beatles had added some melody and harmony, I had been studying accordion since I was 6 years old and a lot of classical music and I just loved melody. I didn't get that guttural, visceral part of rock'n'roll. The Beatles put it all together for me and pretty soon I was turned onto the British invasion and a lot of the wonderful British groups. – the Kinks, the Yardbirds, the Zombies, the Animals, the Stones and the Beatles – and I quickly got turned on to their influences like the blues and Motown."

Carol Kaye of the UK trio, Kaye Sisters: "Before the Beatles, they didn't want to know about English variety acts in America, although they always loved our actors. The Beatles opened up a whole new world and we were able to headline at the Latin Quarter on Broadway. There was a shop that sold nothing but Beatle wigs and photographs. Kids would see my husband in his bowler hat and assume that he must be from England. They'd say, 'Will you give this letter to the Beatles?' They thought there was only one place in England, and that was Liverpool."

Guitarist Vic Juris: "I was in fifth grade and prior to the Beatles' arrival, there was a stir amongst everyone as though we were expecting a volcano to erupt. I had been playing guitar for a year before they came over and when I saw George Harrison on *The Ed Sullivan Show*, I said, 'Wow, that's it'. First, the Beatles made their début on *The Ed Sullivan Show*, then Ed had the Dave Clark Five, the Rolling Stones and Freddie and the Dreamers. Also, you got such great value with the Beatles' records. You knew that the flipside was going to be as good as the hit side. At the time singles were real cheap, 69 cents, so they sold a lot of copies."

American rock'n'roll star Dion: "The British Invasion had an effect on us. New acts were coming in and throwing rock'n'roll back to us. You need new blood to grow and that's what the British Invasion was all about. They were bringing new ideas to the party."

Steve Earle: "I've been a Beatles fan since I was 8 years old and they came over to do *The Ed Sullivan Show*. Everybody now is so busy ripping the Beatles off and I think it's great. They are probably the records that I have listened to most over the years. They elevated pop music to an art form: no one took pop music seriously before them. People got really interested in everything about them and that is because they were really, really, really good."

March 1964 – Can't Buy Me Love/ You Can't Do That (Parlophone R 5114, UK No.1, US No.1, Germany No.24)
John had been hoping that his take on Wilson Pickett, 'You Can't Do That', would be the A-side, but he acknowledged that Paul's 'Can't Buy Me Love' was really good.

The US *Billboard* chart for 4 April 1964 showed the Beatles holding the top five positions with 'Can't Buy Me Love' at No.1 and followed by 'Twist and Shout', 'She Loves You', 'I Want to Hold Your Hand' and 'Please Please Me'. They had another seven entries in the Top 100 and in Canada they did even better by occupying nine places in the Top 10 simultaneously.

The carrots of Wimpole Street, brother and sister Peter and Jane Asher, lived with their parents. Jane was going out with Paul McCartney and he stayed with the Ashers when he was in London. Peter Asher liked his song, 'A World without Love', and McCartney had no plans to use it with the Beatles as John Lennon mocked its opening line, "Please lock me away". Peter and Gordon Waller recorded it, double-tracking their voices for a fuller sound. Their harmonies were good but lacked the razor sharpness of the Everly Brothers. In truth, they were likeable performers but not a whole lot more.

Ironically, Peter and Gordon knocked the Beatles' 'Can't Buy Me Love' from the UK No.1 position, and the single repeated its success in America. The noted songwriter Doc Pomus was to describe 'A World without Love' as his favourite Lennon and McCartney composition: possibly because it is the one that is closest to a typical Brill Building song of the early 60s.

McCartney wrote their melodic follow-up, 'Nobody I Know',

which again did well, but his third song for Peter and Gordon, 'I Don't Want To See You Again', was weaker and a poor seller, although it still made the US Top 20. Despite what is thought, Lennon and McCartney did not give that many unrecorded songs to other artists. Contrast this with Smokey Robinson at Motown who wrote whole albums for other performers.

At the end of April 1964, the Beatles played the NME *Pollwinners Concert* at Wembley. UK agent and manager, Ken Pitt, later to discover David Bowie: "Brian Epstein knew nothing about management, which was a great advantage because he was managing artists who knew nothing about the business either. The Beatles were new and revolutionary and it was right that the person who represented them should also be an innocent at large. He was a very charming man who worked very, very hard in those months when he came down from the North to try and interest people in London. I liked Brian Epstein very much. When I was launching Manfred Mann, we did a show with the Beatles at Wembley and Brian walked right across the arena to tell me how good Manfred Mann was."

British manager and agent Bunny Lewis: "If I can use an old-fashioned term, Brian Epstein was more of a gentleman than most managers. He was very civilised. He was extremely talented as a manager and he only slipped up because of the enormous property which the Beatles became. It went right out of his scope in that they were making millions out of T-shirts and merchandise, which he didn't know a lot about. Still, you can't be all things to all men and he handled them beautifully."

Hal Carter, who worked for Larry Parnes: "It was very difficult to get directly to Brian Epstein because he had so many assistants whereas Larry Parnes did it all himself. Eppy got a lot of things for nothing because just being 'Brian Epstein, the Manager of the Beatles' meant that people made him offers. He was never completely sure of himself whereas Parnes had grit and arrogance and self-belief – all his acts were subordinate to him, he was the star. Parnes could handle everything but Eppy got emotionally involved. Eppy went into show business to meet people and to have friends. He hadn't come into it for the money and he soon found out about the piranha fish – and the piranhas are as big as whales in America."

Aaron Williams of the Merseybeats: "I went back one night to Brian Epstein's house in Belgravia and there was John, Ringo and Viv

Prince from the Pretty Things. John was sitting on a chair against the wall and Brian was sitting on the floor. John was saying, 'Here, boy, have another biscuit', treating him like a dog, and Brian was going along with it. It wasn't being done seriously, but John was certainly mocking him."

In March 1964 John Lennon's first book *In His Own Write* was published, featuring stories, poems and drawings. He was interviewed by Kenneth Allsop on the BBC-TV programme, *Tonight*. In April, John attended a literary luncheon at Foyle's. Not usually at a loss for words, all he said was, "Thank you very much, and God bless you."

Roger McGough: "I don't remember John ever sitting down and talking with me but we both liked wordplay and he did it with those Stanley Unwin type books, *In His Own Write* and *A Spaniard in the Works*. I didn't particularly like them. There were too many cruel jokes about spastics and disability. We weren't as PC then as we are now but even back then, it was a little shocking."

Although everything was happening so quickly for the Beatles, they were capable of writing and recording quality material and Brian Epstein ensured their creativity was encouraged by talented associates. Their first film *A Hard Day's Night* was written by Alun Owen and directed by Richard Lester in 1964.

Alun Owen: "I met Brian Epstein at his office in Moorfields in Liverpool with his brother Clive. They were planning to make a small budget film for the Beatles principally aimed at the British market. Brian asked me if I would write the film and Dick Lester, whom I'd worked with several times, was to be the director. I went with the Beatles to Dublin and Paris and saw an extraordinary reaction in Paris because so many people were shouting, 'Ringo! Ringo!' He couldn't understand what was going on. While I was thinking about the film, the whole thing exploded for them in America. There was then pressure to make it a big budget film and shoot it in colour but we resisted that because we saw it as a black and white subject – rather like a French *nouvelle vague* film, if you like. I was aware that the Beatles weren't actors and so I didn't write long speeches and they spoke in sentences of five or six words each. Later on, I saw that John Lennon would have been capable of something more. Ringo emerged as the star of the film because he had such a remarkable face."

Film producer Denis O'Dell: "I was aware of the bad pop films, vehicles just to make a bit of money, but I got a call from Bud Ornstein at United Artists. He said, 'These guys won't last and we want to make this cheaply and quickly, so will you produce it?' I said I didn't want to but my kids said, 'Are you serious?' I called him back and said that I would do it for 8 weeks. Well, I was on it for 5 months and it was such a joy. Richard Lester was great and we did it in a modern style and took some chances, like not using back projections, which was the normal way of shooting moving scenes on a train. I said, 'How about if I got a real train? Could you cope with that?' and he said, 'I never thought I'd hear that from an Englishman.' The only major change was that they had wanted to shoot it in Liverpool. I would have loved to have done that but we didn't have the money. We couldn't have supported film crews at hotels in Liverpool for 6 or 7 weeks. It was shot in London purely for financial reasons."

Part of Lester's expertise lay in surrounding the Beatles with well-known character actors such as Norman Rossington: "I loved being in *A Hard Day's Night*. Alun Owen wanted as many Liverpool people as possible in that film and he wrote that part of Norm especially for me. That doesn't happen very often. Of course a lot of writers say 'That's a Norman Rossington part' and I end up doing it."

Denis O'Dell: "On a normal picture, you can control the crowd by putting up ropes but I thought we wouldn't fight it. Whenever we were overwhelmed by crowds, we returned to the studio to shoot interiors. I wanted the nearest studio to London. I tried Merton Park at Wimbledon but that was too difficult. Twickenham was ideal but it had been closed for years. I asked the owners if I could reopen it. They agreed for £15,000, and so I built sets. We were run off the streets as soon as the kids were out of school, and so we went back to the studio. We always did a full day's work and the studio never looked back after that."

Gordon Millings worked for his father, the tailor Dougie Millings: "When the Beatles' suits were sent to be cleaned, they would regularly come back with pieces missing. Replacements were constantly being made. They would take two or three sets on tour and we would keep the same number as spares. We made all the suits for *A Hard Day's Night* and *Help!* and the TV specials. The movies meant extra suits for the stunt doubles. Arthur Newman, who was the wardrobe master for the films, worked very closely with us. They would also buy day wear from us and on one occasion, Paul was in the shop for a fitting and was spotted by a couple of kids. In no time at all, a sizeable crowd was outside the shop and we had to call the police to get the street cleared."

Film critic Barry Norman: "Tommy Steele's and Cliff Richard's films look horribly dated now but they were perfectly acceptable at the time. *A Hard Day's Night* was the best of the Beatles' films. A hell of that is due to Richard Lester, who was a very inventive director and they were lucky to have him. It had movement, energy and verve, which were exactly what the boys needed. That is what you felt about them – lively and full of *joie de vivre* and so Richard Lester and the Beatles were a perfect match. He had the good sense to get the best possible actors around. It disguised the fact that the leading men weren't really actors and they carried them through the film."

Did it bother Victor Spinetti that the Beatles weren't trained actors? "Not at all. I had worked in Joan Littlewood's Theatre Workshop for 6 years and some nights she would tell someone to play my part and some nights somebody else. I was used to improvising. They didn't keep to the script in *A Hard Day's Night* but they cut out many of the outtakes, isn't that sad? I walked round the set in my furry sweater and I said, 'You're late for rehearsals. I'm a director.' John said, 'You're not a director. You're Victor Spinetti playing the part of a director.' I said, 'I am a director, I have an award in my office'. John said, 'Office? You haven't even got a dressing room.' I hit Ringo's cymbals and Ringo lent across and said to John, 'He's fingering me cymbals. John.' John said, 'He must be a director as all directors are famous cymbal fingerers.' That was filmed, it was all improvised but sadly, it wasn't used.

Film critic Mark Kermode: "*A Hard Day's Night* is a very smart, knockabout romp that is excitingly done, even though we have seen the set pieces so many times, they still look fresh and original. The Beatles weren't the world's most brilliant actors but they were funny. They were really, really great deadpan comedians. Actually, the best performances they ever did were at their press conferences. They were incredibly funny, and they were sharper than anyone else in the room and were totally unbothered by the camera."

Film critic Ramsey Campbell: "*A Hard Day's Night* had a vitality and urgency that was new to rock'n'roll films. It was shot pretty fast and its roughness is to its credit. It is like the French New Wave, that is: a low budget film using natural light and sound and miles away from the artificial, studio-bound, glossy American films of the day. The New Wave took their lead from the low-budgeted B-films of the 40s, and *A Hard Day's Night* is much closer to its spirit than those which are nominally similar like *The Loneliness of the Long Distance Runner*. That film looks very dated now, whereas *A Hard Day's Night* is still remarkably fresh. Even though it was scripted by Alun Owen, it has an improvised feel as though they are making it up as they go along. A few weeks ago I saw another film of the 60s, *Catch Us If You Can*, which was dire and very leaden, even though it was directed by John Boorman, who was to make *Point Blank* and *The Emerald Forest*. The film lacked the energy of *A Hard Day's Night* and, of course, he was working with the Dave Clark Five rather than the Beatles. Without the Beatles, there would have been a vacuum in *A Hard Day's Night* and I can't think of any other band of the 60s who could have pulled it off so well."

George Melly: "The structure of *A Hard Day's Night* was partially down to Dick Lester and partially to Alun Owen, who was the most important television playwright of the time. The previous films about pop stars had followed a formula – a middle-class girlfriend and an auntie figure who disapproved to start with but ended up tapping her foot – but Alun Owen, who had lived in Liverpool practically all his life, recognised the dilemma of the Beatles. They were suddenly projected from being layabouts to local heroes and then to international heroes and the script was about the trap it set for them, about being imprisoned by fame. It was high-spirited with very inventive photography, and it was about the real dilemma when you can't move along with ordinary people and you become totally isolated. They were in prison on the train, in prison in the hotel, in prison everywhere."

Film director, Peter Bogdanovich: "Within 24 hours of them appearing on *The Ed Sullivan Show*, the Beatles had changed everything. They had opened the floodgates. It was never my music of choice as I was already deeply into Sinatra and later Louis Armstrong and jazz in general. I was never a rock'n'roll aficionado but *A Hard Day's Night* was irresistible and you didn't have to be a rock'n'roll fan to like the Beatles. They have proved to be irresistible throughout the decades and they have directed the course of our lives. They are a phenomenon. They are almost outside music – they are just 'The Beatles'."

Mark Kermode: "I saw *A Hard Day's Night* just 2 days ago because my daughter is doing a project about the 60s. I hadn't seen it for a long time and the main thing I'd forgotten is how much the story about Paul McCartney's grandfather, who's 'very clean', is woven into all of this. You think about the performance numbers in that film, which are really great, and the classic scene of running off the train and into the taxi. There are lots of references to eating bad sandwiches and sitting on grotty trains and having to look after Paul's grandfather. There is all the wacky stuff, all the experimental stuff, all the fun stuff and all the poppy stuff in the film, and yet at the same they are threading a traditional narrative through it. What purpose does it serve? It has a sense of being a proper film so it ought to have a proper story about Paul's difficult grandfather."

There were premières for *A Hard Day's Night* in London and Liverpool. Clive Epstein: "There was a wonderful occasion when the Beatles came back to Liverpool for the première of *A Hard Day's Night*. The streets of Liverpool were lined all the way from Speke airport to Castle Street. Castle Street looked exactly the same as it would have done for Liverpool winning the Cup Final. We were all immensely proud and those of us who were close to Brian could hardly believe it was happening. It was an extraordinary period in our lives."

Roger McGuinn of the Byrds: "Once we saw the Beatles in *A Hard Day's Night*, we wanted to be like them and that included getting suits with velvet collars. We went to Mr. Parker's Closet in south central Los Angeles and we bought some black suits with velvet collars. We wore them on stage and we had them at Ciro's. We would hang them on the racks at Ciro's and go home in our jeans. One day we returned and the suits were gone. I told John Lennon later on that somebody had stolen our suits. He said, 'I wish somebody had stolen ours.'"

In the US, George Harrison had bought a 12-string guitar, which he used in *A Hard Day's Night*. Roger McGuinn: "George Harrison was playing a Rickenbacker 12 string and he gave me the idea for getting one too. His method of playing lead was to play up and down the G string as he got more punch out of it. I emulated that style and it sounded really good."

Dave Pegg, bass player with Fairport Convention: "George Harrison didn't have the best technique in the world but he managed to get a style of his own. As well as admiring people with tremendous technique, I have an admiration for people who have a great understanding of what not to play, and George was in that category. Somebody who is sensitive to a song, whether he is a drummer, a guitarist, saxophonist or a good singer, will know what *not* to do. Some guitarists can say more in a handful of notes than others will in 2 hours' worth."

The Barron Knights parodied the Beatles and their contemporaries in 'Call Up the Groups' (1964) and 'Pop Go the Workers' (1965). Pete Langford: "Dick James was very strict with us. We wanted to do a Barron Knights' parody of a Beatles' song as we had parodied everybody else. He said, 'Definitely no, and don't come back because I will never allow it.' We had to do our parody on songs he didn't publish, that is, 'Love Me Do' and 'Twist and Shout'. Paul has told me since that he loved our parodies but he couldn't swing it with Dick James."

Sonny Curtis of the Crickets: "Lou Adler was a record producer who got me a deal with Dimension Records. The Beatles were hitting America and so he and I wrote 'The Beatle I Want to be' together. It was so early that the record company didn't realise how the Beatles spelt their name and put 'BEETLES' on the label."

Buzz Cason of the Crickets: "I was in England in 1964 with the Crickets when *A Hard Day's Night* film broke out and I remember Glen D. Hardin going out and meeting them one night but I didn't want to stay out. I'm not sure where he went, could have been the Speakeasy, but some place in London. Glen went to meet them and John Lennon recognised him. Glen came back about 5 a.m. and said to me, 'You blew it, man. I've been with the Beatles. You losers have been asleep.'"

The Beatles' name was a nod to the Crickets, who were quickly off the mark as their 1964 album, *California Sun,* included 'Please Please Me', 'I Saw Her Standing There', 'From Me To You', 'I Want to Hold Your Hand' and 'She Loves You' as well as a song the Beatles recorded, 'Money'. The arrangement of their 1964 hit single, 'La Bamba', also owed much to 'Twist and Shout'. The mutual admiration continued as Paul McCartney was later to buy Buddy Holly's song catalogue and he sometimes sang on stage with the Crickets, producing their 1988 single, 'T-Shirt'.

Sonny Curtis of the Crickets made solo recordings: "I was sitting around the apartment one night playing 'All My Loving' fingerstyle on the guitar. Snuff Garrett said, 'I like that. Let's do a whole album like that.' The next day I was in the studio so I didn't have time to arrange anything and was groping for something to play. *Beatle Hits, Flamenco Style* is a nice album though, not earth-shattering, but pretty good for what it is."

Jack Good, the pioneering TV director of *6.5 Special* and *Oh Boy!* made a TV special, *Around the Beatles*, and P.J. Proby was brought to the UK for a guest appearance: "When I knew I was coming, I felt I had to do something like the Beatles, so I took all the old songs I knew and worked out which ones would fit in with their sound. 'Hold me, yeah, oooo'. We recorded it in a small studio at IBC with Big Jim Sullivan on lead, Jimmy Page on rhythm, Ginger Baker on drums, Charles Blackwell on piano and Jimmy Powell on harmonica. When the TV programme was recorded, Paul McCartney said, 'This is P.J. Proby, our best friend and a big star from the USA' and I was neither of those things. I'd known Paul for 15 days and I wasn't a star in America. I'd been a motorcycle delivery boy, a stuntman and a songwriter. Paul said all that and I had to live up to it."

The Beatles kept on touring. In June 1964 it was John, Paul, George and Jimmy Nicol on a world tour while Ringo recovered from tonsillitis. Ringo Starr joined them in Melbourne. "Normally no one would think twice about a group having a 'dep' drummer," said their press officer Tony Barrow, "and it proves the point that the Beatles were unique. Everybody expected to see all four members and Jimmy Nicol was only brought in so that thousands of fans on the other side of the world would not be disappointed."

Debby Delmore, daughter of Alton from the Delmore Brothers: "After my dad died in 1964, we moved to a new neighborhood and I wouldn't even tell my new friends that my father had gone – they all thought he was still alive. We lived in an 8 x 48 mobile home and the air conditioner was in the front. I would go to the back of the mobile home, shut the door where I couldn't get any air conditioning and listen to my Beatle records. Their music was the only thing that would console me. I suppose I had a breakdown but they didn't use words like that then. I just had to get through it. Daddy always told me that music was a gift from God and so since then, every time that I have been sad, I have put on some music. Music is therapeutic and my father taught me that."

June 1964 – Long Tall Sally EP (Parlophone GEP 8913, 6/64)
Side 1: Long Tall Sally/ I Call Your Name
Side 2: Slow Down/ Matchbox
There were two UK No.1's from the film, 'Can't Buy Me Love' and 'A Hard Day's Night' itself. The soundtrack album was another colossal seller and, as if that wasn't enough, the Beatles issued a four-track rock'n'roll EP of previously unissued material, *Long Tall Sally*. They

paid tribute to Little Richard, Larry Williams and Carl Perkins and also included the Lennon and McCartney song 'I Call Your Name'.

At the British Library in Euston Road, you can see John Lennon's original draft for the song, 'A Hard Day's Night' and Paul's handwritten lyric for 'Yesterday'. Andy Linehan, the curator of popular music at the National Sound Archive: "We have a number of handwritten Beatles' lyrics that came to us from Hunter Davies and they are in the Big Gallery. The impact of the Beatles was such that they belong there with Shakespeare and Magna Carta. They are a great attraction for visitors. We have 'A Hard Day's Night' as a work in progress. John Lennon grabbed the nearest thing to hand to write some lyrics, which was a birthday card to Julian. The lyric had just snapped into his head. On the other hand, 'Yesterday' is a late draft and McCartney may have written it to remind him of the words for the recording."

Author Hunter Davies: "About 30 years ago, I picked up on the floor of Abbey Road, and they also gave me, scraps of paper on which they'd done the lyrics and they would have been burned by one of the cleaners. When Sotheby's held a Beatles memorabilia sale, I found that the stuff I had was more valuable than my house. I gave them to the British Museum and now they're in the British Library."

Graham Lyle of Gallagher and Lyle: "The 60s was a real heyday for British songwriting and these days the British have lost a lot of ground. I know how difficult it is to write a song like 'A Hard Day's Night'. It may not be saying a lot emotionally but it is a strongly built vehicle. When you have a strong song, you can play it on the mouth organ and it still works."

July 1964 – A Hard Day's Night/ Things We Said Today (Parlophone R 5160, UK No.1, US No.1, Germany No.2)
July 1964 – A Hard Day's Night LP (Parlophone PMC 1230)
Produced by George Martin, 13 tracks – 30 minutes 40 seconds
Side 1: A Hard Day's Night/ I Should Have Known Better/ If I Fell/ I'm Happy Just to Dance with You/ And I Love Her/ Tell Me Why/ Can't Buy Me Love
Side 2: Anytime at All/ I'll Cry Instead/ Things We Said Today/ When I Get Home/ You Can't Do That/ I'll be Back

A Hard Day's Night is the only album to contain solely Lennon and McCartney compositions, although the thirteen songs amount to 30 minutes playing time. It is a vibrant, rock'n'roll album with no fancy trickery. The songs include 'I Should Have Known Better', 'And I Love Her' and 'If I Fell' from the film, and such non-film favourites as 'Things We Said Today' and 'You Can't Do That'. Ignoring the film and simply taking this as a beat group album, *A Hard Day's Night* shows just how great the Beatles were.

I asked a leading photographer Eamonn McCabe to comment on the photo strip cover of *A Hard Day's Night*. "Modern groups would shun the cover of *A Hard Day's Night* and would want something more adventurous, but it gave the feeling of a movie. The black-and-white pictures look as though they've been set up as a spread of little pictures from a movie. Each Beatle has a line and there are five pictures in a line. In a way, it also looks like early booth photography. It is very stunning and I like the colour on the edge of the LP cover."

Gary Walker from the Walker Brothers: "No one had seen anything like them. They had long hair and strange accents and they were writing stuff that was really good. The one I really love is 'Tell Me Why' on *A Hard Day's Night*. The Beatles made everybody start writing because all we had been doing was covering songs. When we played in Hollywood clubs, we would always have to do the No.1 record. The Beatles did covers too, of course, and they did them great."

Richard Thompson: "The Beatles started the idea that you could be both the band and the songwriters. Usually you had a team of songwriters that would be writing stuff and the band would take the songs and record them. This was a new thing, and then the Rolling Stones had to do it and then everybody else. It has been that way ever since. Your credibility lies in writing your own material. The standard of songs fell because not every band is as good as the Beatles."

John McNally of the Searchers: "Brian Epstein wished he'd signed us and he gave us a Lennon and McCartney song, 'Things We Said Today'. He wanted us to record it but there were so many problems with our management and with him that, in the end, the Beatles put it out as a B-side to 'A Hard Day's Night'. We've never done it because we've stayed away from songs that were popular by other artists."

José Feliciano: "There are so many vocal versions of 'And I Love Her' and so I thought it would be fun to do it as an instrumental. I was fantasising that I might get to hang out with them if they liked it. I never met them as a group although I did hang out with them individually. Paul and Linda were very kind to me and he is a really good person."

Neville Marten of Marty Wilde's Wildcats: "I was turned onto music by George Harrison. John and Paul were casual, easy-going musicians but George was very studious, always taking great care, and I thought, 'That's the guy I want to be'. It was said that the Stones could play and the Beatles could write songs but George Harrison played some lovely guitar on their records. The solo in 'Something' is a classic, a song within a song. 'And I Love Her' on the classical guitar is an absolute example of understanding an instrument as it relates to a song, which is what many guitarists fail to understand today."

Justin Currie of Del Amitri: "The *Hard Day's Night* album is their masterpiece. I love 'I'll Be Back', even though it's terribly obvious, and the melody and countermelody of 'If I Fell' is quite extraordinary. They out-brother the Everly Brothers on that one. The album is dominated by Lennon in the same way as *Sgt. Pepper* is dominated by McCartney. It is the height of Lennon's rocker period but inside the rocker's voice is an incredibly soft centre which was unusual as rock was usually macho. Gene Vincent had the same kind of vulnerability. Elvis is great at that stuff too – I love 'I'm Left, You're Right, She's Gone' but usually it is that film actor's thing: nobody really wants to play a loser."

In 1981 Nils Lofgren covered 'Anytime At All' and he has often performed it on stage. "It is very difficult to cover a Beatles song as no one can do a better version than theirs and I certainly didn't. I loved that lyric, which symbolised to me what the Beatles were all about which is being both incredibly soulful and simple at the same time. It has a plain, simple lyric but it is a way of expressing love and passion for someone in a real soulful way. Lennon had an ability to do that and no one else did."

John Lennon's biographer, Ray Coleman: "The sound of the Beatles to me is the sound of John Lennon's voice. I thought it was very, very special. I particularly fancied 'You Can't Do That' which John sang with that raw, earthy feeling that he alone had in the group. I thought it should have been an A-side, although 'Can't Buy Me Love' was very good. The lyrics are very much John Lennon of that period. They talk of the things you can't do, which was a theme of John Lennon's life, things you can't do that nevertheless he did."

Barbara Dickson was in the original production of *John Paul George Ringo...And Bert,* which opened at the Liverpool Everyman in 1974: "I played tambourine and wore a duffle coat and I had to go outside the theatre with Bert and a couple of guys in the band and busk

'I Should Have Known Better'. It's a great song for busking and we got very generously treated by the Merseyside crowd."

July 1964 – It's For You – Cilla Black (UK No.7)
Paul McCartney, piano. John Lennon and Paul McCartney, co- arrangers
In August the Beatles started a full tour of the US and Canada. Supporting act Jackie DeShannon: "Brian Epstein knew Al Bennett who was running Liberty Records and I felt very lucky in getting on those shows. It was God looking down and saying, 'Let's do something for Jackie.' A lot of my demos had come through Dick James Music and so they were familiar with my work. When we opened at the Cow Palace, San Francisco, I was nervous at meeting them but Paul got out of the limo and said, 'I know your music. We heard it all the time when we went to the publishers.'."

American record producer Huey P. Meaux: "I liked the way the little chicks fainted at their concerts – it was mass hypnotism. I had the exclusive on the Beatles merchandising in Texas and there were roomfuls of plastic Beatle beach bags which contained transistor radios and a few other things. You could sell anything with the word 'Beatles' and those items are worth hundreds of dollars now. They tore Houston upside down and the only way we could get them to Dallas was by armoured car."

BBC presenter Brian Matthew: "We landed in Houston and there were some very funny little airfields in America. Some were no more than dirt strips with a couple of buildings. Houston was like that. There was a gang of kids to meet the Beatles and they not only surrounded the plane, they jumped onto it. They were on the wings, flicking cigarette butts about and it was terribly dangerous. We weren't allowed off. We were locked in the plane and Ringo was standing by the door, making us laugh by saying, 'Beatles and children first.' There was a modicum of security and they cleared the kids from the plane and we were allowed out."

Tony Barrow: "There were fan problems with the Beatles from the word go. It wasn't so much fear that the Beatles would be harmed, although if a large number of hysterical kids had climbed on a stage, and that could have happened. The real fear was that the fans would harm themselves; that they would fall into orchestra pits or fall off airport balconies. On one American tour, the top of the Beatles' limousine was severely dented by kids climbing all over it. We arrived in one Texas city on a charter flight in the middle of the night. Kids appeared from nowhere and they were climbing all over the wings before the engines had stopped. It would have been very dangerous if one of those kids had lit a cigarette. Fan control wasn't simply to keep these kids away from their idols: it was also to protect them from damage to themselves."

Jackie DeShannon: "The shows were fun for me. They weren't fun if you were thinking of 30,000 people who hadn't come to see you but you didn't take it personally. I loved every minute of it. I did rousing songs like 'Shout' and I was thrilled to be playing to that many people. I was in the middle of the show and Brian Epstein moved me to closing the first half. I'd been able to get control of the crowd and get them listening to me and no one was more in love with that Merseybeat sound than me. Obviously, having my child would be one of the big events of my life but being on that tour would be up there in the Top 5. What a great honour it was."

On 17 September 1964 the Beatles played the Municipal Stadium, Kansas City, Missouri. Robert Reynolds of the Mavericks: "My grandfather was the manager of the Muehlbach Hotel. It was a famous hotel and it had been a host to some Presidents. He told my parents that they could be in the lobby when the Beatles came and it would be closed to everyone else. My grandfather checked them in and he said that Paul was grumpy, but everyone is entitled to a bad day. My grandfather was besieged with neighbours who wanted anything they could get from the Beatles. He was asked for cigarette butts but there weren't enough to go round. My grandfather and my grandmother smoked a few cigarettes and passed out some phony butts. They were approached by a marketing company to sell their bedsheets, which were then clipped into one-inch swatches and applied to a card which certified them as the official bedsheets of the Beatles. They authenticated the bedsheets using the letterhead from the hotel. I've since bought a set for myself."

Scott McCarl of the Raspberries: "We went to see them at the baseball stadium in Kansas City. Tom and I got our first jobs ever so that we could afford the tickets. It was a Thursday night show and I can see it now. The movie *A Hard Day's Night* had just come out. They said, 'Did you like the film?', and there was a huge roar. That was great. John was banging away on the stage and the heel came off his boot but he didn't care, he kept on banging. They were Elvis and everybody else turbocharged. There was no real problem with the sound: I could hear them as well as I could on the *Hollywood Bowl* album."

Jackie DeShannon: "I don't remember talking about songwriting with them but we did have pillow fights. I played *Monopoly* with George and he won. They were separated from us in the plane. We couldn't go to them but they could come back to us. John played me 'I'm A Loser', just the first part of the song, and it was brilliant. George came back too and he wanted me to play 'When You Walk in the Room' as he wasn't sure how a bit of it went. They are a wonderful example of a group coming up through the mire by playing in Germany and having all those experiences. They had the experience of playing on stage for a long time: people don't have that today. They had earned their stripes and they knew a lot of genres of music. It comes across in their music and those songs have lasted for over 40 years."

In October, the Beatles undertook their only UK tour of the year. Among the guests were the Tamla-Motown singer, Mary Wells, and a new signing by Brian Epstein, Michael Haslam, who had been discovered by the writer and broadcaster, Godfrey Winn. Michael Haslam: "Mary Wells used to keep playing George's version of 'Do You Want to Know a Secret' and George used to hate that. He hated hearing his voice."

Louise Harrison: "Our parents were always in control and they answered the thousands of fan letters to George as best they could. They took things in their stride. Lots of Beatle fans got letters from my parents and have kept them to this day. When I meet them, they pull them out and say that they have been carrying them around for years. I feel very proud of what they did."

P.J. Proby followed 'Hold Me' with another oldie, 'Together'. "I was singing 'Together' on an acoustic guitar and I decided to arrange it the way that I thought John and Paul would do it. They were a total influence for my first year and a half in Britain. Even though I went straight from them into Broadway songs, my influence was much more the Beatles than Elvis Presley or Vic Damone."

October 1964 – I Knew Right Away – Alma Cogan (Columbia DB 7390)
Paul McCartney, tambourine
Alma Cogan was a 50s hit-maker, known as the girl with a giggle. Although still a big concert attraction in the 60s, her chart days were over. She dated Brian Epstein and, apparently, John Lennon had a crush on her. Paul McCartney happened to be around when she recorded this B-side, her own song, and he played tambourine.

December 1964 – I Feel Fine/ She's a Woman (Parlophone R 5200, 12/64, UK No.1, US No.1, Germany No.3) (B-side also made No.4 in US.)
In November the Beatles released a new single, 'I Feel Fine', which became the Christmas No.1. It opened innovatively with John Lennon's guitar feedback. Guitarist John Jorgenson: "They tried new sounds on every record like the sound of the guitar at the start of 'I Feel Fine'. It is supposedly the first intentional use of feedback but even after the feedback, there is John Lennon's full-bodied Gibson J160E which was an acoustic guitar with an electric pick-up and plugged into a Vox amp. It sounds like the electric piano that Ray Charles plays on 'What'd I Say', the riff too is really similar and the drum part on 'I Feel Fine' is very similar to 'What'd I Say' as well."

The opening riff is also similar to Bobby Parker's 'Watch Your Step' and when I met the rhythm and blues singer on a blues package, he wasn't overawed to be in Liverpool: quite the reverse. He hadn't a good word for the Beatles, claiming that they owed him royalties. I presumed that he hadn't been able to sue because he'd be out of pocket if he lost, and so he nursed a grudge.

John said in interviews that 'I Feel Fine' was the record with the first feedback anywhere – "I claim it for the Beatles, before Hendrix, before the Who, before anyone – the first feedback on any record." Maybe. In his autobiography, *X-Ray*, Ray Davies writes about the Kinks appearing before screaming Beatle fans in Bournemouth in August 1964 and gaining attention by Dave turning up his amplifier and the high-pitched frequency cut right through the screams of the Beatles' fans." Ray comments that John Lennon was watching in the wings. But anyway, what about Johnny 'Guitar' Watson's 'Space Guitar' from 1954, which is full of distortion and feedback and 10 years ahead of its time.

Earl Okin: "When the Beatles' singles came out, we often thought that is not as good as the last one but they needed three or four hearings and then stayed there forever. A lot of record companies said, 'Can you do something similar to your last hit?', but they were in a strong enough position to keep doing something different. Their fans went along with them and so they were able to do that."

Curtis Stigers: "If I do a Beatles tune, it has to be something that you would never think I would do. The problem with making a jazz record and putting in modern pop songs is that most people recommend songs that are jazzy. I prefer to have a great song and make it jazz.

The obvious ones are 'Michelle' because of the chords or 'Something', which already is a little jazzy. I would prefer to take a rock'n'roll song like 'I Feel Fine' and then do something jazzy with it. I would take it to a different place and try not to make it sound goofy."

December 1964 – Beatles for Sale LP (Parlophone PMC 1240)
Produced by George Martin, 14 tracks – 34 minutes 13 seconds
Side 1: No Reply/ I'm a Loser/ Baby's in Black/ Rock and Roll Music/ I'll Follow the Sun/ Mr. Moonlight/ Kansas City/ Hey-Hey-Hey-Hey!
Side 2: Eight Days a Week/ Words of Love/ Honey Don't/ Every Little Thing/ I Don't Want to Spoil the Party/ What You're Doing/ Everybody's Trying to Be My Baby

The title of their second album of the year, *Beatles for Sale*, sounds like a take on 'Can't Buy Me Love'. The semi-apologetic sleeve notes from Derek Taylor suggested that the Beatles weren't overkeen on the album: "It isn't a pot-boiling, quick-sale, any-old-thing-will-do-for-Christmas mixture." Was Derek Taylor making the case for the defence before anyone had heard it? Still, he also said, somewhat prophetically, "The kids of AD 2000 will draw from the music much the same sense of well-being and warmth as we do today."

The album didn't contain the best of Lennon and McCartney's songwriting, although there are good songs on there. The Dylan influence can be heard on John Lennon's 'I'm a Loser'. Note some sloppy songwriting though, as the emphasis on "before a fall" is wrong, and unusually for the Beatles, there is a fadeout ending.

The McCartney song, the folky 'I'll Follow the Sun' gives us a taster of his later work such as his first solo album. When Paul had been banned from driving for speeding, he had a driver who complained that he was working "eight days a week". Cue for song.

US TV reporter Larry Kane: "When I was flying with the Beatles over Kansas, they had a rough version of 'Eight Days a Week' on a portable recorder and they played it to me. They wanted me to help out with a couple of words. That was fun. I can't remember what the words were but I always wish it had been credited to 'Lennon, McCartney and Kane'."

'Baby's in Black' sounds like it was derived from a children's rhyme, although I haven't been able to trace it. Perhaps it's a variant on "Oh Dear, What Can the Matter Be".

For the cover versions, John chose 'Rock and Roll Music' and 'Mr.

Moonlight', Paul 'Kansas City' (merged with Little Richard's 'Hey, Hey, Hey, Hey', though not credited on the original sleeve), George 'Everybody's Trying to be My Baby' (with too much echo) and Ringo: 'Honey Don't', the latter two coming from Carl Perkins. John and Paul harmonised on a delightful version of Buddy Holly's 'Words of Love', but the best cover – John Lennon's rasping version of Little Willie John's 'Leave My Kitten Alone' – was left off the album.

The cover of Dr. Feelgood and the Interns' 'Mr. Moonlight' is not the Beatles' finest hour, and another Liverpool cover by the Merseybeats and released almost a year earlier is far sharper. It's a pity that Billy Preston wasn't around when the Beatles recorded 'Mr. Moonlight': he would have transformed it.

Eamonn McCabe: "I get the feeling that when the photographer was working on the *Beatles for Sale* cover, something happened, and he was brave enough to run with the picture even though it had its faults. Actually, it adds atmosphere. We don't know what the orange and green is – could be two people walking by – it looks like a long lens shot from across the street or across a park, certainly outdoors, and somebody got in the way, but it doesn't spoil it. I like the picture because a long lens has been used and it has a feeling of journalism. The back cover reflects it as well: they've stayed in the same place and the shot looks down on them."

Carl Perkins: "I went to England for the first time in May 1964 with Chuck Berry and at the end of the tour, the Beatles gave a party for me: they wanted to meet me and I certainly wanted to meet them. 'I Want to Hold Your Hand' was very big at the time and I found them to be really down-to-earth, super-talented people, very nice and very witty too. I loved the clothes they were wearing, those spiked heel boots, but they needed haircuts. John said, 'Oh no, we don't do haircuts.' I was in the studio when they recorded 'Honey Don't', 'Matchbox' and 'Everybody's Trying to Be My Baby'. I played a little on the songs as they rehearsed them. Nothing I played with the Beatles was ever released: we were just jamming around and I don't think the tapes were rolling."

Rory Gallagher: "I liked the Beatles a lot, particularly the way they revived an interest in Carl Perkins and Buddy Holly. Most of the string bending came from Paul, and John was a very powerful rhythm player. George Harrison was an underrated slide player, very accurate and very good in the Carl Perkins vein. He worked within the song and he had unusual phrases and didn't fit into the Eric Clapton/ Jeff Beck area. He could play great ethnic rock'n'roll and rockabilly guitar. However, I thought the greatest guitar player from Liverpool was Brian Griffiths of the Big Three – a dangerous player and extremely good. There's a great solo on 'Don't Start Running Away'."

Carl Perkins: "It's hard for me to realise that I influenced people like George Harrison and Eric Clapton with my simple guitar licks as they play so much better than I do. They tell me that I caused them to pick up their guitars, but, man, they have run off and left me."

Charlie Reid from the Proclaimers: "One of the greatest things about the Beatles was those three part harmonies. They did them great early on and even towards the end. I love the forcefulness of their songs, I love the directness, I love the humour, I love the subtlety. 'Ticket to Ride' is one of the greatest records ever made. There's some fantastic drumming on that. I like their covers and there's a wonderful lightness of touch about 'Words of Love' on *Beatles for Sale*. They were popular music aristocracy."

There is a short verse 'The Moldy Moldy Man' in John Lennon's *In His Own Write* that might well have led to 'Nowhere Man': it is the same thought. Nick Heyward: "Take 'Nowhere Man'. I liked the fact that John Lennon was sitting there feeling nowhere and yet he can still write a song from nowhere. It's that self-deprecating humour that he had. He was bang on with that."

On the short documentary issued with the remasters, John Lennon says, "My voice is killing me" while he is recording 'No Reply'. You can understand why as this is an impassioned performance. It is like one of those paranoid Del Shannon hits and the line "That's a lie" is scary. It could easily have been a hit single. Brian Epstein was keen for Tommy Quickly to make the Top 10 and he placed his faith in 'No Reply', which he would record with the Remo Four. Rhythm guitarist Don Andrew from the Remo Four: "Everything was right for Tommy to have a No.1 hit. The Lennon and McCartney songwriter tag and a reasonable production would have guaranteed it a place in the Top Ten, if not the very top. We recorded the backing first and we double-tracked the guitars, which was the first time we'd done anything other than a straight one-off. We added extra percussion and Paul McCartney was playing tambourine. John Lennon was clinking Coke bottles together. It was a great rocking backing track and all Tommy had to do was add the vocal. It was a combination of nerves and drink and Tommy couldn't take it. He strained his lungs out but he couldn't sing in tune. Tony Hatch was tearing out his hair and, although he must have had some finished tracks, it was never released."

December 1964 – Another Beatles Christmas Record Flexidisc (Fan Club, 12/64)
Sounding like Spike Jones and his City Slickers, the Beatles started their second Christmas flexidisc for their fan club members with a wacky instrumental version of 'Jingle Bells'. Clearly, the Beatles have been given a script to read and they add their own comments as they go along, which is often very funny. They conclude with a wacky version of the folk song, 'Can You Wash Your Father's Shirts'.

Another Beatles Christmas Show opened at the Odeon, Hammersmith. For *The Beatles' Christmas Show,* they had combined pantomime with package show but when no one wanted the sketches (or even heard them), why did they persist for a second year?

Michael Haslam was part of the show: "Brian spent a lot of money on the dancing fountains and, on the first night, they flooded the stalls. The show ran too long anyway, so they had to go. He put the Beatles in Eskimo outfits, or thought he did. That sequence worked with the taped backing of their voices and after the first night, there wasn't ever any Beatles in those jackets. I remember one night where they whistled their way through a song instead of singing it, but there was so much screaming that nobody could tell."

Freddie Garrity from Freddie and the Dreamers: "I opened the show at the top of a Christmas Tree, wearing a little tutu and going on as a fairy, swinging onto the stage. I was the comic really and when the Beatles did a sketch, you couldn't hear a thing. It was just noise, noise, noise. I didn't know John well but I sensed that he was the Beatles. He was sharp-witted and aggressive verbally."

The compère was Jimmy Savile: "It was the best and the easiest job in the world. I hardly uttered a word and the *NME* said, 'You could hardly say Jimmy Savile was overworked because all he does is rush on the stage.' I had to introduce the Beatles and the noise was cacophonous. It was the most heady, thrilling sound in the world and all I did was emulate the guitar playing action of the three Beatles and Ringo on the drums. I did that by their rostrums and I whipped the people up into a fever. I didn't miss a minute of their performances. People would say, 'You've seen the show before, why are you standing there?' and I would say, 'We're watching something that ain't gonna happen again, baby, and I'm not going to miss a second of this.'"

Jazz musician Mike Cotton: "We backed Elkie Brooks and all I recall is 3,000 little girls screaming their heads off for two shows a night. The Beatles clowned around the whole time and Paul grabbed my trumpet for a photograph that was used on the cover of *The Beatles Book*. I would point at it and say, 'Look at that trumpet. It's mine.' In contrast to all that, Eric Clapton, who was in the Yardbirds, was sitting in the pub and saying, 'I've got to get out of this band.'"

The Beatles' chauffeur, Alf Bicknell: "The greatest getaways were at the Hammersmith Odeon. It was off the stage, into the car, doors open – towels, Coke and ciggies all there – and then out and round to Hammersmith Broadway. We used to break all records going round there – I've ended up with all four boys on one side as we went round corners and there were plenty of profanities but it had to be that way. We were a mile down the road before the fans realised we had gone. It was always hairy, but I didn't mind."

David Stark, editor of *Songlink International* but then a young fan: "I remember 'Please Please Me' being No.1 and thinking, 'What is this amazing sound?' I was hooked forever. My parents took myself and my brother to *Another Beatles' Christmas Show* at Hammersmith Odeon on 4 January 1965. It says in my diary in huge letters, 'BEATLES!' It was a crazy show, you could hardly hear anything but there were sketches as well and all sorts of guest stars. It was my first pop show. My next big one was the Who at the Saville Theatre with Jimi Hendrix in support, which was promoted by Brian Epstein."

Chris Dreja of the Yardbirds: "The Beatles had heard of us and liked what we were doing and invited us onto the Christmas show. The Beatles played Yetis – remember *Dr Who and the Yetis*? – and they were running around with Yeti boots on. After every performance, two blokes used to come in from either side of the wings with 8 foot brooms to sweep up all the sweets that had been chucked on stage at the Beatles. Lennon came into our dressing room and he had a lump of coal that had been gift-wrapped, it was the size of my hand. It was dangerous even in those days. Remember those old English pennies? They used to throw those and it hurt if you got one on the end of your nose from 50 feet. Sid from the Rebel Rousers got one in his eye one night. John Lennon would pretend to play amidst this terrible row. I remember him announcing 'Baby's in Blackpool' and 'A Hard

Dave Clark' and all that. John Lennon knew that we were looking for material and he thought Chuck Jackson's 'The Breaking Point' would be very good for us. He was right but we never did it. It shows that there was a good feeling as we were all helping each other."

The Yardbirds made it a few months later with 'For Your Love'. Songwriter Graham Gouldman: "I was with Kevin Godley in the Mockingbirds. We had a deal with EMI and we recorded 'For Your Love' and 'That's How It's Gonna Stay'. EMI rejected 'For Your Love' and took 'That's How It's Gonna Stay'. Harvey Lisberg, our manager, said, "For Your Love' is too good to waste. I'm going to get it to the Beatles.' I told him that the Beatles were writing their own songs and wouldn't want this, but he told a publisher about the song and that guy loved it as well. He said that there was a rhythm and blues band looking for material and they needed something more commercial. He played it to them and they recorded it right away."

In December 1964 'I Feel Fine' and its B-side, 'She's a Woman' were included on the US album, *Beatles '65*. Record producer Joe Boyd: "When the *Beatles '65* album came out, I can remember a group of folk singers in Boston – Geoff Muldaur, Jim Kweskin, Eric Von Schmidt and a bunch of other people – sitting around and listening to that record. They'd take the needle off and put it back to the beginning of 'She's a Woman' again and again and again. We must have listened to that song fifteen times in a row. We couldn't believe what an incredible imagination had produced that melody and that way of tackling it vocally. It was a staggering song."

CHAPTER 5

Watch What You Do (1965)

*Death of Winston Churchill – Cigarette ads no longer allowed on TV
– President Lyndon Johnson sends marines to Vietnam – Brady and
Hindley arrested – Pizza Express opens – Miniskirts in fashion.*

When *Another Beatles Christmas Show* finished on 16 January 1965,
the Beatles kept, uncharacteristically, out of the public eye. It was
holidays and a honeymoon as Ringo Starr had married Maureen Cox,
a hairdresser from Liverpool.

In mid-February the Beatles assembled at Abbey Road mostly
recording the songs for their second film and next album, *Help!*

Beatles' chauffeur, Alf Bicknell: "John and Paul had written a song
for Ringo to perform on the *Help!* album, 'If You've Got Trouble'. He
recorded it but they didn't think it had worked out very well. John
and Ringo were sitting in John's dining room with Neil Aspinall and
myself. John was thinking of a song that Ringo could do instead. He
came up with a country song, 'Act Naturally'. Ringo had never sung
'Act Naturally' before but he tried it out with us singing and banging
on the table and decided to do it."

'Act Naturally' was written by Johnny Russell: "I was living in
Fresno, California and my record company asked me to come to LA.
I had to break a date and the girl asked me where I was going. I said,
'They're gonna put me in the movies. They're gonna make a big star
out of me', and it kinda clicked. I never rang the girl back but that was
the one thing I needed to put together a song about the movies, 'Act
Naturally'. It was a No.1 country record for Buck Owens in 1963 and,
luckily for me, Ringo was a big fan of Buck Owens. I wrote Ringo a
letter to say I appreciated him doing the song and that he was welcome
to cut anything else of mine, but he never did. I was very lucky because
they put 'Act Naturally' on the B-side of 'Yesterday', which was a No.1
record in America."

Although George Harrison gets some Bakersville twang on the Beatles' recording of 'Act Naturally', Ringo's vocal is lifeless when compared to Buck Owens'. Still, Buck Owens was flattered and when he came to Liverpool Empire in 1969, he said that he was here "for some pussy and to meet the Beatles." I hasten to add that he did not say this from the stage: I am merely repeating backstage gossip.

In late February, the Beatles flew to the Bahamas to start filming on the as-yet-untitled *Help!* and then moved to Austria and completed filming on Salisbury Plain and at the Twickenham studios. One provisional title was *Eight Arms to Hold You.*

Film critic Ramsey Campbell: "Richard Lester was just right for the Beatles. I don't think *Help!* is any great advance on *A Hard Day's Night* but, it does have a good script by Charles Wood. The Beatles were able to include their own humour in the film and it is like the best *Goon Show* ever made."

Viv Stanshall from the Bonzo Dog Band: "*Help!* was rubbish and it belittled them. It was making them sweet boys and they weren't sweet boys. They should have just been that original R&B band thrashing it out and doing their own stuff."

Actor Patrick Cargill: "Dick Lester was excellent because he had four inexperienced actors to cope with alongside several very experienced actors like Leo McKern, Roy Kinnear, Victor Spinetti and myself. He made himself a fifth Beatle so that he could get on their wavelength. He made it appear as though they had invented what to do, whereas he was still directing it. He got them totally at ease and it was a very clever thing to do."

Victor Spinetti: "We were in the Bahamas doing *Help!* and we came across what we thought was a deserted army hut. All the shutters were closed and there was a tin roof and John said, 'Come and have a look at this, Vic.' Some disabled kids and old people had been locked away in this stinking hut, so we wouldn't see them. That night at dinner, the Governor and the Minister of Finance were there and they were all frightfully grand. One of them said, 'Is that hair real?' and pulled it. We had this dinner with caviar with lots of knives and forks, and John said, 'What are these?', sending them up. The Governor's wife said, 'They don't even know what knives and forks are for.' John pointed to the caviar and said, 'We saw those sick kids and old people this morning. How do you equate that with this?' The Minister of Finance said, 'I am not paid for my work, I do it voluntarily.' John said,

'Ah, in that case, you're doing better than I thought you were doing.' The next day the headlines said 'Beatles Insult Governor' and we were almost run out of the island."

Almost without thinking, Paul McCartney handled the PR side of the Beatles. Norman Jopling from *Record Mirror*: "In 1965 when I had not had anything to do with them for a while, we ran a competition called *Meet the Beatles* and a couple of girls won. I had to drive them to where they were filming *Help!* and we went in my Mini-Cooper. I took them into the studio and the whole place was pandemonium. The Beatles were huge then and I wondered how I was going to do it. They were 30 yards off and when they finished the take, Paul recognised me and said, 'Norman, great to see you, man.' He took the girls and introduced them to the rest of the guys and then he gave me an interview which was on the front page the week after."

Victor Spinetti: "All the producer's relations wanted to come on the set for autographs and they were besieged. The producer came on the set with some guests when Ringo was tied to that machine and I had the laser. Ringo had his hands tied to the machine and his trousers round his ankles. He said, 'Hello, missus, give us a wank, will you?' The producer never brought anyone around again."

April 1965 – Ticket to Ride/ Yes It is (Parlophone R 5265, UK No.1, US No.1, Germany No.2)
The first new release of 1965 wasn't until April when the single 'Ticket to Ride' which was part of the new film, went to No.1. The single would have made No.1 on the first ten seconds alone – an absolutely classic guitar introduction, plus some tremendous drumming from Ringo Starr.

Dave Ballinger from the Barron Knights: "Technically brilliant drummers do not necessarily make good rock drummers. The part that Ringo plays on 'Ticket to Ride' is fantastic. I guess he thought of it, though it might have been Paul. You don't have to be a technical Buddy Rich-type drummer, you just need to be inventive. He did things that I would never have thought of doing."

Dave Mattacks, long-time drummer with Fairport Convention: "Ringo is one of the most important drummers of the 20th century. While he hasn't got any technique to speak of, he realises how important it is for a song to feel good. His feel is absolutely tremendous and he really swings. He got some great sounds on the Beatles' records, it wasn't all production and microphones, a lot of it was down to the way he tuned his kit. Yes, he was very lucky to get in the band and yes, he's a very rich man, but he has a tremendous basic ability. Obviously, there were people playing in a straightforward manner before him but he had a definite feel and he changed pop drumming around. He changed the sound from that of the high-pitched jazz drummers. I think he's tremendous."

Comic actor Rowan Atkinson: "He's a better drummer than me and I'm pretty bad. Oh dear, that sounds terrible, doesn't it? I think he's pretty good, he had a style which was simple and basic and it fitted the style and the time. He was a low profile drummer which was absolutely right for the Beatles. He was an extremely good accompanist whereas in the late 60s, drummers had started to become stars in their own right. He had a great empathy with what the Beatles were doing and he was very modest in his approach to drumming."

Buddy Rich: "Ringo Starr was adequate. No more than that."

Richard Thompson: "Ringo Starr was a lot more than adequate and he was the unsung hero of the Beatles. He was one of the best. He had learnt his trade in Germany and he was a straight four player, a four-four player and a very solid drummer. It must have been very hard for the Beatles to play with all those kids screaming, there weren't good monitors in those days and Ringo held those concerts together. They were following him, he wasn't following them."

Brian Bennett: "Ringo did the job absolutely correctly. If they had had a real whizz-kid on drums, it would have been too sophisticated and complicated and the songs wouldn't have come out as they did. They were great songs and he played them in the only way they could be played. What he did was absolutely right."

Walter Becker from Steely Dan: "At the time of *The Ed Sullivan Show*, I had switched my allegiance to jazz. I was rather snobby, studiously disinterested, when the Beatles first appeared. All the other kids were playing the Beatles' records and as I listened to them, I got interested. I could hear what good songwriters they were and how great their singing was. 'Ticket to Ride' was the first one that really got me. It has a fantastic start and everything about the record is very punchy and very great. The post-World War II period of complacence and conformity had finally exploded into something more intense and real."

Music writer Paul Du Noyer: "George Harrison came out of Liverpool, unlike the other guitar heroes of British rock who were nearly all Home Counties boys like Eric Clapton and Jimmy Page. They had been brought up on the blues but Liverpool was steeped in country music and so Chet Atkins was a bigger influence on George. You can hear that single note picking, rather than long, sustained blues notes, in his early work. It gave the Beatles a very different sound and once it was developed you get 'Ticket to Ride' and 'Day Tripper', which have very intricate guitar playing. George had taken what he had learnt and put it into a new dimension. The southern boys went for the blues and that developed into psychedelia and heavy rock."

The B-side, 'Yes It Is', has the theme and format of a folk song and is in the same vein as 'This Boy'. John Lennon is going through a girl's wardrobe and deciding what she should wear. There are some very pleasant three part harmonies, not to mention George's new guitar sound, effected with a foot-controlled pedal (now known as a wah-wah pedal): they recorded 'I Need You' on the same day with the same effect.

Harry Goodwin was the stills photographer for BBC-TV's *Top of the Pops*. One day, he found John Lennon uncooperative but Paul McCartney intervened. Paul reminded Lennon that the Musicians' Union would only allow a film to be repeated twice and so, if the record stayed on top and they weren't around, the still photographs could be interspersed with the dancers in the studio. "Okay," said Lennon, "where do you want me?" More than anything, Goodwin wanted them pointing, as the pictures could indicate their place in the chart rundown. McCartney took one of Harry's Polo mints, stuck it in his mouth and told him to take a picture. He said, "Harry, we can make some money from this." Harry didn't sell it to Polo, but claimed it could come in useful one day.

In May 1965 Bob Dylan came to the UK for his first British concert tour and was based at the Savoy Hotel in London. When he met the Beatles, he congratulated them on 'I Want to Hold Your Hand' as he thought they were singing "I get high" and hence, alluding to drugs. Could this be why one of the Beatles' next songs, 'It's Only Love' begins provocatively with the words, "I get high"?

Singer/ songwriter Dana Gillespie: "I was sixteen and I met Bob Dylan in London at a reception at the Savoy Hotel. I can't say it was love 'cause I was too young to know what love was but it was awe-inspiring to be hanging out with him. The Stones and the Beatles would come to the Savoy and would play each other their latest recordings and you could see them vying for the spot as the top British band. Everyone was in awe of Dylan and he was one of the few people that both the Stones and the Beatles held in great admiration. When he spoke, everyone sat and listened. John got legless one night and fell asleep on my bed while I was in it. He didn't even know I was there: he was so out of it."

Elizabeth Thomson, co-author of *The Dylan Companion*: "Dylan was very struck by their naïveté when he first met them and it is said that he introduced them to drugs. Lennon went through his Dylan period: 'You've Got to Hide Your Love Away', the acoustic material and the Huck Finn cap. The Beatles were at the Royal Albert Hall when Dylan went electric in 1966 and when he was heckled by the audience, they shouted their approval."

Bob Dylan biographer Michael Gray: "When I saw Lennon in that cap, I never really thought that he was copying Bob Dylan, but that could be right. Lennon and Dylan would have had to bury their egos to be friends as they had the same sharp-mindedness and temperament. They were incapable of friendship as they wouldn't have been able to tolerate the other's input. McCartney didn't share a world view with Dylan and they were never sympatico, and so friendship would be easier. It is interesting that Bob Dylan and Paul Simon did a joint tour a few years ago as they had spent their careers avoiding each other. They wanted the money but they still didn't comprehend each other. On the other hand, George Harrison was a most decent human being and Dylan responded to that. He liked his modesty and his single-minded musicianship."

Protest songwriter P.F. Sloan: "When 'Eve of Destruction' and 'Sins of the Family' were happening, I came to England and I was sitting with Paul McCartney in Scotch of St James. All of a sudden the door opened and light poured into the room and everybody stood there, frozen. The door closed and Paul said, 'That was John.' It was like the opening of *Close Encounters of the Third Kind*. Paul said to me, 'Is there anything to this 'Eve of Destruction' thing? Should we be moving our investments to a different place?'"

The Beatles were influenced by Bob Dylan's poetic imagery and he in turn learnt from them. I doubt if *Sgt Pepper* would have happened without Bob Dylan, nor *Blonde on Blonde* without the Beatles.

Commenting in *Down Beat*, the US jazz critic and songwriter ('Yesterday I Heard the Rain'), Gene Lees remarked; "Paul McCartney is a musical ignoramus, although he has a certain amount of melodic flair. He is not interested in fitting long vowels to long notes, short vowels to short notes, and why should he be? The performances by rock groups are so distorted that fine points of craft are inaudible. Bob Dylan has the worst ear for song of anybody I have ever heard. It may be justified by calling it 'the broken-glass poetry of Bob Dylan', but that's nonsense. Bob Dylan doesn't know a thing about craft."

Cynthia Lennon: "From 1965 everybody was smoking pot and taking drugs. I felt that John was really changing and becoming someone I didn't know. He became a John that I knew a part of, but I didn't know what I was looking at when I saw him being interviewed or heard his music. He became more aggressive, but he had always been argumentative, always ready with the quick, sharp reply."

Barry Miles: "The Beatles were protected because, as Lennon pointed out, it was a conspiracy amongst the broadcasters and journalists because everyone was having a really good time with them. There were girls and drugs and money and why break up a good thing? The Stones, on the other hand, were being purposefully bad. You couldn't pretend they were nice guys because their image was the exact opposite."

Poet and lyricist Pete Brown: "When I was with Allen Ginsberg at the Roundhouse, he said that the Beatles were going to change the world. I said, 'No, they're not that good.' I was into modern jazz and entrenched in be-bop. Of course he was completely right, he felt the tremors and so he was prophetic. He did say that after he had been to Liverpool that Liverpool was incredible: it was like a magic city. There was nothing like it anywhere else and there never will be. Although some people compared it to San Francisco, Liverpool was much nicer as it was to do with people getting in touch with each other and breaking down barriers of class and culture."

Nowadays there is nothing unusual in a young person receiving an award from the Queen. Back in June 1965, many were surprised when the Beatles were awarded MBEs in the Queen's birthday honours. To counter criticism, the award was given for their contribution to British exports. In other words, they were receiving recognition as young businessmen rather than as musicians *per se*. The Prime Minister, Harold Wilson, who was a Merseyside MP, would view this as an astute move in capturing young voters. I did apply to see the papers on these honours under the Freedom of Information Act but was told that nothing was available

Music writer Paul Trynka: "Harold Wilson saw himself as a modern statesman, a technologically forward guy, the new kid on the block and there are exact parallels with Tony Blair. People like the Beatles were part of modern British culture and before that no one would have taken them seriously. It was pop music and it was going to disappear in a year or so. John was as ambitious as any of them. He liked to deride the establishment but he still wanted to be part of it. It is a fairly standard British trait: you want to be part of the establishment but you also want to be separate enough to mock it."

Tony Barrow: "I learnt about the MBEs shortly beforehand from Brian Epstein, who wanted to discuss the PR aspects of it. John Lennon was the least impressed of the four. To him, this was on a par with the Fry's Shooting Star award or whatever. It was just a piece of metal to be picked up, a pop world trophy. Brian was over the moon about the MBEs, but he was disappointed that he didn't get one himself. His contribution to the national economy should have made him first in line."

Clive Epstein: "Brian had made such an enormous contribution to Britain's exports that I think he deserved one. I was surprised that he wasn't awarded one as well but, on the other hand, I can see the justification for just giving them to the Beatles. After all, they were the artists."

At least five holders returned their awards to Buckingham Palace in disgust. In July, when John and Paul received three new Ivor Novello Awards for songwriting, Paul cracked, "Thanks. I hope nobody sends theirs back now."

The Beatles appeared on a traditional variety show, ABC-TV's *Blackpool Night Out*. Lionel Blair: "I worked with Mike and Bernie Winters and the Beatles had taken off. When they were guests on *Blackpool Night Out*, they asked if I would do a dance routine to the new record, which was 'Help!' I did the kick routine to 'Help!' and Brian Epstein liked it so much that he did the Kick tour with the Everly Brothers, Cilla Black and Billy J. Kramer and Lionel Blair and his Dancers. I did a little bit in the film too and it was wonderful being part of that whole thing. Really, the Beatles didn't want to know about dancing. They thought that there was a gay connotation to it. The Kick started my career again. I could not be a tap dancer all my life."

July 1965 – Help!/ I'm Down (Parlophone R 5305, UK No.1, US No.1, Germany No.2)

When the Beatles recorded 'Help!' itself, they had, at last, both a film title and a good song. Actor Patrick Cargill: "I remember them coming in one day and saying that they had written a tune the previous night. They played us 'Help!' and I thought it was terrific. I said, 'That'll go straight to the top of the charts', and of course it did."

John Lennon's 'Help!' was both a tour de force and a *cri de coeur*. By now the Beatles' melodies were becoming more intricate and their lyrics were expanding beyond the me-you-him relationships of 1963.

Victor Spinetti: "They were all down to earth. We were driving to the premiere of *Help!* and when we got to the Pavilion Cinema in London, the kids were screaming and John said, 'Push Paul out first, he's the prettiest.'"

August 1965 – Help! LP (Parlophone PMC 1255)
Produced by George Martin, 14 tracks – 34 minutes 20 seconds
Side 1: Help!/ The Night Before/ You've Got to Hide Your Love Away/ I Need You/ Another Girl/ You're Going to Lose That Girl/ Ticket to Ride
Side 2: Act Naturally/ It's Only Love/ You Like Me Too Much/ Tell Me What You See/ I've Just Seen a Face/ Yesterday/ Dizzy Miss Lizzy

The *Help!* album was released in August 1965. The film score included the two No.1s as well as 'You've Got to Hide Your Love Away' and 'You're Going to Lose That Girl' Apart from Larry Williams' 'Dizzy Miss Lizzy' and Johnny Russell's 'Act Naturally', *Help!* was another album of original material, including two compositions from George Harrison, 'I Need You' and 'You Like Me Too Much'.

Tony Barrow: "To an extent, the Beatles were a performing machine for the songwriting team of Lennon and McCartney. A third party would have to turn out something special to get in there. I do believe that if George had been in a different band altogether, he would have had more songs published and recorded. He might have become a greater songwriter as he would be willing himself to do better. It was discouraging rather than encouraging to be the third songwriter in the Beatles. It was never a matter of whose song was going to go on the A-side, John, Paul or George's. It was a matter of who was having the A-side and who was having the B-side between John and Paul, and that was it. George was mainly tucked away on albums and given token tracks, in the same way that Ringo was given token vocals."

The cover picture had the Beatles doing semaphore although they were spelling N-U-J-V rather than H-E-L-P, which could stand for

'Never underestimate John's vision.' The incidental music for the film was written by Ken Thorne and was not included. Indeed, there were no album notes and nothing to relate the album to the film at all.

Roger Cook who was part of the songwriting team Greenaway and Cook and also sang with Roger Greenaway in David and Jonathan: "I don't think that there is a musician in England who didn't learn something from the Beatles records. How do you do 'reverse echo'? We learnt a lot of tricks from the Beatles, especially as we had their engineer, Geoff Emerick, but you can't say enough about the Beatles. They led the way. Would we have had our first hit in America as David and Jonathan if the Beatles had not already established English artists as being stars? They should have all been Lords for what they did for British music."

Gene Pitney: "I wasn't that impressed when I first heard the Beatles. Andy Wickham, an English guy who worked on the West Coast, played me their first album and I wasn't knocked out because it was largely covers of rock'n'roll things and I knew the originals. I wasn't impressed until sometime later when they started making tempo and key changes. I'd found out the hard way as a songwriter that the whole Top 20 could be played with four chords and if you played a publisher something that went up by more than four notes, he'd say, 'That's all very well but who's going to sing it?' You don't eat if you write those kind of songs, but the Beatles were a big enough entity to get away with it. They could try things out and so they changed the whole way that music was. They advanced it as an art form, and only someone as big as they were could have done it."

Among the Lennon-McCartney songs not included in the film were 'It's Only Love', 'I've Just Seen a Face' and the most covered song of all time, 'Yesterday'. Okay, some maintain it is 'White Christmas', so let's put it this way – 'Yesterday' is the most-covered song of all-time, but 'White Christmas' holds sway for two weeks in December. Paul McCartney displayed his versatility by recording 'Yesterday' and the uninhibited rocker, 'I'm Down', on the same day. In a similar way, they followed 'Yesterday' with a wild rocker, 'Dizzy Miss Lizzy', their customary way for closing an album. The effect is comical and in a sense, 'Dizzy Miss Lizzy' was their nod back to yesterday.

Jason Ringenberg of Jason and the Scorchers: "Even now, I can't really begin to fathom how good the Beatles were. There will never be another Lennon and McCartney ever: they are one of a kind. I loved their country-based stuff best, like 'I've Just Seen a Face', which sounds totally bluegrass. You could also do a country version of 'You've Got to Hide Your Love Away'."

Victor Spinetti: "John invited me up to the recording studio, but I didn't want to bother them. John used to say, 'Only fucking bores turn up.' I did go and they were doing 'You've Got to Hide Your Love Away' and Bacon Buttie Mal would come in and he would pass them around."

Can 'You've Got to Hide Your Love Away' be read as a song about Brian Epstein's sexuality? Music writer Jon Savage: "It's very easy to read it like that. The Searchers' 'He's Got No Love' is equally applicable to Brian and we used it in the *Arena* documentary. Everybody should be able to do what they want and if they don't want to talk about it, then that's their prerogative as well. Later, it came out who was gay and who was bisexual in the period. For me, it just confirmed why I liked those records in the first place."

'It's Only Love' is sometimes cited as the worst Lennon and McCartney song. John himself dismissed it by saying, "Everything rhymed, disgusting lyrics". You can sense that the Beatles are not too happy with it. Listen to the way John sings, "nighttime bright": he is trying to compensate for a bad line.

Ian Hunter from Mott the Hoople: "Paul gets slagged off a lot but if rock'n'roll hadn't been invented, Paul would have been huge anyway. He is the complete song and dance man. He is 'The Long and Winding Road' and 'Maybe I'm Amazed', while John is 'How Do You Sleep'. 'Yesterday' is an amazing song. He is a nice happy guy but with Lennon up his backside, it was a different kettle of fish."

Chris Farlowe: "I was having a drink one night in Scotch of St James with Paul and Julie Felix. He said that he had written a song that week and he thought I could make a great job of it. 'Yesterday' sounded like a good title. He told me to ring him the next day but I got drunk, went home and forgot about it. In the end, I did a really nice version on *The Art Of Chris Farlowe* with Nicky Hopkins on piano."

Billy J. Kramer: "I remember going to the ABC in Blackpool and asking Paul for a song. He played me 'Yesterday' before anyone had heard it and I said, 'Paul, all my singles have been nicey-nicey. I want a real head-banger.' Six months later everyone was having hits with it." Not to worry as he had Top 10 hits with 'Do You Want to Know a Secret?', 'Bad to Me', 'I'll Keep You Satisfied' and 'From a Window', which Billy regards as the best of the Lennon and McCartney songs he was given.

Willie Nelson: "They wrote great songs. 'Yesterday' is my favourite, one of my favourite all-time songs and not just a favourite Beatle song. It is a great piece of literature."

But can it be a great song when you don't find out what happened yesterday?

Willie Nelson: "That's what makes it a great song. In a way, the song is telling you everything. He tells you that his troubles are here to stay. Period. End of story."

Tim Rice: "'Yesterday' is a great song and it is not just because it is a great tune, it is a staggering lyric. The concept of 'How I long for yesterday 'is a brilliant line.' It is so simple and yet it has such brilliant words. The reason why all those Beatle classics are classics are because of the lyrics. 'Do You Want to Know a Secret' is a simple, direct lyric that people can relate to. 'She Loves You' is not a song that people can identify with because it is one step away: it is a bloke singing about somebody else's situation, so that song is not covered as much as 'Yesterday' or 'Here There and Everywhere'. I'm generalising as there are many songs that were only meant to work for them, but it is the lyrics time and time again that determine whether a song is a song for everybody or a song just for the band who did it."

McCartney biographer, Chris Salewicz: "It's said that the line in 'Yesterday': 'I did something wrong, now I long for yesterday', refers to Paul's response to the death of his mother. 'What are we going to do without her money?' was not a revelation with regards to his character, but the kind of remark you come out with at a time like that and kick yourself for later. It's an embarrassed remark, wanting to say something and then saying the wrong thing. It's rather like his remark when John died: 'It's a drag, isn't it?' which was a classic understatement. That word 'drag' should have been lengthened by a thousand years. To me, it was apparent what he was saying."

Blues musician Edgar Winter: "I loved 'Yesterday'. That song is so evocative and the fact that it is not specific is part of its greatness. A great song has to have a universal message and that means that you can bring something to the song, that you can interpret it according to some experiences you've had. If a songwriter can leave something open-ended that is really great."

The keyboard player from Yes, Rick Wakeman: "I've looked at a lot of the Beatles' songs and tried to be analytical and see if there is a pattern as to why they work. There are great wide sweeps of melody. There are never more than two or three ideas in any song, whereas Yes used to throw in hundreds of ideas. Just occasionally you come across someone who can write classics, songs that can be sung by anyone from nine to ninety. Much as I enjoyed all the stuff I did with Yes, there isn't a Yes song that could be sung by that age range. That talent is rare. To write something like 'Yesterday' is something very special."

Sonny Curtis from the Crickets: "Elvis's first records are great but he failed to grow like the Beatles. The Beatles started with 'Love Me Do' and 'Please Please Me', which were very good records, but then every record they came out with was a little bit different and they kept adding new twists. Man, I remember hearing 'Yesterday' and thinking, 'What a great song and what a great idea to do it with a string quartet'. When I heard that, I had to turn the radio off as anything that followed couldn't possibly please me after that. The Beatles wanted to grow while Elvis gave up after a while."

Beatles biographer Steve Turner: "What hit me at the time was the use of the string quartet on 'Yesterday', and that really made the record. It was good to have some older person there in George Martin rather than some zapped-out kid in his twenties. His maturity really helped. I wonder if George would have had sympathy for the Stones' kind of music because there's far more Englishness to the Beatles' music than the Stones. He had a background in classical music and that fed into songs like 'Eleanor Rigby' and 'Yesterday'."

Marianne Faithfull: "Paul McCartney was a great friend of mine and still is. I was at a lot of their sessions and I wanted to record 'Yesterday' with a big choir. Paul was very helpful and supportive. He was in the studio which made me very happy and relaxed, not nervous. He wanted to know what the arranger Mike Leander was doing with his song. I know Paul really liked my version but maybe it was too grandiose. Matt Monro had the hit, but I did it on that TV special *The Music of Lennon and McCartney,* which was a great honour. I was 8 months pregnant at the time and so there is no shot further down than my shoulder." It has been suggested that McCartney also gave Marianne an unrecorded song, 'Etcetera', but she turned it down. "I remember that he did give me a song and I didn't really like it. I don't think it was called 'Etcetera' though."

It's intriguing that so many of the pre-Beatle chart names recorded

120

Lennon and McCartney songs. Not only the rock'n'rollers but also Frank Sinatra and Ella Fitzgerald. Jazz guitarist Barney Kessel: "Who knows what their motives were? It might be that they liked the songs, it might be that their producers insisted that they did them to sell records, it might be that they felt intimidated and said, 'I want to reach younger people so I'm going to do something they will identify with.' If they did those songs for any other reason than that they loved them, then they were not being true to themselves."

In August 1965, the Beatles performed at Shea Stadium, the home of the New York Mets. It set a world record for attendance at a pop concert – 56,000 – although that is paltry by today's standards. Promoter Sid Bernstein: "I called Brian in January 1965. I said, 'Brian, forget Madison Square. Let's go for Shea Stadium. We will sell it out and if we don't, I will pay you for every empty seat.' The supporting acts are a blank to me as everybody was screaming 'Beatles! Beatles!' no matter who was on stage. There was no mention of time in the contract and I didn't realise until later that the Beatles only did 28 minutes. You couldn't hear the music but you could hear the roar of the crowds in the Bronx - Shea Stadium is in Queens. I got the best sound I could, a genius in sound worked upon it, but nobody expected that kind of reaction."

So did Sid Bernstein make a huge profit from the concert? "There were 1,000 press and 55,000 pays, and it was so new that I underestimated my profit. On a gate of $304,000, I made a profit of $6,500. Brian was very upset when he heard that and he wanted to give me a gift. I said, 'Brian, your gift was in giving me the boys.' Years later, John sat with me at a concert I produced for Jimmy Cliff and he said, 'Sid I saw the top of the mountain with Shea.'"

Sid Bernstein didn't make much profit, but there were subsidiary benefits. "I had signed the Young Rascals for management that week and I sat them in the third base dugout at Shea. Long hair was still a novelty and the people in the bleachers thought that the Rascals were the Beatles. We had 2,000 buttons printed saying, 'I am a Rascals fan', and on the scoreboard I had put, 'For the safety of your neighbourhood and yourself, please do not leave your seat. If you do, we will call the concert off.' The director of Shea said, 'You don't have to show that all the time. You can run a commercial.' So I alternated the safety message with 'The Rascals are coming'. My phones were very busy the next day. Record companies who hadn't seen them wanted to sign them.

It was my dream to have a Beatles of the United States but of course there will never be a Beatles of the United States."

Peter Noone, Herman from Herman's Hermits: "What I learnt from the two markets has made me really good at what I do now. There weren't stadiums for pop concerts in England then and so we played Sheffield City Hall and the Liverpool Empire, wonderful places, and I still think they're the best places to play. In America everything was five times bigger and so the buildings and the audiences were five times bigger. I can never remember thinking at the time, 'How do we communicate to all those people?' We just got on with it. We were like a central league team playing in the major league: we would show up and sometimes we would win and sometimes we would lose. Mostly we won and people thought we were brilliant."

Bruce Dickinson of Iron Maiden: "The Beatles played baseball stadiums with Vox AC somethings and 4 by 10 columns, which you would find in small discos or youth clubs now. They were using them as a PA for 50,000 people who were screaming as loud as they could. No one could hear them at all. You would feel justifiably ripped off these days if you turned up to hear a band and you couldn't hear them because the blokes next to you are talking."

On 27 August 1965 the Beatles spent an evening with Elvis Presley. The Beatles were going for world domination but Elvis was making no attempt to reclaim his throne, making movies that were unworthy of his talent.

Tony Barrow: "The long-awaited summit meeting of Elvis Presley and the Beatles was a disappointment. It happened towards the end of the Beatles' 1965 concert tour when they were staying in a rented house high above Los Angeles in Benedict Canyon. The invitation to meet the Beatles came through a trade paper journalist and there was some debate as to whether Elvis should come to them or they should go to Elvis. Eventually, we all drove to Presley's house at Bel-Air and the Beatles were uncharacteristically silent. They didn't know what to expect. Elvis was on the doorstep to greet his guests, and his heavies and henchmen were discretely hidden. The Beatles were led into a very large living room, which was bathed in red and blue, and Elvis handed out guitars and started playing the juke-box. They were playing along to Presley's own records and I remember Paul nipping to and fro between a piano and a guitar. Ringo wasn't involved as he was playing pool with some of Presley's heavies. There was a colour television set, which was a novelty to us, and it was left on the entire time with the sound muted. Occasionally, Elvis would change the channel for no apparent reason. He wasn't watching the telly; it was as though he wanted a new design on the screen. Nobody said anything memorable and there were a few silences. The conversation was stilted and anxious, never properly intimate, even when they were talking about tour disasters and how difficult it was to get in and out of venues. Maybe the whole thing was too engineered for comfort because there in the background hovering were Messrs. Parker and Epstein, and maybe too the postponements had robbed the evening of its magic. There was something missing - to be honest, I'd describe Elvis on that showing as a boring old fart - but I do know that Ringo enjoyed his game of pool."

The Beatles' chauffeur, Alf Bicknell: "It was exciting to arrive and find Elvis on the doorstep shaking your hand and calling you 'Sir'. He said to me, 'You are welcome to my home, sir.' He had an immense hall with a beautiful, brick fireplace, but it wasn't over-the-top luxury. It impressed me to see the number of people that Elvis had working for him. There must have been 10 people there. They took us round Los Angeles over the next few days. We'd go to nightclubs that were closing down for the night and they'd ask the singers to do another set. They were so confident that they were like stars themselves."

Clive Epstein: "There was always a mystique about Elvis but Brian created an image for the Beatles as lads next door, and this is where he succeeded. People could identify with the Beatles because they were on the same wavelength. It wasn't like that with Elvis, Colonel Parker wanted him to be worshipped."

It had been with some reluctance that Elvis Presley met the Beatles at his home in Bel Air in 1965. They failed to win him round as he later denounced them for their subversive views and, somewhat hypocritically, drug-taking. He gave them a name check in his version of 'Never Been to Spain' (1972) and he sang 'Yesterday', 'Hey Jude' and 'Get Back' (in a medley with 'Little Sister') on his return to splendour in Las Vegas.

September 1965 – You've Got to Hide Your Love Away – The Silkie (Fontana TF 603, UK No.28, US No.10)
John Lennon and Paul McCartney, producers
Brian Epstein signed the folk group the Silkie and the Beatles contributed to their cover of 'You've Got to Hide Your Love Away'. Mike Ramsden

from the Silkie: "We had heard 'You've Got To Hide Your Love Away' on their album and we asked if we could do it. They said yes and they wanted to come to the session. John, Paul and George came along. It was a unique situation as it was Paul's arrangement of John's song. We were the first band that they had recorded and Paul played that wah-wah guitar at the beginning. George drummed on the back of his guitar and John was in the booth with the engineer. We had six hours with three Beatles and Jane Asher, who was opening the beers. Afterwards, John rang Brian Epstein and said that it was a No.1. We didn't make the top but we did get a lot of airplays. There is a film of John in a taxi with Bob Dylan and Bob asks what the Silkie are like and John replies, 'Very silky.'"

The Beatles were recording in October 1965 and contributed to a Granada TV special in November, *The Music of Lennon and McCartney*.

P.J. Proby: "I asked John Lennon to write something for me like they had done for Peter and Gordon. We were very tight friends and he gave me 'That Means A Lot'. I said, 'Thanks a million. Now I'd like to ask you something else. Can you get George Martin to arrange and produce it?' He said, 'You never stop, do you?', but he fixed it. I had everything that the Beatles had going for them at that session. I could not have asked for more." The lyric includes the odd line, "Life can be suicide". "Well, that's John's humour. It's a funny line. What was humour to him might not have been funny to the next guy. I understood it and John understood it and that's all we cared about. That's why we got along. We couldn't give a doodly squat about what anybody else thought about it."

On 16 November 1965 Paul went to the Adelphi Cinema, Slough and ended up compèring the show which starred Gene Pitney and Peter and Gordon. Gene Pitney: "I was touring the UK and somebody from the BBC was acting as compère. Over the tannoy, I heard somebody introduce the second half and I thought, 'That's a new voice. I wonder who it is.' I went down this rickety staircase and there was Paul. Not having his own guitar with him, he had turned one upside down so he could play it and he was teaching someone the chords to 'Yesterday'."

The Beatles went on their final UK tour in December 1965. Gary Walker of the Walker Brothers: "We went to see the Beatles at the Finsbury Park Empire, it was towards the end of their live shows in England. Helen Shapiro had come to the show. John said to me, 'Can you come with me to the toilet?' and so I went to the toilet with John

Lennon. We only went in there to hide because she was lurking around the theatre and he didn't want to see her. We talked about music and then George Harrison came in and said the coast was clear. It's bizarre isn't it – I went to the toilet with John Lennon and I don't really know why." (Certainly is: I could ask Helen, I suppose, but in this instance, I prefer the mystery.)

December 1965 – We Can Work It Out/ Day Tripper (Parlophone R 5389, UK No.1, US No.1, Germany No.2) (Both sides listed on UK chart: B-side also made No.5 in US.)
The Beatles released some superlative double-sided singles and they excelled themselves with their Christmas 1965 single, 'We Can Work It Out'/ 'Day Tripper'. It was the first of four occasions on which both sides of a Beatles' single would be listed on the chart.

Although *Help!* had done well, it did give the Beatles a lightweight image compared to what the Stones, the Kinks and the Who were doing at the time. 'Day Tripper' is McCartney's answer to that as his bass playing is so tremendous and it drives the song along. You can tell that the Beatles were having great fun recording this track.

'We Can Work It Out'/ 'Day Tripper' was the last time that a Beatles single would sell more than a million copies in the UK alone. Their top five best-selling UK singles are 'She Loves You', 'I Want to Hold Your Hand' (both over 1.5 million), 'Can't Buy Me Love', 'I Feel Fine' and 'We Can Work It Out'. None were available on albums at time of release. In 1977, Paul McCartney topped them all with over two million UK sales for 'Mull of Kintyre'.

Willy Russell: "I particularly like 'We Can Work It Out' because it combines absolute Lennon with absolute McCartney. McCartney wrote the verses and Lennon added the minor sequence which gives the song its toughness. Paul McCartney's melodic gift with John Lennon's rough edge was an unbeatable combination."

Chris Farlowe: "I got on well with both John and Paul. John would sometimes ring me up and invite me for a drink at the Cromwellian or Scotch of St James. I think they liked me because I was down to earth and said what I thought. The greatest song that they wrote was' We Can Work It Out', which I did on a live album at the Marquee. We had some great black girl singers on it. Paul McCartney said that it was the best version he had ever heard of 'We Can Work It Out', which is a great compliment."

John Jorgenson: "I loved the sound of George Harrison's guitar, especially the sounds at the beginning of 'Day Tripper'. I would take the needle and keep putting it back to the beginning to hear the guitar before anything else came in. I didn't know at the time that they were using double-tracking, so when a guitar is double-tracked it sounds even better. I couldn't work out why I couldn't make my guitar sound like that."

Still, the biggest selling UK single that year came not from the Beatles, but from another Liverpudlian, the comedian Ken Dodd. Then based in America, Paul Gambaccini comments, "With all respect to Ken Dodd, how could 'Tears' have been the No.1 single of 1965? This was the peak of the Beatles, the peak of the Stones, the peak of Motown, the peak of Dylan, and yet now I understand it because I've seen how popular he is."

December 1965 – Rubber Soul LP (Parlophone PMC 1267)
Produced by George Martin, 14 tracks – 34 minutes 50 seconds
Side 1: Drive My Car/ Norwegian Wood (This Bird Has Flown)/ You Won't See Me/ Nowhere Man/ Think for Yourself/ The Word/ Michelle
Side 2: What Goes On/ Girl/ I'm Looking Through You/ In My Life/ Wait/ If I Needed Someone/ Run for Your Life
A review of the Rolling Stones had accused them of playing 'plastic soul'. This phrase amused the Beatles who called their new album *Rubber Soul*, a neat, punning title. It was released the same day as 'We Can Work It Out' and marked another leap forward for the band, taking them into more sophisticated territory. The cover typography heralded psychedelia. The album's mellow tone may be the consequence of marijuana, while *Revolver*, the following year, reflects acid. We know for certain that John and George's first acid trip was when they visited a friendly dentist on 27 March 1965.

Rubber Soul contained some stunning melodies including 'Michelle' and the poignant 'In My Life'. Their humour showed in the 'tit-tit-tit' refrain of 'Girl and the 'beep beep' of 'Drive My Car', although that was lifted from Bo Diddley's 'Road Runner'. How many pop songs before "Think for Yourself" included the word, 'opaque'? I can't think of any. Starting with the sitar in 'Norwegian Wood', Indian influences were coming into their work, instigated by George Harrison.

Rock writer and film-maker, Dominic Priore: "The Beatles dropped acid with the Byrds in 1965 which was a pretty early time to be doing such a thing. They took in influences from the LA scene. The interest in the sitar came from World Pacific Records: Dick Bach who ran the label was into meditation and it was part of the whole folk movement. The Beatles had heard Indian music in restaurants but they took it into their music after they had dropped acid with the Byrds."

Roger McGuinn, lead singer of the Byrds: "We introduced some John Coltrane on the instrumental break for 'Eight Miles High' and - you won't believe this but it's true – we turned the Beatles onto Indian music. We were in a house in Beverly Hills. They had invited us up and we were passing guitars back and forth. We showed them some Ravi Shankar licks and they wondered what it was. We said it was Indian music and they really got into it after that. We turned them onto it!"

Andy Babiuk, author of *Beatles Gear*: "The hardest thing about the sitar is the tuning. Once you tune the instrument the actual technique of playing it is quite easy. Like the mountain dulcimer that Brian Jones used on 'Lady Jane', it is a pre-tuned scale so it is easier to play. There are a lot of 'Norwegian Wood' outtakes and you can hear that the sitar has been overdubbed a couple of times. That was to make the sound thicker on the recording. It makes George sound phenomenal but there is nothing sensational about stopping a tape and punching it in again and the Beatles did that quite a bit. They were the first to introduce an Indian instrument into pop music but it is primitive playing. It fitted the need of the song and what they wanted to do."

Alan Price: "I was in John Lennon's house and he played me the demo of 'Norwegian Wood'. He said that the rest of them were taking the mickey out of him 'cause he was copying Bob Dylan. When I heard the demo, I could understand why they said that."

John Stewart: "We recorded 'Norwegian Wood' in the Kingston Trio 'cause we loved it. That was the only reason we ever did a song. We didn't care that the Beatles had done it and we didn't care that we weren't breaking new ground. Nick and I loved the song and we loved to sing it."

Buddy Rich: "I only pick things that have an appeal to me and I think to an audience. I liked 'Norwegian Wood', 'Something', 'Yesterday' and many of the things that the Beatles recorded. I was a fan of theirs. Jazz is improvisational and though the melody of 'Norwegian Wood' is always there, the soloists will skip around the melody because that's what improvisation is. I didn't get any feedback from them and I wouldn't expect it. Because of royalties, it's to their advantage when I record their music and so I imagine they were very happy about it."

McCartney biographer, Peter Carlin: "There are a lot of songs in that era where Paul is discovering the extent of his authority. Even 'I'm Looking Through You' – 'You were above me, but not today.' That is about Jane Asher who was on a higher social and intellectual plane but now he feels he has transcended that. Paul is a very obstinate guy and he does not comprehend when he is headed in the wrong direction. He doesn't take advice and criticism well."

John Stewart: "I love 'I'm Looking Through You'. It's a great record, great melody and great production. It's just a magical record with that one guitar and the hand percussion on it. *Rubber Soul* is an album that changed my way of thinking about music."

Davey Graham: "I was in the middle of drug addiction and I was having an identity crisis. I was beginning to wonder who I was and when I sang 'I'm Looking Through You', I didn't know if I was talking to myself, or about myself to someone else. There was a personality disorder that I had to overcome."

Steve Earle: "I love 'I'm Looking Through You', but I love the whole of *Rubber Soul*. That is a song I have recorded. Some of their chords are really good. Did they get hold of a Mel Bay chord book and decide to learn every chord in it? There are songs that have every inversion of a key in one song, so it's pretty amazing."

Judy Collins: "I called my album of Beatle songs, *In My Life*. The songs you choose to sing can be as personal as the songs you write and I loved 'In My Life' best of the Beatles' songs and I felt it was suited for me. I had been trained as a classical pianist and as an interpreter and I felt it was a magical thing that I had inherited. It was probably generic."

The original lyric for 'In My Life' contains references to specific places in Liverpool such as the tramsheds: effectively, what John saw on a bus ride to town. Beatles biographer Steve Turner: "From what John said, he thought 'In My Life' was a 'what I did on my holidays' song, so he chopped it down, removing the specific Liverpool references. There is a poem by Charles Lamb which is similar to 'In My Life'. It is included in *Palgrave's Golden Treasury*, which is the sort of book that Mimi would have had on her shelf. The poem from the 18th century is called 'The Old Familiar Faces':

I have had playmates, I have had companions,

In my days of childhood, in my joyful school days -
All, all are gone, the old familiar faces.

Then six verses later it ends:
How some they have died, and some they have left me,
And some are taken from me; all are departed,
All, all are gone, the old, familiar faces."

Richard Thompson: "I love 'In My Life', that is a tremendous song with a very thoughtful lyric. A great tune too, and there are another thirty or forty that I love. At the time I was a bit of a snob, an R&B fan. I dismissed the Rolling Stones as cheap imitations and I was buying imports of real R&B. I thought the Beatles were a bit too poppy for their own good. In retrospect, they get better and better. *Revolver* is probably the best album that anyone has made in popular music."

Bobby Vee's record producer Snuff Garrett: "There was a club in London that burned down after I was there, Scotch of St James. Brian Epstein got me membership and I was having dinner there one night and someone slapped me on the back and said, 'Hello', and it was Paul McCartney. He had been on holiday in Paris and he sang in my ear a song he had just written, and that was when I realised that they wrote individually. He sang 'Michelle' in my ear and I came home and named my new daughter Michelle."

Dr. John: "I didn't like their early records at first, but around the time of 'Michelle', I realised that they were doing some hip stuff. That often happens - sometimes you don't recognise the quality of something when it first hits. They got better too and they influenced a whole generation. They also wiped out the big bands in New Orleans! The club owners just wanted three or four guys."

Chet Atkins: "Their melodies are so wonderful. They wrote some of the greatest music of the century, if not the greatest. I admire them so much and their melodies are even greater than their lyrics. It's quite different in country music. Country writers can come up with clever lyrics but then they throw the melodies on: they don't work hard enough or put their heart into it. That's not true of the Beatles. They were geniuses at writing great melodies whether it be 'Lady Madonna' or 'Michelle'."

Arranger Harry Robinson, the Lord Rockingham of Lord Rockingham's XI: "The strength of Paul McCartney's writing, as opposed to John Lennon's, is that he was a bass guitarist and if you have a very strong left-hand bass line, you have the basis for a good melody.

So Paul was writing from his strength. The longer you are in music, the more you forget and there are simple things you pass over because they are simple. A young songwriter is discovering, say, harmonies that would make a good sound, and they use that as the main part of their piece and a new idea blossoms from it. I'm sure that's how 'Michelle' started 'cause it's got a nice chord shift at the beginning and Paul gives it a very good, very strong harmonic structure emanating from the bass."

The songwriters Roger Greenaway and Roger Cook had a new career as David and Jonathan. Roger Greenaway: "George Martin asked us to do 'Michelle' as the Beatles weren't releasing it as a single. He did the whole orchestral arrangement and worked out our harmonies. Roger Cook has a range of three octaves, he can sing high or low, and I had a high voice. I was perfect for harmonies above him and he was perfect for harmonies below me. We got to No.7 with 'Michelle', while the Overlanders made No.1, but we went on and they didn't."

Roger Cook: "The Overlanders got to No.1 but we had the hit in the States and we got to tour there. When we would turn up at a radio station, there would be hundreds of girls there and the rumour was that we were John and Paul incognito, so girls were screaming at us."

The Byrds' influence on the Beatles is evident on George Harrison's song, 'If I Needed Someone'. The Hollies recorded it for a single: it scraped into the Top 20 but deserved to go higher. Allan Clarke: "The only Beatles number that the Hollies ever did was 'If I Needed Someone'. It was written by George Harrison and we got slated for it. Even George said it was terrible and we didn't like that 'cause it dented our egos. It was a lovely song that had the Hollies' ingredients written all over it but somehow the public didn't accept it. They accepted the Rolling Stones doing a Beatles song but not us. We made a mistake but, not to worry, we had other hits."

Another Hollie, Tony Hicks: "'If I Needed Someone' goes down as one of our biggest mistakes. It wasn't a great version and I don't know why we did it. Why cover a Beatles song? Enough people bought their records anyway. Our record producer Ron Richards was at EMI with George Martin and George said it might suit us. We got a Top 20 record with it but our record was no better than the Beatles, so what's the point? The whole exercise was a waste of time."

Graham Nash: "I was sad that George didn't like it as we certainly didn't want to upset him. We were honouring his songwriting and it was a great song and we did a good job of it. We did it a little too fast but the harmonies are pretty good."

Barbara Dickson: "I recorded 'If I Needed Someone' in 2006 and I thought it was a very good song, very up-tempo and so not as fundamentally thoughtful as some of his songs. I sing it in concert in memory of George Harrison as he gets overlooked so much of the time. If he had been in another band, he could have been as big as Lennon or McCartney but he was overshadowed by them. He was such a sensitive soul and I love him for that."

Record producer Huey P. Meaux, calculatedly, jumped on the bandwagon. "I produced several big records in the early 60s but the Beatles came along and knocked me off the charts. Doug Sahm had been bugging me to make some records with him and I told him, 'Doug, we gotta figure out where the Beatles are coming from. If we don't, we'll starve to death.' I got a case of T-bird wine - it was $1 a bottle and it'd get you drunk in a hurry and keep you drunk for days - and I bought some Beatle records. I went to the Wayfarer Hotel in San Antonio and the clerk said, 'Why do you want three rooms?' and I said, 'I'll be playing these records pretty loud.' I realised that it was all so simple, the Beatles had a beat, and we were not catching onto that. I called Doug, who was also in San Antonio, and I said, 'C'mon over, man, I'm drunk but I've figured it out.' I told him to write some songs with that beat and to grow his hair. He came up with 'She's About a Mover' and 'The Rains Came' and we recorded them at the Gold Star studios in Houston. American DJs would play anything from England, so I called up London Records in New York and I said, 'Put this out. Leave my name off it and we'll call Doug something else.' I thought about knighthoods and the Sir Douglas Quintet sounded perfect. The record made the charts and Doug kept bugging me, 'I want to go on the road, man. When will you tell them it's me?' I told him to keep quiet until the record made the Top 40. Doug was booked for the *Hullabaloo* TV show in New York City, which was mc'd by Trini Lopez. Freddie and the Dreamers were on the show but there was also Doug and me, Vikki Carr from El Paso, and Trini himself. Trini said, 'I can't believe so many people from Texas are on the same show. You've got to let me tell the people.' I said, 'Go ahead,' and that was the night that America learnt the identity of the Sir Douglas Quintet."

December 1965 – The Beatles Third Christmas Record Flexidisc (Fan Club, 12/65)

You have to be in the right frame of mind to enjoy the Beatles' Christmas flexidiscs for their fan club members, but they are often revealing. For one thing, the Beatles were not precious about their material and were prepared to send themselves up. Here they perform a high-spirited, drunken version of 'Yesterday' and return to it at the end of the record to sing new words as 'Christmas Day'. In addition, there is a skiffle treatment of 'Auld Lang Syne', a Scottish Christmas song (from John) and a snatch of the Four Tops' 'It's The Same Old Song' (again from John).

The success of the Beatles had given rise to the success of many other British performers, none more so than the Rolling Stones, a group which had managed to pass a Decca audition. Even though the group members were good friends with the Beatles, their manager Andrew Loog Oldham played on their rivalry in a replay of the old Elvis Presley vs Pat Boone contest. It was north vs south, long hair vs longer hair, conformity vs rebellion. The Rolling Stones was like the Beatles' evil twin but it was, by today's standards, mild stuff. Shock, horror, the Stones were arrested for peeing on a garage wall. "Would you let your daughter marry a Rolling Stone?" was a common headline and while the Beatles had sung 'I Want to Hold Your Hand', the Stones wanted something more. It was all great copy.

Freddy Cannon: "I loved the British records but I idolised the Rolling Stones, who made raw records like Chuck Berry. I am a true rocker and the real raw records are the ones that I like best."

Cyril Neville from the Neville Brothers: "The Rolling Stones actually told people where they had got it from. They brought the blues to Europe. Eric Clapton did the same thing. Hubert Sumlin told me that when Howlin' Wolf was coming to Europe, they didn't include him on the bill and Eric said, 'Well, they should shut it down if you ain't coming.' Okay, these groups stuck their names on some of the songs but they did bring the cats over to Europe. That was real cool."

Dennis Locorriere, former lead singer of Dr. Hook: "A lot of people were asking, 'Are you into the Beatles and the Stones?', but I never took any notice of that. I wasn't going to choose between them. If push came to shove, I would rather keep my Beatle records but I loved the Stones and I loved the Animals and Manfred Mann – Paul Jones made me start playing harmonica – and Eric Burdon made me put down a guitar and go up front. I didn't want to be élitist about any one particular band. This music made me want to be a participant."

Cynthia Lennon: "I never saw John worried by competition but of course he knew it was there, possibly strongest with the Rolling Stones and then with the Bee Gees. The press made up the rivalry between them."

Many music fans in the 60s viewed the Rolling Stones as ripping off the Beatles. Even the Beatles saw them this way as their 'Eleanor Rigby' was followed by their 'Ruby Tuesday', for example. Their extravaganza *Sgt. Pepper's Lonely Hearts Club Band* was followed by *Their Satanic Majesties Request*. The Beatles produced 'All You Need Is Love' for the Summer of Love, the Stones the feeble 'We Love You'. There is one battle that the Stones have won. It may be self-promotion but the public believe they are "the greatest rock and roll band in the world".

When discussing the Beatles and the Stones, one prime difference is that one group was produced by George Martin and the other wasn't. Martin had a strong musical background and was able both to make valid suggestions and to carry out their wishes.

Fellow record producer Stuart Colman: "George Martin is the godfather of producers. Funnily enough, I'm a big fan of comedy as well as American rock'n'roll and his early work with Peter Sellers is unsurpassable. 'I'm So Ashamed', 'Any Old Iron' and *Songs for Swingin' Sellers* are timeless. That alternate take where Peter Sellers does 'She Loves You' as a Cockney dustman is absolute magic."

Mike McCartney: "George Martin was Scaffold's producer, not because of my brother and his chums, but because of his work with Peter Sellers and Spike Milligan. George had recorded *Songs for Swingin' Sellers* and Paul and I had fallen about laughing to those nice little sketches. Do you remember 'Balham - Gateway to the South'? George liked our crazy songs like '2 Day's Monday' and 'Thank U Very Much', which was the first successful one."

Rolf Harris: "George Martin was into weird things long before the Beatles. He did those comedy tracks for Charlie Drake and I was given to George because nobody else could figure out what to do with me. He recognised where the Beatles' charm lay and he gave them the best of his expertise. The combination of their talents and enthusiasm is marvellous."

Ron Goodwin: "George Martin was a first class record producer and a very good musician. He was very well-informed technically about what you can and can't do in a recording studio and he had a wonderful, natural talent for handling people. I've never seen him get upset on a session and I've never seen him upset anybody else. If anything went wrong, George knew how to handle it in such a way that the other person doesn't realise what's happening. He was the ideal producer for the Beatles."

Peter Carlin, biographer of both Brian Wilson and Paul McCartney: "John and Paul were working together on the same creative page and you also had the company guy, George Martin, who was officially the authority figure, but he was game for what they wanted to do. I don't think he ever said no to the Beatles, whereas Brian Wilson constantly had people saying no to him. Brian had to find the wherewithal to resist them and resist their guidance. The other Beach Boys didn't like his creative work at first, they didn't understand it, his father didn't understand it, the record company didn't understand it. A lot of people were saying that he shouldn't be doing that kind of stuff. For a time, he had the emotional strength to say, 'I don't care what you think, I'm going to do what I want.' The Beatles never had those problems."

Raul Malo of the Mavericks: "So many record companies want their artists to stick to the same thing and to make one record again and again. Look at how the Beatles developed as musicians and how their albums changed from record to record, and that should be what it is about. They started as kids and ended as adults. If they'd been doing 'I Saw Her Standing There' over and over again, it would have ruined the band."

Record producer Joe Boyd: "One of the biggest compliments that you can pay to a record producer is that you don't notice him. I know there are producers who very strongly influence a record, like Phil Spector, and I can admire that but I also admire the role of a record producer who makes sure that nothing goes wrong, just keeping away all the negative things that can happen and allowing the music to take place as if it were obvious, as if it were the only way the record could be made. There's no imposition of a heavy hand or a style, it is just music coming at you, something good performed with a lot of energy. You focus on the music and you're not conscious of the producer. George Martin disappeared on those early records, which was a marvellous accomplishment and I will always respect him for that."

EMI record producer Walter Ridley: "When you're making a record, all the elements have to be right. You've got to have a good engineer who can get a good balance and a good producer who can understand what is wanted and can heal the little wounds along the way. He has to have enough faith to battle it out with the boys in the front office who don't like what you do anyway, so it's not easy. You may think that once you've made a record, that's it, but that's not it at all. Somebody has got to be told how to sell the record to the disc-jockeys and unless you have faith and belief, you will never get through. George Martin had a lot of success with very diverse people, the Beatles, Peter Sellers, Cilla Black and Gerry and the Pacemakers, and he knew how to make them all successful."

George Martin is engagingly modest. "Whatever I did shouldn't be stressed too much. I was merely the bloke who interpreted their ideas. The fact that they couldn't read or write music and I could, has absolutely nothing to do with it. Music isn't something which is written down on paper. Music is stuff you hear. It's sound and they thought of those notes. I was purely an interpreter, rather like a Chinese interpreter at the League of Nations. Certainly I taught them all I could in terms of recording techniques and brought an influence of classical music to their work. But the genius was theirs, no doubt about that."

CHAPTER 6
More Popular Than Jesus (1966)

State opening of Parliament televised – Britain's first credit card,
the Barclaycard, introduced – England wins the FIFA World Cup –
Aberfan disaster – China's Cultural Revolution.

In February 1966, Paul McCartney returned to writing for Peter and Gordon. He wanted to know if his songs were strong enough to sell without his name and offered them 'Woman', listing the fictitious Bernard Webb as its writer. This was muddled thinking as there had been several songs which hadn't sold despite 'Lennon-McCartney' on the label. In any event, it was hardly a Webb of deceit as it was revealed by the *NME* that it was McCartney's song. The single made the Top 30 and McCartney had done himself a disservice as it is amongst his best songs and had it been promoted properly, it could easily have been a Top 10 single.

By then, Paul McCartney had become intrigued by electronic music and was impressed with a concert given by Luciano Berio. Paul's friend and biographer Barry Miles recalls, "Paul was the man about town and he was investigating a whole range of things. One night he'd go and listen to Cornelius Cardew playing random music and the next night he would see Sophie Tucker at the Talk of the Town. His range of interest was enormous and it all got filed away in his mind and occasionally you'd notice references to things he had picked up. He was completely open to receiving new information but John, because of his upbringing I guess, was deeply suspicious of anything avant-garde. He was always worried that people were trying to pull one over on him and make him look a fool or show that they were better educated than he was. He came out with that wonderful line about 'avant-garde' being French for 'bullshit', and George Harrison would say 'Avant-garde? 'Aven't got a clue?'"

Beatles biographer Steve Turner: "In 1966, Paul was the avant-garde member of the Beatles because he was the one who was into Antonioni films and art exhibitions. A lot of that was because John was stuck down in Weybridge and not very happy and was lazy by nature. Paul was young and single and accepting invitations around town at a time when London was swinging."

Something radically different was the Beatles' photo session as butchers cutting up dolls. How this assignment came to be approved is beyond me and even odder is the fact that Capitol Records, usually cautious about audience reaction, put one of the images on the cover of the compilation, *Yesterday...And Today*. It could symbolise Capitol's butchery of Beatle records. Capitol had to withdraw 750,000 copies of the notorious sleeve. This was a costly operation at a time when the Beach Boys' brilliant but expensive *Pet Sounds* was seen as another Capitol mistake.

In 1966 Capitol's golden calves – the Beatles and the Beach Boys – were, in their different but related ways giving company executives cause for concern. The executives had no idea what was coming next.

Dennis Locorriere from Dr. Hook: "A lot of things were new then and people could risk doing things that were totally different. The Beatles and the Beach Boys and the others were trying to do things that nobody had done before. It would be totally impossible to act like today. My son said to me, 'It must have been easier to be original back then' and I could see where he was coming from."

Bob Stanley of Saint Etienne: "The Beach Boys would have been the first group that was using sounds that I didn't recognise. Obviously as a kid, I didn't even know what a guitar sounded like. It was just a noise but I was fascinated by the way the records were put together. I had *20 Golden Greats* and when you hear 'Good Vibrations' and 'Heroes and Villains', they are really quite odd. With them and the Beatles, it was also my first brush with strange lyrics."

Kim Fowley: "I was a PR guy working with Derek Taylor on the Beach Boys. Derek Taylor said, 'I want to get these guys out of being one-off bubblegum singles people. I wanted to get the Beatles to come down and genuflect.' The day they came to hear *Pet Sounds* at the Waldorf, John Lennon was quiet. McCartney came in and took over the Canasta game and then said, 'Would you please be quiet while we listen to the album?' Brian Wilson was not only trying to top *Rubber Soul* but also the Four Freshmen and the Hi-Los. A piano was brought in and John and Paul listened and whispered to each other. They went to the piano, played some chords and left. The next day the press said, 'The Beatles visit the Beach Boys to hear their new album.' The PR worked as they had loved the album."

Charlie Reid from the Proclaimers: "You listen to what came before and you can hear what the Beatles were influenced by and then you listen to how they changed it. After *Rubber Soul,* everybody made a *Rubber Soul* record. After *Sgt. Pepper,* everybody made a *Sgt. Pepper* record. They changed everything but not always for the best. Sometimes people who shouldn't have written did write but they also encouraged many talented people to start writing."

The major recording artists wanted to experiment. In May 1966, John and George saw Bob Dylan at the Royal Albert Hall with the musicians who became the Band. Dylan alienated the audience by playing electric rock and the reaction and Dylan's courage must have intrigued them.

The Beatles did not operate in a vacuum. They kept a close watch on the opposition, and not just the Beach Boys. John Sebastian of the Lovin' Spoonful: "I always swore that I would never write a song about being lonely on the road but I had those feelings and I just switched it around to the point of view of the person who has to stay at home. That was 'Darling Be Home Soon' and getting a compliment from McCartney about it was one of the highlights of my career." (An interesting compliment as 'Darling Be Home Soon' is typically McCartneyesque.)

If you listen to the Mamas and the Papas' 'I Saw Her Again', there is a moment where two of them sing "I saw her" before the others. John Phillips: "That's a mistake on 'I Saw Her Again' but it had come off so beautifully that we had to leave it on. It hadn't been released in England but I had a dub of the record with me and I played it to Paul McCartney. He asked me to play it again and then he said, 'That has to be a mistake. No one's that clever.'"

The biggest rival to the Beatles could have been the Byrds but they were hampered by personnel changes. Roger McGuinn: "I was disappointed about that. I was hoping to be in a band like the Beatles: they were a group of friends who got along well and would defend each other. The Byrds were more like a pirate ship and it was every man for himself. It was very cutthroat." When I broadcast this interview, someone contacted me and said, "I was surprised to hear Roger McGuinn call the Byrds 'a pile of shit.'"

Music writer Sid Griffin specialises on those west coast sounds: "The west coast harmony groups have an inter-band history of strife – the Beach Boys, the Byrds, Buffalo Springfield, the Bangles and the Mamas and the Papas had honey-laden vocals, but you wouldn't want any of them to show up at your party. I could never get over this. Go figure."

Byrds biographer John Einarson: "There was a unity to the Beatles that a lot of other bands didn't have and if you look at the Beatles photographs, they are all looking morose or intense or happy: they all looked the same way at the same time. There is a consistency to their moods. The Byrds never had that unity. They were five guys and each one was out for himself. You get that in so many bands – two guys looking cool in Carnaby Street outfits and the others looking like farmers and grinning like idiots. The Beatles had a unity which had developed over the years, whereas the Byrds had come together very quickly."

On 1 May 1966 the Beatles appeared on the NME Pollwinners Concert at the Empire Pool, Wembley. It was to be the last UK appearance in front of a paying audience.

June 1966 – Paperback Writer/ Rain (Parlophone R 5452, UK No.1, US No.1, Germany No.1) (B-side also made No.23 in US.)
In June 1966 the Beatles released their first single of the year, the Chuck Berry-styled A-side 'Paperback Writer', backed by the experimental 'Rain', the first time that the Beatles had used backwards looping. Maybe the origins of 'Paperback Writer' went back to the early 60s. Beat poet and writer Royston Ellis had visited Liverpool and met the Beatles: "We had a conversation about what we wanted to be. I'd had some poetry published but I'd said that I wanted to be a paperback writer. That phrase obviously stuck in Paul's mind and became part of the song." Obviously?

Ian McLagen of the Small Faces: "We were always listening to the Beatles. When 'Rain' came out, we played it at every speed and we even played it backwards. We were really into sound and the Beatles and the Beach Boys were experimenting more than anyone, but we listened to everything. When *Revolver* came out, we went to Ronnie

Lane's flat in Earls Court to hear it and we heard it over and over. It had a great cover from Klaus Voormann. I always loved the Beatles but I loved the Stones first."

Mike Evans from Liverpool Scene: "One of my favourite Beatle tracks is 'Rain', which had the early hint that they were getting into psychedelia. It had an Indian influence before it got terribly specific in George's later work. 'Rain', which was just before *Revolver*, had that droning, hypnotic quality. There's a tremendous promotional film of them standing in a garden and it's piddling down with rain: it's wonderful imagery. I was very much involved with the Liverpool poets at the time and I wrote this instant poem:

All through my childhood
I wanted to be an engine-driver
But when it rained
I wanted to be a Beatle."

In June 1966, the Beatles performed in Germany, supported by Cliff Bennett and the Rebel Rousers. Cliff Bennett: "That was the first European tour that we did and to get the first house out, they had to let the dogs off the leash. The dogs were muzzled though, and the fans did leave! You knew that the audience had come to see the Beatles and you had to be good to keep them entertained. I used to say, 'I know you want to see the Beatles, and so do I, but you're going to have to put up with us for 20 minutes.'"

The Beatles moved on to Japan and the Philippines. Unknowingly, they snubbed the Marcos family which created a furore. Still, in retrospect, it was a good thing to annoy them.

John Lennon was a brilliant interviewee, possibly because he lacked the diplomacy of Paul McCartney. In March 1966 he had told Maureen Cleave in London's *Evening Standard*, "Christianity will go. It will vanish and shrink. I needn't argue with that; I'm right and I will be proved right. We're more popular than Jesus now." The interview was published without controversy in the UK but it led to a backlash in the southern states of America. Beatles' records and memorabilia were publicly burned. The Beatles toured America in August that year, opening with a press conference at which John made a quasi-apology.

The Beatles' press officer, Tony Barrow: "The *Evening Standard* piece was written by a very responsible journalist Maureen Cleave and the quote was published in context. John was making a statement on the world and the fact that a pop group seemed to be drawing more attention than God, certainly there were more people going to pop concerts than attending churches. It was lifted completely out of context and, in that respect, it was a terrible thing for a PR man to read. The Bible belt of America started burning their records and their effigies and when we got to America, John was asked to apologise. It was the first time I had seen him really nervous at a press conference, probably because he didn't know what to say. He said, 'I don't think I've got anything to apologise for but if I have, I'm very sorry.' There was a genuine fear that John might be assassinated by some religious zealot in the South. At one concert, somebody let off a firecracker and the other three Beatles automatically turned to where John was standing because they thought he might have been shot. If he had, I don't think any of us would have been surprised."

Country singer George Hamilton IV: "I think John Lennon meant to say that it was a shame that the Beatles were more popular that Jesus. He was a very bright man and he was commenting on the times we live in where a pop group can have more popularity than Jesus. I don't think he was commenting on how wonderful the Beatles were, he was just commenting on the human condition. It's like in our country. We sometimes elect people to the presidency because they look good on television or have been some famous actor. John was touching on that strange mentality whereby pop stars and movie actors are given more importance than they deserve in comparison to, say, Mother Teresa. His remarks did cause a lot of consternation in the South because a lot of people took it that he was tooting his own horn and saying, 'Isn't it wonderful that we're so popular?' I don't think he meant that at all."

Maybe the most apt comment came from on high. The morning after a Beatle bonfire in Texas, KLUE's transmission tower in Longview, Texas was struck by lightning, damaging their equipment and taking them off air.

No doubt some of the Beatles' new songs would have been difficult to play live but they were not prepared to make the effort. Anyway, the screaming made it impracticable. Mark Lewisohn's book *The Beatles Live!* shows that the Beatles played thirty-three concerts in 1966 but only performed twelve different songs, two of them going back to the Cavern: 'Long Tall Sally' and 'Rock and Roll Music'. They performed 'I Feel Fine', 'She's A Woman', 'I'm Down', 'Day Tripper' and 'Paperback Writer' from singles, plus 'Baby's in Black' (from *Beatles for Sale*), 'Yesterday' (from *Help!*) and 'Nowhere Man' (from *Rubber*

Soul). George sang 'If I Needed Someone' from *Rubber Soul* and Ringo reprised 'I Wanna Be Your Man'. After a return to Shea Stadium, the Beatles made their last concert appearance on their final tour at Candlestick Park, San Francisco on 29 August 1966. They closed the way they had started all those years ago with Little Richard's 'Long Tall Sally'.

Tony Barrow: "Besides all the controversy, they had had enough of touring and they knew this tour would be their last. After Candlestick Park, George Harrison got on the plane and said, 'That's it. I'm not a Beatle anymore'."

Martin Cloonan, an academic who researched a huge project about live music in the UK: "Those all night sessions in Hamburg had turned the Beatles into a fantastic live band with a huge repertoire. However, as a professional outfit on the road, they felt the limitations of audience expectation: they had to sing their hits. They were knuckling down to the demands of showbiz and they were under so much pressure at the time that it must have been easier to do the same songs every night. Things that we take for granted today would not have been possible then, and hearing them at Shea Stadium cannot have been an impressive sonic experience. They could have attempted *Sgt. Pepper* live but it would have been very different from the record. There were no purpose-built venues for music then."

August 1966 – Yellow Submarine/ Eleanor Rigby (Parlophone R 5493, UK No.1, US No.2) (Both sides listed on UK chart: B-side also made No.11 in US)
The second single of the year combined two of Paul McCartney's songs, very different from each other and each very distinctive: 'Eleanor Rigby' sung by Paul and 'Yellow Submarine' sung by Ringo.

There is a gravestone for 'Eleanor Rigby' in St Peter's churchyard in Woolton. John Lennon's schoolfriend, Pete Shotton: "The gravestone is an amazing coincidence. Paul didn't hang around Woolton. He lived in Allerton and we would meet up around Penny Lane. I took part in the writing of 'Eleanor Rigby'. The Beatles and their women, myself and my wife, were all at John's for the weekend. We all had dinner, then the lads went upstairs where John had his tape recorders and his toys, his Scalextric, and his instruments. We were sitting around and smoking weed. Paul said, 'I've got this little tune' and he started playing 'Eleanor Rigby'. We all threw in words though John was subdued and

I had a bigger part in the writing of 'Eleanor Rigby' than he had. I was really getting into it, it was great. Paul sang, 'Father McCartney', and I said, 'Hang on Paul, you can't do that. They'll think it's your dear old dad. You've left him on his own.' He said, 'You're right' and we tried Father McVicar which was quite amusing. I said, 'Give me the phone book', and Ringo handed it to me, and I went through the Mc's and came to McKenzie. I said, 'Try that', and that's how it came about."

Anything else? Pete Shotton:"Paul was stuck as to how it should end. I said, 'Why not have Eleanor Rigby dying as the lonely person and Father McKenzie doing the service?' John said, 'I don't think you understand what we are getting at here, Pete.' I said, 'Sod you' and that ended the session. The next thing I knew was the record with that ending, so it was John who hadn't tuned into the song. I bumped into Paul some years later and he said, 'Pete, what was that song you helped me with?' I said, 'Well, I helped write quite a lot of them, you know.' He said, 'No, you were really helpful on this one', and I am sure he was thinking of 'Eleanor Rigby'."

Songwriter Lionel Bart: "I heard the first versions of some of their songs. For instance 'Eleanor Rigby' was originally called 'Eleanor Bygraves' and I asked them to change it. It was a family affair because we helped each other. If someone had done a good 'un, we'd phone each other about it. I was one of the first people to hear 'Yesterday'. Paul didn't have any lyrics for it then and he called it 'Scrambled Eggs'."

The single had a special significance for Tom McKenzie, a small-time concert promoter who had introduced the Beatles in Northwich, Cheshire in 1962/3: "After they'd been on stage, I might take their guitars or their drumsticks back to them, and John Lennon would say, 'You look after us like a father, Tom', and so I became Father McKenzie. John once asked me what the air raids were like and I told him that there was always an air raid when I was on guard duty. Instead of getting my head down when it was quiet, I used to sit up at night-time darning my socks."

George Melly: "'Eleanor Rigby' seemed to be written out of their experiences in Liverpool. Liverpool was always in their songs but this was about the kind of old woman that I remembered from my childhood and later: very respectable Liverpool women, living in two-up, two-down streets with the doorsteps meticulously holystoned and the church the one solid thing in their lives. There's the loneliness of it and it struck me as a poem from the start. If you read 'Love Me

Do' without the music, it doesn't mean much but if you read 'Eleanor Rigby', it is a poem about someone, which is something unprecedented in popular song. It could have come out of a novel or been written as a poem on its own but they found the perfect tune to go with it. George Martin has to be given credit because he found exactly the right backing, which is an extraordinary mixture of church-like solemnity and humour. I first heard it at a smart party in London. Someone put it on, and I could see Park Road or Mill Street and those houses going down to the river and I could imagine Eleanor Rigby living in one. It was a complete portrait, a thumbnail sketch that was as solid as a Rembrandt drawing."

Julian Lloyd Webber: "People like Bobby Vee used cellos and Adam Faith had those plucked strings but cellos hadn't been used really effectively on rock'n'roll records until the Beatles. George Martin was a very good arranger who knew what he was doing and he loved the sound of the cello. They are used beautifully on 'Yesterday' and especially 'Eleanor Rigby'."

Tommy Steele: "While I was in Liverpool doing *Hans Christian Andersen*, I was on Bob Azurdia's programme on Radio Merseyside in which it was suggested that there should be a statue of the Beatles in the city. I said over the air that I was interested and the Council approached me. I said that, if it was up to me, it should be something that all the people of Liverpool could live with, something that doesn't alienate the citizens down the middle. Fifty per cent of the people living in Liverpool don't want to see four fellers standing around playing guitars and I wanted it to be something that all the people could identify with, hence there's Eleanor Rigby sitting on a bench with her shopping."

Beatles' chauffeur Alf Bicknell: "I attended most of the Beatles' recording sessions for *Rubber Soul* and *Revolver*. I would take them there and then get a restaurant to send food over to the studio. Ringo didn't like onions and Paul loved avocado vinaigrette. I would make tea, play cards or chess, and once I was asked to hold up a song that was written all around an open envelope, I was standing in front of John with the microphone between us. John was laughing so much because I couldn't hold the paper still. I did some sound effects and sang on the chorus of 'Yellow Submarine'. The sound of the anchor going down is me with an old tin bath and a piece of chain standing by a microphone. I can honestly say that I've had a No.1 hit."

The choice of 'Yellow Submarine' is significant. The Beatles were realising that they might be losing younger listeners. After all, wasn't this the reason the Monkees were created? Peter Tork of the Monkees: "The Monkees were created after *A Hard Day's Night* and the producers certainly didn't think, 'The Beatles have gone too far, let's create the Monkees and rectify the situation', which is what you're saying. We simply got the next group of fans who came along. That reference in 'Alternate Title' to 'The four kings of EMI are sitting stately on the floor' is to a Beatles record on a small portable player in the middle of a living room. If I hear it now, it sounds like a line from 'American Pie'."

Whatever. The television series *The Monkees* attracted a huge audience. Their first single 'Last Train to Clarksville' released in America in August 1966, owed much to 'Paperback Writer'. Their zany antics delighted John Lennon who was to call them, "the greatest comic talent since the Marx Brothers". At the time, many regarded the Monkees as synthetic and uninspired but the TV shows have improved with age and John Lennon has a point. Film critic Mark Kermode: "*A Hard Day's Night* is the blueprint for everything you saw the Monkees do. The Monkees didn't rip off the Beatles in general but they certainly did rip off that film."

Davy Jones from the Monkees: "People compared the Monkees to the Beatles and we grabbed at that because we were being mentioned in the same sentence. We had our hair cut in the same way but really we were just two groups with four guys. People would ask, 'Is Paul better than Davy?' or 'Is Mike better than John?', and what was great was that we lowered the age at which kids bought records. I didn't buy a record myself until Johnny Tillotson's 'Poetry in Motion' when I was fifteen and I didn't even have a record-player. No kids ever bought Sinatra's records but 14-year-olds bought the Beatles. We lowered that age to twelve. Since then, there have been other groups, like the Osmonds, who have gone for that market. Kids of seven got turned on by the Muppets and that's great. All this worked out very well for the Monkees but they didn't want to promote me as an individual because I was English. How could America's answer to the Beatles contain someone who was English?"

It was leaked that the Monkees hadn't played on their first album, *The Monkees*. Davy Jones: "Okay, there was some controversy because we didn't play on our first records. We just sang the songs. We didn't want to play on them as it would have meant 6 weeks in the studio.

I don't think it mattered because lots of groups didn't play on their records. You can't tell me that the other Beatles were playing with Paul McCartney on 'Yesterday'."

Beatles biographer Stu Shea: "The Beatles appreciated the Monkees as both musicians and actors. Lennon told a reporter, 'I never miss their shows: you try doing a half-hour show each week and see if you can do it as good.' On their first trip to the UK in 1967, John Lennon had Mike Nesmith as a house guest and Paul McCartney had Micky Dolenz. Mike Nesmith was at the recording session for 'A Day in the Life'. Peter Tork stayed with George and played banjo on *Wonderwall*, but Davy Jones had gone to Manchester to see his sick father and didn't stay with Ringo. The Monkees picked up influences from British bands. 'The Monkees Theme' is really 'Catch Us If You Can' (Dave Clark Five) and 'Last Train to Clarksville' is 'Paperback Writer'."

Peter Tork: "Of course I wouldn't stack our albums against the Beatles or the Stones on a one-to-one comparison but we were third or fourth in terms of quality at the time. I don't think we made anything as good as 'California Dreamin'' or 'Monday Monday' but we have an hour's worth of songs that Mr & Mrs America and Mr & Mrs Great Britain will know. I love the 'Mashup' on *YouTube*. Somebody has taken out our vocals to 'I'm A Believer' and put in the Beatles' singing 'Paperback Writer' and then blended the videos together."

Another rival group was the Walker Brothers. Even more than Scott and John, Gary Walker was convinced that the Walker Brothers would make it. "That was because our music was going to be slower and was going to make people cry as opposed to the Beatles and the Stones. We were doing the Beatle thing in reverse. The girls liked us immediately. John was originally the lead singer but we found out that the songs we were doing suited Scott more."

August 1966 – Got to Get You into My Life – Cliff Bennett and the Rebel Rousers (Parlophone, UK No.6)
Paul McCartney, producer
Chas Hodges of Chas and Dave, then with the Rebel Rousers: "I tend to like the Beatles' tracks that weren't so popular like 'You Won't See Me'. I had known the Beatles for some years and we did a tour with them. They gave us a preview of their new album and they offered a bottle of Scotch to anyone who could come up with a title. I don't know who thought of *Revolver* but they did say that there was a song

on the album that would suit us. That was 'Got to Get You into My Life'. We said, 'Great' and Paul McCartney produced our single."

Cliff Bennett: "When we played in Essen, John and Paul played 'Got to Get You into My Life' to me. John sang the song and Paul did all the da-de-da's for the brass. It sounded great like that. Brian Epstein told me that the Beatles would not release *Revolver* until our single had been out for 10 days. Paul co-produced the session with Dave Paramor. As well as being a great songwriter and performer, Paul had a great recording technique and was very experimental. He was limiting the piano, that's condensing it down, and I didn't know these tricks. He'd picked them up from George Martin and he was passing them to us. The engineers knew what he was talking about and I was in awe of him. I didn't know whether it would be a hit because I haven't got a very commercial ear. We had 'Needles and Pins' in our repertoire long before the Searchers, but I could never see it as a hit. Later on, I turned down 'Proud Mary'."

August 1966 – Revolver LP (Parlophone PMC 7009)
Produced by George Martin, 14 tracks – 35 minutes 11 seconds
Side 1: Taxman/ Eleanor Rigby/ I'm Only Sleeping/ Love You To/ Here, There and Everywhere/ Yellow Submarine/ She Said She Said
Side 2: Good Day Sunshine/ And Your Bird Can Sing/ For No One/ Dr. Robert/ I Want To Tell You/ Got to Get You into My Life/ Tomorrow Never Knows
The Beatles titled their new album, *Revolver*, a gentle pun on the spinning vinyl. More revolutionary was the record itself, not least the striking art nouveau sleeve image by Klaus Voormann featuring the Beatles' faces with collages in their hair. A revival of interest in the drawings of Aubrey Beardsley, including an exhibition at the V&A, was reflected in contemporary psychedelic art, as Klaus Voormann acknowledges: "Yes, I knew him but not from one particular exhibition. I had always adored his drawings. The *Revolver* cover came at a time when I was only doing music and so it was a bit of a switch to do art. John asked me to design the cover and invited me to the studio to hear their music and I was amazed, it was so fantastic. I heard 'Tomorrow Never Knows' where they were playing around with those tape loops and it was incredible. I realised that the cover was going to be even harder than I thought. They hadn't just done another record: they had created another milestone. Lots of groups held back once they

had made it but they never did. They said, 'Now we're here, they're expecting us to be even better' and they did it every time."

The LP cover was to win a Grammy in its own right. Klaus Voorman: "I had felt-tip pens, they were new then, aluminium sticks that smelt terrible and I did sketches of lots of different ideas. Everything else was in colour then. Normally when you go through a record rack, the titles are on the top, but I thought, 'You don't have to do that for the Beatles. They will see the Beatles' heads and know it's them. They are known all over the world.' I got stuck on having lots of hair because that was important. You always have to think of the people who are going to buy the record but it was a really wide range for the Beatles. That is why I didn't get that crazy or surreal. I had to be close to the people so that they would still accept the cover. Some people told me that they had bought the record and put it on the mantelpiece and got scared by George's face because it looked so white with those dark eyes."

Although I generally dislike the way that still photographs have been converted to 3D for the mini-documentaries with the remasters, the effects for the *Revolver* cover work well. Klaus Voormann: "I stuck lots of little pictures in there. I told them to bring me stuff and I would choose from them. I looked through Robert Freeman's photographs. Everybody was there when I showed them the cover at EMI: George Martin and Brian Epstein as well as the Beatles. I put it up and they were quiet. I thought, 'Shit, they are not going to like this.' Then Paul looked closer and said, 'Hey, that's me sitting on a toilet' and George Martin said, 'You can't put that on there.' They started to discuss it and I felt better as silence is bad. Brian Epstein was crying and he said, 'Klaus, this is more than I ever expected. This is so much in line with what they are doing now. You've hit the spot and I love it.'"

Psychedelia hung over *Revolver*, particularly with George Harrison's eastern 'Love You To', the acid-induced 'She Said, She Said' and 'Tomorrow Never Knows'. In contrast, there were the childhood reflections of 'Yellow Submarine', the forlorn beauty of 'Eleanor Rigby' and Paul McCartney's greatest love song 'Here, There and Everywhere'. Originally, I had considered George Harrison's 'Love You To' one of the weaker tracks and then I heard, in 2009, an extended live version from John Jorgenson and changed my mind: the combination of a bangra backbeat with Jeff Beck-styled playing was wonderful. *Revolver* revolved around millions of turntables and set the scene for *Sgt. Pepper*, though many consider it the better album.

Richard Thompson: "I liked the influence of Bob Dylan because it brought lyrics more into the music but I didn't like the Beatles. I thought they were overrated, and in Fairport Convention we only listened to lyric-orientated music: Joni Mitchell, Dylan and the Byrds. It's funny that I should prefer the Beatles in retrospect. I like them now up to *Revolver*, which was their best record. *Sgt. Pepper* was overrated and by the time you get to *The White Album*, it doesn't sound like a band anymore. It's individuals doing their own thing, although there are good bits here and there."

Will Birch, songwriter and drummer with the Kursaal Flyers: "The best Beatles album is *Revolver,* which, in my opinion, is the best pop album of all time. That's partly for the diversity of its material. I'm not a big fan of 'Yellow Submarine' but it is a light-hearted novelty song and has its place on the album. The album has 'Eleanor Rigby', 'Taxman', the futurism of 'Tomorrow Never Knows' and the beautiful melody of 'Here, There and Everywhere'. Is there a greater collection of fourteen new songs? I don't think so."

Bob Stanley of Saint Etienne: "I love 'Rain' and 'She Said She Said' just for the rush of noise. They are phenomenal sounding records, great guitar lines. It is fantastic, compressed noise. The Who were doing something similar but their records didn't have that huge joyous rush that the Beatles had."

Gordon Lightfoot: "I'd been to England and so it was really interesting to see the Beatles and the Rolling Stones on television. With those haircuts, they did indeed look like beetles. The music was good and the consistency was good. I loved 'From Me to You' and 'She Loves You' and I thought the advanced stuff like *Revolver* had some really good songs on it. I liked 'Taxman' but there's not much sense in complaining. The Government always wins."

Ian McNabb: "George Harrison was into Chet Atkins and he was getting to be a really good guitarist around 1966. The lyrics of 'Taxman' can't have sat too well with his Indian gurus as you're not supposed to be bothered with worldly goods if you're into Gita."

Ray Davies, who was similarly tight-fisted, was at No.1 singing about his tax problems in 'Sunny Afternoon'. Many listeners would be thinking, "Well, I'd love to be in a position where I had to pay that much tax, so don't moan about it."

Mark Lewisohn: "I like 'Taxman' for several reasons. First and foremost, it's George Harrison's writing. He had been writing a few songs over the years and although they're very pleasant, there's nothing especially great about them. They hadn't got the depth that Lennon and McCartney's songs had but that changed with 'Taxman', which is a very clever composition and typically George Harrison because the stories of his fascination with money are legion. He always wanted to know what they were owed and what they were earning. The fact that they were paying a great deal in tax rankled George a lot more than it did Paul, John or Ringo, so he wrote this stinging song to show how bitterly he felt about it all and he rounded it off with some of the best playing on any Beatles record. I like to listen to one of the stereo channels of 'Taxman' and then the other because they are both great in different ways. On one channel you've got the rasping lead guitar and on the other you've got the bass line and the beautiful harmonies as well. It's altogether a cracking song and it opens *Revolver*, which many people, me included, think is their best album. It's one of the best opening tracks on an album that I've ever heard."

Ray Coleman: "Paul's gift for wonderful, marvellous, lyrical melodies, always contrasted handsomely with John's talent for raucous rock'n'roll. 'For No One', with its beautiful melody line and Paul's very pretty vocal is a very special track for me."

Nick Heyward: "The seed was sown for me with the Beatles. I loved 'For No One', it is so beautiful. That song had a French horn solo and how many songs of the time had that. Again, it was the Beatles being unique."

Emmylou Harris: "My producer, Brian Ahern, had the Beatles songbook and he said, 'Let's think of some Beatle songs that you might like to do.' 'For No One' was one that I had performed with a piano player in Washington DC on a few shows together. Brian played 'Here, There and Everywhere' on the guitar and I sang it and it seemed like one that might work. It was very early on in my recording career and I was still unsure. I knew it was a good song and I trusted Brian's instinct. I would not have chosen if it hadn't been for his encouragement."

Songwriter Richard Kerr, who wrote 'Mandy': "One of the areas where I am really snobbish is the *Eurovision Song Contest*. I hate the formatted song and the biased voting, the politics of it all. Songs can be too good for *Eurovision* as they are not instant enough. 'Here There and Everywhere' is one of the greatest songs that Lennon and McCartney ever wrote, but it wouldn't have meant a damn thing on *Eurovision*."

Indeed. How do Lennon and McCartney match up to the Great American Songbook? Frank Sinatra's lyricist, Sammy Cahn: "John Lennon and Paul McCartney received the first international award in the Songwriters Hall of Fame and they deserved it. Their songs are here forever. 'Here, There and Everywhere' is an absolutely great composition - great words and great music. Okay, they couldn't write music but then Mr Irving Berlin had no musical ability whatsoever. Jerome Kern said to him, 'Irving, you simply must learn how to write. You should be able to sit down and write your own notes.' He respected Mr. Kern so he started very laboriously to learn to write music. After a month, he said, 'Why, that son of a bitch! While I was learning to write, I could have written 12 new songs.'"

Jazz band leader John Dankworth: "I don't think that you need training to write good songs. There are lots of technically bad musicians who have scaled the heights. Irving Berlin could scarcely play the piano, Noël Coward had to hum his songs to people to get them on paper, and yet they wrote great songs. When you're a musician you like to think that you need a certain amount of expertise to be a good songwriter but it's not true. If you've got it within you, it'll come out. Paul McCartney would be the first to regret that he didn't have more musical knowledge and I don't think it would have harmed him. There must be times now when he wants to play more keyboards or conduct an orchestra or read a score."

Raul Malo of the Mavericks: "Two of my favourite records are *Rubber Soul* and *Revolver,* so I love anything from there. 'And Your Bird Can Sing' is fantastic. There is something special about the guitar and the melody on that."

Music writer Paul Trynka: "The Beatles' version of psychedelia was better than the San Francisco one: it was more coherent and focused. A lot of the bands were derivative and not very creative. Those groups were lifting ideas from jug bands and blues music while the Beatles had got well beyond that. They knew how to write songs when they encountered psychedelia. 'Tomorrow Never Knows' is so far ahead of stuff by the Grateful Dead or the Animals and it had a discipline about it."

Tony Thorpe of the Rubettes: "The Beatles brought a fresh approach to everything they did. Nobody had played guitars like that before, nobody had used them in that orchestral way, nobody had turned the tapes backward, they revolutionised everything. The songs that everybody talks about, 'Yesterday' and the like, are the least of it. With anybody else, that would be everything there is. Nothing like the lyrics of 'Tomorrow Never Knows' had been written before. The whole approach to that track was straight out of John Lennon's head and George Martin was able to pick up on it and do what he did. It's a piece of art, it's a Picasso, it's like a Charlie Parker recording, I can't speak too highly of the man."

Barry Miles: "The line, 'Turn off your mind, relax and float downstream' is from Timothy Leary's book *The Psychedelic Experience,* which in turn was adapted from *Tibetan Book of the Dead* and. Leary was delighted. He thought it was the greatest thing that Lennon should quote him. He thought the Beatles were gods, a mutation into a new super-aware species. That's typical hyperbole from Tim."

John Foxx from Ultravox: "The track that blew me away was 'Tomorrow Never Knows'. I got the album when I was still in Chorley and I went to an art school party and we played it all night. We didn't think much of the other tracks: it was just that one that was so interesting. As soon as I heard it, I knew it contained almost everything that I would want to investigate for the rest of my life. It was fantastic and absolutely beautiful. It had a drum loop which was the precursor of a drum machine and a precursor of sampling as well. It had all those reverse sounds and nobody had done that before. It was intricately put together from tape and synchronised beautifully and there were random elements as well. I suspect that they had been listening to John Cage and those 60s avant-garde ideas and they put that into a pop record which is a phenomenal thing to do. I was enchanted by the whole idea of it and it sounded like music from another planet. It crystallised what the psychedelic bands like Pink Floyd were doing and it was all in one track."

Martyn Ware of Heaven 17: "In the 60s people started thinking about music in different ways and they got away from the concept of the traditional pop song. The idea of a soundscape or a sound experience that is not connected in a coherently structural way has never left us and is something that inspires me to do more interesting structures. The Beatles were early proponents in a very populist field. It is all very well having experimental acoustic types who do things that are purely abstract but to do things like this is remarkable. I liken it to soundtracks for films which don't exist."

'Tomorrow Never Knows' ends with seagulls and a hurdy-gurdy, pre-empting the sounds of *Sgt. Pepper*. ELO's 'Mr. Blue Sky' is inspired by 'Tomorrow Never Knows' as well as the 1996 No.1'Setting Sun' by Noel Gallagher with the Chemical Brothers.

Instead of touring, the Beatles involved themselves with individual projects. John appeared in the Richard Lester film, *How I Won the War,* which starred Michael Crawford and Roy Kinnear. He had his hair cut for the role and wore granny glasses, which he decided to keep. The film had a strong anti-war message, but the conspiracies over a cricket pitch were only going to mystify American audience. It did, however, lead to John Lennon as Gripweed saying, "Can I rub your ball, sir? It'd give me great pleasure."

Film producer, Denis O'Dell: "I went to see Brian Epstein as we were short of money for *How I Won the War* and I wondered if he would be interested in investing. He was really nice and said yes, and I said, 'How would it be if we got John to act in the picture?' He said, 'Why don't you ask him? He's only in the next room.' I told John that he would have to have his hair cut and he said,' Fine.' We made it in Spain and he was very nervous about it but I said, 'Richard will take care of it.' He was terribly homesick when he did it but we got Brian and Ringo to come out and see him and it worked out very well. He did a wonderful death scene."

Film critic Barry Norman: "I don't think that any of them were particularly good actors, although they got by okay. I remember going to interview John Lennon near Belsen when he was making *How I Won the War.* I thought he was impressive and if he had kept on, he might have developed into a very good actor. He was a good looking and attractive young man and he had everything you needed to be a movie star but it was far more lucrative to be a Beatle."

November 1966 – From Head to Toe/ Night Time – The Escorts (Columbia DB 8061)
Paul McCartney, producer
The individual Beatles, especially Paul McCartney, were happy to help their friends with their recordings. Paul worked on the Motown song, 'From Head to Toe' with the Liverpool band, the Escorts. Mike Gregory: "I was with the Escorts and we were working in a small studio in the Old Kent Road. Paddy Chambers had been in the NEMS stable as part of Paddy, Klaus and Gibson and he knew Paul quite well. He bumped into Paul and he asked him to help with our single and, much to our surprise, he said yes. He played tambourine on 'From Head to

Toe' and he supervised my bass sound. He was an outstanding bass player as he could make one note count for about twenty."

Tony Crane of the Merseys: "The Beatles loved 'Sorrow' and George Harrison said it was exactly the way that they would have done it themselves. John Lennon said, 'I've got a song for you lads.' It was 'I'll Be Back' off the LP *A Hard Day's Night*. We knew the song and he said, 'I've got an arrangement which will suit you. It's just like the way you did 'Sorrow'.' However, Lennon's mind was so incredible that he kept coming up with new ways of doing it. We were spoilt for choice and we didn't know which arrangement to take. Lennon wanted to produce it but our recording company said that there were difficulties in getting him to produce it in a different studio for a different label. We didn't do it and I'm sorry that it never happened."

December 1966 – The Beatles Fourth Christmas Record Flexidisc (Fan Club)
This is the best-known of the Beatles' Christmas records as it includes a new Lennon and McCartney song 'Everywhere It's Christmas', an African chant, a story about Podgy the Bear and Jasper, an impersonation of Harry Secombe and Paul's song, 'Please Don't Bring Your Banjo Back'.

December 1966 – A Collection of Beatles Oldies LP (Parlophone PMC 7009)
One new track, Bad Boy
Parlophone didn't issue a compilation album of singles until Christmas 1966 when *A Collection of Beatles Oldies* was released. Following a practice which became commonplace, the album included one new track, in this case an exhilarating revival of Larry Williams' 'Bad Boy'. This LP broke the run of Beatles chart-topping albums, peaking at No.7.

George Harrison had had a life-changing year. He had married Pattie Boyd, whom he met while making *A Hard Day's Night*, in January 1966, and he had spent some time in India and befriended Ravi Shankar. Barred from a club for not wearing a tie, George Harrison saw in the New Year at Lyons Corner House in Coventry Street.

CHAPTER 7
And Now My Life Has Changed (1967)

North Sea oil pumped ashore – Six Day War – Biafran War – Abortion legalised in UK – Pound devalued – Christian Barnard performs first heart transplant, the patient survives for 18 days – Concorde ready at last.

In January 1967 Paul McCartney demonstrated his versatility in two ways. He composed the score for a northern film drama, *The Family Way,* starring Hayley Mills, Hywel Bennett, John Mills and Wilfred Pickles. It was a good if traditional score, arranged by George Martin and incorporating a brass band.

In the same month, some electronic sounds recorded by Paul McCartney were played at the Carnival of Light at the Roundhouse in London. The results have never been released. Paul's friend, the author Barry Miles: "The notion of random sound and different ways of organising sound, particularly the idea of using the whole orchestra as one instrument, comes from John Cage. Paul recorded a random track two years before John did 'Revolution No.9'. It's more or less the same kind of stuff as 'No.9' but it is less structured. It is a lot of banging and shouting with a heavy echo."

February 1967, Mellow Yellow – Donovan (UK No.8, US No.2)
Paul McCartney, whisperer and reveller
February 1967, Penny Lane/ Strawberry Fields Forever (Parlophone R 5570, UK No.2, US No.1)
Hunter Davies: "My book *Here We Go Round the Mulberry Bush* was about to be filmed and I approached Paul to see if he would write some

music for it. He was busy with other projects but in conversation I suggested a serious, hardback biography of the boys. There had only been two lightweight paperbacks previously. He thought it was a good idea but he told me to clear it with Brian Epstein and helped me write a letter to him. When I went to see Brian, he played me the acetate of 'Penny Lane' and 'Strawberry Fields Forever'. The second track was a huge leap forward from anything they had done before. It convinced me that an official biography would be a worthwhile project."

When David Jacobs played 'Strawberry Fields Forever' to his panel on *Juke Box Jury*, they didn't know what to make of it and even doubted its hit potential. Jacobs himself thought the Beatles had made a mistake. It was part of a double-A side single with 'Penny Lane'. If the other A-side had been another experimental track, say 'Tomorrow Never Knows', how well would the single have fared?

George Martin: "'Strawberry Fields Forever' was the beginning of the *Pepper* era. We recorded it with 'Penny Lane' and 'When I'm Sixty-Four' at the same series of sessions just before the end of 1966 and we agreed to get back together after Christmas. We wanted 'Strawberry Fields Forever' and 'Penny Lane' to be part of the album but EMI wanted a single so we didn't include them on *Pepper*."

Bill Drummond of the KLF: "John Lennon might never have been interested in Yoko Ono if he hadn't been to art school, so being there might have been a defining influence in his life. Going to art school introduced him to a lot of things that he didn't know existed, a world outside of Jerry Lee Lewis and Gene Vincent. It opened his eyes to surrealism. For me, 'Strawberry Fields Forever' is the greatest record ever made and he wouldn't have made it if he hadn't gone to art school."

The song's inspiration was a Salvation Army home, Strawberry Field, close to where John had lived. Hughie Jones of the Spinners: "I don't think that John Lennon was really thinking about Strawberry Field when he put those words together. He was thinking about childhood and about freedom such as going into the woods, they were woods rather than fields actually. It was a great place for a little boy and he was thinking about that rather than making meaningful remarks about Salvation Army hostels or children's homes."

George Melly: "Strawberry Field was a reform home for girls, but John was attracted to the title because the idea of Strawberry Fields is a very trippy idea, glowing and glimmering in the sun. The Beatles' hallucinatory songs were unlike anything that had been done before, both as tunes and images, and I'm glad they're there."

Singer/ songwriter Ron Sexsmith: "As a kid, I loved' Strawberry Fields Forever'. It was like a crazy dream. It was like no other record at the time and it still sounds like no other record I've ever heard. I didn't know anything about drugs back then so I had no idea as to how they came up with a song like that. It is beautiful and a masterpiece."

Elizabeth Thomson, co-author of *The Lennon Companion*: "John Lennon supposedly knew at the age of five that he was brilliant and that he had a great writing gift. That business of saying, 'No one I think is in my tree' in 'Strawberry Fields Forever' is his way of saying that he knew he was better than everyone else."

George Martin: "I regard 'Strawberry Fields Forever' as a very great song. It was the beginning of the imaginative, some say psychedelic, way of writing. I prefer to think of it as being complete tone poem imagery and it's more like a modern Debussy. We did two different recordings of 'Strawberry Fields Forever'. They had different arrangements and were in different keys and tempi. John wasn't satisfied with either and he asked me to take the beginning of one and add it to the end of the other. I pointed out the difficulties but he just smiled and said, 'I'm sure you can fix it'. It was a terrible challenge but, with a bit of luck, I found that by reducing the speed of one of the recordings and increasing the other, the tempo change accounted for the intonation change of a half-tone. I put the two recordings together and what you hear today is two separate recordings edited together."

Drummer Dave Mattacks: "The first time I heard 'Strawberry Fields Forever' I thought, 'What a great tune, that's a great song, it's got the best of everything'. It's really interesting melodically and I like everything about it. It changes signatures, there are odd beats and bars here and there but you're not aware of it at the time, it's just a terrific tune with a great performance. Everybody plays tremendously well on it and the sound and the production are great. It's a landmark recording."

Jake Thackray: "The lyrical line of 'Strawberry Fields Forever' is very odd and compelling and so is the chord sequence. There are some bars of 5/4 time which throw you but which work completely."

Beth Nielsen Chapman: "The Beatles came along when I was in fifth grade. I remember being in a friend's house in Germany and hearing 'Penny Lane' and I was jumping on a bed and thinking that I had to own that. That was the first time that I heard music that I wanted to go and buy."

Ralph McTell: "There's a very English feel to 'Penny Lane' and to the *Sgt. Pepper* album which followed. I don't know Penny Lane in Liverpool but I know a Penny Lane in Croydon or wherever. I always imagined somewhere with a street market, lots of little shops and a community of people buzzing backwards and forwards. I thought it was very English and very optimistic."

George Melly: "'Penny Lane' was a Liverpool street that had always intrigued me as a kid and I had real image in my head. The Beatles treated it as a surrealist thing with the nurse selling poppies and the like. I believe that it caused considerable embarrassment to the local fish-shop because people kept going in and ordering 'fish and finger pie'. It was typical of the Beatles to throw that in. They knew that very few would know what they were on about." 'Finger pie' is teenage slang for fingering a female's genitals.

Jake Thackray: "I like the lyrics in 'Penny Lane'. I would love to have written those buggers myself. They're authentic, it's about a street that people know about, and there's a barber's shop and a fire brigade. It's a very, very English, northern song. I also like the vigour of that high, dashing trumpet. It's a stunning record."

Klaus Voormann recommended the Swedish director, Peter Goldman, to the Beatles for the making of promotional films for the single. Tony Bramwell organised the locations and the props: "Klaus Voormann had an idea about a big harp in the open air. It was impossible to make one quickly so we found an old tree in Sevenoaks and we smashed an old piano to pieces and put wires from it to the top of the tree. We strung Christmas balls around the top and it looked surreal. We filmed it in the park for two days and then came to Penny Lane. We got a policeman dressed as a fireman and filmed the barber's shop and the roundabout. The Beatles rode horses in the east end of London and it all cut together very nicely. It was the first time anyone had made a film without miming to the song. Because it was 32mm, we could use laboratory tricks to change the colour and light. It was ground-breaking, just like 'Bohemian Rhapsody' later on. They were the first psychedelic films."

While filming, John bought a poster for a circus in Rochdale in 1943 which led to the song, 'Being For The Benefit Of Mr. Kite'. The lyric is little more than a celebration of the poster, but it fitted perfectly into the psychedelic times.

Documentary filmmaker John Sheppard who made *The Stones in the Park*: "It's very difficult to look at the records that were No.1 during the first part of 1967 in England and sit them alongside the designation Summer of Love. There's 'I'm a Believer', 'Something Stupid', 'Puppet on a String', 'Silence is Golden' and 'Release Me', which committed the cardinal sin of preventing the Beatles getting to No.1 with 'Penny Lane' and 'Strawberry Fields Forever'."

Paul Gambaccini: "When I was living in America, I was constantly amazed at the records you've missed out on and also some of the records which were hits. Jerry Butler is the one who upsets me the most: he never had a hit in England. 'Penny Lane' and 'Strawberry Fields Forever' is the greatest single ever made and I wondered how on earth Engelbert Humperdinck could have kept the Beatles from No.1 but now I know what a sensation he was in England."

Don't expect any misgivings from Engelbert Humperdinck: "I don't feel bad about it at all and, indeed, I feel proud that I kept the Beatles from being No.1. To be in front of them in the charts was totally amazing."

There were some unlikely winners during the Beatle years. Engelbert for one, but the top selling record of 1965 was Ken Dodd's 'Tears' and the biggest-selling album of 1967 was not *Sgt. Pepper* but the soundtrack for *The Sound of Music*.

It has often been suggested that 'Penny Lane' and 'Strawberry Fields Forever' were going to be part of a larger project, an album called *Liverpool*, although I'm not sure where this originated as neither Lennon nor McCartney said so. Willy Russell: "The Beatles were too canny to write straightforward songs about Liverpool or the Cavern. When they do mention somewhere specific like Penny Lane, they transcend the place and it becomes much, much more than a little thoroughfare. They start with something specific and then move on to something gloriously general. Maybe they toyed with writing about the Star-Club or the Cavern but their instinct told them not to. Things like 'All I Want for Christmas Is a Beatle' or 'Cavern Stomp' are iffy novelty records. They would have kept away from that, but it may have found its expression in due course. Later, George Harrison did 'When We Was Fab', which was a lovely song."

There was talk of the Beatles making a new film, *Up Against It*, scripted by the controversial playwright Joe Orton. Music writer Elizabeth Thomson: "If you see the film *Prick Up Your Ears*, you will see

Brian Epstein telling Joe Orton that they can't make *Up Against It*, but it wasn't as straightforward as that. There was a lot of communication back and forth. Orton's diaries tell how he was approached to make the film and he was taken with Brian Epstein and Paul McCartney. *Up Against It* is a very amusing screenplay and I am sure it would have been a very entertaining film, but there would have been an outcry if it had been made. It would have endangered their nice, safe image although in retrospect there is nothing too outrageous in it. The Beatles all got into bed at once, but so did Morecambe and Wise."

During 1967, it was as though the Beatles were at a fancy dress party but not all their fellow musicians had a costume or wanted to be there. Jon Savage: "There was a split by the late-60s – did you become psychedelic, take acid and grow your hair or did you go into cabaret? Some of the bands had been together from the early 60s and they were exhausted. They didn't want to risk losing their audiences and they didn't want to make changes."

The Liverpool bands like Gerry and the Pacemakers and the Searchers felt out of place. Paul Du Noyer: "Most of the Liverpool bands were comprised of earthy, working class lads and not college boys like the southern groups. The southern groups moved into psychedelia as it was more intellectual and well away from the beer and football culture of the north."

The Hollies found themselves under criticism when they recorded 'King Midas in Reverse', although now it sounds as good as anything else they did. Frank Allen of the Searchers: "We were amazed when 'Strawberry Fields Forever' came out. There's no way we could have copied that in the Searchers. We didn't have that kind of originality and we didn't have the writing talent. The same applies to a lot of other bands, but that didn't stop some of them trying to copy the Beatles. The Searchers just knew how to sing nice songs and if we'd taken more care over that, our career would have been ten times more successful."

EMI record producer Walter Ridley: "The problem that I found insurmountable with the Swinging Blue Jeans was that they couldn't write their own hits. In that world, if you can write your own hits, you're there as of right. If you've got to take somebody else's writing, then the very good songs may be taken before they reach you. Elvis Presley had great writers queuing up to give him songs but we didn't have that depth of songwriting talent in this country. The Beatles had an enormous advantage. They weren't the best musicians in the world, they weren't the best singers in the world, they weren't the best performers in the world, but they were the best songwriters in the world. They could write songs that were way ahead of their time, marvellous writing."

June 1967, Sgt. Pepper's Lonely Hearts Club Band LP (Parlophone PMC 7027)
Produced by George Martin, 13 tracks – 39 minutes 43 seconds
Side 1: Sgt. Pepper's Lonely Hearts Club Band/ With a Little Help from My Friends/ Lucy in the Sky with Diamonds/ Getting Better/ Fixing a Hole/ She's Leaving Home/ Being For The Benefit Of Mr. Kite
Side 2: Within You, Without You/ When I'm Sixty-Four/ Lovely Rita/ Good Morning Good Morning/ Sgt. Pepper's Lonely Hearts Club Band (Reprise)/ A Day in the Life

In 1966 the Los Angeles band the Mothers of Invention, masterminded by Frank Zappa, released their double-album, the satirical and experimental *Freak Out!* The single, 'It Can't Happen Here', was greeted with hostility on BBC-TV's *Juke Box Jury* and its chairman David Jacobs said, "We certainly hope it can't happen here." It was clear to the Beatles, however, that Frank Zappa was an excellent musician who wrote great lyrics and had a strong sense of humour.

Barry Miles: "Just after they'd done 'Penny Lane', Paul McCartney told me that they were going to do their own *Freak Out!* It wouldn't be anything like *Freak Out!* but it would have a specific viewpoint. The new album was not going to be a set of tracks slapped together. *Freak Out!* has the overall theme of empowerment of youth and how brown shoes don't make it. The level of political comment in *Sgt. Pepper* is on about the same level as *Freak Out!* although done entirely differently."

Ron Mael of Sparks: "I always loved the Beatles and the ambition of *Sgt. Pepper* is something that every band should aspire to. We never try to write songs like the Beatles but the size and scope of that album is something that we try to do with every album. It is an inspiration and it is encouraging you to do something really important."

The Summer of Love was a spiritual quest for the young, a search incorporating mind-expanding drugs, highly colourful clothes and sexual freedom. The philosophy and lifestyle of Dr Timothy Leary and the availability of contraceptive pills were important contributory factors. These interests highlighted the generation gap. The media told of the happenings (and the Happenings) in New York and San

Francisco. Haight-Ashbury was full of runaway teenagers and tourists but it didn't last long as Dion sang in 'Sanctuary', "Well, I got to Haight, I was a little late". However, it could be argued that the Summer of Love left a dangerous legacy in that it encouraged subsequent generations to tune in and drop out.

If the engine room for the Summer of Love was in San Francisco, numerous groups - the Doors, Grateful Dead and Jefferson Airplane - provided the pistons. Although peace signs were everywhere, so too was conflict. The peaceniks were rebelling against the war in Vietnam and often moving to Canada to escape the draft. American teenagers were rebelling against their parents' values.

The record that both transcended and encapsulated the Summer of Love was English – the Beatles in their new identity as *Sgt. Pepper's Lonely Hearts Club Band.* There's no magic about the Sgt. Pepper name: it was simply "salt and pepper, please" being misheard as "Sgt. Pepper, please". The critic, Kenneth Tynan called the album "A decisive moment in the history of western civilisation." That's sounds pretentious and Tynan was probably using hyperbole to get noticed.

Released on 26 May 1967, the LP topped the album charts for 26 of the remaining 28 weeks of the year. Val Doonican: "I was so proud of my album *Val Doonican Rocks but Gently.* It was arranged by Ken Thorne, a lovely writer who had been involved with the Beatles' movies. We picked all these lovely, sentimental, late-night songs and I don't think I've enjoyed making an album as much as that one. Lovely. It went to No.1 on the album charts and it knocked *Sgt. Pepper* over. Astonishing really, isn't it?"

Adrian Barber, founder member of the Big Three, who was to produce Vanilla Fudge and the Allman Brothers, recalls in his own distinctive way: "I was jealous of the Beatles' success when it first happened and it was not until *Sgt. Pepper* that I appreciated them. It was so far ahead of what I was doing that it entranced me. Chris Huston of the Undertakers asked me to come over to his apartment and he took me into his bedroom, handed me a joint and left me on the bed. I thought I was hallucinating. I thought nobody else could be doing anything like that and only a few thousand people would really understand what they'd done. It was so perfect. It was right, right, right, right down to the three mice in the football helmet in the dirty brassière in the attic." (No, I don't understand that either, but then I've not been hallucinating.)

Beatles press officer Tony Barrow: "I am one of those people who, by and large, plays the earlier stuff, the middle 60s stuff up to *Sgt. Pepper*. It's almost like Old and New Testament with the dividing line at *Sgt. Pepper*. You've got one set of people who concentrate on the 'Before' music and one set on the 'After'. It may be personal memories in my case rather than the magnificence of the music. I associate particular Beatle tunes with things that were happening to us and I had much more contact with the Beatles between 1963 and 1966 than I did afterwards."

Hunter Davies: "I was with Paul one morning on Primrose Hill with his sheepdog Martha – it was the first day of Spring and he remarked how the weather was getting better. He started laughing and told me about when they were touring with Jimmy Nicol depping for Ringo. After each concert, they would ask Jimmy how it was going and he would say, 'It's getting better.' John took the piss out of him and it became the tour joke. As he walked, Paul worked out the first bars of 'Getting Better'. John came round to the house later and they worked on it in Paul's little studio. Then they went into Abbey Road the next day and finished the song."

Billy Kinsley of the Merseybeats "Tony Crane and I were at Abbey Road when they recorded 'Getting Better', some four or five months before it came out. Paul was playing electric piano, John and George guitars, and Ringo drums. We couldn't actually hear what Paul was singing although we were in the studio. They did several takes and consequently we knew every note of the song but none of the lyrics apart from the bit about 'I used to be cruel to my woman'. Before the album came out, we were singing that bit to everyone."

George Martin: "I like to experiment with voices and you can hear it clearly on 'When I'm Sixty-Four'. If you listen to it in stereo, you'll find that there's only an accompaniment on one of the tracks. This boomeranged on me as some foreign copies were pressed that only had this track on the record, which meant that Paul's voice wasn't there. It taught me a lesson and since then, I've put the voice in the centre."

The Beatles, or more specifically Paul McCartney, called the album, *Sgt. Pepper's Lonely Hearts Club Band*. The songs would be performed by this imaginary band and suitable costumes were created. The LP would play like a concert with an overture and a song by Billy Shears, followed by a song by somebody else, and so on, with a reprise of the title song, leading into 'A Day in the Life'.

The packaging for *Sgt. Pepper* was to be unlike that for any other album. It was designed by Peter Blake with his then wife, Jann Haworth. Peter Blake: "I suggested that they had just played a concert in the park. They were posing for a photograph and the crowd behind them was a crowd of fans who had been at the concert. Having decided on this, then, by making cut-outs, the fans could be anybody, dead or alive, real or fictitious. If we wanted Hansel and Gretel, I could paint them and they could be photographed and blown up. I asked the four Beatles for a list and I did one myself. Robert Fraser did a list and I can't remember whether Brian Epstein did one or not. The way that worked out was fascinating. John gave me a list and so did Paul. George suggested only Indian gurus, about six of them, and Ringo said, 'Whatever the others say is fine by me' and didn't suggest anyone. It's an insight into their characters. All kinds of people were suggested. Hitler was there; he is actually in the set-up, but he is covered by the Beatles themselves as we felt he was too controversial. The same applied to Jesus. There were only two of their contemporaries on the cover. Bob Dylan was suggested by John and I put on Dion because he is a great favourite of mine. Presley was left out on purpose because if you were taking the top symbols, he would obviously have to be there. I can't remember why he was excluded. Maybe they felt he wasn't making good records anymore. I can't think why Chuck Berry isn't on there. If I was doing it now, Chuck Berry would definitely be there, so maybe there was an embargo for some reason."

Mike Evans, author of *The Art of the Beatles*: "The cover was created in three dimensions. That whole tableau was created and all those pictures of their heroes or whoever were life-size blow-ups of photographs, stuck onto hardboard and arranged on long wooden poles so that it looked like people actually grouped there. When the picture was taken, whoever was knocking around the studio took souvenirs as nobody thought it had any great significance."

Peter Blake: "The original Madame Tussaud's waxworks of the Beatles were included which were rather old-fashioned. They had little, high-button jackets whereas the Beatles by this time were psychedelic and wearing daffodils. John came to the photographic session with a white silk scarf and a daffodil in his buttonhole and wearing all sorts of badges. They had moved on and the idea was to have this other band, the Beatles, looking at Sgt. Pepper's band. It was commenting that the record really wasn't made by the Beatles at all. The Beatles were just a part of the audience watching Sgt. Pepper."

The cover is extraordinary, perhaps even more so in comparison to the minimal CD packaging of today. There is so much detail in the cover that university theses have been written about it. There are the questions of selection, the various uses of colour and black-and-white, why certain portraits have been used, how the incidental material was determined, and so on. Peter Blake: "*Sgt. Pepper* broke so much ground, not particularly because of me. The Beatles were at their absolute peak and power and I was quite inventive. If we decided to do something, they could go to EMI and say, 'This is what we want to do'. If EMI said, 'No', then they wouldn't get the record. They were very powerful so it meant that we could break through lots of barriers. One thing was the words on the back: another was that it was going to be the first double-album. It ended up as only one record, but it was a double-sleeve. It was meant to be a double-album but the Beatles used 'Strawberry Fields Forever' and 'Penny Lane' for a single, and they didn't have enough to make two albums. I had already worked out the double pocket and that is when I created the sheet of cut-outs. My original idea was to have a little plastic bag full of presents, a sergeant's stripes, some badges and maybe some sweets and this is when EMI put their foot down and said that this was completely impractical. That was the only thing we didn't do so then I designed the insert."

What was the origin of the *Sgt. Pepper* sleeve? For some years, I thought it was Adrian Henri's painting *The Entry of Christ into Liverpool* (1964) but now I know that both are based in different ways on James Ensor's *The Entry of Christ into Brussels* (1889).

Liverpool artist Adrian Henri: "The Beatles were one of the first acts to print lyrics on an album cover. They popularised the idea of printing the lyrics which in turn gave them a totally different significance. It brought the lyrics into the foreground, and the idea of getting a real artist to do the cover was extraordinary. Nobody had thought of asking a painter before, and they did it with Peter Blake and then with Richard Hamilton for *The White Album*."

Peter Blake: "Someone at EMI said that we would have to get permission from all the people on the cover or their families. That in itself was very interesting because Mae West wrote back and said, 'What would I be doing in a Lonely Hearts Club?' The Beatles wrote her a personal letter, which they all signed, in which they said, 'It's not quite like that. We would love you to be there.' Then she agreed.

On the top row, I put in two of the Bowery Boys, but Leo Gorsey wanted a fee. EMI wouldn't pay a fee so he was taken out. You'll see that there's a gap at the top. Brian Epstein later thought, 'We could get rid of all these problems if we put it out in a brown paper envelope instead.'"

Scarcely a month goes by without some magazine or record cover paying homage to the *Sgt. Pepper* cover. Peter Blake: "There have been insulting parodies and there have been flattering parodies. To this day you'll see cardboard cut-outs with photographs which come from the *Sgt. Pepper* idea. Usually I'm flattered, but the one that the Mothers of Invention did on *We're Only In It for the Money* was spiteful. I have never liked Frank Zappa much."

Barry Miles: "Frank Zappa's sleeve wasn't an attack on the Beatles: it was supposed to be humorous. Zappa always said that the Beatles tried to stop it but I was there when McCartney said, 'Sure, go ahead.' McCartney did say that they needed EMI's permission and Zappa didn't understand that as they were the Beatles and they could do anything they wanted. The original Mothers album even had a cut-out where you could clip out a Zappa moustache."

Peter Blake: "There's a whole mythology around the *Sgt. Pepper* sleeve which is extraordinary. As far as I'm concerned, it's all by chance. If they were marijuana plants, it was a joke on me. As it was, the figures were set up at the back, and there was a small stage for the Beatles to stand on and in front of that, at an angle, was a flowerbed. That was subcontracted to a firm, so if there were marijuana plants, and I don't think there were, they brought them in."

There are so many unique features about *Sgt. Pepper*. One was to sequence the songs without bands on the vinyl or pauses between the tracks. The Beatles played around with the running order, so why did they end up putting 'Getting Better' and 'Fixing a Hole' together when they are virtually the same tune?

All this would have counted for little if the music on *Sgt. Pepper* had not been outstandingly original. George Martin: "It's very difficult for me to be impartial, but my favourite Beatles album is *Sgt. Pepper's Lonely Hearts Club*. I do think it is the best thing that they ever did. It was a producer's dream. I was able to do everything I've ever wanted to do and the boys were similarly anxious to make it far out for its time. At the end I wondered if we'd gone too far, if people would think it was pretentious, but fortunately they accepted it."

Rick Wakeman: "I liked the concept of *Sgt. Pepper*. The BBC did a preview, the first play of the whole album and I like millions of others sat glued to the radio. There wasn't much of a story but it was great music and I was gobsmacked. It was pushing the bounds of technology. It really showed you what George Martin could do and in a strange way, it made him the fifth Beatle."

Bob Brunning, a founder member of Fleetwood Mac and later a headmaster: "The Beatles were responsible for me failing my college course. The day that I had to sit my Art final coincided with the release of *Sgt. Pepper*. You could get *Sgt. Pepper* first thing in the morning and I thought it was utterly reasonable to miss my finals to buy *Sgt. Pepper*. I listened to it all day. I went to college the following day and my lecturers said, 'Why didn't you sit your finals yesterday?' I said, '*Sgt. Pepper* was released and I couldn't wait until two in the afternoon.' Very unsympathetically, they failed me and I never had the chance to take it again. I don't regret it: every second of that day was worthwhile."

Jimmy Webb: "*Sgt. Pepper* was only cut on a four-track recorder and it is a testament to George Martin's genius. The recording studio had its own capabilities and *Pet Sounds* was a multi-tracking *tour de force*. The studio became more than just an organ that soaked up and preserved a performance. George Martin and the Beatles were aware of the possibilities and so the studio came into its own. Now the studio is in control, but there was a magical time when there was a symbiosis between art and the recording studio that was very important."

Richard Digance: "George Martin recorded *Sgt. Pepper* on four tracks. Having made records myself, I would have thought that some of that *Sgt. Pepper* stuff would have been impossible on four tracks, but George did it by putting the guitars on one track and the vocals on another and bouncing them across. That was a very sophisticated technique for the early years, and he deserves so much credit for those albums, more than your average fan would ever know."

Alan Parsons: "I originally worked in the department responsible for exporting copies of master tapes to foreign countries and was lucky to be among the first to hear the Beatles' new product. Listening to *Pepper* made me want to get into this wonderful art form for myself. They had a remarkable knack of fooling us on first hearing when it looked like they had blown it, but after two or three plays, we would be totally transfixed. I can remember thinking that 'We Can Work It Out' was the end of their career and then realising it was a work of genius."

Record producer Stuart Colman: "*Sgt. Pepper* contains my favourite Beatle track which is 'Fixing a Hole'. It's beautiful, and mind images whisk across the speakers while I'm listening to it. It's got all sorts of colouring in there and the Beatles were magical about doing things like that. I've never paid much attention to the so-called drug references on *Sgt. Pepper*. I just enjoy it as a Beatles record and I'm sure that's how the Beatles meant it to be in the first place."

Documentary filmmaker John Sheppard: "Since the war, LSD had been deployed in a whole range of experiments by doctors. Sometimes it was used to disorientate prisoners, sometimes it was therapeutic. There were guinea pigs around who claimed to have had a profound experience. Up until the mid-60s, the role of drugs in England was confined to a group of people inhabiting the raffish fringes of London society. 1967 changed all that, and *Sgt. Pepper* gave it some public attention. As the comedian Robin Williams says, 'If you can remember the 60s, you weren't really there.'"

George Harrison commented in 1968, "We can jump around and try new things which others can't or won't. Like drugs. People doing ordinary jobs just couldn't give the time we did to looking into all that." I'd never appreciated that the Beatles were doing this as a public service. Thanks, fellers.

Ray Coleman: "There was a chameleon quality to John Lennon. He was an experimenter in every way. He experimented with drugs and he wanted to push his mind, his brain and his body to the limit. When he drank, he drank too much and he did everything to excess. Even his appearance. He kept fooling us all the time, particularly when you judge the music that came out of the different parts of his life. I found him fascinating."

Tony Thorpe of the Rubettes: "I still think that the Beatles are underrated because everybody talks about their massive fan following and their wonderful tunes but the Beatles changed everything. It was John Lennon's avant-garde mentality that was the main push and the fact that George Martin was able to pick up on it and complement it so perfectly. 'Tomorrow Never Knows', 'Strawberry Fields Forever' and 'Lucy in the Sky with Diamonds' were plucked out of thin air. There was nothing before that to give them even the slightest idea of what to do. It wasn't jazz, it wasn't straight music, it wasn't rock – it was nothing else but the Beatles. It was totally unique and completely original, and they were revolutionising lyrics and chord structures and the way the studio could be used. Flipping heck, what an achievement. They turned popular music into art."

George Martin: "The thought that 'Lucy in the Sky with Diamonds' deliberately stood for LSD is rubbish. John Lennon wasn't like that at all and people credit him with too much subtlety. He liked to shock people and if he'd really wanted to write about drugs, he would have done so, straight out. You'd never have been in any doubt as to what he was singing about."

Alistair Taylor, who worked for NEMS Enterprises: "'Lucy in the Sky with Diamonds' doesn't stand for LSD as I happened to be there when Julian brought that drawing back from school but if you listen to the song, he must have been out of his head when he wrote it."

On the other hand, around the same time, Jimi Hendrix recorded a song, 'The Stars that play with Laughing Sam's Dice'. Did Lennon and Hendrix both decide to put LSD into song titles? It's possible. My own theory is that the picture exists, yes, but John saw the potential of the L-S-D in its title.

Roger McGough of Scaffold: "I always thought that Procol Harum's lyrics were daft. I wrote one like theirs that starts 'You're as bored as butterscotch', and it goes on and on like that. I was at Paul McCartney's in St John's Wood, staying there with his brother, Mike. Mike told Paul that this was a good poem and Paul put music to it. Mike sang it on one of the albums. Lyrically, it's crap but it sounded great when Paul sang it."

George Melly: "There was a certain moment in the Beatles' development when they took LSD and it utterly changed their music and their imagery. Now, you can say that LSD was a very bad thing, and certainly it was for some people. There are some who 'blew their minds' and became casualties, but, treated as a help towards art, in the Beatles' case and in some other cases, it changed their visual approach to life. I only took LSD once, I didn't like it much, but I did hallucinate. Here were four creative figures who previously had to rely on the world as seen by everybody else. Okay, a joint blurs things a bit, but it doesn't do much. After LSD in which the wallpaper fills up with kissing mouths and sofas become hippopotamuses, a stream of consciousness was released which went into the songs. I would say that 'A Day in the Life' was their richest, drug-created invention. It's partially about drugs of course, but it's doomy, a bad trip, whereas 'Eleanor Rigby' is beautiful and cheerful and pretty. 'A Day in the Life' also emphasises the bad side of drugs, the despair and the doom that can come out of them, but it is a considerable work of art and it would not have been created without LSD. Whether art is justified by this way of living, I don't know. I'd give it the benefit of the doubt because, without it, we wouldn't have had their best song."

Because drug terminology was often adapted from standard speech, it was easy enough for songwriters to protest, "Of course it's not about drugs. We weren't thinking of that at all." However, Paul has said in interviews, though not at the time, that when they came up with the line, "I'd love to turn you on", they gave each other "a little look".

After hearing the *Sgt. Pepper* album, the Director of Sound Broadcasting, Frank Gillard, wrote to Sir Joseph Lockwood, the chairman of EMI: "I never thought the day would come when we would have to put a ban on an EMI record but sadly that is what has happened over this track. We have listened to it over and over again with great care, and we cannot avoid coming to the conclusion that the words 'I'd love to turn you on' followed by that mounting montage of sound, could have a rather sinister meaning."

He continued, "The recording may have been made in innocence and good faith, but we must take account of the interpretation that young people would inevitably put upon it. 'Turned on' is a phrase which can be used in many different circumstances, but it is currently much in vogue in the jargon of the drug-addicts. We do not feel that we can take the responsibility of appearing to favour or encourage these unfortunate habits, and that is why we shall not be playing the recording in any of our programmes on radio or television."

Evidently Frank Gillard was not aware that scores of EMI records had been banned over the years. John Peel soon found himself in trouble for violating the ban and playing 'A Day in the Life', but I suspect that he did it deliberately.

Music writer, Paul Du Noyer: "'A Day in the Life' is a good example of a pure John song with a pure Paul song in the middle. That is done to very good effect. They often wrote in fragments so they had bits lying around. Paul had this incomplete notion of describing his bus ride to school through Liverpool and it seemed to fit this idea of the dreamy 'Day in the Life'."

Beatles biographer, Mark Hertsgaard: "'A Day in the Life' has to be their single greatest masterpiece, showing the sensibilities of each man. John had a wonderful cosmic lyric about status, hierarchy and false gods with a warning about unhappiness if one goes chasing them. Paul's contribution brings it down to the level of the common man and makes it more human. The orchestral crescendo has the world spinning out of control and it is a wonderful mixture."

George Martin: "After the strings at the end of 'A Day in the Life', we added a special dog whistle which is an 18 kilocycle note that you won't be able to hear. We thought it would be nice to include something especially for dogs. We also wanted some noise at the end so that people would wonder what the hell it was. It didn't mean anything but people found that by playing the damn thing backwards, they could make out a four letter word. I was amazed when I was first told about it but Paul tried it out and, sure enough, it was there." If you didn't have an auto-return, the final sounds would play on and on for hours.

The range and depth of music on *Sgt. Pepper* was very impressive, but not all the songs were new. Paul McCartney had written his first version of 'When I'm Sixty-Four' in Liverpool and had once performed it during a power cut at the Cavern. The song answers the question, 'Will you love me tomorrow?' Comic actor, Bernard Cribbins: "George Martin rang me and said, 'I've got a song called 'When I'm Sixty-Four', would you like to have a go at it?' It's a very nice love song and if you ignore the tune, which is very good anyway, you'll find it is one of the loveliest poems ever written. My record wasn't very well received, but I still think we made a very good recording."

Kenny Ball: "I know that John Lennon never liked jazz, but I loved the Beatles' stuff. The way they worked out those harmonies was almost churchlike, wasn't it? It was a different style of harmony as well, 13 bars in a row instead of 16, so it made you think a little bit. 'When I'm Sixty-Four' intrigued me because it reminded me of an old jazz tune called 'Jazz Me Blues', the first two bars are more or less the same. I always felt that McCartney had a feeling for trad jazz. 'Honey Pie' was very much in that vein. We had a go at 'When I'm Sixty-Four', but we only got to No.48."

'When I'm Sixty-Four' is a picture of family life and so is the drama of 'She's Leaving Home', a poignant ballad inspired by a story in the *Daily Mirror*. It was arranged by Mike Leander as George Martin was busy with Cilla Black and McCartney was impatient. It's an intriguing song as McCartney is imaging the situation from both sides. No doubt helped by John saying, "Now this is what Mimi would think..."

A song about a female traffic warden, 'Lovely Rita', is pure fun, the evidence being that all four Beatles play comb and paper. Paul wrote the song after speaking to a female warden, Meta Davis, and she occasionally talks about it in the press.

Despite the many types of music, *Sgt. Pepper* works as a coherent whole. In order to preserve that entity, no singles were released from the album. This meant that some great songs were up for grabs, none more so than 'With a Little Help from My Friends', a UK No.1 for Joe Cocker. Joe Elliott of Def Leppard: "Joe Cocker's vocal on 'With a Little Help from My Friends' is mind-blowing and I prefer it to the Beatles' version. They had so much passion in their performances and their songwriting ability was second to none. It is the ultimate blueprint. We sound nothing like the Beatles at all, but the structure of their songs is a huge influence on all our work."

Joe Brown: "The worst thing I ever did was to record cover jobs because that's when my recording career started to go down the drain. I should have stuck to country-based things like 'A Picture of You' and music hall songs like 'I'm Henry the Eighth, I Am', because all that was peculiar to Joe Brown. I knew when I did 'With a Little Help from My Friends' that I shouldn't do it, but you get talked into things and it was a good record and a great song. I preferred Ringo's version to mine because Ringo had a lovely, out-of-tune, soulful voice which was great. It sounded like he needed friends, which was what the song was all about. The Beatles were very clever like that."

Whilst the Beatles were making *Sgt. Pepper*, Hunter Davies was researching his official biography of the band. "When I saw the Beatles, I would tell them what I had been doing. They were very interested when I said, 'I've been to Hamburg and seen Astrid,' but they fell silent when I said, 'I've been to Liverpool to see Pete Best.' I said, 'He's slicing bread for £18 a week,' and they changed the subject. A few weeks later I was in John's house, and John brought up the topic of Pete saying, 'We were bastards. We were scared, we were so mean, we didn't tell him face-to-face that we didn't want him any more. We let Brian do the dirty work and we were ashamed, so John was ashamed of himself."

The biography, *The Beatles,* is important for several different reasons, not least because Hunter Davies watched John and Paul writing. "I was around Abbey Road during those 3 months when they were doing *Sgt. Pepper* and I would go around to Paul's house at two in the afternoon, have a walk with him and Martha or whatever around Primrose Hill, and come back and muck around. We would have tea and then John would arrive. Then they'd go into Paul's little eyrie at the top of the house and they would play tunes to each other and because it was the *Sgt. Pepper* days they'd work on something for that evening. I would see the beginning and the middle, and now and again, the whole of a song. I watched it happening and then in the evening I'd go to Abbey Road and see it being recorded. I wish I'd taken better notes and I wish I could have tape recorded my interviews. I don't like tape recording; it doubles your effort, doubles your time so I never did it. I couldn't really use a tape recorder in Abbey Road anyway as it would have been an interference. It might also have been an intrusion in their homes when they were talking to each other. Instead, I'd get out my little notebook and it's the same kind of notebook that I'm using all these years later. If it was a group thing, say like the shoot for the *Sgt. Pepper* photograph, I would rush straight home and write down at my typewriter everything I remembered happening from that evening."

The second side of the album opened with George Harrison's 'Within You, Without You', which featured George with Indian musicians. Victor Spinetti: "I said to George Harrison, 'I can't get it together with Eastern music', and he said, 'Vic, don't listen to it. Let it happen to you. Western music is all maths, but Eastern music is the flow and you can jump in and out whenever you want.'"

July 1967, All You Need Is Love/ Baby, You're A Rich Man (Parlophone R 5620, UK No.1, US No.1)
'All You Need is Love', a Beatles' single linked specifically to the Summer of Love, was seen by an estimated 400 million viewers when they performed it live on the TV programme, *Our World* on 25 June 1967, broadcast worldwide by satellite.

Andy Babiuk, author of *Beatles Gear*: "It was the psychedelic era. They said, 'We'll have a mural on the house, we'll have the car decorated and we'll have the guitars painted.' George's Stratocaster was the most distinctive of them. Paul painted his Rickenbacker bass. John commissioned The Fool to do something and Ringo put something on his drumhead. They did that for 'All You Need Is Love', but John didn't use his guitar. You can see it at his feet. He was the only one performing live: the vocal was live but everyone else was playing to a track."

Marc Bolan: "Repetition comes into my songs a lot because my lyrics are so obscure that they need to be hammered home. You need to hear them eight or nine times before they make sense. I don't see anything wrong with that. Some artists repeat the simplest lyrics about forty times over. Look at 'All You Need Is Love'."

Barry Miles: "John knew that he had to keep the song really simple as most of the viewers wouldn't have English as their first language or understand much at all. It wasn't really thought of as a single, more for the TV show, and it was very effective, though these days it looks corny. People were walking around the studio carrying signs that said, 'Love' in all these different languages. It was an important message for its time."

Victor Spinetti and, in case you're wondering, he is talking to me: "If you love the Beatles and their music, you have a great burden to carry, but it is a joyous burden as you have to live up to that. There are no songs of hate there, no songs of revenge, no songs of kill the faggot, kill the Jew, none of that. It is an avalanche of poetry and melody. Listen, my darling, if anyone tells you to listen to a record which says 'Kill this' or 'Murder that', tell them to fuck off. They burned John's records because they said he was more popular than Jesus, but they should have burned all the others. We should all be lovers and I said to John, 'What's your best lyric?' and he said, 'That's easy, Vic, 'All You Need Is Love'."

Songwriter and arranger Les Reed: "In general, the public want the 4/4 beat and you don't generally stick in a 5/4. Burt Bacharach, who was a trained musician, would stick one in without even thinking about it, and the Beatles did it in 'All You Need Is Love' because it felt right. That's what matters. It doesn't matter how many beats you have in a bar: if it feels right, then why not?"

John Lennon's friend Pete Shotton: "Paul would have been very happy being a Beatle all his life, but John thought that there was more to life than that. He had a lot of time on his hands. If he could write a song in 10 minutes, what would he do for the rest of the day? He jumped from reading *Treasure Island* to reading Marx and Nietzsche. He was forming political opinions all the time and I remember him saying, 'Between capitalism and communism, I think communism is the better way.' He was certainly one for having opinions that were cast in stone and 3 weeks later, he was saying the complete opposite. I couldn't keep up with him."

Tony Palmer: "We always think that the music of our youth is a golden age, but there is no doubt in my mind that the short period from 1966 to 1972 was a phenomenal moment in popular music history. I made a film some years later with Aaron Copland, and he said, 'In a 100 years' time, if people want to know what it was like to be alive and well and living in the 1960s either in western Europe or America, they are not going to listen to my music. They are going to listen to the Beatles because that tells you what the time was like.' The difference between then and now is this – we have Bono and Sting parading around the rain forests and saving the planet, but you don't hear it in their music. In the 60s you absolutely heard it in the music. They used music in order to try and change the world."

The B-side of 'All You Need Is Love', 'Baby, You're A Rich Man', is about money not being everything. It is surrealistic and yet commercial but it is more highly rated now than it was at the time. Bill Nelson from Be Bop Deluxe: "I loved jazz guitar and I looked down a bit on the earlier Beatles stuff and then, when they did *Rubber Soul* and *Revolver* and became more experimental, they got my attention. Now I love the early stuff as well as I can see the value of it. I was a teenage jazz snob. I liked George Harrison as he was a big fan of Chet Atkins and he played a Gretsch Chet Atkins guitar which I lusted after when I had cheap guitars. The production was so inspiring. My all-time favourite is 'Baby, You're A Rich Man'. I just love the vibe of it."

Klaus Voormann recalled his final meeting with George Harrison: "That last day I met him, he had had a video of himself when he went to the dentist to have a tooth out and he was singing, 'How does it feel to be one of the beautiful people?'"

August 1967, We Love You – The Rolling Stones (Decca F 12654, UK No.8)
John Lennon and Paul McCartney, backing vocals
To support the protest at the arrest of two of the Rolling Stones on drug offences, John and Paul added backing vocals to their single, 'We Love You'. It taps into the same groove as 'All You Need Is Love' but is nowhere near as effective. Still, context is everything. Shortly after 'All You Need Is Love' was released, I saw Scaffold with their comic show about P.C. Plod. They ended the show with 'All You Need Is Plod'.

As 1967 progressed, George Harrison appeared to be leading the Beatles as they became involved with Indian religion and mysticism.

They were intrigued by transcendental meditation (TM) as promoted by Maharishi Mahesh Yogi. The average pop-picker was mystified, and the Beatles were in danger of leaving their audience behind as well as Brian Epstein and George Martin.

George Melly: "I'm bored very quickly by Indian music on account of what appears to be its monotony. I know that it isn't monotonous. I know that if I understood it, I would find it marvellous. The thing about drugs is that they make everything less boring and more significant, so that the Beatles were able to listen to Indian music for hours at a time without ever looking at their watches and it seeped into their own music. It went with the incense and the bells and the pot and the LSD and the kaftans, all the 60s images which now seem extremely tiresome and dated, but, in the case of the Beatles, their genius was strong enough to give continuous validity to their music of the period."

Donovan: "When we were experimenting, we weren't taking drugs to get high, but to explore inner worlds, which would lead to serious meditation. Drugs became a problem, but not for us, but because the world thought that we were promoting it. Before we discovered that meditation was the safe way, we were trying these extraordinary ways of entering the inner world. That was the great discovery in the 60s. By the way, LSD was legal until 1966. I don't call them drugs: I call them holy plants. We didn't write songs on drugs, but what we explored in the inner world, we brought to our work afterwards."

Barry Miles: "I never liked the Mahirishi although I never met him. Allen Ginsburg said he had been criticised in India for charging for his teachings and for his connections with right-wing politicians. The main criticism was that he had commercialised the business. I spoke to Lennon about this and he said, 'What's wrong with being commercial? We're the most commercial band on earth.' There's no arguing with that. I said, 'But he takes a tithe off people's earnings', and he said, 'No bastard's going to get a golden castle out of me.'"

Quite improbably, Bangor in North Wales became the most fashionable place in the world as the Beatles and their entourage headed there – by train! – to study with Maharishi. Marianne Faithfull: "It was strange to go Bangor and I can't really figure out why I was there. I wanted to go and I felt that it was some sort of spiritual quest. I'm very glad I went but it was incredibly sad because Brian Epstein died and so it was very intense. I didn't have a great connection with the Maharishi although I think he was a very good man and did good work. Mediation is not really for me although I have used it occasionally."

Donovan: "I was in America and I saw on the news that the Beatles had gone to meet an Indian teacher called Maharishi in Bangor, and that intrigued me. Some friends in California told me that he was giving a lecture in a school hall so I went there. There was something good about him, and I got initiated in the lower flats of Beverly Hills, on the flatlands there, and I found that meditation was incredible. It is amazing to go within yourself and drop down your heart rate and your physical functions to a very calm level: you gain a lot of power from that. I have thanked Maharishi for that ever since. Maharishi said, 'Come to India,' and I said, 'I'd love to.' The aide said, 'There is someone else to see you,' and he said, 'Who is it?' The aide said, 'The Grateful Dead.' He laughed and said, 'They should not call themselves The Grateful Dead. They should call themselves The Grateful Living.' I liked this man: he was a joker, he was funny."

Brian Epstein was found dead in his bed over the bank holiday weekend in August 1967 and no-one can say with certainty why he died. At the time, the Beatles were seeking inner peace in Bangor with the Maharishi. The Beatles were encouraged by the Maharishi to have nice thoughts about Brian, and John's comments to the press seemed out of place, rather like Paul's "It's a drag" after John's assassination in 1980.

Clive Epstein: "Brian was not distressed but he was sorry that the touring days were over. He felt that he couldn't make the same contributions to the Beatles' everyday life as he had done. Obviously there were going to be new singles and new albums but that didn't absorb as much of Brian's time as touring. Also, many of NEMS Enterprises' other bands were not featuring as frequently in the charts. He was a little uncertain about his own career so that is why he devoted more time to the Saville Theatre and the possibility of producing films."

Billy J. Kramer: "Brian Epstein saw my future in films. He wanted me to go to RADA for a year. I thought it was funny because he used to say, 'Billy, you'll never get anywhere if you speak as badly as that' and I would reply, 'Brian, if people won't accept me for what I am, that's it.' He was annoyed when I put on weight but when I lost it, he came to see me at the Shakespeare in Liverpool and he said, 'It's water under the bridge now. I can see you're working hard and I'm going to put you back on top again.' On the Saturday he left me a letter at the stage door which said, 'I'm not coming tonight because my father died recently and I don't like leaving my mother, but I shall not forget what I said to you.' I finished at the Shakespeare and went to Stockton-on-Tees. I got shaved and had a bath and got ready for the show when I saw on TV that Brian had died. It was a very sad loss to the business because he was a very thoughtful man. We had our differences but he always remembered my birthday and sent Christmas cards to my parents. After my mother died, he went round and took my father out and made sure he was all right. I'm very grateful for that."

Brian O'Hara from the Fourmost: "Brian Epstein was a shy, sensitive man and we liked him very much. The Beatles took the mickey out of him all the time and they knew he was the sort of man who could be hurt by one word. We didn't see him very much in the months before he died because he became more and more involved with making Cilla Black a TV star. He wanted us to record 'Simon Smith and his Amazing Dancing Bear' and we turned it down because it was unlike anything that had ever appeared in the charts."

Tony Barrow: "Brian Epstein's death was a tremendous shock to me and yet, at the same time, it wasn't. If someone had said to me, 'How long do you think Brian Epstein is going to last?', I would have said, 'Well, honestly, I think he will be dead within the next 5 years at the rate he's working.' Some people say that he took his own life, but I have never subscribed to that theory. They say that he was depressed because the Beatles had stopped touring and he had less to occupy his mind. On the contrary, I would say that he regarded it as a new challenge, to pursue new directions with them as a non-touring act and I can't imagine him wanting to do away with himself. Like anybody else in the business, he lived on his nerves and he had a lot of things going for him: several of his artists were highly successful, his personal life was okay, and I don't think he was depressed. On the contrary, he was very positive about things and looking forward to a good future with his artists."

Yankel Feather: "Brian would come into the club and have a double brandy and then he would have another double brandy and then he would take sleeping pills. People who take sleeping pills are going to make mistakes, I've done it myself. You think, 'Have I taken that one?', and you take another. I am sure it was an accident."

Alistair Taylor: "Brian was not depressed. The last time I spoke to him, he was full of plans for a tour by the Four Tops and I was not concerned about his welfare. I was called to his house when his secretary thought something was up and I saw him lying in the bedroom. He used to take pills and I believe his overdose was a terrible accident. I will never accept that he committed suicide. The inquest came up with 'accidental death' and that'll do for me. If he had planned to commit suicide, why was he planning for the Four Tops' tour, why was he working through correspondence in his bedroom, and, most importantly, how could he do that to his mother? Brian was too considerate for that."

Johnny Rogan: "There are so many functions that a manager has to perform and it comes down to personality in the end. Many of the desired qualities for a manager are mutually exclusive. There is no blueprint. Some managers are indulgent and treat their artists like children. Others have them running around, and both are good managers. A good manager will be getting success for the artist and doing it in whatever styles that suits their personalities the best. You can be a sugar daddy manager but if you are naturally aggressive like Don Arden, you are an autocrat and you can still make lots of money. Expansionism was the name of the game for both Larry Parnes and Brian Epstein. Brian has been criticised for one thing, and one thing only - people say he should have made more money for the Beatles. Integrity was his watchword. He didn't bother with tax avoidance schemes, which was a good thing."

Music writer Paul Trynka: "How can anyone criticise Brian Epstein? Look at his rivals. Mike Jeffrey managed the Animals, and their money disappeared in the Cayman Islands. Andrew Loog Oldham signed a deal with Allen Klein that even now he does not fully understand and the Rolling Stones' money disappeared. Look at Colonel Parker and what happened to Elvis' money, so yes, Brian Epstein was not aware of the kind of money that could be made from merchandising but nobody was, and he still got a slice of the action. There are managers who came later and cut better deals than Epstein but Epstein was the first rock band manager and he was vital to the band. It is easy with the hindsight to criticise him but he did a great job and it wouldn't have worked without him."

Tony Barrow: "I would question the comments about the Beatles being lost without Brian as prior to his death, they had decided to form Apple and to manage themselves. Brian would be pushed into the background, remaining as a friend. It is wrong to say that they had lost him at a critical time."

John Lennon's close friend Pete Shotton holds a similar view: "I was involved with Apple in 1967 and 1968. The Beatles had finished touring by then and I was friendly with all four of them. They were looking to start Apple. They had a lot of money that they either had to pay in tax or put in a new venture. They thought Apple would be fun, fun, fun. They were splitting away from Brian Epstein at the time. This is an important point that has been missed over the years – they were setting up Apple and not involving Brian Epstein. He was losing his babies, they were not touring, and they didn't need him in the recording studio. He was surplus to requirements. Brian was a bit of a suit although they loved him and Apple was going to be a hippie heaven."

September 1967, Smiley Smile – The Beach Boys (Brother ST 9001)
Paul McCartney, munching on vegetables in 'Vegetables'.
Well, it could be anyone. Possibly the most ridiculous guest appearance ever on record.

Scott Bennett from Brian Wilson's band: "The Beatles are my bread and butter, the template from which all else stems. They were only a few American groups that penetrated at the time. *Pet Sounds* topped the album charts in Britain but it was a weak seller in America. Smart people were telling Brian Wilson that he was brilliant but even his record label and the rest of his band didn't dig him. The Beatles were kicking his ass all over the charts and he must have felt like throwing in the towel, but he made *Smile*, which was a really challenging record. His version of psychedelia was the Ringling Brothers meets Aaron Copland. It was like he and Van Dyke Parks were living in the 1860s not the 1960s."

October 1967, Catcall – Chris Barber Band
Paul McCartney, organ, catcalls, producer
Jazz band leader Chris Barber: "I said to Paul, 'You've got these tunes. Have you got one that you haven't used or do you write instrumentals?' He had 'Catcall' and our record was like one of their in-jokes, like the end of 'All You Need Is Love', because he said, 'The idea is that the band is playing this tune and about three-quarters of the way through, someone on the talkback says, 'No, it's rotten. Play it some other way.' We do that and then an audience starts cheering and it fades out, so what the record-buyers have bought is a rejected take. His whole idea was a gag based around this nice little tune. Brian Auger played the

right-hand side of the organ, and Paul played the left and gave a loud yell. You can hear Paul's voice when the band starts playing at the right tempo and everyone cheers. Vic Briggs, who was a guitarist with the Animals, is on it while Viv Prince, the drummer with the Pretty Things, drops a cymbal and makes general noises and yells."

November 1967, Hello Goodbye/ I Am the Walrus (Parlophone R 5655, UK No.1, US No.1)
Alistair Taylor: "Paul sat me at his old, hand-carved harmonium. He told me to hit any note on the keyboard and he'd do the same. Whenever he said a word, I was to say the opposite, and from all this he would compose a melody. The words were things like 'black, white' and 'hello, goodbye'. I can't remember what Paul's tune was but a short while later he arrived at the office with a demo of the latest single: 'Hello Goodbye'."

The arrangement of 'Hello Goodbye' with its feeling of a carnival ride is better than the song. It is a song of contradictions, which you also get in 'All You Need Is Love'. The record has a great fadeout, anticipating 'Hey Jude'.

Rick Wakeman: "'I Am the Walrus' is absolutely stunning and illustrates the remarkable empathy between George Martin and the Beatles. He was another ace in the pack and an important catalyst. The Beatles had no formal musical training, but they knew what they wanted and they were able to convey those ideas to someone who could translate them: George Martin. I experienced the same thing with Jon Anderson in Yes. He has had no formal training but he knows what he wants to do."

Pete Shotton: "John was on the piano and writing 'I Am the Walrus' and he said to me, 'What was that silly song we used to sing about yellow matter custard?' I said it was a horrible poem:
'Yellow matter custard, green slop pie,
All mixed together with a dead dog's eye,
Slap it on a butty ten foot thick,
And then wash it down with a cup of cold sick.'
He wrote it down and said to me, 'Let the fuckers work that one out.'"

Documentary film-maker Tony Palmer: "I did once have a long conversation with John about 'I Am the Walrus'. He admitted that he hadn't a clue as to what it was about but the words and the melody flowed and he felt it was right at the time. That is a sufficient explanation."

Pete Shotton: "John used to receive sacks of mail but he wouldn't read it. He would have a lucky dip from time-to-time and he picked one out from a kid at Quarry Bank. He wrote to say that the English teacher was playing their records and asking the kids to analyse them. We cracked up laughing. We rebelled at school and got suspended for a while and now they were proud of him."

Rick Wakeman: "I don't think that there is a musician around who doesn't appreciate Lennon and McCartney if they are really being honest as they changed the face of music. You can't help but like them for so many reasons. My favourite period is around *Sgt. Pepper* and my favourite track of all time is 'I Am the Walrus'. That is a work of art. Technically, it was remarkable, especially when you consider the limited technology that was available"

Eric Burdon from the Animals: "There was a wild party one night and John Lennon said to me, 'Go for it, Eggman', so I don't know if that is a reference to me or not. I do remember taking that single to San Francisco and going to the house where the Grateful Dead lived and putting in on their superb hi-fi system which had been built by some top engineers. I played it over and over and our minds were blown. The Grateful Dead were the cutting edge of San Francisco's radicalism and here they were listening to a Beatles cut and saying, 'This is so psychedelic, where did that come from?"

And why was Eric Burdon called the Eggman? "Use your imagination."

This is one of the few times when John Lennon's surrealism is put into the Beatles' songs. Possibly the Eggman is not Eric Burdon, but one of Lewis Carroll's characters, Humpty Dumpty. In Lewis Carroll, the Walrus mystifies his charges with word games, hence John Lennon admitting to be the Walrus. Lennon did say that it could have been "I am the pudding basin", but it couldn't: he knew what he was doing.

Paul Du Noyer: "John liked to stay close to his roots which were in basic 50s rock'n'roll and above all, very powerful and very simple music. The only time he strayed from that was during the psychedelic era, around the time of 'I Am the Walrus', when everything became multi-layered and more complex. It became more abstract but that was a phase as he returned to very basic rock'n'roll. John felt that as long as he didn't stray too far from that music that he loved he wouldn't go far wrong."

'I Am the Walrus' includes a reference to letting your knickers down. Tom Sloan, the Head of BBC Light Entertainment, wrote to his managers: "In the Beatles film so far uncompleted, they sing a number called 'I Am the Walrus'. A disc has now been issued. The lyrics contain a very offensive passage and after talking to Anna Instone, we have both agreed not to play it on radio or television. Although not officially banned, it will not be heard on *Top of the Pops* or *Juke Box Jury*. I should be grateful if you would ensure that any other possible outlets are similarly blocked off."

December 1967, Magical Mystery Tour EP (Parlophone MMT 1, UK No.2 on singles chart)
Magical Mystery Tour/ Your Mother Should Know/ I Am the Walrus / The Fool on the Hill/ Flying/ Blue Jay Way
Paul McCartney biographer, Chris Salewicz: "Paul's father was a disciplinarian who believed in the work ethic in that traditional, particularly northern, way, and he passed that down to Paul. What do you do when something goes wrong? You work, you find something else to do. That's what Paul does: he just gets on with it. When Brian Epstein died, he set up *Magical Mystery Tour* and when the Beatles split up, he formed another group."

If Brian Epstein had still been alive, he might have persuaded them against *Magical Mystery Tour*. Film producer Denis O'Dell: "The idea was that each of the Beatles would write and direct their own section on something they had loved for years, and then they would join it. I would write segues to cover the whole thing and it would last 90 minutes. I had been there two weeks and Paul suddenly said that he wanted to shoot it. We did it then as an ad lib thing which was a shame as the idea was great. It would have been fun and a new way of working and good for them at the time."

Tony Barrow: "There was an entourage following the coach. Half of Fleet Street took to their cars and drove down to the west country. Driving in the west country is now relatively easy, but then there were B-roads rather than motorways. At one point, we started a huge traffic jam because the coach could not turn; the lock wasn't sufficient for it to go over this tiny bridge. We were stuck, not able to go forwards or backwards, because of traffic on either side."

Chris Salewicz: "It was very much Paul's project and it was inspired by a visit he'd made to San Francisco the previous April when he'd seen Ken Kesey's Merry Pranksters, as celebrated in Tom Wolfe's book. You know, you're either on the bus or you're not. He'd been very inspired by that quasi-comic adventure."

Tony Barrow: "Ivor Cutler was on the *Magical Mystery Tour*. I had discovered him before a lot of Englishmen because I had known him in my pre-Beatle, Decca days. I'd been involved in writing sleeve notes for his records and classics like 'Gruts for Tea' were well-known to me. I was delighted when I heard that he was going to be involved in *Magical Mystery Tour* because I thought the amalgamation of his humour with John Lennon's would be quite something. As it was, an awful lot of stuff took place behind the scenes after the cameras had stopped rolling for the day. It was a great pity because they were hilarious together."

Ivor Cutler played Buster Bloodvessel in *Magical Mystery Tour*: "The Beatles asked me to come on their *Magical Mystery Tour* and as I thought it would be worth doing, I did it. They said that they knew my work and I understand, from what I have read in newspapers, that I was an influence on John Lennon. George Melly included me in an article in *The Times* on John Lennon's influences. It was sociologically very interesting to see how the Beatles related with the rest of the people on the coach. I was fascinated. They did it very, very well and I was impressed with their ability to be themselves. The critical response to *Magical Mystery Tour* didn't come as a complete surprise to me. It's not the way I would have made a film, but I'm not into making cheap jibes or anything like that."

Victor Spinetti: "*Magical Mystery Tour* was berated by the press, 'How dare these long haired louts think they can direct their own movie?', but that movie was years ahead of *Monty Python*. If they had gone to Cambridge, everybody would have said, 'Brilliant.' Because they were the Beatles, they were ready to be knocked. There is some wonderful stuff in that film and the songs are great. They were all directors. John sent me a note: 'Can you do that thing you did in *Oh! What a Lovely War*. P.S. Have you got any uppers?' They wanted me to be the courier but I couldn't as I was in a show in London."

Sam Spoons from the Bonzo Dog Band: "As *Magical Mystery Tour* is one of the least interesting things that the Beatles ever did, it's a pity to be associated with something that was a flop. It was not put together well but it wasn't much of an idea in the first place. The concept of filming a tour has been done a lot better since. I ended up being cut out of it as they didn't use the sequence I was in. I was sitting around at Christmas with a lot of my family and friends and I found it deeply embarrassing as (a) they didn't enjoy the show anyway and (b) they never saw me on the screen. You can forget it as far as I'm concerned."

Magical Mystery Tour was shown on BBC-TV over Christmas 1967 and was poorly received. Amateurish, poorly scripted, embarrassing, pointless – these were the favourable comments. Only *The Guardian* liked it. Critics were looking for a plot when there wasn't one. It was the first time that the Beatles had been widely criticised. However, the years have been kind to *Magical, Mystery Tour* and it has improved with the years.

Denis O'Dell: "Paul was the one who did the work on the film as the others dropped by the wayside and I put an editor on it who understood music, Roy Benson. I was talking with an American company to take it first, but Paul wanted to repay the BBC for their loyalty to the Beatles, but they didn't repay him by broadcasting it in black and white. I was 100 per cent against this, but it didn't matter much. I sold it around the colleges and universities in America and it made money, but it should have had a better life."

Noted rock writer and Paul McCartney biographer, Chris Salewicz: "I was very lucky in being able to see *Magical Mystery Tour* when it was shown on Boxing Day and again when it was repeated on New Year's Day in colour. Very few people had colour TV then, but I had a friend who worked for the BBC with a colour set, and it was a revelation. But, even when I saw it on Boxing Day, I liked it very much. We perceived things in black-and-white in those days and it fitted in completely. It went out at the wrong time as people wanted to relax after Christmas. However, it fitted in totally with the genre of the times, *Play for Today*, with that core of faintly wacky, bit pretentious, rather surrealistic, unstructured plays. I don't see what the problem is with *Magical Mystery Tour*. I think it's a good film and the review in *The Guardian* was highly favourable."

Tony Barrow: "I was sorry that when *Magical Mystery Tour* was on TV, it was slammed and slated by critics from every quarter. They were expecting a massive epic, which is the one thing it was never meant to be. *Magical Mystery Tour* was ahead of its time. It was a late 60s progression from the *Goon Show*, but people weren't ready for it, least of all the television critics. Although the music for *Magical Mystery Tour* did not contain the finest music that Lennon and McCartney ever wrote or that the Beatles ever played, it had some fabulous stuff in it. The title song wasn't too bad at all and you've got the marvellous extremes of 'Fool on the Hill' and 'I Am the Walrus'. I was in the back of the coach, so it's like a home movie for me. If it had been directed more professionally and with more thought, it could have been a *Not the Nine O'Clock News* or *Monty Python* or whatever."

Viv Stanshall, the lead singer of the Bonzo Dog Band: "We were involved in a scene with a load of strippers, so it was great, come on! I wanted to do some Chandleresque nonsense. At the time I was not particularly well read and I wish I had read Dashiell Hammett. I thought *Magical Mystery Tour* was a very good effort. It wasn't lit very well and had technical faults but it had 'I Am the Walrus' and some wonderful songs. They had a go with *Magical Mystery Tour* and that's all one can do."

Neil Innes from the Bonzos: "The launch party for *Magical Mystery Tour* was in fancy dress and Viv had a yellow plastic mac that he covered with plastic fried eggs to go as the Eggman, and Paul was very jealous. The Beach Boys were there and we all got up for a 20 minute version of 'Oh Carol' with George on bongos. Viv was moaning to John and Paul about how our producer would only give us 3 hours at a time in the studio, which led to Paul producing 'I'm the Urban Spaceman' for us."

Few, though, criticised the music for *Magical Mystery Tour*. The six-track, double EP included 'Fool on the Hill' and 'I Am the Walrus'. The EP set was listed on the singles chart and only kept from No.1 by the Beatles 'Hello Goodbye'. As the B-side of 'Hello Goodbye' was 'I Am the Walrus', the Beatles effectively had the same record at No.1 and No.2!

The packaging for the EP set was exceptional, but it was used differently in the US as additional, previously released tracks were added to make a new album. Tony Barrow: "*Magical Mystery Tour* was a pair of EP records in a sleeve which contained a cartoon story book based upon the show. It was something that I edited and worked on in collaboration with Paul. I remember him saying *Rupert Bear* style, which is the way we did it – that is, not balloons, but words under the pictures. While the film was being edited in one little room in Soho, Paul and I were in another room getting that book together and he spent more time on it than I ever imagined. It pleased me greatly because I thought that he would lose all interest after they'd finished filming because there were so many disasters on that. The whole production was an ad-lib affair and I thought they might all clear off to India and I would be left to put the book together and somebody else the film, but Paul saw it through to its conclusion."

Mark Lewisohn: "The song 'Magical Mystery Tour' itself has some nice sound effects. There is the sound of a car which goes from the left speaker to the right speaker, which was taped by one of the engineers from Abbey Road leaning over a bridge on the M1. All that 'Roll up, roll up' was speeded up from the tempo at which it was recorded."

George Melly: "'Your Mother Should Know' has the feel of the Grafton Rooms, which is a Liverpool dance-hall from my youth. It's brilliantly captured that feeling of dressing-up and ballroom dancing to Mrs Wilf Hamer. Those songs will last as long as people have a means of playing them."

Out of keeping with the rest of *Magical Mystery Tour*, 'The Fool on the Hill' is another classy ballad from Paul McCartney, usually taken as a romantic song but it's not necessarily so. Like 'Yesterday', you are not sure what is going on. Who is the "man with a thousand voices"?

The instrumental, 'Flying', credited to all four Beatles is a strong piece of film music including Duane Eddy-styled guitar, John on the Mellotron and some chanting by the band. George Harrison offered the swirling sounds of the mystical 'Blue Jay Way', which is about waiting for Derek Taylor to arrive at his rented house in Los Angeles one foggy night. The overall sound with the phased vocals is not far from the Incredible String Band.

Mike Heron of the Incredible String Band: "It's sometimes said that we influenced the Beatles, but I've met Paul McCartney and he never said, 'You influenced us', so I don't think we did. I loved anything that George Harrison did. It's very clever to write song that are commercially acceptable and yet have spiritual messages. I've tried to do that but he was a master at it."

December 1967, The Beatles Fifth Christmas Record Flexidisc (Fan Club)
Another new seasonal song, 'Christmas Time Is Here Again', recurs throughout the fan club single, later recorded in 1999 as a 4-minute song by Ringo Starr. Other song snatches are 'Get One of Those for Your Trousers' (a parody of the Wonderloaf ad) and 'Plenty of Jam Jars'. There is a Goons-styled sketch where they arrive at Broadcasting House, and John plays a Scottish poet on 'When Christmas Time Is O'er'. Victor Spinetti, Mal Evans and George Martin are also featured on this faux broadcast and it illustrates that the Beatles would have

made a better job of the satire on *The Who Sell-Out* (1968) than the Who did.

On the whole, we can see that Paul McCartney was buoyant and full of confidence during 1967 while John was depressed. John was capable of truly eccentric behaviour, undoubtedly fuelled by drugs, but not a million miles from his true personality. What if this story had been made public at the time? Pete Shotton: "We spent the whole night together and we had the house to ourselves as Cyn was in Italy with her mother and we had been hanging round the house. We used to take substances in the attic where his tapes and his toys were and he was circling his arms in front of me and he said, 'Something is happening. I am Jesus Christ, I am back again.' I said, 'Couldn't you be happy just being John Lennon?' He said, 'You must get the inner circle together tomorrow to make the announcement.' We fell asleep on the floor after discussing it. He believed it all right and I have my doubts if he ever stopped believing it. We fell asleep and the housekeeper came round at 8 a.m. and we made phone calls, and everyone converged at the Apple office. John sat behind the desk, the focal point of the office, and he said, 'I am Jesus Christ, I am back again.' They went, 'Oh yeah', and were blasé about it. I said, 'What shall we do now?', and someone suggested the pub. It was busy in the pub and John sat on a bench next to some feller. This bloke said, 'You're John Lennon and it's nice to meet you.' John said, 'Well, actually, I am Jesus Christ.' This feller said, without being phased at all, 'Well, I liked your last record anyway.' We had a beer and went back to the office and the next night he met Yoko and there was a very quick turnaround. He stayed with her that night and Jesus Christ got forgotten then."

Whatever we may think of the Beatles' eccentricities, 1967 is generally regarded as their creative peak. 'Penny Lane'/ 'Strawberry Fields Forever' is a contender for the greatest single ever made, while the wildly inventive *Sgt. Pepper* has been voted the best rock album on many polls. Even by today's rock critics.

CHAPTER 8

Don't Upset the Apple Cart (1968)

"I'm Backing Britain" campaign – Assassinations of Martin Luther King and Bobby Kennedy – Luxury liner, QE2, launched – Student protest in France – Invasion of Czechoslovakia – Two-tier postal service introduced.

In January 1968, there was a hive of activity, both personally and professionally around the Beatles. John Lennon was reunited, albeit rather spikily, with his father, Freddie. The Beatles' new business venture Apple opened for business at 95 Wigmore Street, close to Oxford Street in London. On paper at least, it seemed like a good idea...

There was a press reception to launch their signing, Grapefruit, the name coming from John Lennon and the title of a book of poems by Yoko Ono. A single on RCA, 'Dear Delilah', was released as there was no Apple label as yet. Although the Beatles were to offer Grapefruit encouragement, they did not play on their records. For their album, *Around Grapefruit* (1968), Lennon and McCartney produced 'Lullaby' to which strings were added for their album. Lennon suggested the horn arrangement on 'C'mon Marianne' and McCartney produced 'Yes'.

Starting in March 1968, Cilla Black's new BBC-TV series, *Cilla*, attracted audiences of 7 million. Cilla Black recalls, "Paul McCartney said to me, 'How are you going to open your TV show?' and I said, 'I don't know.' It was a problem because variety shows like *The Billy Cotton Band Show* had dirty big openings with big band arrangements. He said, 'I think you should have a friendly song, a more intimate thing, and I'll write you one.' Paul wrote 'Step Inside Love' and he had the idea of beginning the show with opening doors. When I first sang it live on the telly, I forgot the words because I was so nervous. I made up some words and thought it didn't matter because no one had heard the song before. Paul was watching the show and was upset because he thought the producers had been at me to change his lyrics."

March 1968, And the Sun Will Shine/ The Dog Presides – Paul Jones (Columbia DB 8379)
Paul McCartney, drums
Having left Manfred Mann, Paul Jones formed his own supergroup for a single – Jeff Beck (guitar), Paul Samwell-Smith (bass), Paul McCartney (drums) and himself on harmonica – which was produced by Peter Asher. "Paul McCartney wanted to play drums and Peter Asher told me he was good," says Paul Jones, "When we did 'The Dog Presides', Paul went 'Ay, ay, its one of those songs." Session men were known as Cromwell's army and the Ironsides in the song are session men working for the dog (EMI).

March 1968, Lady Madonna/ The Inner Light (Parlophone R 5675, UK No.1, US No.4)
The Beatles' first single of the year, 'Lady Madonna' was released in March and went to the top. It was a Paul McCartney song, inspired by Humphrey Lyttelton's 1956 hit, 'Bad Penny Blues'. This could have been a 'My Sweet Lord'/ 'He's So Fine' moment for McCartney.

Humphrey Lyttelton: "A number of idiots came up to me and said, 'They've borrowed the introduction to 'Bad Penny Blues'. What are you going to do?' They wanted me to sue them but I told them not to be so stupid. You can't copyright a rhythm and the rhythm was all they'd used. Anyway, we'd borrowed it from Dan Burley. It was absolutely stupid and I've never had any sympathy with the notion of 'Here are some guys, they're worth a fortune, let's try and get some of it by suing them'. In fact, I was very complimented. Although, none of the Beatles cared for traditional jazz, they all knew and liked 'Bad Penny Blues' because it was a bluesy, skiffley thing, rather than a trad exercise."

Note too the nursery rhyme reference to 'Three Blind Mice' in 'Lady Madonna'. Both that and 'I Am the Walrus' refer to nursery rhymes but it's not out of the ordinary as many popular songs contain such references. The B-side, George Harrison's 'The Inner Light' set the teachings of Tao Te Ching to music, and the backing had been recorded at the EMI studios in Bombay.

At the end of February 1968, the Beatles flew to India and headed for the Maharishi's base in Rishikesh. Ringo and Maureen only stayed a few days, Ringo likening the place to Butlin's (surely not).

Donovan: "Going to India was excellent for songwriting. I wrote 'Lord of the Reedy River' which was a dream that I had there. It was a magnificent experience to be in a tropical land on the banks of the Ganges under tropical stars with peacocks flying through the jungle, monkeys jumping on the table and taking your breakfast, and elephants roaming the forests. This was amazing. Nobody can go to India without being influenced."

Dory Previn: "When John went to India, somebody told me that he was sitting on a bank of the Ganges and he was playing 'Goodbye Charlie', which Pat Boone recorded. Someone said to him, 'Why are you singing that? Who wrote it?' and he said, 'It's by Dory and André Previn and it's my favourite film song.' I thought that was terrific."

By April 1968, all the Beatles were back in London. Donovan: "It cannot have done anyone any harm to have met Maharishi but there was some trouble in India. I had a great time but there was controversy between the Beatles and Maharishi. I wasn't involved and if the truth be known, it seemed like something extremely human happened and Maharishi crossed over the line between teacher and pupil. We found out that he was a man, not a god, and this was important. It destroyed the Beatles' faith in the man but it didn't destroy their faith in meditation."

Donovan is alluding to the ill feelings because the Maharishi apparently made overtures to Mia Farrow's sister, the Prudence of 'Dear Prudence'. "Why are you leaving?" asked the Maharishi. "If you're so bloody cosmic, you should know," replied John. Later, John said that the Beatles relied on him for the dirty work, but where was John when Pete Best was sacked?

Those who have had world acclaim often find no satisfaction in it, hence the considerable number of star names who have taken up religion or cults. The Beatles' mysticism was, however, unusual in that many fans - and musicians - followed them. This indicates the extent and the depth of their popularity.

May 1968, McGough and McGear LP (Parlophone PCS 7047)
Paul McCartney, producer
Paul McCartney produced this mixture of original poems and music for two of Scaffold: his brother, Mike, and Roger McGough. Jimi Hendrix

plays guitar on 'Ex-Art Student', the title indicative of the LP's market. McCartney himself plays bass and keyboards on occasion but he is not to the fore. He and Jane Asher supply backing vocals.

Paul McCartney had an Old English sheepdog, Martha, and he was to record 'Martha My Dear' for *The White Album*. Roger McGough of Scaffold: "I had a dog called Bran and Paul's dog, Martha, was his mother. I would regularly jog through Sefton Park with him and one day, two young girls jumped out at us. By then, I always carried a pen for autographs but it wasn't me they wanted. They had an ink pad and they pressed one of Bran's paws into their autograph books."

Apple was besieged with tapes from young hopefuls. I can vouch for this as I was to visit Apple with the folk singer, Timon, later Tymon Dogg, and I saw them piled up in Peter Asher's office. "Are you going to play them all?" I asked. "How can I?" he replied. As far as I know, no one was signed as a result of these tapes and Apple's most successful signing, Mary Hopkin, had won the ITV talent competition, *Opportunity Knocks*.

Rather cleverly, the fact that the Beatles didn't want to make a third film was turned into a creative opportunity. A crack team of animators were recruited for *Yellow Submarine*, a feature length film that was premièred in London in July 1968.

The Beatles showed little interest in the project, even though it was getting them out of a hole, and film producer Denis O'Dell, although not officially working on the project, spoke to them: "I did try and persuade the Beatles to take more interest in *Yellow Submarine*. I went to see some of the stuff that they were shooting as they wanted the Beatles for the dialogue. It was really good animation and the art work was terrific, so I told the Beatles that they must not have idiots doing their voices, they must do it themselves. They wouldn't hear of it. Eventually they saw some of it and appreciated the quality of it, so they added the end sequence. I think, in the end, that they would have liked to have done it and if they had, they would have invented so much stuff."

Roger McGough: "I was brought in as the 13th or 14th scriptwriter for *Yellow Submarine* and I followed the man who wrote *Love Story*, Erich Segal. Though it was about Liverpool, nobody from the city had been working on it and the script had been targeted at US audiences. The script was full of Americanisms – Ringo was making jokes about bagels and bar mitzvahs – and so my job was to make it more Liverpudlian. I also wrote some scenes like the Sea of Monsters. I was paid $1,000 which was the original agreed fee, and they wouldn't budge on not paying for extra work. Also, I didn't get a credit which is very annoying. I'd like to be there."

Film critic Ramsey Campbell: "*Yellow Submarine* is one of the great animated features. It was very innovative and it included techniques which were being shown for the first time in a film on commercial release as opposed to something from a film school. Without the peg of the Beatles, the film would never have been made, so we must be grateful for that."

Music publisher David Stark, then a teenage fan: "My friend and I gate-crashed the *Yellow Submarine* première at the London Pavilion. I told someone that Clive Epstein had invited us. They went to find him and I saw Dick James and I said, 'Is Clive here?' and he said, 'No, he is stuck in Liverpool and can't make it.' The cinema manager said, 'You know people, so you can stay.' We were standing at the back of the circle and suddenly all the Beatles came in and they sat in the front. There were a couple of seats behind Paul and John and so we sat there. Keith Richards was in the third seat along and he said, 'Mick and Marianne are in New York, so you're all right there, mate.' I had the Beatles in front of me for the whole of the film and it was incredible. I loved the film. It was well ahead of its time, but it was a psychedelic film with a psychedelic audience and so it went down very well. It got some mediocre reviews and didn't last too long at the local cinemas, but I thought it was great. I loved 'Hey Bulldog' and told Paul that it was a good one."

Yellow Submarine was undoubtedly a better film than *Magical Mystery Tour*, but the new songs were better in *Magical Mystery Tour*. The evidence that the songs were not highly rated is that the soundtrack album was not issued until some months later because EMI preferred to push *The White Album*. Who today would release an album after the film had been and gone?

Although the film contains many Beatle favourites, there were only four new songs on the soundtrack of *Yellow Submarine*. The cheerful 'All Together Now' is ostensibly a children's song but does contain the line, "Can I take my friends to bed?" The song had been recorded for *Sgt. Pepper* but not used.

And talk about having your own agenda, how about this? George Harrison's 'Only a Northern Song' is an early example of post-modernism. A disgruntled George is commenting on Lennon and

McCartney and his own relationship with Northern Songs. Now we would say it was a typical George Harrison rant and a peculiar thing to make public.

EMI historian Brian Southall: "'Only a Northern Song' was George's dig at Northern Songs having his publishing. John and Paul as co-owners and directors and shareholders in Northern Songs earned almost as much as George Harrison did from his songs and that caused resentment. George felt he had been conned and it is true that he wasn't given any independent advice. Seemingly, every lawyer and every accountant who advised the Beatles was retained by NEMS, which was Brian Epstein's management company."

On the fadeout of another George Harrison song, 'It's All Too Much', George Harrison sings, "With your long blonde hair and eyes of blue" twice, a clear nod to the Merseys' 'Sorrow' and also to Pattie Boyd, whom he'd recently married.

Although the Beatles hadn't been keen to contribute to *Yellow Submarine*, they did have their own projects.

John Lennon's play with Victor Spinetti, *In His Own Write*, was ready for the National Theatre. Victor Spinetti: "This young girl came into my dressing room and said that she had written a play based on John's book, *In His Own Write*. She had cut out the pages, put them in a different order and stuck them in an exercise book. I said, 'John has written fantasy and you have to put some reality in the middle of all that.' I went to see Kenneth Tynan at the National Theatre and he said that we must do it. I told John that the National wanted to do a play based on his books. He said, 'They must be mad.' I said, 'I can think of a way to do it. Let's do it together.' It was December 1966 and John said, 'Hey Vic let's go somewhere warm.' I thought he meant another room but we ended up in Africa."

Unlikely as it sounds, Spinetti and Lennon developed a workable script. Victor Spinetti: "We went to Africa and when we came back with the script, Laurence Olivier said to me, 'My dear baby, you will have to direct it as none of us understand it.' Olivier wanted to meet John Lennon and so the next day Olivier was on the steps and the car arrived with John and Yoko, white suits, hair and glasses. Olivier said to me, 'Which one is which, my dear baby? I cannot tell them apart.' They had tea in his office and he said, 'My dear Johnny', and John said, 'I haven't been called Johnny since I was at school', and he said, 'If this play is made into a film, the theatre will own 60% of the film rights.'

John didn't move. He said, 'Don't you have people that you pay to talk about these kind of things who can talk to the people that I pay to talk about these kind of things?' Olivier was livid. When they left he said, 'What a ridiculous pair, and what is this ridiculous line in the script, 'I wandered humbly as a sock'?' I said, 'It is John's version of 'I wandered lonely as a cloud.'' He said, 'Are you telling me that a Beatle has heard of Wordsworth?' Oh god, yes. They were long haired gits to him."

Apple rocked the establishment by opening premises in 3 Saville Row in Mayfair, an address synonymous with bespoke tailoring. Apple opened a boutique but within weeks, they were giving the clothes away.

Apple was full of problems, but the record label had an enviable roster of artists - the Beatles (still with Parlophone numbers), Mary Hopkin, Billy Preston (the singer/ pianist who had worked with Little Richard), Jackie Lomax (the lead singer of the Liverpool band, the Undertakers), Doris Troy, Badfinger, James Taylor and the Black Dyke Mills Band (a colliery band not really living up to its name). James Taylor, surprised to be making an album, was frantically trying to complete enough songs. Apple was the first record label to be owned by pop stars - a common occurrence nowadays - and it was soon followed by the Moody Blues' Threshold imprint.

August 1968, Hey Jude/ Revolution (Parlophone R 5722, UK No.1, US No.1)
Following the break-up of John Lennon's marriage, Paul had gone to see Cynthia and Julian one day and on the way home, had the idea for 'Hey Jude', a message of encouragement to John's son, as it were.

Apple's first release (though with a Parlophone number), 'Hey Jude' was more than twice the length of most singles and it became the longest record to make No.1. Songwriter and producer Jimmy Webb: "I know that 'MacArthur Park' preceded 'Hey Jude' because 'MacArthur Park' was 7 minutes 20 seconds long and when 'Hey Jude' came out, it was 7 minutes 21 seconds. I no longer had the longest hit single."

Cutting engineer George Peckham: "'Hey Jude' was a very big challenge as three minute singles were the norm. It was in mono so you could snuggle the grooves closer together but the volume had to come down to avoid velocity movements. If you listen to it now, the tambourine cuts through in the loudest part. We limited it so that it didn't jump too far. 'Hey Jude' is quiet at first which allows you to put more volume in the space that is left. I managed to gain some ground there."

Paul Gambaccini: "By 1968 the Beatles' work can easily be divided into the creative efforts of its individual members with 'Hey Jude' being Paul's song. The single of 'Hey Jude', which was shown on David Frost's TV show, totally sums up the Beatles' appeal. They performed 'Hey Jude' completely surrounded by a wide cross-section of society, a real mixed bunch, and yet all of them are singing along to 'Hey Jude'."

It is extraordinary what some people remember. Roddy Frame of Aztec Camera: "My sisters were listening to the Beatles and Stones and had Paul McCartney posters on the walls. I heard 'Hey Jude' one morning on the radio as I was eating my toast and it was cold and I was getting ready for school, but it was like a spiritual experience. I knew that there was something special about it, and so from a very early age, I wanted to be a musician."

Blues guitarist Joe Bonamassa: "My favourite Beatles track would be 'Hey Jude', but I was not influenced by the Beatles until I was older. They wrote the book on songwriting but at the time I preferred Free to the Beatles. Then I listened to *Sgt. Pepper* and *Abbey Road* and realised how hard it would be to pull that off today with Pro-Tools, and yet these guys were doing it on four track, genius. People will remember the Beatles a thousand years from now because you can pick up an acoustic guitar and play 'Hey Jude' or 'Love Me Do'. Those songs work with an orchestra, with the four piece Beatles, and with a single guy on an acoustic guitar. Having all those elements come together is genius songwriting."

Ric Sanders, violinist with Fairport Convention: "'Hey Jude' was a phenomenal tune. In pop music you don't often get tunes that can be played totally on their own as a single, melodic line in the same way that you might play a folk tune or an Irish air like 'The Londonderry Air'. You can do that with 'Hey Jude'. Folk melodies are autonomous; they don't require rhythm or harmony to make them work. I play an Irish air called 'A Lark in the Clear Air', it's a single note melody and it works beautifully on its own. A lot of pop tunes are punctuated by rhythm and harmony and there are even gaps. If you take 'A Hard Day's Night', for instance, you couldn't play it as a solo even though it's great, fantastic pop music. That tune hasn't got the same lyricism as 'Hey Jude'. There are too many gaps or turnaround bars where the harmony takes it round to start the next line."

The dynamic B-side, 'Revolution', was also recorded with a

doowop treatment on *The White Album*. Tony Thorpe of the Rubettes: "Everything John Lennon did was totally unique. He had a completely different approach to everything. He was the first one to use massively distorted, vicious guitar sounds, ones that would have been called ugly at first, yet he made them work in 'Revolution'. It's ridiculously overdriven and it's not a smooth, sweet overdrive like Eddie Van Halen. He was making a statement in the way he played."

In 'Revolution', Lennon is considering his political position and looking at anarchism, but he is not sure whether he wants to be counted in or out. Student revolutionary Tariq Ali: "John had written 'Revolution' which our music critic in *Black Dwarf* described as 'pathetic'. John wrote to the magazine complaining about the review and I contacted him proposing a lengthy interview. He wondered at first if people would take him seriously but we did the interview. The next day he rang to say that he had been so inspired that he had written 'Power to the People'. We started to meet regularly and Yoko introduced me to Japanese cuisine. John always regretted not going on anti-war demos and apparently Brian Epstein had told them that anything like that would bring about a ban on them visiting the States. That was absolute nonsense as many people in the US were erupting against the war as well. I really miss him and I know he would be with us against this war in Afghanistan."

Jon Savage: "The fact that we didn't go into Vietnam made English psychedelia very different. In a way, American psychedelia is so powerful because they were reacting against the war. Group members were drafted and it was a terrible time. The whole of psychedelic rock in America is counterpointed by these violent demonstrations against the Pentagon or in Chicago or elsewhere. People felt incredibly strongly about it and that was a generational rallying call too. Think of the contrast with 'It's All Too Much' in *Yellow Submarine* where George Harrison sings, 'Show me that I'm everywhere and get me home for tea.'"

August 1968, Those Were the Days/ Turn! Turn! Turn! – Mary Hopkin (Apple 2, UK No.1, US No.2)
Paul McCartney, producer
'Hey Jude' was replaced at the top by Apple's second release, Paul McCartney's production of 'Those Were the Days' for Mary Hopkin. Surprisingly, this song was covered by the hitmaker Sandie Shaw for Pye

and Apple took ads in the music papers which said, "Listen to Sandie Shaw's version and make your choice." Not much peace and love there.

August 1968, Sour Milk Sea/ The Eagle Laughs at You – Jackie Lomax (Apple 3)
Producer: George Harrison. George plays rhythm guitar on both titles, and Paul plays bass and Ringo drums on 'Sour Milk Sea'.
How could this single fail? An excellent vocalist from the Undertakers, a George Harrison song, and Eric Clapton on lead guitar. Jackie Lomax: "I was signed to Apple Publishing with a view to writing songs for other artists to record. George Harrison heard my stuff and wanted me to work with him. I had to wait for him to come back from India where they had been with Maharishi. George had written 'Sour Milk Sea' out there about the ages of the world. They believe that every 26,000 years, the world changes. In between there is a just a sour milk sea where nothing happens. It was a heavy driving rock song at a time when everyone was doing ballads and we thought it would be a hit. Apple released four singles on the same day and mine got lost in the crush."

August 1968, Thingumybob/ Yellow Submarine – John Foster & Sons Ltd Black Dyke Mills Band (Apple 4)
Paul McCartney, producer
McCartney wrote 'Thingumbybob' for an ITV comedy series written by Kenneth Cope and starring Stanley Holloway, but he wasn't satisfied with the recording by the George Martin Orchestra (which was eventually released in 2001). He felt it would sound better with a brass band and being Paul McCartney, he could employ the best, the Black Dyke Mills Band. The single was recorded in Victoria Hall, Bradford and was said to have been conducted by Geoffrey Brand and Paul McCartney. Just how do two people conduct an orchestra? With difficulty, I would have thought. Nice arrangement of 'Yellow Submarine' on the B-side. McCartney used the band on *Back to the Egg* (1979).

The authorised biography by Hunter Davies, *The Beatles*, appeared in September: it was very good but largely uncritical. Hunter Davies: "The only thing I don't tell the truth about in the book is the groupies but everyone knows that they are one of the reasons for forming a band. At Brian Epstein's country home one evening, he rang a club in London asking them to send down a few boys. They told him that he had left it rather late and all they had left was rubbish. This was done with a credit card with me listening to the entire conversation, not knowing that such clubs existed."

Beatles biographer Steve Turner: "I liked Hunter Davies' book because it's very straight-forward, it's not pretentious. It's like the Anthony Scaduto book on Bob Dylan: they were all-round journalists and they were tackling this popular music subject, but they treated it in the same way they would have treated a book on a bank robber; they went in for quotes and details. It's a very good book for its time. I remember John saying that you shouldn't use the word 'just' in a song and also, I remember Hunter Davies saying that it was funny that, when they were in India, their minds went back to Liverpool. They wrote a lot of songs about childhood and Liverpool when they were in another country, another culture. I suppose that as a writer, he was interested in how they wrote and as a Northerner; he knew all about their background and could relate to it."

However, the Beatles were moving so fast that it was already out of date. Brian Epstein had died while Hunter was writing the book. *Magical Mystery Tour* was the Beatles' first sign of vulnerability, while John and Yoko had been charged with possession of cannabis. Jane Asher's engagement to Paul McCartney was over. There have now been hundreds of books on the Beatles and Jane Asher is one of the few major players who has not told her story. Hunter Davies: "I admire Jane Asher for not cashing in. Everybody, who met the Beatles for 2 minutes, whether they did the gardening, the cleaning, the driving or worked in the Apple office, has written their memoirs. As a Beatles' fan, I find there's a little nugget in all of those books, but most of it is flim-flam. Whereas Jane was engaged to Paul and had several songs written for her and Paul lived with her in Wimpole Street."

October 1968, I'm The Urban Spaceman – Bonzo Dog Band (Liberty 15144, UK No.5)
Paul McCartney (as Apollo C. Vermouth), producer
Writing a musical takes 2 or 3 years out of your life, and McCartney, in particular, preferred one-off projects. He produced the only hit single by the Bonzo Dog Band, 'I'm the Urban Spaceman'. It was written by Neil Innes: "Our producer was a very kind man but he was very keen on getting things done quickly and we would think, 'Hang on, we haven't finished yet.' Paul said that he would produce us and he did produce 'I'm the Urban Spaceman'. He sat down at the piano and said,

'I've just written this' and it was the first time that anyone outside his circle had heard 'Hey Jude'. I thought, 'What is he doing? He's wasting time.' He played ukulele on 'Urban Spaceman' and our manager's wife said, 'What's that? A poor man's violin?', and he said, 'No, a rich man's ukulele.' He helped Viv record that horrible thing at the end, which was a trumpet mouthpiece with a length of garden hose and a funnel on the end which Viv swung over his head. The engineer couldn't see how to record it and Paul said to put a microphone in each corner of the studio and we got that wonderful effect. We didn't want to ride on his name as producer and so we dubbed him Apollo C. Vermouth with his blessing."

In November, the BBC-TV series, *Omnibus*, broadcast Tony Palmer's documentary, *All My Loving,* which featured many rock stars including the Beatles. Tony Palmer: "I made a film about Benjamin Britten and I was the golden boy for that weekend. Huw Wheldon said, 'We would like you to make a film that explains rock'n'roll.' Huw knew that there was far more to it than gyrating nubiles on *Top of the Pops* or what you saw on that dreadful, moronic programme, *Juke Box Jury*. I had met John Lennon when I was representing *Varsity*, the Cambridge University paper in October 1963. I rang up and left a message for him, and within a day I was having lunch with him and getting a complete ear-bashing about the appalling state of pop music on television. He said that I had a responsibility to do something about this. He said, 'I'm going to give you a list of people who can't get onto television, either because their act is too outrageous or they won't do 3-minute pop songs or they don't want to appear on *Juke Box Jury*. I'll make the introductions, and you make the film. That was *All My Loving*, and it was a wonderful opportunity. It was a tough time – Vietnam, people being assassinated, riots in Grosvenor Square and so on – but it was the perfect moment. They all wanted to speak. Paul McCartney said, 'We have some power and we want to use it for the good.' He couldn't have said that on *Juke Box Jury*. I think the significance of *All My Loving* is not that it is a particularly good or bad film, but that it broke the shackles of what rock and roll was being held in until that moment."

November 1968, Wonderwall Music – George Harrison LP (Apple SAPCOR 1)
Apple's first album. The film, *Wonderwall,* looks ridiculous now: well, it looked ridiculous then, but it was a psychedelic love story starring Jane Birkin, Jack MacGowran and that famed hippie, Irene Handl.

Nonsense of course, but an interesting curio and it gave Oasis a song title. Film director Joe Massot: "I asked George at the opening of the Beatles' boutique if he would like to do the music for *Wonderwall*. I told him that it was a silent film and his music would provide the emotion for the characters. Quincy Jones told me that it was the greatest soundtrack he had heard but the movie was too far out for some audiences. It did well in London though."

Peter Tork of the Monkees: "Mickey Dolenz and I met John and Paul and George at the Speakeasy one night in London and that was very pleasant. They were very friendly and the next day George took me to visit Ringo. George showed us his sitar and we had a lovely time. George did a soundtrack album for *Wonderwall* and if you see the movie and hear any banjo playing, that'll be me. George didn't play banjo. I was playing a five-string banjo that Paul had."

Although at the forefront of popular music, the Beatles were always aware of what other musicians were doing. Rock writer John Einarson: "Both Eric Clapton and George Harrison were very impressed with the first Band album, *Music from Big Pink*. Clapton wanted to quit Cream and Harrison played it to George Martin. The Band synthesized so many styles: mountain music, gospel, country and Canada too in a very unique way. The ultimate is their second album where everything came together. Look at the picture with their families on that first album. You would think it was a gathering from a village in the Ozarks, but it is from southern Ontario. They have a grizzled Arkansas look about them."

November 1968 – The Beatles (known as The White Album) 2LP (Parlophone PMC 7067)
Produced by George Martin, 30 tracks – 1 hour 33 minutes 43 seconds
Side 1: Back in the USSR/ Dear Prudence/ Glass Onion/ Ob-La-Di, Ob-La-Da/ Wild Honey Pie/ The Continuing Story of Bungalow Bill/ While My Guitar Gently Weeps/ Happiness Is a Warm Gun
Side 2: Martha My Dear/ I'm So Tired/ Blackbird/ Piggies/ Rocky Racoon/ Don't Pass Me By/ Why Don't We Do It in the Road/ I Will/ Julia
Side 3: Birthday/ Yer Blues/ Mother Nature's Son/ Everybody's Got Something To Hide Except For Me And My Monkey/ Sexy Sadie/ Helter Skelter/ Long Long Long
Side 4: Revolution 1/ Honey Pie/ Savoy Truffle/ Cry Baby Cry/ Revolution 9/ Good Night

After being Sgt. Pepper's Lonely Hearts Club Band on the last LP, the Fab Four simply called the new offering, *The Beatles*. They wrote most of their double-album while they were in Rishikesh. Because of its packaging, the record has come to be known as *The White Album*. The original title had been *A Doll's House,* but then Family used that phrase.

The white packaging, designed by Richard Hamilton, represents a clean slate. Peter Blake: "There are three basic branches of Pop Art. One started in America, I started one here and the other was with Richard Hamilton, Edward Paolozzi and members of the ICA independent group. Richard Hamilton did the sleeve for *The White Album*, which was a reaction to *Sgt. Pepper*. *Sgt. Pepper* was highly coloured, very complicated and over-excited. Richard Hamilton decided upon a plain, white cover, which was a brilliant idea and a total contrast. All it had on the front was a serial number so that the first copies were limited, unique editions. It started at No.1 and went into hundreds of thousands. Inside was a poster which was a collage of the Beatles, but the outside was perfectly plain, white, shiny cardboard. I think our two sleeves work in conjunction."

The concept of the Beatles as a group, however, was as fictional as Sgt. Pepper's band. John, Paul and George's songs for *The White Album* are distinctive and separate, although John charitably calls Paul 'the walrus' during 'Glass Onion', seemingly to puncture a Beatles' myth. They didn't solely work with themselves and George, for example, asked Eric Clapton to play the solo on 'While My Guitar Gently Weeps'.

George Martin: "I didn't like *The White Album* very much. They'd turned up with thirty-six songs after their Indian trip and they were pretty insistent that every song was to be included. I wanted to make it a single album and I stressed to the boys that whilst they could record whatever they liked, we should weed out the stuff that wasn't up to scratch and make a really super single album. I didn't learn until later the reason why they were so insistent. It was a contractual one. By this time, the contractual negotiations were above my head and I didn't know that their current contract with EMI stipulated a number of years or a number of titles, whichever was the earlier. So the boys, in an effort to get rid of the contract were shoving out titles as quickly as they could. This was on the advice of the people governing them and there was a sinister motive behind that album."

There were, however, plenty of happy times in the studio. Jimmy Webb: "I went to a session one night in Trident 3 where the booth is upstairs and the studio is down below. They were cutting 'Honey Pie'. Paul was playing the piano on one side of the studio and Linda was sitting on the bench with her arms around his neck. He had a sweater tied around his neck and they looked charming. He was doing a great job playing piano. George Harrison was playing bass and was standing in the centre of the studio, and then over on the right was John Lennon, sitting down on the floor with some candles and holding an acoustic guitar. I couldn't see Ringo as the drum booth was tucked underneath the control room, but I could hear him. It was fascinating and they played a joke on me as after they had finished a take, Paul came and introduced me to George Martin and Geoff Emerick as 'Tom Dowd from Atlantic Records'. I was so terrified and so overawed by where I was that I did not correct this impression, and they proceeded to treat me as though I were Tom Dowd. They were asking me what I thought of this guitar solo and that guitar solo and I was doing the best I could. I didn't want to disappoint them by telling them that I was only Jimmy Webb! Finally, after what I thought was entirely too much of it, George Harrison tapped me on the shoulder and said, 'By the way, man, I loved those strings on 'MacArthur Park'."

Although it is inconsistent, *The White Album* contains many excellent songs and performances. Their Beach Boys' pastiche 'Back in the USSR' is so good that you long for a whole album in this vein. That track features Paul McCartney on drums as Ringo had walked out after an argument. 'The Continuing Story of Bungalow Bill' could be mistaken for a Syd Barrett song. Paul McCartney wrote a light-hearted reggae song with 'Ob-La-Di, Ob-La-Da', based on a phrase from a Nigerian conga player based in London, Jimmy Scott, who took them to task in the *NME*.

Paul had been expecting the Who's 'I Can See for Miles' to be the heaviest rock track ever and he was disappointed when he heard it. In response, he wrote the manic 'Helter Skelter' and a longer version was not released. As it is, the stereo version of 'Helter Skelter' is a minute longer than the mono and includes the final line, "I've got blisters on me fingers."

'Helter Skelter' achieved notoriety because Charles Manson used the song as a blueprint for serial killing. John ironically wrote 'Happiness is a Warm Gun', having read in a magazine that a warm gun was one that had just been fired. The song, amusingly, contains a reference to donating something to the National Trust. John wasn't thinking ahead to the future of Mendips: this was contemporary slang for opening your bowels.

Simon Nicol: "The first gig we did under the name of Fairport Convention was the day that *Sgt. Pepper* was released. It was a memorable day for me though I was much more gobsmacked by *The White Album*. I had to go out for a long walk after I'd played *The White Album* to let it soak in. I thought 'Dear Prudence' was great."

Donovan: "*The White Album* came out of the Indian experience, and I was involved with two songs in particular. I showed John Lennon the finger-styled guitar playing that I had learned from the folk scene: it comes from the Carter Family and it is called clawhammer. When anybody learns a new style, they write differently and he wrote 'Julia' and 'Dear Prudence' from this. My influence is obvious on 'Dear Prudence'. Paul would not sit down and learn it like a good boy but would peer over our shoulders and pick up little bits as shown in 'Blackbird'. He was like a sponge and absorbed things by listening. In return, George introduced me to Indian music and he gave me a tambura, and it is still making music. I put it on 'Hurdy Gurdy Man' and it is the drone in between the verses. George did write a verse for that song, but because of the guitar solo, we didn't include it on the record. I include it in my concerts now. Yeah, George."

Richard Digance: "*The White Album* is my favourite album, and one of my party-pieces is 'Blackbird'. If there are any guitarists reading this who have tried 'Blackbird' and don't know how to do it, I'll let you in on the secret. It's impossible to play with conventional tuning and Paul McCartney tunes his guitar in a different way. You drop the two E-strings down a tone to D and use the second and fourth strings and suddenly 'Blackbird' takes shape. It's a well structured song, but if you don't know that, you won't be able to play it."

Harmonica player Judd Lander from the Liverpool band, the Hideaways: "The Beatles had so much money then. When I was in London, I stayed with Neil Aspinall in a beautiful flat that the Beatles had bought him as a present, with a Bentley Continental too. Neil showed me into his massive bedroom and I rang my mum in Aintree and told her than we could fit our house into his bedroom. Neil came back with an acetate of 'Blackbird' at 2 a.m. one morning and he said, 'Have a listen to this.' He said that they were going to do another mix and then he threw the acetate into the bin."

John Lennon sang a stinging vocal on 'Yer Blues', the bluesiest record that the Beatles ever made. Blues legend, B.B. King, who calls his guitar, Lucille: "I like the Beatles' songs so much that I hope one day to do an instrumental version on Lucille. I'd never sing them as my voice would never make it. I met George Harrison and he was a wonderful man. John Lennon said in an interview that he wanted to play guitar like B.B. King. I mentioned that to a record producer called Bill Szymczyk, who knew him. He called him and said, 'Here's John Lennon' and John said, 'When have you got time to give me lessons?'"

The White Album also contains John's tender tribute to his mother 'Julia', his thinly disguised attack on the Maharishi 'Sexy Sadie' and the downbeat 'I'm So Tired' (cursing Sir Walter Raleigh for introducing tobacco to the UK) which were all excellent, while Paul was at his lyrical best on 'I Will', 'Blackbird' and 'Mother Nature's Son'.

Although written in India, George Harrison's songwriting was returning to its English roots as evidenced by his attack on eating meat, 'Piggies' (George's mum gave him the line, "What they need's a damn good whacking!"). George Harrison knew that Eric Clapton was having trouble with his teeth, and as a joke, he wrote a lyric around boxes of assorted chocolates, 'Savoy Truffle'.

Ringo wrote a maudlin country song 'Don't Pass Me By', an odd subject for someone who was not used to songwriting and one he had written in 1963. Its theme 'Don't rush to conclusions' owes something to Hank Williams as Luke the Drifter. The track sounds even more maudlin in mono as the speed was botched.

There's much inconsequential material on *The White Album* such as 'Wild Honey Pie' (as opposed to the cheerful pre-war pastiche 'Honey Pie'), 'Everybody's Got Something to Hide Except for Me and My Monkey' and 'Why Don't We Do It in the Road', although even John's self-indulgent 'Revolution 9' has its advocates. There is a snatch of an uncredited song, 'Can You Take Me Back', from Paul McCartney.

Mick Groves of the Spinners: "The Beatles' talent culminated in *Sgt. Pepper*. I thought *The White Album* was full of the rubbishy bits that an artist must produce eventually. They filled up a double-album because they knew they could sell anything in those days. I remember the sculptor Arthur Dooley saying that when he became the flavour-of-the-month in Liverpool, he would take a piece of driftwood, whitewash it, stick a few nails in it, and sell it to the professors at the University. They would buy it because it was Arthur Dooley."

'Revolution 9' was a piece of avant-garde music that was bought by millions. It is full of sound effects, a choir, gossip, backwards voices and a bingo caller. Liverpool artist Adrian Henri: "I'm not too fond of *The White Album*. It was too self-consciously arty in the way that a lot of John and Yoko's stuff was. Up until then, I thought that the Beatles had a good balance between being poets and good writers and being rock'n'rollers and great entertainers, but by *The White Album*, they had lost their way. 'Revolution 9' was just experimentation. It was a collage and there was a lot of that around at the time. I was doing cut-up poems, which had been around since 1917, and William Burroughs was writing cut-up novels. I can hear William Burroughs' influence in 'Revolution 9'. They were disrupting reality by trying to make you see something different by presenting it in this chopped up, edited way. It's not a revolution in the sense of throwing bombs, but more a revolution in thinking and hearing and seeing."

In *The Observer*, Tony Palmer said that almost every track was a send up of a send up, effectively making this the first post-modern album. There is some justification for this as there are knowing references throughout the album – 'Strawberry Fields Forever', 'Fool On The Hill', Elvis Presley, Donovan, Little Richard, Blind Lemon Jefferson and B.B.King. 'Good Night' showed that they could do schmaltz as well as Engelbert and they could also rock as well as Chuck Berry and the Beach Boys.

As the Beatles did not release singles from *The White Album*, the songs were fair game for anyone. Graham Knight, bass player with Marmlade: "We weren't writing anything decent in Marmalade, but we wrote B-sides and things. Dick James played us the acetate of 'Ob-La-Di, Ob-La-Da' and we thought it was great. He said, 'You can have it. I won't give it to anyone else.' But, of course he gave it to twenty-seven different acts. We rush recorded it in the middle of the night during a week of cabaret in the north east. Our manager, who was in America at the time, kept sending us telegrams telling us not to do it. He didn't think that we should record a Beatles song. We expected it to be a hit because we had done well with 'Lovin' Things', 'Mary Anne' and 'Baby Make it Soon' but we didn't think it would go to No.1. We got no feedback from the Beatles. There had been so many covers by that time that I shouldn't think they'd have been very interested."

The White Album's failings are as significant as its triumphs. Since then, several acts have made long, sprawling albums flowing with ideas and over-indulgence. the Clash's thirty-six track *Sandinista!* (1980), Prince's *Emancipation* (1996), and Prefab Sprout's *Jordan: The Comeback* (2001).

The White Album was very influenced by current modern art. Indeed, you could see its very basic cover appealing to Yoko Ono. Peter Blake: "I met Yoko Ono when she came over and did a show at the Indica Gallery. That was where John met her. I taught at the Royal College and she asked me to recommend two students. They ended up building the whole thing for her. I saw a lot of the pieces and I have since thought that they were very self-concerned, rather cruel pieces. I didn't like the art she made, but it certainly affected John. She sent John on mad errands and this was her negative side and very bad for John. The positive side was that he loved her and was very happy with her most of the time. He deserved someone to love, so in the long run she was pretty good for him."

Yoko Ono's reputation was as an avant-garde artist and filmmaker and her infamous film of 365 bottoms included Michael Aspel's. George Melly: "I was asked to be one of Yoko Ono's bottoms but I declined. I thought my bottom was not a very pretty object. I accept that wasn't the purpose of the film, but I thought it was too silly to walk on a treadmill and have my bottom photographed. I wasn't ashamed of showing my bottom but I thought the whole thing was phony and silly."

Ray Coleman: "The Beatles stopped touring in 1966 and John felt very, very restless, which is why Yoko was so interesting to him, quite apart from the physical attraction which was obviously there. He was mentally drawn to her and her adventurous spirit touched a chord in John. He was desperate for something new. The Beatles were very famous, they'd triumphed in America and were very, very rich, so all the hurdles had been overcome. With Yoko, he moved into a totally new life."

May Pang became John and Yoko's assistant. "I was in awe of John and Yoko when I first met them. They wanted me to work on two movies with them, *Up Your Legs Forever* and *Fly*. *Up Your Legs Forever* was an idea of Yoko's in which people would donate their legs for peace. I was calling all sorts of interesting people like Andy Warhol and Jackie Onassis but it was too way out for me. She wanted 365 legs, one for each day of the year, but we didn't get that many."

Sylvain Sylvain of the New York Dolls: "I was in a John and Yoko film *Up Your Legs Forever*. They shot you from your toes to your torso. Billy Murcia and I were hanging out in Central Park and we were by the fountain and this scout came round and said, 'Hey, do you guys want to be in a John Lennon movie?' We were smoking joints and we went round the corner and got paid $1. John Lennon gave me a *Screw* magazine, which is a sex magazine. He was working with someone from the magazine and it was great to get that."

It is doubtful if the film ever promoted peace as so few people have seen it, nor the subsequent works – *Fly* and *Erection* – that May Pang was also involved with. "I particularly like *Apotheosis*, which is one of John's. For five minutes you are watching nothing but a blank screen and then the blue rises above the top of the clouds and you see the sun shine."

George Melly: "Yoko Ono brought out a side of John Lennon that he was unaware of. She made him kinder and nicer to people and, indeed, when he left her and went raving off for a year by himself, he reverted to his tough, Liverpool street persona. He was smashing windows and getting terribly drunk and staying up all night. I don't think she was a bad influence on him but there is something pretentiously avant-garde about the bed-ins and the handing out of acorns to world leaders. I doubt if he would have done that by himself. All this symbolic minimalist art is derived from Marcel Duchamp, so it wasn't original either. I don't want to be too harsh because he undoubtedly loved her and he wrote some interesting songs while he was with her. Whether he would have stayed with the Beatles without her is another question, but she was certainly a catalyst for him leaving."

Yoko Ono sat in on the recording sessions, even contributing to 'The Continuing Story of Bungalow Bill'. Many saw Yoko as splitting up their favourite group and so she became very unpopular. Bob Monkhouse underlined the public's mood with insulting Yoko Ono jokes on *The Golden Shot*. Yoko is often said to have precipitated the break-up of the Beatles. Barry Miles: "Mainly, it was John's fault, not Yoko's. He was the one who insisted she sat next to him on the piano stool and she even had to go with him to the toilet. Maybe she should have realised that she was doing tremendous damage to the creative camaraderie, the special sort of magic that they had when they were being creative, but she didn't. John would have never stood for somebody else's girlfriend or wife being there, but as long as it was him, it was all right. 'We are Joko', basically."

Music writer Paul Trynka: "A lot of people don't like Yoko's art but she was very cutting edge. It was very difficult for her as a woman in those surroundings. She did split up the Beatles but you can blame that on John as much as Yoko. She didn't want him out of the band, but John felt that Yoko was an escape route as the band had run its course. John was very bolshie but he lacked confidence and did need somebody to rely on."

Adrian Henri: "Artistically they were a disaster for each other. They were very happy and idyllic as a couple, but they brought out the worst in each other's art. She brought out a narcissistic, self-indulgent streak in his writing, and her work got more trivial, all this crawling in and out of bags, for example. She lost the artistic toughness that she had in her New York period. She also lost the company of other very good artists like Dick Higgins while he lost his Liverpool sarcasm and scepticism."

November 1968, Unfinished Music – John Lennon and Yoko Ono LP (Apple SAPCOR 2)
John and Yoko's first joint album was a 30 minute LP of sound effects, *Two Virgins*. It had the infamous nude cover for which they might have been prosecuted. A *Private Eye* cover had John Lennon saying, "I tell you, officer, it won't stand up in court." Cutting engineer George Peckham: "Those albums were fun and it was always a wind-up with John. He could throw you completely. Yoko was artistic in her own way and John was 100% behind her. We sent a copy to Richard Williams, who was based at Island Records. Back then, they would often press one side of music and the other would be a standard metal plate that had a 1K tone. Richard Williams thought it was a double album and without ringing anybody at Apple, he played the four sides. He commented in *Melody Maker* that the tone fluctuates from time-to-time but maintains the interest. We thought, 'What double album?' They were not meant to be played. I told Richard that he had sat through two tone sides – he was the joke, not us. John loved the review to pieces."

John and Yoko appeared with the Rolling Stones in their *Rock And Roll Circus*. David Stark: "The Stones parodied the Beatles' covers with *Their Satanic Majesties Request* and *Beggars Banquet*. When they finished *Beggars Banquet*, they made the *Rock And Roll Circus* TV concert. The *NME* had a draw for tickets and I won a couple and it was a fantastic experience. We wore smocks and colourful gear and it was in a TV studio in Stambridge Park in Wembley in December 1968. There was little security back then and at one point I went to the loo and walked past a group of Lennon, Jagger, Townshend and Clapton."

December 1968, James Taylor – James Taylor LP (Apple SAPCOR 3)
Paul McCartney, bass on 'Carolina In My Mind'.
The album includes Taylor's composition, 'Something in the Way She Moves'. A few months later, we have George Harrison's 'Something'.

Billy Kinsley of the Merseybeats, then working on sessions at Apple: "I liked to sit in Derek Taylor's office: he was like a guru and he told great stories. We walked in once and James Taylor was sitting in the window, and a photograph of him sitting there was used on the album cover. When he stood up, he was a giant. I thought from the start that his songs were different. The Beatles missed his potential really, and the same with Delaney and Bonnie. They had thousands of their first album pressed but the Beatles hadn't signed a contract with them. They signed elsewhere with the same record and Apple had to give their albums away. That is typical of the chaos."

December 1968, The Beatles' 1968 Christmas Record.
The Liverpool DJ, Kenny Everett, who had found fame with his zany approach on Radio London and then Radio 1. The most memorable moment is when George introduces the novelty singer, Tiny Tim, doing his version of 'Nowhere Man'. Paul sings an all-seasonal song of goodwill, 'Happy Christmas, Happy New Year': John reads a couple of poems and Ringo links it together.

Somewhat out of character, George Harrison had invited some American Hell's Angels to visit them at Apple. He probably thought that they would never come. They arrived in December 1968 and intimidated everyone. There was a bizarre Christmas party for the children, hosted by Hell's Angels and with John and Yoko as Father and Mother Christmas. Still, someone far more scary than a whole chapter of Hell's Angels was about to descend on Apple.

Pete Shotton: "Apple was a mad house and terribly confusing. Each of the Beatles had different ideas and the Beatles would come in on different days. We had four part-time bosses. I was 25 years old and had run a little supermarket on the south coast and John asked me to run Apple! We were all going to have a good time but the Apple went pear-shaped. I wish I had put my foot down and said, 'You need a suit; you need someone who is business minded and has had experience.' Their attitude was if it didn't make money but broke even, that was all that mattered. They didn't realise that you had to make profits to develop and so their concept of business was negligible."

CHAPTER 9

And in the End (1969)

Neil Armstrong walks upon the moon – Much violence in Northern Ireland – Charles Manson's Hollywood killings – East End gangsters Reg and Ronnie Kray jailed – Films include Butch Cassidy and the Sundance Kid *(Paul Newman and Robert Redford),* Easy Rider *(Peter Fonda and Dennis Hopper) and* The Italian Job *(Michael Caine and three Minis).*

January 1969, Yellow Submarine LP (Apple PCS 7070, UK3)
Produced by George Martin, 12 tracks, 39 minutes 28 seconds
Side 1: Yellow Submarine / Only a Northern Song/ All Together Now/ Hey Bulldog/ It's All Too Much/ All You Need Is Love
Side 2: Orchestral pieces from George Martin (Pepperland/Medley - Sea of Time & Sea of Holes/ Sea of Monsters/ March of the Meanies/ Pepperland Laid Waste/ Yellow Submarine in Pepperland)

At long last, the soundtrack for *Yellow Submarine*, featuring the four new songs, the title song and 'All You Need Is Love', was released. On the second side, George Martin's lushly orchestrated score is good, but is typical of film music and not especially memorable, the best moments being the dark 'Sea of Monsters' and the Michel Legrand-styled waltz, 'Sea of Time'.

You sense that EMI had a reluctance to release this album as the back sleeve features Tony Palmer's review for *The White Album*, while some notes from Derek Taylor tells us nothing about the album in hand. How perverse is that? It was a disappointing package, but several bands took up the idea of a cartoon cover, notably the Flamin' Groovies and the Move.

After *Help!* which seemed so long ago, the Beatles had a contract to make two more films that they fulfilled ingeniously. The cartoon

211

film, *Yellow Submarine,* was followed by a documentary on the making of an album, *Let It Be*. They would, as it were, be killing two birds with one stone.

George Martin: "*Let It Be* was going to be a live album of new material. It would have to be an open-air event but there were no halls in Britain that were large enough. We thought about Africa, but not America because that would have been too expensive. In the end, we went to the film studios at Twickenham with the cameras following us around. The idea then was to make a TV documentary about the making of an album, but as they were a film short on their contract, it became a full-length feature. John was still very determined that it should be a live album. He said that there were to be no echoes, no overdubs and none of my 'jiggery-pokery'. It was to be an 'honest album' in that if they didn't get the song right the first time, they'd record it again and again until they did. It was awful to do. We did take after take after take and John would be asking me if Take 67 was better than Take 39. I put together an album which captured this documentary approach and included their mistakes and interjections. When it was over, John took the tapes to America."

The intention was the Beatles would create an album from scratch, one that would hopefully be of the same standard as *A Hard Day's Night* and *Sgt. Pepper*. They did come to *Let It Be* with good songs at first, but it soon fell apart. Any expectations they may have had were soon dashed as the daily sessions became intolerable and often brought out the worst in them. There was little of the famed Beatle wit and repartee. It was like the *Big Brother* house with music and that comparison is not as fatuous as it sounds: this was reality TV long before the term was invented. It illustrated that the presence of a camera all day and every day is unbearable, even for those as accustomed to the limelight as the Beatles. The frictions between the individual Beatles were evident in *Let It Be*, which, as it happened, wasn't released until after the split.

Bob Stanley from St Etienne: "I rate the Beatles really highly. Their story can't be beaten. If anybody comes up with unseen photos of the Beatles, they always look great. It is like some special thing that was hanging over them and they couldn't do anything wrong. Even those strange pantomime pictures work. Look at the Stones and consider how many mediocre album tracks they did. Right at the very end, the Beatles did some bad stuff but even that is part of the story as it was all starting to fade. The story is perfect."

The version of 'Let It Be' on *Let It Be...Naked* features John Lennon on bass: it could have been Klaus Voormann: "When they were recording 'Let It Be', Paul said, 'C'mon, Klaus, you play bass' but I said, 'No, no. You're the bass player with the Beatles.' I couldn't do it. Actually, I did once play with them in Hamburg. They were doing 'I'm in Love Again' and Stuart gave me his bass guitar which had a long lead and I sat in the audience and played."

Beatles' biographer Hunter Davies: "Six months after the book came out, I was in Portugal with my wife and two children, who were very young and not at school. Paul and Linda came out to stay with us and we'd never met Linda. When I left London, Paul was engaged to Jane whom we'd met and they'd been to our house for tea. Paul and Linda stayed with us for 2 weeks and it came out that my first Christian name is Edward – my full name is Edward Hunter Davies – and Paul laughed hysterically. I said, 'You needn't laugh: your first name isn't Paul but James.' He'd brought his guitar and he used to play it in the lavatory. He came back one day and he played to me a song and the song went: 'There you go, Eddie, Eddie, Eddie, There you go Eddie, Eddie, you've gone.' It was quite funny but I forgot about it for about 10 years. Then I heard a bootleg from the *Let It Be* sessions and I could hear Paul playing this tune and telling John, 'I've got a new song.' He'd written another four lines and as one of the lines was 'You think you're in with the in-crowd', it wasn't very flattering. Still, it sounded good to me. As Apple and EMI are going mad remixing things, one of these days, it'll suddenly appear and I'll be so proud to have a Beatles song in my honour."

The *Let It Be* sessions concluded with a glorious sequence in which the Beatles gave a free concert with Billy Preston on Apple's flat roof in January 1969. Rather like Eric Clapton had been introduced to the Beatles' sessions for *The White Album* by George Harrison, this time he thought of reducing the tension by asking Billy Preston.

Georgie Fame: "The Beatles didn't really need a piano player in the band - Paul is pretty good in his simple fashion and George Martin helped out with the more intricate things, but I loved it when Billy Preston joined them. He's one of my favourite keyboard players and he did a great job. Not many people had heard an electric piano being played the way he played it. It sounds like a Hohner 'cause it has a fairly metallic sound. It added another dimension to the band and it was perfect for that 'Get Back' wallop."

February 1969, Rosetta/ Just Like Before – Fourmost (CBS 4041)
Paul McCartney, producer (both sides) and piano
The Fourmost hadn't had a hit for some years and had moved into cabaret, and Paul worked with them on a revival of 'Rosetta'. Joey Bower of the Fourmost: "We used to do mouth music where we would mimic the sound of the instruments with our mouths. Paul McCartney said that 'Rosetta' was his dad's favourite song, and would we do it for him? He booked the session and at 9 o'clock there was no sign of him: 10 o'clock, no sign: 11 o'clock, no sign and we thought that he wasn't going to show. He turned up at half-eleven and said, 'Sorry, I'm late. I had two songs in my head and I had to get them down.' He went to the piano and played us 'The Long and Winding Road' and 'Let It Be', and so we were the first people to hear them." Well, maybe not as he appears to have been trying them on everyone.

Billy Hatton, also from the Fourmost: "Dave Lovelady is a good pianist and he was going to do the Earl Hines' stuff on 'Rosetta', and we said, 'Play it badly', which he did. He was sounding like Les Dawson. As we expected, Paul said, 'Come on, I'll do that' and so we had Paul playing on the record as well as producing it. The Beatles did some mouth music in 'Lady Madonna', and they had seen us doing the mouth music on stage. The idea came from the Mills Brothers."

Another Fourmost, Joey Bower: "'Rosetta' had been made privately for Paul's dad but someone in his organisation played it for CBS and they wanted to put it out. It had one of Brian O'Hara's songs on the other side. We had made that with Paul as well and Apple took the publishing." Rather amusingly, Brian O'Hara wrote the B-side under the pseudonym, A. Benny.

March 1969, Post Card – Mary Hopkin LP (Apple SAPCOR 5, UK No.3, US No.28)
Paul McCartney, producer, plus some guitar, bass and percussion.

March 1969, Goodbye/ Sparrow – Mary Hopkin (UK No.2, US13)
Producer: Paul McCartney. McCartney plays guitar, bass and slaps his thighs for percussion on A-side: bass on B-side.
Benny Gallagher, then a writer for Apple Publishing with Graham Lyle: "Paul sent a note round saying that he wanted Apple to be a successful publishing company and he wanted all of us to write for Mary Hopkin. I had to go to Scotland and I was walking along the coastline with my

dog. I got an idea for 'Sparrow' and I phoned Graham and he finished it off in London. They sent us a chocolate cake for winning the Song for Mary and then invited us to the studio. They kept asking us what we thought. Normally that doesn't happen as the writers are cut out of the picture. It was a good place – shame that it didn't carry on."

Graham Lyle: "Of the Beatles, Paul showed the most enthusiasm for us, we were really his boys, and he was so encouraging. He would take a song and say, 'That's a strong point', or 'This needs strengthening.' He made us work at it, and Apple was like the Brill Building for us. It made us realise that if we put in the hours and really thought about what we were doing, we could make a living from it. We shouldn't wait for inspiration. We were asked to write for Mary Hopkin whose voice was wonderful, distinctive and unusual. It also had a soulful quality about it. She liked our material and McCartney was producing, so what more could you want? We ended up with the B-sides of three of her singles. That was a big thing because we had done nothing up until then. It started us off."

Tymon Dogg from Joe Strummer's band: "My time with Apple was pretty short-lived and I did no more than record some demos for them. It gave me an opportunity to sit on a piano stool with Paul McCartney and have him play piano on a number, 'Something New Everyday', but he could have been doing that on every demo in London for all I know. Nothing was ever released as Apple was falling apart before it got started. Nobody ever signed anything. James Taylor never signed anything. Nobody was running the place and it wasn't very businesslike."

Peter Asher: "I can remembering James Taylor coming up with 'Something in the Way She Moves' which is a very beautiful song about his sister Kate. That was on the initial tape he gave me and was one of the reasons I signed him. I played that to the Beatles and obviously that line stuck with George and in an elaborate coincidence, he wrote an entirely different and another amazingly great song but with that same line. That is why he just called his song 'Something'."

Following the Beatles' lead, the Moody Blues set up their own label, Threshold, and they re-recorded Tymon Dogg with 'And Now She Says She's Young'. "It didn't bother me that I didn't have any records out with Apple. There are people who have had hits who are cleaning windows now. That it's a good thing to have hit records is a fallacy, and that is why you saw people in the 70s doing horrible cabaret gigs after their hits. I have a great love of the beauty of songs and I've still got that burning in me. It is possible that someone could have written 1% of my songs and become a millionaire, but that's destiny."

Tommy James from the Shondells: "When the Beatles started publishing songs with Apple, they wanted to write songs for other artists. George Harrison and Grapefruit wrote us a bunch of great songs that were really up-tempo like 'Mony Mony' and sent them to us. We were flattered to get them but we had moved onto 'Crimson and Clover' by then."

March 1969, Is This What You Want – Jackie Lomax LP (Apple SAPCOR 6)
Mostly produced by George Harrison with Ringo Starr on drums
When Jackie Lomax's album was issued on CD in 1991, Billy Kinsley from the Merseybeats was on the bonus cuts. "'Going Back to Liverpool' was great because George Harrison produced it. George was a wonderful producer as he was very methodical and never looked at his watch: he just wanted everything to be precisely right. Paul could be like that too, but he also went for feel. If it sounded okay, that was fine. 'Going Back to Liverpool' featured the Jackie Lomax band which was Jackie, myself, Pete Clarke, Tim Rennick on guitar, Chris Hatfield from Waterloo on piano and organ, and Billy Preston on Hammond. It's a wonderful track and I remember doing the backing vocals with George, Billy and Tim. That is when I realised how high George could get with his falsetto. We had a competition to see who could get the highest, but I can't remember who won."

In March 1969, the American impresario, Sid Bernstein, who had put the Beatles on at Carnegie Hall and Shea Stadium, offered the Beatles $4m for a series of concerts in major US cities with his band, the Rascals, in support. The Beatles turned it down but I wondered if Sid had the $4m if the Beatles had said yes. No, he told me, but I could have got it within a week. Sid missed his calling: he should have bought some English football clubs.

Enter Allen Klein. The antagonistic accountant was at the top of the music business, having managed Sam Cooke, Herman's Hermits and latterly, the Rolling Stones. With Allen Klein, you were either friend or foe, and if you were a friend, a significant part of your earnings would go to him in commission. He got results, and maybe that is why John Lennon favoured him, despite warnings from his embittered clients, the Rolling Stones.

Peter Noone, Herman of Herman's Hermits: "We came from Manchester and my mum and dad lived in Liverpool. I was out in America on my own and I believed anyone who told me that they could make me money. Allen Klein was like a wide boy with a suitcase full of ties saying, 'Here comes Peter Noone. I'll con him' Nobody would say anything nice about him. He was a cheat and liar. I've said that before and I was hoping he would sue me, and as he didn't, he must be a cheat and liar."

"He's had a bad press," says May Pang, but he had more than that as he has done time for tax evasion, "There is something of the gangster about him, sure, but he wasn't a total gangster like some of the record moguls. He genuinely loved the music and he was a brilliant man who did a lot of good because Apple was in such disarray before he came along and he renegotiated the Beatles' contracts. I loved working for the music publishing side of his business and even now I love to see who wrote a particular song."

Alan White, drummer with the Plastic Ono Band: "I used to go into London and would hang around Apple as that was a very cool place. Lots of things were happening there. George Harrison had a pink room with a desk in the corner and nothing else. We would sit on the floor. Derek Taylor's room was like an all day disco with flashing lights and he was the PR guy. Allen Klein came in and he was a control freak. Once you got past that, he was all right, but you didn't mess with him at all. I was a young guy and he was wielding all the sticks."

Benny Gallagher: "No one was steering Apple. People were taking advantage of the Beatles, it was all coming out of their pockets, and they were abusing expenses. They called in Allen Klein just as our songwriting contract was about to expire."

Quite often, Billy Kinsley would go to Apple not knowing what would happen. "We were there every day, rehearsing or just jamming and sometimes Donovan would pop in. Pete Clarke kept his drum-kit at Apple and he gave me some drum lessons. Pete is a very competent teacher, and I learnt a lot from him. I remember Paul McCartney walking in and jamming with us on piano. He said, 'I wrote this last night. What do you think?' I was on drums and he started, 'You never give me your money' and so I was the first person to play drums on that song. After he left, Pete Clarke said to me, 'Did you listen to the words? It's got to be about Allen Klein.' It was a sarcastic song and the bad feelings were obvious by then. Paul didn't care for Klein and even if the Eastmans hadn't been there, I don't think he would have wanted him."

But Klein had to make some changes. Billy Kinsley: "John Lennon had made the statement, 'If we carry on like this, we'll be broke in 6 months', so somebody had to do something. I was there when Allen Klein came and although I didn't like the look of the guy, he did make a lot of necessary changes. A lot of people were being paid to do nothing, and you needed a businessman to say, 'You're doing nothing, you've got to go.' It was at the same time that the Beatles were breaking up and we were working independently with both Paul and George. There was some animosity between them and I was very sad about that as I'd grown up with the Beatles. I loved their music but being there in the Apple days was not very encouraging. I'd been there at the beginning and I was there at the end."

What was an example of the animosity? Billy Kinsley: "Something silly really. George Harrison had a big bar of Cadbury's Fruit and Nut and he gave pieces to me, Pete Clarke and Derek Taylor. Paul McCartney walked in and saw us all eating chocolate and wanted some. George, very deliberately, put the last piece in his mouth. It's childish, and I've done things like that in the Merseybeats, but Paul was really annoyed that George didn't give him his last piece of Fruit and Nut."

There's another song that might also convey the tensions at Apple. Billy Kinsley: "The Jackie Lomax band was jamming in a little studio in the basement of Apple. Paul McCartney walked in and he was going to record us a couple of weeks later. He said, 'What songs have you got?', and Jackie played a few. Paul said, 'Let's do something now', and so we started a 12-bar rock'n'roll song like 'Long Tall Sally' and 'I'm Down' and then Paul goes, 'You used to come around, baby, knockin' at my door, Giving me your lovin' which you don't give me no more. Oh no, oh no.' I did the next verse and then Jackie or Tim Rennick did another. That, for me, was the end of it."

Only it wasn't. Billy Kinsley: "Pete Clarke takes everything in and he remembered the first verse which Paul had written. In 1972 Pete and I were set to go to America as Gerry Marsden's new band, his new Pacemakers if you like. Gerry was looking for songs, so Clarkey said to me, 'What about that one that Paul wrote the first verse to? Why don't you finish that?' I did, and I made it less of a 12-bar by sticking in a couple of minor keys. We demoed the song and forgot about it, and then 4 years later with Liverpool Express, we wanted some new songs and recorded it, and it turned out great. We recorded it very quickly because it's best to do rock'n'roll songs like that. Then I thought we couldn't put it out as McCartney had written the first verse. Where would we stand with that? I told Mike McCartney and I said, 'Will you ask him what the situation is?' He rang me back within half an hour and said, 'Our kid says, "Don't worry about it. He doesn't remember it and it's your song." Really, I wanted it to be McCartney – Kinsley - Clarke. It didn't go on the first Liverpool Express album but it was a B-side of a single. That was the end of it again until the day after John Lennon died and the *Daily Express* headline said; 'John Lennon Murdered – Oh No'. You could see the connection with Ono. Then it hit me. I didn't realise until then that Paul had been making a statement."

June 1969, Thumbin' a Ride – Jackie Lomax (US Apple 1807, released in UK Feb 70 on Apple 23)
Paul McCartney, producer and backing vocals
Paul McCartney married Linda Eastman on 12 March 1969. Billy Kinsley: "Pete Clarke and I were at Apple rehearsing and recording with Jackie Lomax and then the news leaked out that Paul was getting married the next day. We assumed that the session with Paul would be cancelled and so we drove back to Liverpool for the weekend. In the papers the next day there was a photo of Paul playing Pete Clarke's drum kit that we had left a few hours before. Someone had the presence of mind to think that the photo must be the wrong way round because Paul is playing the kit right-handed. They turned the picture round, trying to be clever, but they weren't being clever as he was playing a right-handed kit. We got a phone call saying that the session was still on. We returned to London and Paul spent the night recording 'Thumbin' a Ride', and Linda wasn't there."

'Thumbin' a Ride' had originally been recorded by the Coasters. Billy Kinsley: "It was Paul's idea to do that. It was a great arrangement and I'm playing bass and doing backing vocals with Paul, Jackie and Billy Preston. Paul is very easy to work with in the studio, very relaxed. You could get very uptight about working with someone like that but he gets you relaxed. He'd laugh off mistakes, and that takes away the tension."

Peter Asher, now an Apple producer, was given a Lennon and McCartney song, 'Two of Us'. Billy Kinsley: "Mortimer was an American band that Apple had signed, and they didn't have a bass player and a drummer: it was a band of acoustic guitars and congas. They were good singers and they had a Lennon and McCartney song called 'Two Of Us', which the Beatles hadn't released. I had to work out a bass line as there is no bass on the Beatles' recording. George Harrison plays a rough bass line on his guitar, so their version's a bit strange. The session went fine, but Mortimer didn't have any releases on Apple. Klein was booting out everybody by then."

The Beatles' predicament did not always affect their creativity as there are some, but not many, good songs in *Let It Be*. Paul's 'Get Back' can be taken as a message to the others. He wrote 'The Long and Winding Road', which, strangely, became the Beatles' biggest-selling single in the US.

Alistair Taylor: "I was very privileged to see Paul sitting at the piano at three in the morning in the middle of the big studio at Abbey Road. He was picking out a melody on the piano and I said, 'I like that. It's a fabulous melody', and he said, 'It's just an idea'. I told him that my wife, Lesley, would love it and he told the engineer to put the tape on. He recorded 'The Long and Winding Road' then and there, it's full of la-la's as he'd only written a few lines, and it was fantastic. He gave me a copy for her."

April 1969, Get Back/ Don't Let Me Down (Apple R 5777, UK No.1, US No.1)
Mick Groves of the Spinners: "I think it was fantastic when they recorded 'Get Back' because all bands go through that, that is, 'Can we get back to where it was all happening when we were working together?' That's the thing that gets to bands, if only you could get back to the ideals that brought you together in the first place. I'm sure that song was a personal message to the rest of the Beatles. Paul was saying, 'Come on, lads, let's get our heads together and get back to what made us a good band in Hamburg and Liverpool.'"

American blues rocker George Thorogood: "The thing I like about Ray Davies, Pete Townshend and Mick Jagger is that they paid a lot of attention to Chuck Berry. People don't give them enough credit for that and consider them all hard rock bands. Chuck Berry is very funny when he wants to be and there is a lot of humour in their lyrics. 'Lola' sounds like something Chuck Berry would write. The very name of Loretta in 'Get Back' is very like Chuck Berry and the rhythm's the same, but the Stones had a step up on the Beatles as far as humour goes. The words of '19th Nervous Breakdown' and 'Satisfaction' are both very funny. Mick Jagger is seen as the master showman these days but he has written some very clever lyrics over the years."

May 1969, Unfinished Music No.2 – Life with the Lions LP – John Lennon and Yoko Ono (Zapple 01)
Together, John and Yoko made experimental films, albums and lithographs, maintaining a high public profile. Now involved in music publishing but then a fan, David Stark recalls, "I had a letter published in *Disc* when they released *Life with the Lions* and *Disc* had written, 'Why would anyone want to buy this album by John and Yoko? It is garbage.' I wrote in their defence that it was cosmic and wonderful. I came home from school the next day and found a letter in scrawled handwriting – 'Dear David, Thanks for the kind words, John and Yoko' – as the letter had been published with my address. I felt guilty as I hadn't heard the album! A while later, I gatecrashed the première for *The Magic Christian*. I told them about *Disc* and they thought it was hilarious that I had never heard the record. There is also the famous picture of John and Yoko outside Marylebone Magistrates Court when they got busted by the police. If you look carefully, you can see me standing behind John. I am the Zelig of Rock." Indeed. David should be recruited by the security forces to test breaches in their systems.

May 1969, Electronic Sound – George Harrison LP (Zapple 02)
In 1975, Lou Reed took a lot of flak for his *Metal Machine Music* but here's George Harrison playing on his synthesiser in 1969 without a melody in sight. In 2010 Lou Reed was touring with *Metal Machine Music*, presumably because people had been telling him how good it really is. Maybe George's album would have been rediscovered too.

May 1969, The Ballad of John and Yoko/ Old Brown Shoe (Apple R 5786, UK No.1, US No.8)
The years may have passed but John and Paul still took inspiration from Chuck Berry. Both Paul's heartfelt plea to the group, 'Get Back', and John's autobiographical 'The Ballad of John and Yoko' were written in his musical style. Although John and Paul had personal differences, they worked on 'The Ballad of John and Yoko' together: George and Ringo were away and John wanted to release the topical song quickly. Paul played guitar and drums and added his voice to the last words of

the lines. Although it looked like a vanity project, 'The Ballad of John and Yoko' was a No.1 for the Beatles in the summer of 69, but many thought his usage of the word 'Christ' was blasphemous. Even odder though was the reference to "Gibraltar near Spain", but still, lyrics have to fit.

Barry Miles: "Even when John and Paul were supposedly not talking to each other, John took 'The Ballad of John and Yoko' round to Paul. They were being commercial as the songwriting team generated most of their income. John wasn't going to throw it away over an argument about Klein. They would be in the middle of a terrible argument and John would pull his glasses down and look over the top and say,' It's only me' and defuse the whole thing."

Beatles biographer Mark Hertsgaard: "John wrote 'The Ballad of John and Yoko' when he had just come back from his honeymoon. The relationship between John and Paul was strained and they were at loggerheads over who should take Brian's place. The other two were away and John couldn't wait so he went to Paul's house telling him to come into the studio and play drums. After the second take, John is heard to say, 'You could go a bit faster, Ringo' and Paul comes back with 'OK, George.' The atmosphere was very professional but there was no electricity like the early days. They are like a married couple heading for the divorce courts and knowing they are going to bed together for the last time."

June 1969, My Dark Hour – Steve Miller Band (Capitol CL 15604)
Paul McCartney (as Paul Ramon), bass, drums, backing vocals
Aptly, Paul McCartney worked on 'My Dark Hour' the very day that Allen Klein was trying to persuade him to sign a management contract. Beatle fans will forever argue over Klein's merits but although he resolved the mess that was Apple, he intensified the split between Paul and the others. Paul, who married Linda Eastman in March 1969, wanted the Beatles to be represented by the Eastman family.

The Lennon and McCartney songs were valuable copyrights and many businessmen wanted to control them. EMI historian, Brian Southall: "Brian Epstein's death started the breakup of the Beatles. There was a split in management and there were lots of drugs around. Dick James was of the old school and had had enough of it. He saw the Lennon and McCartney partnership falling apart and he and his partner Charles Silver, who founded the company with him, decided to sell their stake in Northern Songs. They sold their shares to Lord Grade at ATV. Dick James didn't tell the Beatles what he was doing. He felt that they would never bid themselves as they were in disarray. As it happens, they launched a counterbid through their lawyers and a battle went on for control. A city consortium owned 14% and whoever secured that would have control of Northern Songs. Allen Klein structured a deal that was acceptable to all parties, but it fell apart when Lennon and McCartney realised that they would have little freedom in the future. John Lennon wasn't going to be told what to do by 'fat arses'. He walked out of the room and that was the end of their bid. The consortium then rang Lord Grade."

There was also the renewal of the Beatles' contract with EMI and the desire for better rates on their existing catalogue. Barry Miles: "There was a side to John Lennon that was quite commercial. When the time came for the renegotiation of their contracts with EMI, he wasn't going to screw it up. Klein said, 'You mustn't say anything about leaving the Beatles', and he didn't. It was ultimately McCartney who let it slip."

June 1969, That's the Way God Planned It/ What About You – Billy Preston (Apple 1, UK No.11)
George Harrison, producer

July 1969, Give Peace a Chance/ Remember Love – Plastic Ono Band (Apple 13, UK No.2, US No.14)
'Give Peace a Chance' was recorded by John and Yoko and a party of friends in a hotel room in Montreal and released under the name of the Plastic Ono Band. John had succeeded in writing a chant like 'We Shall Overcome' that could be used at peace rallies.

Paul Du Noyer: "John said on more than one occasion that he wanted to add his voice to the anti-Vietnam war movement. Partly it was a songwriter's vanity – he saw the impact of this great anthem 'We Shall Overcome' on the news and he wanted to write something with as much impact as that. Again, he had always wanted to write a big Christmas song, and he did that too. You could say that they were self-conscious efforts to get the whole world singing along."

Pete Seeger: "I can't say that I know much about the Beatles. I've only heard a few of their songs but some of them are really great. I happened to hear 'Give Peace a Chance' from a young woman guitar-picker just two days before I was going to a big peace demonstration in Washington on 11 November 1969. When I first heard it, I thought, 'That's a namby-pamby song, it doesn't have enough bite or militancy for me.' When I got there, I was faced with half a million people and I felt I needed a slow, slow song. I hadn't learnt anything but that one phrase but I tried it and, by gosh, it worked better and better as I kept going. Brother Kirkpatrick, Peter, Paul and Mary, and Mitch Miller came up to help me out. Before we knew it, we had half a million people swaying back and forth, like a huge ballet with children on their parents' shoulders. So 'Give Peace a Chance' is a very special song for me."

Although John Lennon wrote 'Give Peace a Chance', it still has Lennon and McCartney on the label. Paul Du Noyer: "I'm sure that Paul listened to John's solo work very closely, far more closely than John listened to Paul's stuff, mainly because he is competitive. John wasn't greatly interested in anything outside his own music, but Paul liked to keep up with everything. He was always extremely generous in his opinions about John, and I am prepared to give him the benefit of the doubt and say it is because he did admire what John did. Given the martyrdom of John Lennon, it became next to impossible for him to say anything critical about John. He would always say that 'Give Peace a Chance' was one of the greatest anthems of the century."

Hughie Jones of the Spinners: "I'd love to have seen the Beatles tackling more anti-war and social subjects. 'She's Leaving Home' was a social subject and very important but I would have liked some more anti-war things. 'Give Peace a Chance', 'Imagine' and that one about having no time for fussing and fighting are good examples, but I don't think they spent enough time on the subject. 'Give Peace a Chance' is very good but it's no more than a chant. Peace is the strongest possible subject for a song and once you've heard Eric Bogle's 'And the Band Played Waltzing Matilda', you will never, ever forget it. They could have written songs like that if they'd worked at it."

*August 1969, Hare Krishna Mantra/ Prayer to the Spiritual Masters –
Radha Krishna Temple (London) (UK No.12)*
George Harrison, producer

*August 1969, That's the Way God Planned It – Billy Preston (LP, Apple
SAPCOR 9)*
George Harrison, producer

August 1969, Songs for a Tailor – Jack Bruce LP (Polydor 583 058)
George Harrison (as L'Angelo Misterioso), rhythm guitar on 'Never Tell
Your Mother She's Out of Tune'
The festivals, Monterey and Woodstock, showed how rock music could
be marketed to a huge, young, mostly hippie, audience. The British
weather was an imponderable factor for all open air events in the UK,
although Woodstock had been no picnic. A promoter could lose a lot
of money, especially if the barriers came crashing down and the bands
wanted to be paid.

Although John and Yoko attended but didn't perform at the Isle
of Wight Festival in 1969, they did work as the Plastic Ono Band a
fortnight later at the Toronto Peace Festival. They planted acorns for
peace, promoted Bagism and even said they were both having sex
change operations (they didn't).

Tom Paxton, who had written and recorded a song about Lennon,
'Crazy John' was playing at the Isle of Wight festival. "Bob Dylan
brought me back to this secluded backstage rendezvous to which only
the invited could go. Shortly afterwards, John, George and Ringo
showed up with their ladies and Bob introduced me to John. He said,
'John, I want you to meet Tom Paxton' and John said, 'Oh, Crazy
John', which was a wonderful tribute. That night, during the concert
with the band and Dylan, I sat with John and Yoko in the press area and
something happened that I have never forgotten. Security was intense,
so there wasn't anyone there who wasn't in some way connected with
the music business. Even so, a fellow leaned over from behind and
asked John and Yoko for his autograph. John very politely and very
quietly said, 'No, if I start, I'll never get to stop' and the guy burst out
with profanity, spewing hate all over John's head. He called him every
name you could think of. Two minutes later, he came back, practically
crawling on his belly. Throughout this entire barrage, John sat with
his head bowed, looking at the ground. When it was all over, I said,
'Does that happen a lot?' and he said, 'Every time I leave the house.' I
thought, 'My god, what a price to pay.'"

A few weeks later, Kim Fowley introduced the Plastic Ono Band
at the Toronto Rock'n'Roll Festival: "John Lennon was in his white
suit throwing up and he was supposed to be on stage. He told me to
distract the audience. I had seen the film, *The Miracle of Our Lady of
Fatima*, where the villagers light candles when Our Lady comes down.
I thought of that and I asked 22,000 people to light matches or use

their lighters to give John a ritualistic welcome. It gave him a religious glow when he came on, and it worked. Everybody takes their lighters to festivals now, but that was the first time it was done."

In 2009, I was fortunate enough to interview two musicians – Klaus Voormann (bass) and Alan White (drums) – about the event.

Klaus Voormann:" John called me and said that he was going to form the Plastic Ono Band for a concert the next day and I thought, 'That sounds strange, better be careful: maybe we will have to play naked on stage or something.'"

Alan White: "...or in a bag. John called me and I thought it was a friend who was joking. I said, 'No, no' and put the phone down. He called me back 10 minutes later and said, 'No, really, this is John Lennon and can you be at the airport in the morning? We are doing the gig tomorrow.' We all got on the plane and there had been no rehearsals, nothing."

Klaus Voormann: "I had no idea who this drummer was! He was like a little boy speaking Newcastle and I couldn't understand a word."

Alan White: "John saw me playing in a club and he must have thought, He's a young guy and he's pretty good. That's what happened. I'd done some work with Billy Fury and Alan Price, but this was a huge stepping-stone in my career."

Despite the hurried booking, the fans knew when they were arriving. Alan White: "Allen Klein was in the car with us going from the airport to the gig and we had fans or journalists following us, chasing the car. Allen Klein gave the tyre iron to the driver and said, 'Throw it out of the window and we'll get rid of them.' He meant it too. I said, 'What are you talking about?' He wanted us to hit the car next to us and we could have killed somebody. Don't you remember that?" Klaus Voormann: "No, I think I must have been in that other car!"

And then there is the drama of the performance itself.

Klaus Voormann: "We had one amplifier in the dressing room: we all plugged into one little amp and you had a snare and a high-hat, and that was it."

Alan White: "That's why John says, 'We've never played together before.'"

Klaus Voormann: "John threw up too. I was hoping he hadn't thrown up on his nice white suit."

Alan White: "It was one of John's first solo things and even though it was chaotic, I knew it was important."

Klaus Voormann: "Here we have a Beatle, someone who has been in the best band in the world, and he makes his first solo appearance with a band that has never played before. It was so ridiculous."

Alan White: "I think we did a pretty good job of covering everything up. I like the spontaneity of it."

John and Yoko stayed with the Canadian rock'n'roll star, Ronnie Hawkins: "John was in Canada signing lithographs and Ritchie Yorke, who was a journalist for *Rolling Stone*, was playing one of my records, 'Down in the Alley'. I hadn't intended to play him my stuff 'cause everybody in the world does that. Everybody's on the hype. He listened to it a couple of times and he really liked it. He did a promo for the record company saying that it was his favourite song of the year and that it combined the old with the new."

September 1969, Abbey Road LP (Apple PCS 7008, UK No.1, US No.1)
Produced by George Martin, 17 tracks – 47 minutes 23 seconds
Side 1: Come Together/ Something/ Maxwell's Silver Hammer/ Oh! Darling/ Octopus's Garden/ I Want You (She's So Heavy)
Side 2: Here Comes the Sun/ Because/ You Never Give Me Your Money/ Sun King/ Mean Mr. Mustard/ Polythene Pam/ She Came In Through the Bathroom Window/ Golden Slumbers/ Carry That Weight/ The End/ Her Majesty

Considering that 1969 was to be the Beatles' last full year together, the Beatles were extremely active. After *Let It Be* had been filmed, they set about what was to be their final album, the much more disciplined *Abbey Road,* although several songs had been featured in the *Let It Be* rehearsals. It is, however, so much more together than *Let It Be.* The second side of the album was taken up by a suite of songs, largely written by Paul McCartney, which encompasses some of their finest work.

They had thought of calling the album, *Everest,* but as no one wanted to go to the Himalayas for a photoshoot, it was changed to *Abbey Road.* It was apt, the scene of their greatest achievements, unlike the Stones who recorded in several studios.

Ian Macmillan's photograph of the four Beatles on a zebra crossing outside Abbey Road has made this another iconic album sleeve and because of its simplicity, it is also among the most copied. The first was Booker T and the MG's *McLemore Avenue* and there has been New

York City's *Soulful Road*. Other albums named after studios have been Creedence Clearwater Revival's *Cosmo's Factory* and Eric Clapton's *461 Ocean Boulevard*. Benny Hill, Hinge and Bracket, *The Red Hot Chili Peppers, Seinfield, The Young Ones* and *The Simpsons* have all parodied the sleeve, and as the best tribute of all, the EMI Studios were renamed Abbey Road.

Photographer Eamonn McCabe: "The hardest thing in our world is getting time with famous people. With *Abbey Road*, they may have been in the building for the whole day and the photographer was told that he could have them for 15 minutes. What do you do with the Beatles in 15 minutes? Well, the photographer had the bright idea of getting them to walk across that zebra crossing and it has immediacy to it. There are people looking at what's going on, and there's a police van probably protecting the Beatles. It's a very simple picture, and the photographer is elevated, probably on a ladder, looking down at the road, because if he was at street level he would be looking at the bodies, and that's how you get the effect of the stripes in the zebra crossing."

George Martin: "*Let It Be* was a very uncomfortable time. I was losing control of the boys and they were losing control of themselves. I thought it was the end of everything and so I was quite happily surprised when they asked me to make another album with them. They realised that they didn't like *Let It Be* and they asked me to come and take over. They wanted me to exert control the way I did in the *Pepper* days. So I did and *Abbey Road* proved to be a very happy album. They'd been disliking each other and having punch-ups, but now they came together and collaborated very well. I was very pleased that the group went out on a note of harmony and not one of discord." Precisely. What better swan song could a band have than *Abbey Road*?

Billy Bob Thornton: "I like George Harrison's songs, and 'Here Comes the Sun' is one of my favourite Beatles songs. It's a fantastic song. George seized his chance on *Abbey Road*: 'Quick, while the others aren't looking!'"

Cutting engineer George Peckham: "Paul didn't want George to do too many songs, but John would say, 'Hang on, give him a chance, that's not a bad number.' John was on his side and Paul was putting him down." Having said that, John almost went out of his way *not* to play on George's songs. Lennon is not on 'Long Long Long', 'Savoy Truffle', 'Here Comes The Sun' and 'I Me Mine'

Donovan: "All psychedelia points to one thing and one thing only:

there is a spiritual path that the world needs and it was the singers and painters and dancers and filmmakers and poets that presented this path to the world. Now the doors of perception are open and George pointed the way by singing, 'Here comes the sun, And I say, It's all right.'"

Richie Havens: "I thought 'Here Comes the Sun' was the happiest, simplest, clearest wishing well for the world of all the songs that they had ever done. It is a message for all of us. The sun is going to come up tomorrow, no matter what. You've got to be prepared, it's going to be all right. Things are not as hard as you're making it. That was the message of the time that needed to be heard. I said that to George and he said, 'It is a song about finding the light, the real light, the sun.'"

Steve Harley of Cockney Rebel, who took 'Here Comes the Sun' into the Top 10 in 1976. "'Here Comes the Sun' is a fine example of a well-crafted pop song, like 'Waterloo Sunset'. George has this weekend hippie, euphoric state on his version whereas I was saying that I could understand what he was writing even if he couldn't. Mine's apocalyptic. I wanted 16 to a bar on the ride cymbal and lots of accents, I saw it as a song of impending doom."

Joey Bower from the Fourmost: "The Beatles gave us a tape of their new album and said, 'Pick what you like.' We chose 'Maxwell's Silver Hammer' but we should have gone for 'Something'. How did we overlook that? Our record was played on *Juke Box Jury* and Cliff Richard was on the panel. He said, 'It's not a hit but I'd love to have been in the studio while they were making it as it sounds like they were having a great time.'"

The Fourmost's single was released under the new name of Format. Billy Hatton: "CBS thought we should put it out under a different name and then if it was a hit, we could say, 'Na- na-na-na-na, it's us'. I did a quick bit of mouth music, a trombone, in 'Maxwell's Silver Hammer'. That record is just us as we were, not taking things too seriously."

Today most people regard the song 'Maxwell's Silver Hammer' as, at best, inconsequential and, at worst, sadistic. It is therefore surprising to read William Mann's critique of *Abbey Road* in *The Times* when it was released. He thought 'Come Together' and 'Something' were only "minor pleasures. For mass appeal, I would have pinned greater hopes on 'Maxwell's Silver Hammer', a neo-vaudeville comic song about a jocular murderer and Ringo Starr's 'Octopus's Garden' which might be called 'Son Of Yellow Submarine' and like 'Maxwell', delights the teeny-bopper in all of us."

Eric Stewart of 10cc had a hit with 'Donna' that appeared to be based on 'Oh! Darling' from *Abbey Road*. "Paul McCartney has said to me a few times, 'Where are my royalties for 'Donna'?', but I tell him he can afford it. The song didn't come from him actually. In the 50s there was another screaming song just like that, but I can't remember the title of it. We both got the idea from that." (There are elements of Jackie Wilson in there, so possibly it was 'Doggin' Around' or 'A Woman, A Lover, A Friend'.)

Even more unrefined than 'Oh! Darling' is John Lennon's 'I Want You (She's So Heavy)'. The 7 minute track which ends unexpectedly uses extreme repetition to ram home its lustful message. John Lennon's tormented lead vocal is as exciting as 'Twist and Shout' and the backing, which includes Lennon on synthesiser and Billy Preston on organ, is superb. McCartney enjoyed the track so much that there is an unissued take with him on lead vocal.

The Beatles' harmonies can be heard on 'Because' (which John had written after playing the 'Moonlight Sonata' backwards) and 'Sun King' (which, cod Italian notwithstanding, sounds suspiciously close to 'Albatross'). We know that the Beatles liked Fleetwood Mac as they approached them to join Apple Records.

Mark Wirtz wrote and recorded 'Excerpt From A Teenage Opera' for singer Keith West: "Paul McCartney told me that Side 2 of *Abbey Road* had been inspired by some of my stuff. The Beatles and I shared the same engineer Geoff Emerick and so there was a kinship there. I loved *Tommy* but there were very few efforts in the spirit of what I had in mind. The Pretty Things did a good job with *S.F. Sorrow* and Pink Floyd's *The Wall* is fabulous, fantastic, but it was the Who that took the Rock Opera to the finishing line. I don't count *Jesus Christ Superstar* as that is a conventional musical with some rock instrumentation."

On *Abbey Road,* one song bleeds into another and earlier sections are reprised. The pieces are held together and there are back references to what we have heard earlier. George Martin: "There's far more of me on *Abbey Road* than on any of their other albums. The symphonic piece on side two was my idea and, to be quite honest, John didn't approve. He only wrote a little of it and he preferred the rock'n'roll things on side one."

Alan Parsons: "*Abbey Road* was really a compilation of solo work and most days there would only be one or two of them in the studio.

It was done very quickly in 8 weeks and it was Paul's idea to have the symphonic piece which we called 'The Long One'. I can remember Paul saying in George's absence that 'Something' was the best thing he'd written but I don't know if he said this to his face. George would have been well pleased to know that."

Paul McCartney biographer, Chris Salewicz: "The Apple Scruffs were girls who used to hang out at Apple. They were not groupies, just particularly obsessive fans. One of them broke into Paul's house in St John's Wood and took a number of things including one of the few photographs Paul had of his father. He asked the girls to find out what they could do about this and the photograph did reappear, hence the song 'She Came in Through the Bathroom Window'. Actually, she came in through the bathroom window up a ladder, and Paul said it couldn't be a girl because 'girls can't climb ladders'."

Liverpool artist and painter Adrian Henri knew Polythene Pam: "The girl was actually called Polythene Pat, but they changed her name. She was one of the original hardcore Beatle fans whom they knew by name and they would give her a lift. She was one of the original Cavern dwellers and she used to eat polythene: it wasn't a bizarre sexual thing or anything, she just ate polythene. I was in America when I first heard 'Polythene Pam'. It was weird hearing a bit of obscure Liverpool history on a jukebox in New York."

Abbey Road was rounded off with a cheeky and short, Paul McCartney song, 'Her Majesty'. As far as I know, this was the first album to have an uncredited track, and now with bonus tracks on CDs and Easter eggs on DVDs, such things are commonplace. Once again, the Beatles had started something.

But even the quality of *Abbey Road* could not entice the Beatles to stay together as a musical unit. They preferred their individual projects.

October 1969, Something/ Come Together (Parlophone R 5814, UK No.4, US No.1)
The single of 'Something' and 'Come Together' came from *Abbey Road*. It only reached No.4, probably because most fans had bought the album. At first both sides were shown on the US chart with 'Something' at No.11 and 'Come Together' at No.10. 'Come Together' climbed to No.2, only to be replaced the following week by 'Something' at No.2, By then, *Billboard* had realised that listing different sides of the same record separately was daft. The following week, they amalgamated the

sales and so, after 7 weeks, the Beatles had another US No.1.

John Lennon wrote the suggestively titled 'Come Together' but borrowed a couple of phrases from Chuck Berry's 'You Can't Catch Me' (1956). Considering that Chuck Berry had done so well from the British beat groups, it should have been brushed aside, but not a bit of it.

Music writer Paul Du Noyer: "John Lennon called Chuck Berry another name for rock'n'roll, so that's how high he regarded him. Chuck Berry was a great words man and his songs are like movie scripts, detailed and precise. John would have certainly known what he was doing when he wrote 'Come Together' and it was one of his lapses in judgment. He didn't realise that Chuck Berry had a very opportunistic publisher working for him, Morris Levy who was a real sharp customer. At one time in the 1950s, he had even tried to copyright the term, rock'n'roll, so that anyone who used it would have to pay him a royalty." As part of the settlement, John Lennon agreed to eat humble pie and record 'You Can't Catch Me' on his 1975 album, *Rock'n'Roll*.

Chris Rea: "'Something' is just gorgeous – classic George Harrison and classic Beatles. He was my favourite Beatle but if one of them had been missing, it mightn't have happened like it did. Ringo was an antidote to the others, like flesh and blood, and his drumming is superb. It is more than technical, he has good blues feel, you know. You can get Cornell Dupree or B.B. King to play three notes on the guitar and it does more to you than 1,000 notes from a guitarist who has practiced very hard. Ringo's drumming was like that."

'Something' was easily the most covered song on *Abbey Road*, being famously recorded by Frank Sinatra. In concert, Sinatra called it a Lennon and McCartney song, causing George to reflect, "He was very old by then and we probably all looked the same to him." Still, Frank did call it "the greatest love song ever written". George's sister, Louise Harrison: "George wasn't particularly made up that Frank Sinatra had recorded 'Something'. Once I was staying with him at the Plaza in New York and he spent the night hiding from Frank's guys who were after him. Sinatra wanted him to write a whole album for him and he felt that these weren't the sort of people you said no to."

Between them, the Beatles had written 200 songs in 7 years, many of them undeniable classics, but how did they shape up against the composers of previous generations like Rodgers and Hart and Cole Porter?

Orchestra leader Stanley Black: "I am strictly a middle-of-the-road man. My ideal artists are Frank Sinatra and Ella Fitzgerald, so when the Beatles burst upon the scene, I wasn't entirely grabbed by their music. It took somebody else's recording, an American singer called Keely Smith, to make me realise, for the first time, that they wrote wonderful songs. The Beatles never grabbed me as performers but they did as songwriters."

Jazz guitarist Barney Kessel: "I wouldn't rate the Beatles at all. I wouldn't go across the street to see them. It's not my music and it's not for me. It doesn't stack up to Duke Ellington or Cole Porter. There's no malice in what I say. It's like saying 'I don't care for peppermint or tobacco or a certain kind of candy bar', it doesn't mean I hate it."

George Melly: "They haven't got the glittering, chromium sophistication of Cole Porter, but their songs will last as long. There's room for more than one kind of song-writing in the world and into the Beatles' songs go things that were certainly not in Cole Porter's. There's the influence of George Formby on 'When I'm Sixty-Four' and the portrayal of provincial Liverpool. There's room for that as well as Cole Porter's Manhattan or Paris."

Barney Kessel: "Frank Sinatra and Ella Fitzgerald recorded Beatle songs but who can say what their motives were? Very often they have to work from the standpoint of what a producer wants them to record, they are being paid a fee for that. The producer says, 'Look, we are paying you what you want. Now, give us the chance to sell some records. This is what I want you to do.' It might be that they liked those songs, it might be that they insisted upon recording them, it might be that they felt intimidated and wanted to reach younger people. They are intimidated by not sticking to their values. To me, good music is timeless, just like Shakespeare, just like the Rolls-Royce, just like Keats and Byron, just like Lord Olivier. These things transcend time. Time does not deteriorate their worth. If Frank Sinatra or Ella Fitzgerald recorded those songs for any other reason than they wanted to do them, then they were not being true to themselves."

Curtis Stigers: "Tony Bennett threw up before he went in the studio because of the things that he had to sing for Mitch Miller at Columbia. Sinatra did 'Something' and you gather that it may not have been the best choice, you know, when he says 'Jack' in the middle of it. There are some questionable decisions when these pop jazz singers were trying to stay in vogue. They couldn't compete with the Beatles and the Stones and perhaps they should have taken the decade off and gone to the beach."

October 1969, Cold Turkey/ Don't Worry Kyoko – Plastic Ono Band (Apple 1001, UK No.14, US No.30)
The second Plastic Ono Band single was 'Cold Turkey'. John had offered it to the Beatles but they had turned it down. It was a step too far. The phrase was not in common usage but it was a harrowing song about drug withdrawal, foreshadowing John's first solo album and it could not hope to be a major success. John Lennon was to return his MBE in protest over "Britain's involvement in the Nigeria-Biafra thing, against our support of America in Vietnam and against 'Cold Turkey' slipping down the charts".

October 1969, Wedding Album – John Ono Lennon and Yoko Ono Lennon LP (Apple SAPCOR 11)
A ridiculous story started in the States suggesting that Paul McCartney had been dead for over 2 years and that the Beatles' records were scattered with clues. It started with the *Abbey Road* cover where Paul is out of step with his bandmates – how unusual! Paul was barefoot, like a corpse (so it went), John was the minister, George the gravedigger and Ringo the funeral director.

Paul had his back to the camera on the back cover of *Sgt. Pepper*; John is said to mumble "I buried Paul" at the end of 'Strawberry Fields Forever': the number plate of a car on the cover of *Abbey Road* is 281 F and Paul would have been 28 IF he were alive, and so on. Paul denied that he was dead, but nobody believed him.

Beatles writer and lecturer on *Paul Is Dead*, Joel Glazier: "The *Abbey Road* cover led to the discovery of clues as to whether Paul was dead. On the front cover, Paul was the one who was out of step, Paul was the one who was barefoot which is how people are buried in India, and Paul had his cigarette in the wrong hand. People said that a double had taken his place. These were the clues that started it and people started to search the other albums for more clues - and found them! Some clues can be explained away but you've still got hundreds of others to account for. Paul could have given us absolute, conclusive proof that he was still alive, but he never chose to do that."

George Martin: "I started getting letters about how obvious it was that Paul was dead and why were we covering it up. Paul was round at my place one afternoon and we had a good laugh about it, but it wasn't so funny to be woken in the middle of the night by some little girl in Wisconsin wanting to know if he was still alive."

Tony Barrow: "There were rumours all through the years that one of the Beatles had been killed in a road crash or fallen off a cliff or whatever. Some of them were from fans ringing up the press so that the press would ring me and thereby find out where the Beatles were. If the press asked me if Paul was in a crash in Edinburgh, I would say, 'No, he's in Paris.' After many unfounded rumours, things came to a head when a lot of people said they could prove that the Beatles themselves were admitting that Paul McCartney had died and had been replaced. It was a fascinating story, but totally without foundation."

The *Sgt. Pepper* cover was a rich source for clues. Peter Blake: "A young boy who was helping asked if he could make a guitar in hyacinths. It seemed a nice, simple, lovely idea so I said, 'Yes, that's fine'. If you look at the little, white guitar now, you can read 'Paul?' which was one of the things around the time of the rumour that Paul was dead."

Paul Gambaccini: "Even if Paul wasn't dead, the Beatles were! The Beatles knew that *Abbey Road* was going to be their last goodbye: the last track to be listed was even called 'The End'. It was a very good goodbye: the Beatles were in their death throes, but they could still cut it."

December 1969, Live Peace in Toronto – The Plastic Ono Band (Apple CORE 2001)
Despite the hurried formation of the band, John Lennon was presumably happy with the result as he released it as an album.

December 1969, Come and Get It – Badfinger (Apple 2, UK No.4, US No.7, Germany No.34)
Paul McCartney, producer, piano, maracas
Ringo Starr appeared in the films, *Candy* and *The Magic Christian*, which was funded by Apple. Denis O'Dell: "Terry Southern came to Apple with *The Magic Christian* and he wanted to make it as a film very badly. I thought it would have been good for Apple, but there was not enough money in that part of the company. Terry Southern, Joe McGrath and I got it financed through British Commonwealth. It had bad reviews and the company lost money, and the film has

changed hands so many times that I don't know who owns it now. It would make a marvellous DVD as it has Ringo and Peter Sellers in it, a lot of guest stars, and Paul and Badfinger's music. Peter Sellers loved making films but he had a terrible attitude to life. One day he fired a continuity girl because she was wearing purple on the set. He would get so despondent about things."

Joey Molland of Badfinger: "Paul McCartney wrote 'Come and Get It' for *The Magic Christian* but he was nice enough to give us the song. I'm sure he wouldn't have given it to a group on any other label. He was going to do it himself but as we had had a semi-success with 'Maybe Tomorrow', he thought it was a good idea. He let the band write the other music for the film and the band has three songs in the film."

In January 1970, Badfinger had a Top 10 hit with 'Come and Get It'. If anything, it shows the strength of the song and the performance as the record had little promotion because Apple was in such disarray. The music for the film is the best thing about it and the worst things about it are Peter Sellers' unfocused performance and Ringo Starr's somnambulistic acting. Ringo is, however, far worse in *Candy*. On the face of it, *Candy* had the best cast in the world including Richard Burton, James Coburn and Marlon Brando. Terry Southern, who could write cutting satire about the 60s deserved better than the messes that were *The Magic Christian* and *Candy*.

December 1969, The Beatles' Seventh Christmas Record (and the last one too: for the fan club)
Kenny Everett produced the final Christmas record for the fan club. All four Beatles contribute separately with John being interviewed by a childish Yoko. They sing the avant-garde 'Happy Christmas', while Paul comes out with the reggae-like 'This Is to Wish You'. Ringo plugs *The Magic Christian* and sings a snatch of a Christmas song, 'Mama's Little Boy' while George has a short and daft Christmas message.

December 1969, No One's Gonna Change Our World – Various Artists (Starline SRS 5013).
The Beatles contribute 'Across the Universe'
Spike Milligan had suggested to EMI the idea for a charity album, a rare event at the time, for the World Wildlife Fund. The Beatles contributed a new song, 'Across the Universe'. Hunter Davies: "When I interviewed

John at home, he would often be drunk, stoned or hung-over. One time out by pool, we heard a police siren with its two-tone wailing and John started playing with the sound that eventually became the riff for 'Across the Universe'."

Barbara Dickson: "My favourite of their songs is 'Across the Universe' without a doubt. That is a great John Lennon song, although I don't like everything he did. Controversially, I don't care for 'Imagine'. It's too sentimental but usually I love his words. I love Paul's tunes so together they were magic. Neither was as great without the other. Lennon was not as melodious, although he has had his moments, and the same with Paul, who is often not a good lyricist. It was a fantastic gift to popular culture that these two boys got together and sat on single beds in hotel rooms and wrote those songs, songs that everybody considers to be legendary."

The dream was over. The Beatles' close friend, Barry Miles: "The Beatles encapsulate the 60s so perfectly. They started pretty much in 1960 and broke up at the end of the decade. They both led everything and embraced everything. They were great spokesmen for the psychedelic period. They wore incredible clothes. They picked all that up from the circles they were moving in and they were brilliant at absorbing street culture. In Liverpool they were moving around the art students and picking stuff up from the poets and then transforming it into something much more universal. They did that in London as well. They were very astute at picking up even the slightest little vibes, and it seemed that they had invented things although they very rarely had. By the end of that decade I was absolutely worn out and I think the Beatles were too. We'd done too much. It wasn't just drugs. It had been tremendously exciting. You leapt out of bed in the morning and there was so much to do and it was a wonderful period."

Paul, more than the others, wanted the Beatles to continue, but probably only on his terms. Look, however, at the front page of the *Daily Mirror* for 20 March 1971 – the headline is "The New Beatle" and the new Beatle is Klaus Voormann. I had this with me when I was talking to Klaus Voormann and Alan White in 2009.

Klaus Voormann: "Wonderful! Great!"

Me: "Did you know that this was going to be in the paper?"

Klaus Voormann: "No, no, of course not. The papers invent lots of things and they said I was going to replace Paul. Perhaps I should have done that!"

Alan White: "Admit it, Klaus, you played bass on everything, and Paul was just sitting in the background! "

Klaus Voormann: "I wouldn't have liked it anyway. The breakup was the most natural thing to happen to the band. They were so close for such a long time that it just had to happen. It was not fair to ask them to stay together just because the fans wanted them to."

So the 1960s ended with the Beatles on the verge of collapse. No one's gonna change our world was right – there was no need for anyone to do that, they were perfectly capable of messing it up by themselves. The break-up was presented as a permanent split. These days, groups often disband for a few years and come back together for a new album and a world tour, the Rolling Stones being a prime example. Why didn't the Beatles think of that?

CHAPTER 10

You Know How Hard It Can Be (1970)

UK voting age lowered to 18 – Edward Heath becomes Prime Minister – Radioactive leaks at Windscale – Arab guerrillas hijack UK plane – Death of Charles de Gaulle.

January 1970, All That I've Got – Billy Preston (Apple 21)
George Harrison, producer
February 1970, How the Web was Woven/ Thumbin' a Ride – Jackie Lomax (Apple 23)
George Harrison, producer (A-side): Paul McCartney, producer (B-side)
John and Yoko had their hair cut short and faced controversy with their erotic lithographs in the London Arts Gallery, eight of which were confiscated by the police. John's obsession with sex is apparent throughout his work and it was no surprise that Kenneth Tynan asked him to contribute to the erotic stage revue, *Oh, Calcutta!* Following the success of *In His Own Write*, John Lennon knew theatre folk and he would easily have found someone to stage a musical, if he (and/or Paul) wrote one.

Music writer Stephen Citron: "Lennon and McCartney have some lovely harmonies in their songs and it would have been nice if they had tried a musical. It takes discipline to do that as you have to work the songs into a story. *Hair* did a lot of the things that I could imagine Lennon and McCartney doing. It talks about freedom, gurus, Indian influences, honesty and the spirit of young people and it is also a great musical. 'Aquarius' is a standard and is very much like a Beatles song and 'Let the Sunshine in' could have been a Lennon anthem."

Maybe, but John Lennon did see *Hair* in London and wasn't impressed. He told the journalist, Ray Connolly, in 1971, "No musicals. I loathe musicals. I never did have a plan for doing one. I think they're just horrible. Even *Hair*."

Februry 1970, Instant Karma!/ Who Has Seen the Wind – Plastic Ono Band (Apple 1003. UK No.5, US No.3)
On 27 January 1970, John wrote and recorded a new song. 'Instant Karma!' which he made with the American record producer Phil Spector, another client of Allen Klein's. The Plastic Ono Band promoted it on *Top of the Pops*, the first time a Beatle had been live on the programme since 1966.

Music writer Paul Du Noyer: "John didn't like his own voice as he thought it was too hard and dry and nasal, which it is if you compare it to Paul's which is softer, rounder and more musical. His is a harder edged, rock'n'roll voice. John went for the reverb out of self-consciousness and out of a love for the early Elvis and the Phil Spector sound which was drenched in echo. You get it in full on 'Instant Karma!'."

February 1970, The Magic Christian – Original soundtrack with Badfinger and Ken Thorne and his Orchestra (Pye NSPL 28133)
Ringo went to the States for the opening of *The Magic Christian* and appeared on the TV comedy show, *Rowan and Martin's Laugh-In*.
February 1970, Ain't That Cute/ Vaya Con Dios – Doris Troy (Apple 24)
George Harrison, producer (both sides) and guitar (B-side)

March 1970, Govinda/ Govinda Jai Jai – Radha Krishna Temple (Apple 25, UK No.23)
George Harrison, producer
March 1970, Let It Be/ You Know My Name (Look Up the Number) (Apple R 5833, UK No.1, US No.1)
McCartney biographer Chris Salewicz: "Paul wrote 'Let It Be' about his mother. It was a very difficult time for Paul within the Beatles. He would lie in bed tossing and turning and trying to go to sleep. One night, when he did go to sleep, he had a dream in which Mother Mary came to him 'speaking words of wisdom'."

Bruce Dickinson of Iron Maiden: "My favourite Beatles' track by a million miles is 'Let It Be'. I find it amazingly uplifting. It is like a hymn and I like some hymns."

Beatles biographer Steven Stark: "People who have lost their mother tend to take any subsequent loss very badly, and Paul wrote 'Let It Be' at the time that the band was breaking up and he dreamed about his mother. Paul went off to Scotland for 5 or 6 months and was inconsolable. It was not just the money – it was the music, the friendship and the great ride that they'd had. He took it harder than the others."

It is possible that Paul McCartney had not intended 'Let It Be' for the Beatles. Atlantic record producer Jerry Wexler: "The Beatles sent me an acetate of 'Let It Be' for Aretha Franklin. She recorded it but when it came to release time, she never approved it. She said, 'I don't want that out.' A year went by and we had this beautiful record in the can and finally the Beatles decided that enough was enough, and they wanted to release their own version and sent a legal notice restricting us from putting out the record. That was their right. I can't validate this but I think Aretha's would have been a huge smash. Aretha never showed any regret or remorse. She never would say anything like that and it would have served no purpose if she had."

Mr Bean himself, Rowan Atkinson: "We never had a television in our house until I was 14 because my parents didn't approve of it. I was at university for most of the 70s and I caught up with the Beatles there. I went to two universities and spent 6 years there, and the one particular track that was always with me was 'Let It Be'. When I was doing my electrical engineering exams at Newcastle University, I had a superstition about playing 'Let It Be' just before I went to bed. I had it spooled up on a tape recorder. I use to press 'Play' at a quarter to eleven, listen to 'Let It Be' and then go to sleep. For some reason it used to make me cry slightly and I still blink when I hear it. As I got the top degree in my year, the Beatles can bring you luck."

The B-side of 'Let It Be' was a pastiche of lounge jazz, 'You Know My Name (Look Up the Number)'. It was the Beatles at their silliest and included John Lennon grumbling in French. It is as though the Bonzo Dog Band had decided to record the Shadows' 'What a Lovely Tune'. McCartney has often spoken of his affection for this record, possibly because it was made when all four Beatles were enjoying themselves.

Denis O'Dell: "When I was producing *The Magic Christian*, I started getting strange calls from the States like, 'We know your name, now we're going to get your number.' My wife went berserk. Over one weekend, I said, 'I will answer all the calls.' True enough, I got a call. I kept them talking and it turned out to be five guys from a candle factory in Philadelphia. They put the fear of God in me, and they turned up 2 weeks later on my doorstep. It was shortly after the murder of Roman Polanski's wife. This was all done with love, but it was very hairy at the time."

David Stark: "One Saturday night when I was about 17, I was with my friend Vince and we thought that we would ask Ringo for a drink. We knew which street he lived in but not which house. We knocked on the first door and it was Lulu and Maurice Gibb's. She said, 'Just down the end on the right.' and was very nice. Can you imagine that today? There were no gates, just a big drive with a few cars, and we rang the bell and Ringo came to the door. 'Hello, boys', he said and we looked like bedraggled hippies. We asked him to come out for a drink and he said, 'Thanks very much but we have a few people over tonight.' I could see Eric Clapton walking behind him in the hall."

March 1970, Leon Russell – Leon Russell LP (US Shelter SHE 1001: UK A&M AMLS 982)
George Harrison, guitar: Ringo Starr, drums
March 1970, Sentimental Journey – Ringo Starr LP (Apple PCS 7101)
Paul McCartney, arranger Star Dust
Ringo's first solo album was a collection of standards. It's pleasant and has some good arrangements, but Ringo was out of his depth. The cover, showing his local pub in Liverpool, suggested that he was simply doing an album of pub songs.
April 1970, McCartney – Paul McCartney LP (Apple PCS 7102)
From time-to-time one of the Beatles wanted to announce that he was leaving the group, but he was talked out of it by the others. An official announcement came with the release of Paul's first solo album, *McCartney*, in April 1970. The press release that accompanied the album included an interview with McCartney which made it clear that the Beatles were finished. John was furious as he felt that the group had been disbanded solely to market Paul's solo album and, in any event, they were on the verge of releasing *Let It Be*.

The McCartney album has its moments but mostly it was a friendly, fragmented affair. There are some good songs ('Maybe I'm Amazed', 'Every Night' and a song that the Beatles almost released, 'Teddy Boy') but mostly, it is like a whole album of 'Her Majesty'.

April 1970, Delaney and Bonnie on Tour LP (Atlantic 2400 013)
George Harrison, guitar
May 1970, Let It Be LP (Apple PCS 7096)
Produced by Phil Spector, 12 tracks – 35 minutes 13 seconds
Side 1: Two of Us/ Dig a Pony/ Across the Universe/ I Me Mine/ Dig It/
Let It Be/ Maggie Mae
Side 2: I've Got a Feeling/ The One After 909/ The Long and Winding
Road/ For You Blue/ Get Back

There are hours and hours of Beatle outtakes from their *Let It Be* sessions in January 1969. A proposed album had been put together by Glyn Johns under George Martin's supervision, but the Beatles had rejected that. Things reached an impasse when John Lennon passed the tapes to Phil Spector. It was a unique task for the record producer and considering the speed with which he produced the final album, it is doubtful that he did more than dip into the original tapes. This is unfortunate as a diligent producer could have put together an intriguing album, admittedly of a band disintegrating. The snippets of pop and rock'n'roll covers could have been used very entertainingly.

Instead, Phil Spector's approach largely followed Glyn Johns' track listing and he polished the tracks as much as he could, sometimes adding additional musicians. Lennon approved the results, this from a man who had stressed that *Let It Be* should be the Beatles with no adornments.

Just as John Lennon closed the roof-top session with the words, "I hope we passed the audition", Spector hadn't had a hit of late and had nothing to lose. Indeed, he had everything to gain as it was likely that he would produce both John and George's solo work. His first single with John Lennon 'Instant Karma!' had been rush-released and was a Top 10 hit.

The Wall of Sound that Spector had pioneered for the Crystals, the Ronettes, the Righteous Brothers, and Ike and Tina Turner was not appropriate here, but he bathed 'The Long and Winding Road' with a huge orchestral setting. McCartney knew nothing of this until the record was released and vented his displeasure publicly.

Ironically, the public loved the new version and as a single, it became the Beatles' biggest-ever hit in the US, replacing 'Bridge Over Troubled Water' at No.1. The B-side, 'For You (Blue)', was written by George Harrison, and had Lennon on slide guitar and McCartney playing a metallic-sounding piano.

The sleeve note for the *Let It Be* album refers, with some irony, to "the warmth and freshness of a live performance", and the album had sumptuous packaging. The glossy book contained photographs from the sessions plus some of their banter. You can sense their jousting from the jokes that are included between the tracks on the short album. There are references to the vintage entertainer, Wee Georgie Wood and the *Carry On* actor, Charles Hawtrey. What has 'Hark the Herald Angels Sing' got to do with 'Let It Be', and why does it segue into a snatch of the old Liverpool folk song, 'Maggie Mae'?

George Martin: "The tapes had rather shocked John and he asked Phil Spector to overdub them, which was in direct contradiction to all he had said. He kept it very quiet and the first thing I knew was when the album came out. I was pretty annoyed and so was Paul who didn't know about the album either. The album credit reads 'Produced by Phil Spector' but I wanted it changed to 'Produced by George Martin. Over-produced by Phil Spector.' I don't think there is anything you can point to in the Beatles' records I made that wasn't tasteful, but 'The Long and Winding Road' was BBC-TV music like Mantovani and Mike Sammes Singers."

Mike Sammes: "We did a vocal backing on nearly every British record of the period, and I think they would be less interesting records without us. I had a phone call from someone who wanted to use eight voices on 'The Long and Winding Road' and we went in and did the sessions. It wasn't our problem. We just went in and did what Phil Spector wanted."

The new arrangement for 'The Long and Winding Road' meant that it could have been a big-voiced ballad of any decade, even the 1930s. Cutting engineer George Peckham: "Phil Spector was a very strange character. He did have a gun in a holster and he kept himself separated from everyone but John. Even George was wary of him. His Wall of Sound had been fantastic, but here he was putting backing vocals on 'The Long and Winding Road.' He added swamping echo to the strings. It was polished in a way that didn't gel with the Beatles and Paul was upset about it."

Swamp rocker Tony Joe White: "There are so many songs that are right there. They did a lot of slow ballads like 'The Long and Winding Road'. I loved the chord changes in it and the words are unforgettable. It's really beautiful writing. They could make people jump up and down and they could also do quiet little masterpieces. Brilliant."

And here's an intriguing quote. Cynthia Lennon: "I have many, many favourites but I think 'Here, There and Everywhere' and 'Fool on the Hill' are very beautiful. I love 'The Long and Winding Road' because it seems to apply to my life. I suppose everyone picks the ones that are apt to themselves." Why is it intriguing? John's wife, Cynthia has chosen three Paul McCartney songs.

Tony Barrow: "'The Long and Winding Road' has very special memories for me because it summed up everything. I had heard the song in a very incomplete form when Paul was writing it and the melody had stayed with me. It came out when the Beatles were saying in public, and not just behind the scenes, that they had disbanded and were not working together anymore. It seemed to me symbolic that they had reached the end of a very long and very winding road. There had been a lot of hell in working with the Beatles but there was a lot of heaven as well, and this long and winding road was reaching the end of the rainbow."

The *Let It Be* album starts well with a cheerful rocker, 'Two of Us', and for all its quirkiness, George Harrison's 'I Me Mine' is a good track and possibly a comment on his fellow Beatles. The Beatles had recorded 'The One After 909' in 1963 and rejected it, so they knew it wasn't much more than an enjoyable but perfunctory song. 'I've Got a Feeling' is okay and it shows that the Beatles could be Canned Heat if they wished. 'Dig A Pony' and 'Dig It' are fragmentary: they're good to hear once, but there's little substance. The album included 'Across the Universe', this time slowed down and with orchestral accompaniment.

Outside of the Liverpool folk song, 'Maggie Mae' there were no covers on the album but among the unissued tracks is a complete take of the Crickets' 'Maybe Baby'. Paul McCartney later revived this as the title song for a 1999 film starring Hugh Laurie and written by Ben Elton.

The *Let It Be* album and film were released in 1970: the album was slight for a month's recording but it came with a photograph album of the recordings that was badly bound and soon fell to pieces. The final cost of the film was in the region of £180,000 which was minimal then. United Artists' share of the music tracks paid for the entire film in 3 days, that is, before anyone had seen the film.

On the cover, the hirsute Beatles look like they are auditioning for the Dubliners. Photographer Eamonn McCabe: "This is the first of the Beatles' covers that has got four action pictures on it. They're all working or singing, and even though Ringo is not actually shown doing anything, you get the feeling that he's banging his drums. I like the rawness of this, 'Let's put the four guys on the cover and show what they can do.' I really enjoyed that sequence on the roof of the Apple building and the cover photographs capture it for me."

Let It Be was one of the first rock documentaries to be given a cinema release. Film critic Ramsey Campbell: "*Let It Be* was an unusually honest film to get a commercial release. You knew that something was going wrong and there was an undercurrent of growing hostility."

Richard Thompson: "I can appreciate why any band breaks up. People want different things at different times and it is easier to work together when you're younger. After a certain point, your egos get too big and you want different things. In many ways, it is unrealistic for a band to be together for more than 5 years because everyone is pulling in different directions. It's like a marriage. A marriage is often artificially held together when the individuals don't have anything that they can relate to each other."

August 1970, Get Back – Doris Troy (Apple 28)
George Harrison, guitar
September 1970, My Sweet Lord/ Long As I Got My Baby – Billy Preston (Apple 29)
George Harrison and Billy Preston, producers
Billy Preston's version of 'My Sweet Lord' was issued before George's.
September 1970, Doris Troy – Doris Troy LP (Apple SAPCOR 13)
George Harrison, producer (Ain't That Cute) and guitar: Ringo Starr, drums
September 1970, Encouraging Words – Billy Preston LP (Apple SAPCOR 14)
George Harrison and Billy Preston, producers
September 1970, Tell The Truth – Derek and the Dominoes (US Atco 6780)
George Harrison, guitar
September 1970, Beaucoups of Blues – Ringo Starr LP (Apple PAS 10002)
Ringo's second solo album in a year, this time a country record made with top Nashville musicians.
September 1970, The Worst of Ashton, Gardner and Dyke LP (Capitol EST 563)

George Harrison (as George O'Hara Smith), guitar on I'm Your Spiritual Breadman
November 1970, Stephen Stills – Stephen Stills LP (Atlantic 2401 004)
Ringo Starr (as Richie Starr) on To a Flame and We Are Not Helpless
Novmber 1970, All Things Must Pass – George Harrison 3LP (Apple STCH 639)

George Harrison was undoubtedly the happiest to be freed from the Beatles. He enjoyed working with other musicians, and he had several songs that he had not been able to use with the Beatles. What's more, he no longer had to submit his material for Lennon and McCartney's scrutiny.

So George Harrison began his solo career by releasing a triple-album boxed set, *All Things Must Pass*. It sold at £5, twice the cost of other LPs, and yet it topped *Melody Maker's* album charts. It included many excellent musicians (Eric Clapton, Ringo Starr, Billy Preston, Badfinger) and a No.1 song 'My Sweet Lord', but the 100 minute set could have been condensed onto two albums.

Drummer Alan White, later with Yes: "When I did 'My Sweet Lord', George said, 'Alan, you play drums.' Ringo was standing right there, and George was asking me to play drums! I said, 'But Ringo's here' and he said, 'No, no, I want you to play, and Ringo will play tambourine.' Ringo didn't mind. I live in Seattle and we went to see Ringo in a winery with his band. I walked into the dressing room and he said, 'You're that bloody drummer. Can I have my photograph taken with you?'"

John York of the Byrds: "I don't think songwriting gets better than the Beatles. The Beatles were given a unique opportunity where they had millions of people who really wanted to hear whatever they did and to their credit they always gave us something wonderful. They never sat back on their laurels. You listen to any Beatles record and you will find that George always wanted a different guitar sound. They never did anything that was boring and were always really cool, it's totally remarkable. There was a power struggle and a hierarchy and George was relegated to two songs on a disc and that helped him grow as an artist in a strange sense so that when he put out *All Things Must Pass*, everyone went 'Wow', because he had been held down. They played together for several years in conditions where they could barely hear each other so they really know how to listen to each other. They were playing and singing at the same time in the studio which is really courageous."

George Harrison was sued for plagiarism over 'My Sweet Lord'. Had he copied the New York girl group hit from 1963, the Chiffons' 'He's So Fine'? It would be a record that Phil Spector knew well so why hadn't he said, "Hey, George, that's a bit close." As it happens, he didn't and Allen Klein, vindictively, bought the publishing rights to 'He's So Fine' so that he could sue the former Beatle. George lost the case but the judge ruled that he should purchase 'He's So Fine' from Klein at the price he paid for it, a clever judgment which ensured that Klein didn't profit from his malicious action.

Alan White: "I don't agree that George had copied the Chiffons' 'He's So Fine' for 'My Sweet Lord'. That song changed so much in the studio and to me, it was and always will be legitimate. George was the sweetest guy in the world. A really, really great guy and he wouldn't harm anyone or anything. The vibe and the atmosphere when we recorded 'My Sweet Lord' were incredible. We played music all day every day for 3 weeks and it was a great group of people."

December 1970, John Lennon/ Plastic Ono Band LP (Apple PCS 7124)
December 1970, Yoko Ono/ Plastic Ono Band LP (Apple SAPCOR 17)
John Lennon and Yoko Ono, producers
John's first album since the Beatles split, *John Lennon/Plastic Ono Band*, was astonishing though many found its stark music unlistenable and Yoko's album even more so. Following analysis with Dr Arthur Janov, Lennon screamed his way through such primal therapy rockers as 'Mother' and 'God' in which he said that he didn't believe in Beatles, whatever that might mean.

American songwriter Dory Previn: "The Beatles were brilliant, some kind of cosmic accident. Yoko came to see me perform when she was separated from John and she told me that he knew my albums. He heard 'Twenty Mile Zone', the one where I was screaming in the dark, and then wrote 'Mother', his thing about screaming. I know I was influenced by them and it's good to think that he was influenced to an extent by me." I've only met Dory Previn once and spoken to her for half an hour, but it is revealing that every time I mention somebody else, the answer is still about her.

Beatles biographer Steven Stark: "I think 'Mother' showed John Lennon's true feelings for his mother and there are many references to mothers in the Beatles' music. It's not something that you find in rock'n'roll generally, at least not about your own mother."

Elizabeth Thomson, co-editor of *The Lennon Companion*: "You can sense the beginnings of punk in the pared-down, back to basics sound of John Lennon's first solo album. It's a remarkable album and I listen to it a lot. Tracks like 'God' are not entertaining but they are incredibly powerful and thought-provoking. It's totally different from the second side of *Abbey Road*, which was only a year earlier."

In one song, John proclaimed that a working class hero was something to be, and it is a pity that we don't know how Paul, George and Ringo viewed this song when they first heard it. Lennon's half-sister, Julia Baird: "I thought John was sending people up with 'Working Class Hero'. Mimi would say, 'John, why are you talking with that awful accent?' and he would say, 'Mimi, that's what they want to hear, I let them hear it.'"

The album became notorious because of the four-letter words in 'Working Class Hero'. John might have hoped to be the first rock star to include profanity on an album but he was beaten by the folk-based singer/ songwriter, Al Stewart with *Love Chronicles*.

Country Joe McDonald of Country Joe and the Fish: "It was easy for Paul to fit into high society but John remembered his roots in Liverpool. A working class hero is something to be, which means it was something to aspire to, but really a working class hero is nothing to be. I grew up in a radical working class family and Joe Hill was a working class hero and he was shot by a firing squad. There aren't too many living Medal of Honour winners. Usually you're dead. Nelson Mandela is perhaps a working class hero but he was in jail for 27 years so he paid his dues."

Ray Coleman: "All the cockiness and aggression was a cover-up really. Under John's tough nut exterior was a heart of gold. He was a sentimental man and by the age of 17, having had the dramatic break up of his parents' marriage, the death of his Uncle George and the death of his mother, he had an enormous chip on his shoulder. All this influenced him but, underneath it all, as we found out in his music, he was a softie."

Several rock stars including Don Everly and Paul Simon made similarly introspective albums, but the fashion was short-lived. The contrast between Lennon's album and *McCartney* was all too evident.

The Beatles disbanded in April 1970, but what would have happened if they hadn't? This could have been the album they never made, largely basing it on tracks they recorded individually during the following year. I've called it *Finishing School*. Their first album, *Please Please Me*, showed them looking over the balcony at EMI House, the cover of this one would show them 7 years later in the same pose, a photograph which does exist.

Side One

(1) COME AND GET IT (Paul McCartney) (2.30)

Paul recorded this demo for Badfinger in July 1969 while the Beatles were recording *Abbey Road*. It sounds like a Beatles song and it was included on *Anthology 3* in 1996.

(2) INSTANT KARMA (John Lennon) (3.20)

In 1970 John Lennon wrote, recorded and released this Top 10 single within a week for the Plastic Ono Band.

(3) NOT GUILTY (George Harrison) (3.20)

By 1969 George Harrison was facing criticism for persuading the other Beatles to follow the Maharishi and he wrote a spirited defence, 'Not Guilty'. The Beatles took 102 takes to get the song right and even then it didn't appear until *Anthology 3* in 1996.

(4) ANOTHER DAY (Paul McCartney) (3.40)

A delightful picture of suburban life, typical McCartney and his first solo Top 10 single in February 1971.

(5) MY SWEET LORD (George Harrison) (4.30)

At a guess this would have been the single from my fictitious album. George was the first Beatle to have a solo No.1 and it prevented 'Another Day' from making the top. George is at his most mystical on this track and Eric Clapton plays the stinging lead guitar.

(6) GOD (John Lennon) (4.10)

John Lennon would not have been too happy with the sentiment of 'My Sweet Lord' as this track from his first solo album, *John Lennon / Plastic Ono Band*, indicates.

Side Two

(1) POWER TO THE PEOPLE (John Lennon) (3.20)

The Beatles sometimes started the sides of their albums with John Lennon's agit prop, e.g. 'Revolution' on *The White Album* and 'Come Together' on *Abbey Road*. Here's another example.

(2) MAYBE I'M AMAZED (Paul McCartney) (3.40)

A great ballad from Paul's first solo album, *McCartney*. A worthy successor to 'The Long and Winding Road' and 'Let It Be'.

(3) IT DON'T COME EASY (Ringo Starr) (3.00)

Ringo's first solo single and a Top 10 hit in April 1971. It shows how he had developed as a songwriter and George Harrison is featured as well as Klaus Voormann and Stephen Stills.

(4) I LIVE FOR YOU (George Harrison) (3.35)

A stunning George Harrison song discarded from his *All Things Must Pass* sessions. It was eventually issued as a bonus track on the CD version of *All Things Must Pass* in 2001.

(5) BABY PLEASE DON'T GO (John Lennon) (4.30)

John Lennon screamed his way through 'I Want You (She's So Heavy)' on *Abbey Road* and he did a similar thing with this rock'n'roll number from the Olympics during the sessions for the *Imagine* LP in 1971. A good song to end *Finishing School*, but then...

...after a 20 second gap...

(6) THE LOVELY LINDA (Paul McCartney) (0.45)

Just like 'Her Majesty' on *Abbey Road*, *Finishing School* concludes with this fragment of a song from the *McCartney* album.

CHAPTER 11
It Don't Come Easy (1971)

1971 – Barriers at Ibrox stadium collapse, killing 66 – Decimal currency introduced – CAMRA formed – Internment with trial reinstated in Northern Ireland – Space Hoppers in UK stores – 'Workaholics' diagnosed.

George Melly: "Their genius was while they were together and it couldn't be otherwise because their individual faults then surfaced over their virtues. When they were together, there was something critical going on, a critical check which kept the balance between them. Once they'd split up, Paul's tendency towards sentimentality was given full reign, Lennon's change-the-world Messianic arrogance came out, and George became less accessible with his interest in oriental music. The magic that they had together no longer worked. I think Lennon produced the best work singly just as McCartney produced the most popular. McCartney's work entered the mainstream, while Lennon, possibly through Yoko Ono, produced thoughtful, bitter, angry work, but there was nothing with that extraordinary knife-edge between knowingness and innocence that happened when they were the Beatles. There is 'Imagine', I suppose, which is a beautiful vision of what the world could be like if it wasn't a swamp full of monsters."

Adrian Henri of the Liverpool Scene: "I don't think any of them singly did anything that was as remotely good as what they did together. There's something very special about the chemistry that people have for each other. It's like love or marriage and part of it is the fights and disliking the same people, or whatever. It's all part of togetherness. I was in a band for three years and I know what it's like. Suddenly four of us would hate the fifth member and it would go on for a month and then stop for no reason and it would be your turn. What looks like Lennon slagging off McCartney, and vice versa, is part of that thing.

It's the same for people who've been in the army or the trenches as that kind of closeness develops."

If Paul was dismayed by the behaviour of his former partner, John Lennon, worse was to come. In 1971, John Lennon made the *Imagine* album with Phil Spector. The title song is about harmony and peace but 'How Do You Sleep' showed the tension between John and Paul. To add fuel to the fire, George Harrison was playing slide guitar, implying that George was siding as well as sliding with John.

Drummer Alan White: "I went into the kitchen in Tittenhurst Park and John said that these were the lyrics for the album. He said, 'Some of these are very heavy, especially 'How Do You Sleep'.' That was all about Paul, but I said, 'That's fine, it's a great song.'"

Richard Thompson: "Even though it was painful for them, it was probably better to work in partnership. Paul McCartney rounded off John Lennon's hard edge while he put more grit into what McCartney was doing, and they both needed that. What they did consequently is therefore less interesting, particularly for McCartney. He needs someone to smash him over the head and tell him to play rock'n'roll."

Paul McCartney

Paul McCartney's 1971 Top 10 single 'Another Day' was a catchy song about a working girl - standard Macca fare - but the albums, *Ram* (1971), *Wild Life* (1971) and *Red Rose Speedway* (1973), were lightweight compared to his time with the Beatles. Now working with his wife Linda and other musicians as Wings, he stirred controversy with 'Give Ireland Back to the Irish' and playing safe, followed it with the children's song, 'Mary Had a Little Lamb' and then the cod-reggae of 'C Moon', all in 1972.

Denny Laine of Wings: "I wasn't happy about 'Give Ireland Back to the Irish', because I thought it was too political and I don't think it makes the situation any better. I'm not criticising Paul though - if he wants to write about Ireland, then good luck to him. We followed it with 'Mary had a Little Lamb', which was a nice song for kids, but seemed wrong for the direction of the band."

McCartney hit his stride in 1973 with the romantic ballad, 'My Love' and a James Bond theme 'Live and Let Die', produced by George Martin, and his best Wings album, *Band on the Run*. 'Live and Let Die' was ideal for spectacular stage effects and has become the most dynamic number in McCartney's concerts.

Tim Rice: "There is only so far you can go with lyrics like 'Uncle Albert/ Admiral Halsey'. It may have been No.1 in America but I don't think many cabaret singers thought of putting it into the act. I hate to criticise one of the greatest songwriters of all-time but he got less cover versions in his later career not because the tunes were falling off, but because he went for rather obscure lyrics like 'Listen to What the Man Said' and 'Jet'. The lyrics are great fun but they don't make sense. 'Band on the Run' is a great tune and the words work in the context of that particular record but you aren't going to get great adult entertainers doing lyrics as obscure as that."

McCartney biographer Chris Salewicz: "McCartney is incredibly prolific. He will get up in the morning and write a song, and then write another, but he can't tell which ones are the good ones. He needs someone around him to say, 'No, forget that.' That was a function that both George Martin and John Lennon had. The musicians in Wings were not going to tell him that what he was doing was a load of rubbish."

Denny Laine: "*Band on the Run* was just two of us initially and then we added people to it afterwards. The backing tracks were put together very quickly and added to in London. It had a really good feel because it was just the two of us. It wasn't meant to be anything revolutionary, but it worked, the chemistry was there. We've done other albums that didn't have that combination."

Mike McCartney: "Our kid was producing the *McGear* album and at the end of the sessions, I was offered a TV booking for Scaffold getting back together again. I was wondering what we could do, and Paul said, 'I've always liked 'Liverpool Lou', why don't you do that?' We got hold of some versions from the BBC, one by Dominic Behan and one by Delaney and Bonnie. We didn't think much of them and we found another way to do it. Out of all the versions of 'Liverpool Lou', ours was the success, which shows how absolutely brilliant my brother is at putting the right interpretation on the right song."

Other big singles followed with 'Listen to What the Man Said', 'Let 'Em In', an answer to his critics with 'Silly Love Songs', and a single that sold 2 million in the UK alone, 'Mull of Kintyre' (1977). Denny Laine: "Paul came up with the chorus for 'Mull of Kintyre' and we got a bit inebriated one day and wrote the rest. It was about the area we were living in and so we thought it was appropriate. It was a folky thing that anybody could have written and the fact that it was us made it such a hit. Also, the pipe band changed the song a lot from its original conception and gave it some magic."

Music writer John Tobler: "'Mull of Kintyre' was an utterly pathetic song and the video was even worse. Wings hadn't got a drummer or a lead guitarist at the time, so they had this thing where they were standing in a field playing guitars - pretty convincing for a start! When I saw the video, I said, 'There's going to be a lot of pipers coming over the hill in a minute' and sure enough, there they were. We lap up this sort of thing in the UK but it was too contrived for America."

George Hamilton IV: "There's the expression 'horses for courses' but it's amazing that 'Streets of London' and 'Mull of Kintyre' were No.1 in England and are hardly heard of in America. When I went into a session to record 'Mull of Kintyre' in Nashville, we passed out the chord sheets and one of the leading Nashville session players looked at the sheet and said, 'Hey, man, you misspelt this.' I said, 'What?' He said, 'Mule of Kintyre, you got two l's in it.'"

On the advice of his father-in-law, McCartney acquired important musical copyrights, the most significant MPL purchase being Buddy Holly's publishing catalogue. Sonny West, who wrote 'Oh Boy!' and 'Rave On': "My songs picked up a lot in the 70s after Paul McCartney bought the Buddy Holly catalogue. He promoted the songs a lot more and probably took care of the books a lot better. That was the best thing that happened to me. It helped me out an awful lot and it has allowed me to do a few more things that I wanted to do."

Ralph McTell: "Billy Connolly invited me along to the opening of the *The Buddy Holly Story* and I turned up without an invitation. I'm 6 foot 2, but four huge bouncers were on the door and I was never going to get past them. Fortunately, someone inside recognised me and I was invited in. As I was making my way towards the bar, Paul came up and said, 'Hello, Ralph, nice to see you.' I had never met the guy. I didn't even know that he would know who I was. What a smashing geezer."

Mark Lewisohn: "Paul McCartney owns thousands of songs, but he doesn't have the catalogue that he really wants, the Beatles' catalogue, I am pretty certain now that he never will. It is out of his reach: even Paul McCartney couldn't afford to buy the catalogue."

At the time, McCartney wanted to establish himself with Wings and was somewhat reluctant to perform Beatle songs. Guitarist Laurence Juber from Wings: "There would be a couple of acoustic guitars on stage and once in a while, he might pick one up and play 'Michelle' and it was great to see Paul play a Beatle song. That would have been how he wrote it and it was great to see the chord changes that he used. Magic, really. I regard the tours as more like an education than a gig for me. I picked up so much that has been really invaluable by watching him first hand."

The *Tug of War* album in 1982 was co-produced with George Martin and Paul worked with Stevie Wonder ('Ebony and Ivory') and Michael Jackson ('The Girl Is Mine') as well as Carl Perkins. Although Carl recorded none of their songs, he provided the strongest personal link between rock'n'roll stars and the Beatles. They recorded several of his songs, both as the Beatles and in their solo careers, and Paul McCartney recorded a duet with him, 'Get It', in Montserrat in 1982. During the session, Paul told Carl a dirty joke and Carl's laugh has been added to the track, which is featured on the *Tug Of War* album. In 1984 George, Ringo and Eric Clapton were among the musicians paying tribute to Carl Perkins in *A Rockabilly Session - Carl Perkins and Friends* for Channel 4.

Although Paul McCartney's film, *Give My Regards to Broad Street* (1984) was poorly scripted, the excellent score included another Top 10 single, 'No More Lonely Nights'. Film critic Barry Norman: "Paul did *Give My Regards to Broad Street* which was a disaster. I remember George Harrison saying Paul had written the script on the back of a postage stamp and that had upset him."

McCartney's album of rock'n'roll standards, *Choba C CCCP*, for the Russian market deserved a standard UK release, and the public wasn't impressed by *Press to Play* (1986). He and Gerry Marsden contributed to the charity single for Hillsborough, 'Ferry Cross the Mersey' and a line of his vocal from 'Let It Be' was dubbed onto the single for Ferry Aid. Paul balanced cheerful guest roles in TV series (*Bread*) with major world tours and he appeared on both the Live Aid concerts (the first with a non-functioning mic). For the *Imagine - John Lennon* tribute in Liverpool in 1990, Paul went full circle with a segued 'Love Me Do' and 'P.S. I Love You', while Ringo sang 'I Call Your Name'.

Colin Vearncombe of Black: "Macca's a working class dude and he won't let you forget it and the thing that gets to him is that he is not taken as seriously as John Lennon, but when did he write words that you could really believe in? McCartney was the superior musician, but when he was with Lennon, he must have sometimes been afraid to play him his songs and there has been no one like that for him since. What did Lennon think when he first heard 'Lovely Rita, meter maid'? Did he say, 'Come on, grow up. 'Honey Pie', pleeze!' Lennon once said, 'We were a decent rock and roll band for 15 minutes' and that is a deep truth. He wasn't into art rock. Why do so many British rockers end up as music hall? Look at the Kinks, McCartney, even Spandau Ballet. Only Keith Richards has never betrayed his love of what got him into it in the first place. He never did stupid stuff."

Barry Miles: "Around 1992, I arranged for Allen Ginsberg to meet up with Paul again and Paul showed him his poems. Allen by that time was a teacher at a Brooklyn college and the first thing he did was whip out his pen and start correcting them. Paul couldn't believe it. I don't think anyone had corrected him since John Lennon. That's his problem: there is no one to say no to him."

Adam Faith's songwriter, Johnny Worth: "I like the Beatles and anyone who says that they don't is either acting out of sour grapes or a fool. They are the great success story of our age but I don't feel that John Lennon had too much to do with it. I think the Beatles were, and always will be, Paul McCartney. His mark is all over them, everywhere you look. I don't feel that the Beatles would have succeeded if he hadn't been in the group. He is the catalyst and the others could have been anybody. I know that's a big charge to make, but I feel that McCartney is a genius whereas Lennon happened to be a very good songwriter, of which there are many, and he was very fortunate to be in the same band as Paul McCartney. There are many others who don't get the laudatory praise that John Lennon gets. If I can make a parallel, President Kennedy is rated as one of the great statesmen of our time – well, not to me he isn't. Before his assassination I don't recall anyone saying that he was one of the greatest statesmen who ever lived, but all of a sudden when a man is unfortunately and horrendously killed, they become sanctified, and attachments are made to their character and ability that far outstrip the truth."

John Lennon's biographer, Ray Coleman: "There's no question in my mind that John was the architect of the group. He was the most creative and the most intelligent and as his life proved after the Beatles ended, he was a questing and restless spirit. If he has been worshipped more than the others, it's only because it's what he was due. In my view, he was the greatest."

It's hard to say but probably Paul McCartney missed working with John Lennon far more than John missed working with Paul. No matter how much hurt and public humiliation he had received from John (and those comments must have hurt), he would have forgiven everything and worked with him again. They came close to it a couple of times, notably in 1974 when they were in a studio in Los Angeles with Stevie Wonder, Nilsson and a few other musicians. A jam session emerged, the songs including 'Lucille', 'Stand by Me', 'Cupid' and 'Take This Hammer', but it is nowhere near as enticing as it sounds. The sound balance is poor but even if it was better, I don't think the music would amount to much.

Considering that he has to manage a vast financial empire, MPL, Paul McCartney has been involved with many musical projects. He wrote his *Liverpool Oratorio* with the classical composer and conductor, Carl Davis. (It's officially called *Paul McCartney's Liverpool Oratorio*, and I wonder what Carl Davis really thinks about this.) It received its première in Liverpool Cathedral in 1991 and has been performed around the world. As the title suggests, Paul wrote about his childhood experiences in *Liverpool Oratorio*. The fault may be mine but I have difficulty in listening to opera sung in English. Lines about "sagging off school" sound slight in such an impressive musical setting, but similar remarks can be made about many operas. Also, there were no great McCartney melodies in the oratorio, a strange criticism to be sure. Paul followed this with other classical works, notably a 75 minute piece about the mystery of life, *Standing Stone* (1997). By way of contrast, there has also been experimental rock such as his *Liverpool Sound Collage* (2000) with Super Furry Animals and various collaborations with Youth under the name of The Fireman.

As well as the Beatles and his solo work, Paul McCartney's legacy will include the foundation of the Liverpool Institute for Performing Arts (LIPA) in Mount Street. This is in the glorious building of his old school, Liverpool Institute, which at the time of McCartney's vision, was run-down. LIPA opened in 1996 and it can be viewed as the start of the regeneration of the city.

The productions that the students stage for the public in the Paul McCartney Auditorium (no less) are of a very high standard – in recent years, I have seen Sondheim musicals, a Ben Elton and Andrew Lloyd Webber premiere and productions of *Hair, Sweet Charity* and *A Chorus Line*. Nowadays LIPA graduates are involved with theatre and music shows all over the world. Years ago, while waiting for a play to start, I would read the programme to see how many of the actors had been in *Brookside* or *The Bill*: now I check it out for LIPA. Their musical successes have included Rageev, the Wombats, the Zutons and their first No.1 artist, Sandi Thom.

Linda McCartney was a campaigner for healthy food and her products are still being manufactured. She died from cancer in 1998 and an album, *Wild Prairie*, produced by Paul, was released to acknowledge her musical contribution. As for her singing voice, you will find on *YouTube*, her backing vocals for 'Hey Jude', isolated from McCartney and his band. Still, everyone has off nights.

Paul's second marriage was far less idyllic. Right from the moment, Paul McCartney romanced the former model, Heather Mills, there had been excessive tabloid coverage. They were married in 2003, separated in 2006 and divorced in 2008. The settlement cost McCartney £24 million as well as much of his dignity, especially when full details of the agreement were shown on line. McCartney biographer, Peter Carlin: "Bad things happen to everybody and I am sorry it happened to him, and I guess to her as it didn't work out for either of them. He got a great album out of it, *Memory Almost Full*. His back was against the wall and his music got good. He knows how to take a sad song and make it better: it's God's gift to that guy. There is a lot of autobiography and introspection on that album and some songs are about his childhood and growing up. 'The End of the End' is about death and is very unsentimental. He wants songs to be sung on the day he dies. He knows his contribution to the world."

McCartney's lavish stage shows are becoming more and more Beatlecentric, even up to 70% at times. From interviews and press reports, it is evident that Paul McCartney has turned into the world's biggest Beatle fan and he collects memorabilia out of the price range of most fans. He may want to buy his songs but his continued success only pushes the price up.

John Lennon

Although released in 1971, 'Imagine' was not released as a single until 1975 and even then, it did not acquire its mythic status until after John Lennon's death in 1980. Now it is regarded as his most meaningful and greatest song.

Songwriter Barry Mason: "Some people think 'Imagine' is cheesy but it is sensational. It is like a young boy saying, 'Imagine the world could be like this.' How could you knock those words?"

George Hamilton IV: "When I first heard 'Imagine', I loved its melody and I started to learn it. When I considered the lyrics more closely, I realised that I didn't agree with its theology. Maybe I'm mistaken, I come from the Bible belt, but the lines say, 'Imagine no heaven' and 'Imagine no hell'. It's all very well to dwell on peace-and-beauty-and-I-love-you-and-let's-not-harm-each-other, but I feel very strongly that there is a heaven and a hell and that Jesus Christ died for me. That's important to me, so if 'Imagine' means what I think it does, I don't agree with it."

American gospel singer Billy Blackwood: "'Imagine' seems to be saying that if you could do away with all the restraints, then there would be a freedom available to human beings that would increase the quality of our lives. John Lennon might have looked at religion and seen bonds and burdens but he failed to realise that God said 'He who knows the Son will be free. The truth will make them free.' There is a freedom in Christ to help us with the ills of the world and the consequences of our mistakes. The casting off of restraints does not lead to freedom, and psychologists know that we need guidelines and parameters within which to live our lives. If we do away with those, we overdose on freedom and we would soon find out that this is not the freedom we long for."

Mick Groves of the Spinners: "'Imagine' is a peace song so it interests me greatly. I sing in the last verse, 'Imagine all the people sharing all the wealth' although on the single John sings 'the world'. I remember him doing a show for Lord Grade on television from America. Lennon's band was the highlight of the cabaret and they came on with back-to-front masks and he sang 'Imagine all the people sharing all the wealth' to all these people covered in jewels. That appeals to me, being a socialist."

The *Imagine* album in 1971 was more melodic and commercial than his first solo album, although it bristled with political invective ('Gimme Some Truth') and couldn't have been made by anyone else. 'Jealous Guy' should have been released as a single, but John and Yoko did have hits with 'Instant Karma!', 'Power to the People' and 'Happy Xmas (War Is Over)', all produced by Phil Spector.

John and Yoko settled in America and because of a drugs conviction in 1968, he was refused a Green Card. John knew that if he left the country, he couldn't return. Lennon biographer Ray Coleman: "The American thing happened by accident. John and Yoko went there to get access to Kyoko, her daughter from a previous marriage, and they decided that they liked it. There was no conscious decision to stay until they were there. John found the artistic climate so powerful, although he didn't expect to have to stay in America for nine years."

John's political activity took centre stage in the double-album *Sometime in New York City* (1972), which didn't help with his request for a Green Card. It was followed by two patchy albums, *Mind Games* (1973) and *Walls and Bridges* (1974), though his duet with Elton John, 'Whatever Gets You Thru the Night', was a US No.1.

Beatles biographer Elizabeth Thomson: "John Lennon complained that George Martin and the Beatles spent more time perfecting Paul's songs than his. However, when he had the opportunity of perfecting things, he never did it. I do wonder if some stars realise when they've done something very bad. The out-of-tune singers on 'Mind Games' are outrageous. How could anyone who has worked in a studio for almost 15 years not realise that this is an assault on our ears?"

When their marriage became strained, Yoko Ono had the oddest solution. She spoke to May Pang who worked for them: "Yoko came into my office and said, 'Listen, you know that John and I are not getting along. He's going to start seeing other people.' I thought, 'My God, who am I going to work for, her or him?' I'd no idea what was going on. She continued, 'I know John likes you, you don't have a boyfriend and it would be perfect if you went out with him. It would be good for you too and you would treat him nice. Would you want him to go out with someone who would not treat him nice?' She suggested the same thing to John while he was shaving and he told me, 'I almost cut my throat at that moment.' She was handing over her husband to someone else. I resisted at first but she wanted me to start that night. I was with John during his famous 'lost weekend', which was a lot more creative than people think. The few wild incidents were blown out of proportion. He was even considering writing with Paul again and, if he hadn't gone back with Yoko, I would have pushed for it."

Too much echo spoilt his 1975 *Rock'n'Roll* album but his revival of Ben E. King's 'Stand By Me' was magnificent. May Pang: "When John started making *Rock'n'Roll*, he told Phil Spector to take control. He said, 'I just want to be a member of the band, one of the boys. I don't want to produce it.' I had a gut feeling something was wrong when twenty-seven musicians came to the first date when we were expecting eight. Everyone got drunk that night and very little got done. It was a pity because John had gone through a period of not being sure about himself. It had taken him a year to get over *Something in New York City* and go back to the recording studio. He didn't feel that he had a strong enough voice and he used to say, 'Put on the echo, Phil, and mess it up for me.' 'Stand by Me' was great. He was sitting on a chair and I was sitting at his feet when he cut it. I am credited as 'Mother Superior' on the album. John used to say, 'If May taps her feet, it's a good one.'"

Soul singer Ben E. King: "When I heard that John Lennon had done 'Stand By Me', I said, 'That's great'. He copied my version line for line, word for word, and it had a good feeling. He didn't try to do anything cute with it and he sang it with a lot of sincerity. I hope he heard that I'd done 'Imagine'."

John was often criticised for spending as much time on Yoko's work as his own. Here she is defended by John's girlfriend, May Pang: "Yoko thought that she was a very good songwriter. She felt that she was on the same level as John, if not better. When John did an album, she wanted to do one as well. Some of her songs are very good: 'I Want My Love to Rest Tonight' on *Approximately Infinite Universe* is wonderful."

1980's *Double Fantasy* included 'Just like Starting Over', 'Woman' and 'Beautiful Boy'. John Lennon was killed in December 1980, and he was an easy target because he wasn't surrounded by bodyguards. May Pang: "John was intrigued by Greta Garbo. She lived in the next building to us and so wanted to be alone that not even John Lennon could see her. John loved celebrity. We attended an American Film Institute dinner honouring James Cagney and that room was filled with famous actors like Mae West, Kirk Douglas, John Wayne and Steve McQueen. John was a kid in a candy store that night. Maybe that's why he always said yes to a request for an autograph. If someone asked him for an autograph, he would say yes. He didn't build a wall around himself."

And maybe that cost him his life. John Lennon was shot dead in the Dakota building in New York on 8 December 1980. Loudon Wainwright: "'Not John' is a strange song of mine. It's more of a departure. The idea was to make the event into a folk song with just the names and the places and the incidents which happened. The tune is based on an old American folk song about the murder of President McKinley. It is just the details – five bullets, vigils at the Dakota, Chapman's wife was Japanese – and you had a vigil in Liverpool and then a riot. John would have liked that. The idea was to take this and make a folk song out of it. We'll know in 50 years time if I was successful."

Tony Barrow: "Unfortunately, I've got this gut feeling that we hadn't by any means heard the best from John Lennon. He hadn't passed his peak, he had a long way to go and that's a great pity. Mark Chapman didn't just kill a legendary performer: he prevented the world from hearing a lot more of his music. There are rumours that he was going to come back over here. Maybe he would have done that and I suspect he would come back to his musical roots and that would have inspired him. We don't know."

George Harrison

All Things Must Pass was followed by another triple-LP as George organised the *Concert for Bangladesh,* the first major event to combine rock and charity. Ravi Shankar had asked him to do something for the famine in Bangladesh and he organised two concerts on 1 August 1971 at Madison Square Garden. It featured Bob Dylan, Leon Russell, Eric Clapton, Ringo Starr and Billy Preston and it gave a wonderful lift to large rock events after the disaster following the Rolling Stones at Altamont. It led the way for other major charity rock concerts and when Bob Geldof planned Live Aid, one of the first people he asked for advice was George Harrison.

Blues guitarist Joe Bonamassa: "We've got the *Concert for Bangladesh* on the bus. I love George and I would put him up in the same league as Lennon and McCartney as 'While My Guitar Gently Weeps' and 'All Things Must Pass' are classics. He co-wrote 'Badge' with Eric Clapton, which is a great song. We've got *Woodstock* back there and Joe Cocker is doing 'With a Little Help from My Friends', so no matter who sings a Beatles song, it works if the singer's any good."

George Harrison had Top 10 singles with 'Bangladesh' and 'Give Me Love (Give Me Peace on Earth)'. *Living in the Material World* (1973), *Dark Horse* (1974), *Extra Texture* (1975), *33 And A Third* (1976), a punning title to link the record speed with his age, and *George Harrison* (1979) were good rather than great albums. *Somewhere in England* (1981), which included his tribute to John Lennon 'All Those Years Ago', was better, but the very title *Gone Troppo* (1982) suggested that his muse was on vacation.

Another tribute to Beatle days was 'When We Was Fab' (1988), the video being made by Kevin Godley and Lol Creme. Godley recalls, "That was a lot of fun. I remember that we had George against the wall in the *Sgt Pepper* outfit with multiple arms and legs, a pseudo-Indian religious vibe with all sorts of mad things happening. It was a hoot of a shoot. George could laugh at himself and it was great fun."

When *Monty Python's Life of Brian* lost its funding, George Harrison stepped in and his company, HandMade, had a significant impact on the British film industry. He occasionally played bit parts or contributed to soundtracks such as *Time Bandits* and *Shanghai Surprise*. Vicki Brown: "George lives 5 minutes away from us and he was doing the soundtrack for *Shanghai Surprise*. He asked me to help to demo a song for Madonna. He had worked out some great harmonies and we did the duet. Two weeks later, the producers wanted Whitney Houston to do it instead, but he said, 'I think you should do it.' We sang it on the soundtrack but they didn't release it as the film flopped."

Peter Doggett: "During the making of *Shanghai Surprise*, George was horrified to find he had to intercede between Madonna and Sean Penn. The film had appalling reviews, so he decided against releasing a soundtrack album. Only about 100 promotional copies of the single with Vicki Brown were pressed, so they have become collectors' items. Even though he included some songs from the film on his *Cloud Nine* album, he re-recorded them, almost as though he wanted to exorcise the whole ghastly experience from his mind."

Both Paul and George were involved with Duane Eddy's 1987 album, *Duane Eddy, His Twangy Guitar and the Rebels*. Paul wrote and produced 'Rockestra Theme'. Duane Eddy: "I ran into Jeff Lynne when I was doing a rock festival in Switzerland with the Art of Noise and he offered to help with an LP. I rang Jeff later but he was working with George Harrison and he wasn't sure whether he could do it. He rang back a couple of days later to say that George wanted to record with me and he was so excited that he would put his own album on hold for a couple of weeks. They came and worked with me and we did three songs." 'Rockestra Theme' was written and produced by Paul McCartney, while 'The Trembler', written by Duane and Ravi Shankar, featured George on slide guitar.

Released at the same time as Paul's *Press to Play* in 1987, *Cloud Nine* was a commercial success, particularly with its No.2 single, 'Got My Mind Set on You'. George's good-nature came over on his sensational album with Jeff Lynne, Tom Petty, Bob Dylan and Roy Orbison as *The Traveling Wilburys, Vol.1*, although the follow-up, without Orbison who had died, was mediocre. George developed an interest in the ukulele and in George Formby, in particular, and even attended a meeting of the George Formby Society in Blackpool.

Klaus Voormann recalls going to see him in 2001: "George Harrison was in Austria and he was in bad shape. It was a lovely day and the sun was shining and we were sitting outside. Olivia explained about his treatment and it took him ages to come down because he was so weak. He couldn't get up easily and getting shaved and dressed was agony for him. He wore a gardening hat and he took it off and he had no hair, but he was happy. He was laughing. His concern was to make me feel good. It was the opposite of what I expected, that is, for me to try and make him feel good. He said, 'If I die, that's okay, and if I live on, that's okay too. My body in not important, that is just my shell. My spirit will stay with you always.' It was lovely that he felt like that. It helped him so much that he wasn't scared. He was still fighting for his life but he knew he was going somewhere better. If everybody could feel that way, it would be great."

'Goodnight, George' at the end of the CD *Fate's Right Hand* by the singer/songwriter Rodney Crowell is a reference to George Harrison. "We were rehearsing the song 'This Too Will Pass' and I got a phone call from my daughter Hannah who lives in Los Angeles and is an incredible Beatles fan. She was in tears because George had died. I went back and told Pat Buchanan and Michael Rhodes who were on the session with me and as we were recording the play-out at the end, I just said, 'Goodnight, George'. It was just an emotional thing. We went into the control room and Pat had tears down his face and he said, 'Do you realise how similar this song is to *All Things Must Pass*?' I hadn't thought about it until that moment, but he's right. We left 'Goodnight, George' on the song and decided to end the record that way."

In 2009, the Birkenhead singer/songwriter, Dean Johnson, took an uncompleted lyric by George Harrison and fashioned it into a full song, 'Silence Is Its Own Reward'. It was done sensitively but after it appeared on *YouTube,* Johnson was ordered to stop performing the song. He has rewritten the lyric so that none of Harrison's original words are retained.

Ringo Starr

The astonishing thing about Ringo Starr's solo career is that he has made so many albums. Ringo must have surprised himself as *Ringo the 4th* was his sixth album. Unexpectedly, he often lets someone else play drums. Some of his albums tax the tolerance of even the most ardent Beatles fans and when he tried to prevent one album being released because it was substandard, I wondered how he could tell. Nevertheless, Ringo has a likeable, good-natured voice and the producer who has understood that best is Richard Perry who made the best-selling album, *Ringo* (1973).

Peter Doggett: "When the Beatles split up, everyone thought that Ringo would have the hardest time and yet, at one stage, he was the most successful of the four. He hasn't been able to keep it up, but he has made some very good records. I like his B-side 'Early 1970' which is about the break-up of the Beatles and so is very close to his heart. The title track of his Nashville album *Beaucoups of Blues*, is very good and so is '$15 Draw' from the same album. His best tracks are usually when one of the other Beatles has given him some assistance such as 'I'm the Greatest' with John and 'Photograph' with George. Obviously, you are buying the personality as much as the voice, but the quality of his vocals is still okay."

Ringo Starr played Frank Zappa in the experimental film, *200 Motels*, directed by Tony Palmer. "I'd filmed Frank Zappa for *All My Loving* and he had appeared on a TV programme I had called *How It Is,* so we knew each other pretty well. I was rung up by his manager Herb Cohen who said that they would be in London and they wanted to tell me about *200 Motels*. Zappa wanted United Artists to finance the film. They said 'No', but the compromise suggested by Herb Cohen was that they brought in a safe pair of hands and I was the safe pair of hands. The script was a suitcase full of loose bits of paper and so I had to sort out an incoherent jumble. The first tune was called 'Penis Dimension' so I thought I am on a hiding to nothing here, but I liked Frank and thought it was going to be fun. The script called for multiple Frank Zappas so I said, 'Let's do something really daft and get Ringo Starr.' Derek Taylor put it to Ringo who thought it was too funny for words."

Ringo met his future wife, Bond girl Barbara Bach, on the set of the film, *Caveman* (1981). Film critic Barry Norman: "Ringo was an endearing and enchanting character and I liked him very much personally. *Caveman* is an example of 'Well, the Beatles are over and how do you fill the time?'"

Well, he soon knew the answer to that question. Ringo has won acclaim for his All-Starr Band. It's a Greatest Hits concert as the musicians play Ringo's successes as well as their own. Over the years, I'm surprised to have collected six albums of Ringo Starr and his All-Starr

Bands. The first from 1989 featured Clarence Clemons (saxophonist with Bruce Springsteen), Rick Danko and Levon Helm (Band), Dr. John, Nils Lofgren, Billy Preston and Joe Walsh (Eagles). That's a heavy duty line-up, and along the way, Ringo has played with Jack Bruce, Eric Carmen, Paul Carrack, Dave Edmunds, Timothy B. Schmit (Eagles) and his son, Zak Starkey (Oasis and the Who). Unlike Bill Wyman's Rhythm Kings which tends to draw on the same body of artists, Ringo prefers to vary his All-Starr bands. The most recent versions have not been as star-studded – mostly American rockers from the 70s who may come cheap – but that's the recession for you.

Nils Lofgren: "We went to a party with Ringo at Tittenhurst and Jeff Beck was there. Jeff is not a big jammer but he is the greatest living guitarist now that Hendrix has gone. We were jamming and sure enough Ringo joined in. It was a real thrill for me. We kept in touch and we got to be friends. He sat in with my band in the UK and then in 1989, he wanted me to be part of the All-Starr band. His attitude was 'Don't hold back, develop your personality.' It was like a round robin and it was very unique and exciting. You can't find a better drummer than Ringo. His feel is amazing and there are some very unusual drum patterns that other drummers weren't coming up with. He is underrated and he is very solid and has a great ability to play what's right for a song. He doesn't feel that you have to do fills automatically."

There is a generation that know Ringo more for the children's TV series, *Thomas the Tank Engine* than for music, but in the last few years, Ringo has lost the plot. He was the star guest for Liverpool's opening celebrations as the European Capital of Culture 2008. He appeared at two events, drumming on top of St George's Hall and singing at the Echo Arena. That passed uneventfully but a couple of days later, he appeared on Jonathan Ross's TV show and, given an opportunity to praise the city, he admitted that he wasn't as impressed with Liverpool as he had made out when he was there. I suspect it was a joke, akin to his comments on returning from India, but it went wrong. Angry comments were made on local radio and in the local papers. His head was cut off the topiary of the Beatles at South Parkway station, but it has now been restored.

A few months later, he announced on his website that he was no longer signing autographs but he was telling us this with "peace and love".

CHAPTER 12

Beatlemania 2.0

I. The Beatles Themselves

Since the Beatles disbanded, they have had five Top 10 hits ('Yesterday', 'Love Me Do', 'Baby It's You', 'Free As a Bird', 'Real Love'), three more in the Top 20 ('Hey Jude', 'Back in the USSR', 'Beatles Movie Medley') and all their reissued singles have at least made the Top 75. As for albums, there have been two *Live at the BBC* sets, three *Anthology* sets, *Yellow Submarine* (film soundtrack), *Let It Be...Naked*, *Love*, and all those Beatle *Remasters*. In 2000, the hits collection, *1*, sold 31 million copies around the world. There has been endless repackaging including the 60s American albums on CD, though why have the Beatles and their representatives supported hotchpotch collections that they loathed at the time?

The Beatles' catalogue took some time to come to CD but the albums were issued in batches in 1987 with the reissue of *Sgt. Pepper* cleverly timed for 1 June, thus enabling the marketing slogan to be "It was 20 years ago today." This reissue made No.3 on the album charts, but, of the others, only *The White Album* made the Top 20. Since that time, the Beatles have chosen to leave the original albums as they were, rather than repackage them with bonus tracks à la Beach Boys, David Bowie and Elvis Costello. Even in 2009, the *Remasters* retained the tracks in their original order without outtakes or alternative versions.

In 1995, the first *Anthology* cover by Klaus Voormann tore off Pete Best's head. Klaus Voormann: "It was coincidence, not on purpose, but maybe it does portray the feeling that we all had. I know Pete Best was in the Beatles but he was always somehow on the outside. He was a sweet guy but living in a different world. The cover was harder to do than *Revolver* because Neil Aspinall had to communicate with everyone and they were all over the world. I thought of having a cover with a big piece ripped off and if it says 'BE' and a head, the people will know it's them. He said, 'No, it has to be the four heads and the name, Beatles.' I wanted a little boy with a spray guy writing 'Anthology' across the whole thing, but he didn't want that either. People didn't really get the final result which was supposed to represent a big billboard. That was a bit of a shame, but I still like it."

The first *Anthology* included a new track, 'Free as a Bird' and the second one had 'Real Love'. A third track, 'Now and Then', was dropped from the third set. 'Free as a Bird' was a John Lennon demo expanded into a full song with additional accompaniment from Paul, George and Ringo. It was skilfully produced by Jeff Lynne and the result is more like ELO than the Beatles. The track has often been criticised but it is usually criticism of the remaining Beatles doing something so tacky in the first place.

Kevin Godley recalled making the video for 'Real Love' with his business partner, Lol Creme: "I didn't do much shooting for that other than filming each member of the band in super slow motion, just to match some film of John by Yoko shot many years ago also in super slow motion. So I then had the full band doing the same thing. We dropped a white piano into the Mersey in super slow motion. That was when we had budgets for these things. It wasn't a special effect. It was unplayable before it hit the Mersey as it was seriously doctored before it went in.

On his 1999 album, *Social Studies*, Loudon Wainwright wrote 'What Gives', his commentary on duets with dead people. "When I first heard 'Free as a Bird', I thought it wasn't one of their best and it was an example of a commission. National Public Radio asked me to write a song about it, and I thought of the videos of Nat and Natalie Cole, the magic of technology. It is death, rock'n'roll and money. The single was not very good technically. Elton John can do a Coca-Cola commercial with Humphrey Bogart and it is the way things are. There is something cynical about it. I wouldn't like anyone to do that to me, and I suspect that John Lennon wouldn't like it either, but I don't know of course. There was the audacity of it: it was John's demo, and presumably if he had wanted it out, he would have put it out. People do it with books and plays. Samuel Beckett had very specific instructions about how his plays were to be done and there are law suits if people disregard his wishes. I can't imagine that Hank Williams would get a kick out of that duet with his son. It's the money guys. That has been what a lot of music is about. They are proud that they have manipulated everybody."

Brian Nash, Nasher from Frankie Goes To Hollywood, released a song about McCartney in 2003. "When the *Anthology* was coming out, my attitude was leave it alone, people know who the Beatles are and if collectors want to hear ten versions of 'I Am the Walrus', fair play, let them have it, but they were dressing it up as something it wasn't. You can't release records with dead people on them like 'Free as a Bird' and 'Real Love'. They were using a dead man's vocals to make money for the corporation. Around the same time, Paul wanted to have his name first on some of the Lennon and McCartney songs he had written on his own. Let it go - you were in the Beatles, move on, grow old gracefully. He should be a producer because his grasp of melody and songwriting is second to none. Why not pass it on, isn't that what we're here for? He doesn't want to do that, he wants to make sure that people remember his past."

Beatles biographer Steve Turner: "Funnily enough, the *Anthologies* are not albums that I want to listen to for pleasure. They are more like research tools or listening to a radio documentary. I don't think there was much on the *Anthologies* that made you doubt the Beatles' original decisions. They were wise to discard what they did. Maybe they could have done a good version of 'Come and Get It'. You can see how 'What's the New Mary Jane?' was developing from improvisations. There's some kind of gobbledygook where Paul's using wrong tenses and wrong words which may have something to do with being in India: it's the way someone from India might speak in English if it's been learnt as a second language."

In 2003, the *Let It Be* tapes were remixed and deSpectorised for *Let It Be...Naked*, which came with a 20 minute film documentary. The CD included a different take of 'Don't Let Me Down' and deleted 'Dig It' and 'Maggie Mae'. Oddly though, the *Let It Be* film is not available on DVD and, sooner or later, it is bound to be released in a double package with outtakes.

After much negotiation, the Beatles' catalogue was remixed and reworked for the acrobatic troupe, Cirque du Soleil, and the resulting show, *Love*, which opened in 2006, has been a resounding success in Las Vegas. The new look 'I Am the Walrus' worked extremely well in *Love*.

Charlie Reid of the Proclaimers: "I haven't bought the Beatles' *Remasters* yet but I am tempted to do it. I tend to think, Come on, how much have they already made out of people buying those tracks in different formats? They show you what true talent is. They were very good when they started and they became sublime within a couple of years."

For the *Remasters,* all the original albums including the American version of *Magical Mystery Tour* were issued in stereo, both in a boxed package and separately, with the albums up to *The White Album* also available in mono but only together in the box. In a rare moment of generosity, the original stereo mixes of *A Hard Day's Night* and *Help!* have been included with the mono albums. The double *Past Masters* CDs collected singles and tracks not on the original albums. The original artwork and liner notes were retained, albeit much reduced in size, and there were recording notes and historical essays. They were packaged in cardboard rather than jewel cases and each CD included a short documentary in QuickTime about the making of the album. The interviews with the Beatles and George Martin have come from the *Anthology* TV series.

Retaining the mono versions was important as that was how most people heard the tracks in the 60s. They first heard them in mono on the radio and certainly up to 1965, stereo record players were a luxury and largely confined to classical musical and orchestral MOR recordings. Nobody listened to the music on headphones: the music filled the room, and it was impossible to play an LP in a car. In a sense, the mono versions are the real versions of the hit singles and albums as that was what we heard and what we bought, and what the Beatles intended. The first stereo mixes were done later by George Martin and his team with no input from the Beatles themselves.

II. Plays, Films and Rutles

A star-studded film musical of *Sgt. Pepper's Lonely Heart Club Band* was made in 1988 with the Bee Gees, Peter Frampton and Paul Nicholas. The film was produced by Robert Stigwood, who was hoping to follow his success with *Saturday Night Fever* and *Grease*, but his good luck left him. Paul Nicholas: "The film of *Sgt. Pepper's Lonely Hearts Club Band* was dire. It was a rotten script and the whole thing was a let-down. The director did his best but if things are naff in the script, they'll be naff on the screen. I had a great time doing it 'cause I was living in Hollywood for 5 months, but, as a piece of work, it was rubbish."

Although I largely agree, it wasn't total rubbish and there are some good individual performances, produced, incidentally, by George Martin and engineered by Geoff Emerick. Is it a worst concept than *We Will Rock You* or *Mamma Mia!*, so maybe, just maybe, it was before its time. Singer/songwriter John Stewart, who was in the final sequence, told me, "*Sgt. Pepper's Lonely Hearts Club Band* was a terrible movie. It was trying to do the Beatles without the Beatles and it was incongruous to stick Earth, Wind and Fire into a Beatles movie. It had no integrity and you can't fool kids. To do a movie with that story was absolutely bound for disaster. I was in the big party at the end where we all sang. I got to meet George Martin and stand next to George Burns. It was a day of Georges."

Even stranger was Lou Reizner's production *All This and World War Two,* a 1976 documentary that showed World War II newsreel footage to a soundtrack of heavily orchestrated covers of Beatle songs. The Beatles' songs are largely about love and peace, so what was the point? Still there were some good performances, especially Frankie Valli's 'A Day in the Life'.

Stage plays around the Beatles' story started with Willy Russell's *John, Paul, George, Ringo...and Bert* in 1974. Barbara Dickson: "George Martin told me how much he had enjoyed the music but I didn't know that at the time. There were lots of comments from people who thought the play was hard-hitting. It didn't pull its punches and I suppose if somebody wrote a very strong and intense statement about my life and career, I mightn't be too pleased."

Willy Russell: "I don't think I wrote any fiction in *John, Paul, George, Ringo...and Bert* but I did invent the bulk of the dialogue. I took the spirit of the event and then invented the dialogue rather than going through biographies and press reports and lifting it verbatim. I suppose anyone who lived through the early 60s with a guitar is a Bert, especially in Liverpool. I'm always meeting people who had some connection with the Beatles and my idea was to tell Bert's story. He'd played three gigs with them but he didn't know enough chords."

Barbara Dickson: "Willy Russell had asked me to do this because my particular strengths were in singing a different type of material, and he thought it would work and that it would pay off to have a woman singing these songs in a particular way. I enjoyed all the show and I loved the action that was going around me but I suppose my favourite song was 'Penny Lane'. The show made me realise that I could do virtually anything I wanted."

Willy Russell: "*John, Paul, George, Ringo...and Bert* was in the West End for a year and George Harrison went to the last Saturday matinee. He left a note saying he had to leave early because there were more people looking at him than at the stage and it was unfair to the actors. I don't know if that was true but I would find it monumentally difficult to watch anyone portraying myself on stage. John Lennon sent a few nice messages to George Costigan but Paul McCartney saw some excerpts on TV, decided that he was being portrayed mischievously and prevented it from being staged in America. Two years later I mentioned this when I was interviewed for the *Sunday Times* about *Breezeblock Park*. Paul read it and invited me round and surprisingly, he asked me to write a film for him. Even though he objected to *John, Paul, George, Ringo...and Bert*, he liked something about my writing. I watched him work with Wings at his studio in a barn in Scotland, which was a fantastic experience, and he wanted me to write a film which would feature the current line-up of Wings going out and playing tiny clubs and avoiding the hoo-ha of mega stardom. The script is about a solo singer playing vast dates who walks out in the middle of a concert. He doesn't carry any money and he is trapped in a motorway café by having ordered food and not being able to pay for it. He teams up with a band that has been thrown out of a pub. Paul wanted a happy ending and I didn't as I'd said he had to go back and sort out his problems, but the discussions were all good-natured. He then went to Tokyo, that line-up of Wings fell apart and the script gathered dust in someone's office."

In 1981 the Everyman Theatre in Liverpool, staged *Lennon*, starring Mark McGann: "I was a part-time actor at the Everyman when Ken Campbell was there as artistic director and he greatly encouraged me. There was a band on stage during one of the productions and, almost as a joke, I got up and did 'Revolution' with them in a wig and glasses, the whole Lennonesque thing. Ken liked that and he had an idea for doing a play about Lennon but he put it on the back burner as he wasn't sure how to end it. Bob Eaton took over from Ken Campbell and during the transition, John Lennon was shot dead. It was just fate that they had that script and they now knew how to end it. There have been many plays about John Lennon but this was the first and it has become the definitive one."

Mark McGann won plaudits for his portrayal as Lennon and he still performs as Lennon at special events such as the Beatles Convention in Liverpool. I've seen hundreds of Lennons and to my mind, he is the best. "I don't think it is a perfect impersonation but it's not meant to be. For example, I can get my speaking voice lower than it is normally, but it is not as low as Lennon's. Also, I was doing a lot more songs than John Lennon normally would in an evening and you have to have something of your own vocal timbre in there to get you through, to protect your voice for a long run. I haven't played Lennon on stage in a play for some years but I do like doing the occasional concert. In fact, it's really great to sing those songs."

The play had an unforeseen effect on Johnny Worth, who wrote hits for Adam Faith and Eden Kane: "I went to see the *Lennon* play and it convinced me that he was the lesser light of the Beatles, a songwriter who, in his whole life, had only written a few truly memorable songs. If you think that 'Strawberry Fields Forever' is one of the great songs of our time, you belong to a minority. It's only thought of that way by fans of John Lennon, of which, of course, there are millions. However, I don't think there's a granny or young person anywhere who doesn't know who Paul McCartney is. Paul made the world sing over and over again and he is one of the great writers of the century, like Irving Berlin and Richard Rodgers. That doesn't mean that Lennon should be diminished by comparison but there has to be an order of things."

Perhaps Johnny Worth would prefer something less reverential. In 1978, Eric Idle and Neil Innes combined their talents as the Rutles for the mock TV documentary, *All You Need Is Cash*. Neil Innes: "I think the time was exactly right for what we did. Everyone saw the joke and got right into it. It would be a lovely joke today to pretend that the Beatles never existed and there were only the Rutles. There are even tribute acts to the Rutles and doing quite well."

The programme's humour stands up well and the soundtrack was particularly good. Neil Innes: "I wrote the songs from vague memories of the various stages they went through. When I was at art school, 'Love Me Do' came out and I remembered that period clearly. I wrote the songs and then when we came to record them, I listened very carefully to the production techniques on their records, and I was amazed to find little bongos tapping away when I thought they were just simple band line-ups. I had no idea that they had put so much into it. Then we had the question of what song goes with what skit. A cheap idea was the parody of *A Hard Day's Night* because it is black and white and is just running about Benny-Hill like. That led to the first spoofette with 'I Must Be in Love'. The hardest song to write was 'Hold My Hand' where I was trying to remember what my first date was like, you know, the intensity of that first contact. 'Piggy in the Middle' was easy by comparison."

The trick was to get close to the Beatles' songs without plagiarism. Neil Innes: "'I Must Be In Love' is obviously 'Love Me Do' with a different chord structure, but when George heard 'With a Girl like You', he said, 'That's a bit close.' I said, it was different and he said, "Well you can always stand up in court with your guitar.' They took all in good part and we never had any trouble with them but later it cost me £5,000 to fight ATV with a musicologist who said that there was no case to answer. My lawyers reckoned that we would get costs but I wound up giving them 50% of my royalties."

The Rutles records stand up very well in their own right. They are almost as enjoyable as the Beatles' records and they also make you laugh, because of the sheer cheek and the whole audacity of the project. Mike McCartney: "I hadn't seen *The Rutles* for some years and it was a really nice pleasure to see it again recently. I love the bit where Eric Idle interviews Roger McGough at the Atlantic Tower Hotel. He says, 'So you personally knew the Rutles...' and talks so much that Roger never gets a chance to speak. It's a wonderful scene, and the whole thing is full of great observations. The Beatles phenomenon was extraordinary in that normal relationships with the public became almost impossible and common sense went out of the window. The Beatles reduced presidents and royalty to gibbering idiots."

Neil Innes: "George Harrison was the most pro-*The Rutles* as he thought it was a good way of telling the Beatles story in a roundabout way and having fun at the same time. Paul was annoyed because he had *London Town* out at the same time and in every interview he would be asked about the Rutles. He would say, 'It's all fun but what about *London Town*?' Eric Idle met Paul at a dinner party and said that he was a bit tense, but Ringo was okay and John was intrigued. They did let us have some footage for the film, so in effect they endorsed it."

The 1994 film, *Backbeat*, told of the relationship between John Lennon and Stu Sutcliffe and the accompanying book was written by Alan Clayson and Pauline Sutcliffe. It considers the various explanations for the brain haemorrhage which killed Stu Sutcliffe. They write, "One of the more infamous biographical portrayals of another ex-Beatle has it that Sutcliffe shuffled off this mortal coil as the result of an altercation with John on a Hamburg street." Now, it would appear that Pauline Sutcliffe is agreeing with this "infamous" biography, presumably Albert Goldman's. How can she be so sure that "John had viciously kicked my brother in the head" as she had dismissed it earlier and, indeed, claimed not to know the underlying cause for his death? How does Macmillan, which has published both

Backbeat and *The Beatles' Shadow*, justify this change of heart?

Backbeat though captured the spirit of the time and its director Iain Softley transferred it to the stage in 2010 where it had a short run in the West End. It could have been a hit but they got it wrong. I couldn't care less how explicit a production is but once you have prostitutes giving the Beatles blow-jobs, not to mention the strong language, you are losing the coach parties. It was good fun and spirited but the producers should have considered the qualities which turn a production into a 'must see' event.

Then, in 2012, *Let It Be* came to London's West End in which a tribute band goes through the costume changes and presents forty of the Beatles' hits chronologically. It was very well done, especially when you consider that the Beatles did not want to do *Pepper* on stage themselves but I found it too predictable. Still, if you want a good night out, singing along to your favourites, you can do far worse.

In March 2016 I was fortunate enough to see the first performance of *The Sessions,* a remarkable re-staging of the Beatles at Abbey Road – and I really mean that. It was so extraordinary that a lot of the time I was thinking, how did they do that? Forty-five musicians were involved including two sets of Beatles. The *modus operandi* was to recreate how the Beatles sounded in the studio and this was very effective indeed.

The fab faux performed on the stage but see-through curtains were all around the stage on which graphics, news items, session information and live footage were projected. There were two large screens to the side which showed the actual live performance. In the first half, the curtains were up for 'All You Need Is Love' and 'Yellow Submarine' but otherwise we watched everything through a gauze. I've never been to a show like that before.

The second half opened with *Sgt. Pepper* and the curtains were raised much of the time. I wasn't sure about the dancers – seven people in a large sheet swaying to "I am the eggman" or four dancing policemen - but corny as this was, it fitted in with the psychedelic spirit of the times.

Geoff Emerick was the creative consultant and in the mixing booth with two engineers, but the narration, such as there was, came from the actor playing George Martin – he looked right – long and lean and always wearing white shirt and grey trousers.

There was such a large marketing stall that I realised that this must be destined for arenas everywhere, but it was not to be. There was another night at the Royal Albert Hall, but soon the performances were cancelled or at least postponed until 2017. What had gone wrong? Technically it seemed fine but maybe the ticket sales meant it was losing money. I saw it in the Echo Arena in Liverpool. About 6,000 people were there but then that is only half full.

III. Books

The Beatles biographies have included Philip Norman's *Shout!* (1981), Peter Brown's *The Love You Make (1983)* and Ray Coleman's *Lennon* (1984), Albert Goldman ignored superb work from his researchers for his personal attack on John Lennon in *The Lives of John Lennon* (1988), which, in turn, was ignored by fans.

Cynthia Lennon: "I've read a number of Beatle books and I find it extremely annoying if the facts aren't straight. I find myself so far removed from it sometimes that it's as though they were writing about somebody else. I don't like the situation where people who know me and my friends deliberately distort our lives. With Ray Coleman, I tried to put the record straight as much as possible."

Mike McCartney: "There are two ways of approaching life. I tried to be positive when I was writing about my brother and his mates in the *Thank U Very Much* book. I could have written a *Paulie Dearest* or done a 'Goldman' because it is so easy to paint the negative side of anybody. I worry about the honest books not getting enough sales to give them credibility with the computers at the publishing houses. I'm hoping that God will take care of it in the end, I'm sure He will, but so many books are based on unsubstantiated stories and the authors twist things around. It's like having a lovely, innocent conversation with a newspaperman and then finding it's become something else in print."

Denny Laine: "I was writing a book about my days in Wings and it came out, in a condensed version, in *The Sun*. They had taken sections out of the book and had made it look as though I was slagging off Paul McCartney. It was not true: he knows it too and that's all that matters to me."

Alistair Taylor: "I was terribly upset by Peter Brown's book, which I had unknowingly contributed to. He told me that he was writing a book about the 60s and it wasn't about the Beatles specifically. On that basis, I agreed, along with a string of colleagues. I shouldn't think Peter Brown has many friends left."

Steven Gaines, who co-wrote *The Love You Make* with Peter

Brown: "There are a lot of people who are children when it comes to the Beatles. If they hear something bad about them, it's like being told there's no Santa Claus. They were four wonderful but ordinary guys who had problems and had tremendous difficulty in dealing with the fame and the pressures on them. We're not little boys anymore and so we should be able to take an honest look at the Beatles."

Beatles biographer Bob Spitz: "Albert Goldman had no regard for John Lennon as a performer, let alone as a person. I think that is a great misrepresentation of the biographer's art and he should not have undertaken the project."

John Lennon biographer Ray Coleman: "I was a close friend of John Lennon's and a great admirer of his and so I knew that some reviews would say that I leaned far too much towards supporting him and not enough towards criticising him. They said the book suffered because it was written by a friend. Well, if that's the worst thing they can say, I am delighted. I don't think it is a bad thing that a journalist friend did a comprehensive biography."

Philip Norman's biography, *Shout!* (1981) is a well-regarded history of the Beatles but it is highly opinionated, stating clearly that Lennon was the genius in the group. Over the year Norman has been softening his views so that when the 860-page *Paul McCartney: The Biography* (2016) was published, Paul was on an equal footing with John. Is this a genuine conversion or is it for expediency? My main gripe is that Norman is always reluctant to give his sources so we don't know what his original research is and what is taken from elsewhere, for example, Barry Miles' official biography of Paul, *Many Years From Now* (1997) and, naturally, Mark Lewisohn's books.

Howard Sounes' biography of Paul McCartney, *Fab* (2010) covers familiar ground but he hits the motherlode with first-hand accounts of Paul's temper tantrums. I knew Paul could get angry but I didn't know the wherefores and the whys until I read this book.

The Beatle books continue to be published at a startling rate and there is even the large and opinionated assessment by two academics, Mike Brocken and Melissa Davis, of hundreds of books, *The Beatles Bibliography*, published in Colorado in 2012. I found this book stimulating but then I enjoy reading opinions which differ from my own providing they are well argued. The intention is to publish regular updates and I look forward to their assessment of *Tune In*.

Tune In is the first part of Mark Lewisohn's highly readable and brilliantly researched study of the Beatles' background and history. There are two editions and I would recommend the two-volume set which takes 1,700 pages to reach the end of 1962. It is a social history of Liverpool and a history of popular music as well as being totally informative about the Beatles and every page grabs my attention. Lewisohn does not pull his punches and although the text is largely reverential, he gives candid details of what happened in Hamburg. *Tune In* will be the definitive text of the Beatles' early years but that is not going to prevent many more books being published.

As far as I know McCartney and Starr have not read through the text and although Lewisohn has interviewed them in the past, they did not help directly with the book. The book I would love to see now is *The Beatles Read Tune In* where Paul and Ringo plough through the text, commenting as they go along as I am sure it would stimulate many memories. It is possible that they would disown it as they might feel it puts too many private details into the public arena. I don't know but I do know that Ray Davies has disowned Johnny Rogan's biography, *Ray Davies: A Complicated Life*. To have written about his mother's hygiene was certainly insensitive, but if as an author, Rogan has this information, should he hold back?

IV. Sounding like the Beatles

Around the late 70s, the time of the Rutles as it happens, many of the new bands were determined not to sound like the Beatles. Especially in Liverpool. How could you aim to be the best band in the city when the Beatles had already come from there?

Ian McNabb from Icicle Works: "When I started in a band in 1975, the Beatles were a curse as the shadow that they cast was just too huge. If you tried to get a record deal, people would say, 'Oh, Beatles' which killed it for us. What goes around comes around and towards the end of the 70s when the New Wave was around, you had successful bands from Liverpool like Wah! Heat, Echo and the Bunnymen and the Teardrop Explodes and it was a baptism of fire. It killed off the Beatles comparison as most of the Liverpool bands sounded like they came from Los Angeles or New York. The spell was broken. People didn't speak about the Beatles very much in the 80s: they were always there but there wasn't too much made of it. Then Oasis came along and that got a new generation into it, and now you can't move for Beatles."

On the B-side of their debut single, the Clash sang, "No Beatles,

Elvis or the Rolling Stones in 1977." Glen Matlock was supposedly ditched from the Sex Pistols for talking about the Beatles, but the Beatles were integral to punk from the start. The Damned did 'Help!' as a B-side, the Rezillos sang 'I Wanna Be Your Man', and Siouxsie and the Banshees performed 'Twist and Shout', 'Helter Skelter' and 'Blue Jay Way'. In 1983, they went to No.3 with 'Dear Prudence'. In an interview with Paul Weller's mum, she revealed how he collected the monthly *Beatles Book*. The Jam's 1980 No.1, 'Start', took its rhythm from 'Taxman' and was also strongly influenced by the Who.

Music writer Paul Morley: "I've had an ambivalent relationship with the Beatles over the years because in the 70s and 80s you had to race away from them as their influence was so all-pervading that they had become heritage. They had become anti- what the original idea or spirit was. The Clash line of 'No Beatles, no Rolling Stones' was right as you turned against them but I couldn't maintain that level of indifference or ignorance towards them. Because they were the first, they had managed to both grab the history and be the history. The Beatles were Picassos without a doubt but they also came from Liverpool with the self-confidence of local energy and they were good at the con trick of creating the illusion of just how great they were. As a result the rest of the world started to believe them. This is not necessarily disparaging them: they created this wonderful sense of illusion that this brilliant, multi-tiered palace of pop music had come out of the minds of these extraordinary Liverpudlians."

Over in America, the Flamin' Groovies' 'Let the Boy Rock And Roll' sounded like a George Harrison outtake. The Knack named themselves after a Dick Lester film and looked and sounded like the Beatles.

In the late 70s and early 80s, Chris Difford and Glenn Tilbrook of Squeeze must have tired of the number of times they were compared to Lennon and McCartney, but although Squeeze recorded for as long as the Beatles, only a few of their hits are remembered today and relatively few artists have covered them.

Neil Innes: "I think the word 'Rutle' should be a verb meaning to copy someone you admire and in that case, the Beatles are Rutles as they copied artists like Eddie Cochran and Gene Vincent. Oasis are Rutles because they copied the Beatles."

In more recent times, Oasis has been the defining British band, yet their songs are full of Beatle references, and their career has been fashioned around a Beatles' B-side, 'Rain'. It is not unfair to call them a tribute band but they have only hammered out a certain type of Beatle song: they have no 'Eleanor Rigby'. Although they have borrowed from the Beatles and their subsequent solo careers, they have not developed any of this into a new sound. Even Noel Gallagher's sparklingly funny interviews owe something to John Lennon. This is not a Scouser knocking Mancs, by the way: I would say this irrespective of their origin. And two ironies: Oasis lost a court case in which they were accused of plagiarising Neil Innes, creator of the Rutles, and the Beatles' remasters were issued the week that Oasis split up.

Music writer Paolo Hewitt: "There are obvious reference points with Oasis but Noel Gallagher is taking the piss a lot of the time. When he put that piano like 'Imagine' at the start of 'Don't Look Back in Anger', he knew what he was doing and he was doing it to wind people up. He is like all the great songwriters, assimilating their influences and turning them into something else. Even though you can hear tinges of those influences, you can hear his music all the time. He has far more going for him than copying the Beatles."

Jon Savage: "Oasis became a business and their problem was very simple. They kept referencing the Beatles. Within 10 years, the Beatles changed incredibly and Oasis hardly changed a jot. Their trick, and it was a good one, was to source 'Rain'. That sound, that particularly psychedelic moment, is Liam's vocal. It's such a wonderful moment, but they didn't do that spirit any justice."

As well as the vocals, Oasis has followed the Beatles' fashions, circa 1965. Ian McNabb: "The Beatles were four very charismatic people who didn't hide behind sunglasses. They actually communicated and had two incredible singers as well as songwriters. Oasis tends to do the shouty Lennon helium sort of thing. The Beatles never had guitars that sounded like that so Oasis have never sounded like the Beatles, but there was a lot of that Lennony vocal thing going on. There was a lot of that before Oasis. The La's did it here. Listeners like to find something from the past to identify with: it helps them to like something new a lot better."

Andrew Gold: "My favourite tracks are around the time of *Beatles For Sale* and *Rubber Soul*, you know, 'Drive My Car' and 'We Can Work It Out', when they were really starting to get creative. I was listening to the radio like crazy and I was listening to the Beach Boys, the Byrds and Bob Dylan and also Motown and Burt Bacharach. It was the soundtrack of my life and it was such a turning point. The music of the 20s and 30s wasn't echoing around in the 60s. Even the 40s had gone, but the music from the 60s is still very much in evidence today. There is still a lot of Beatle-influenced stuff and I am not just talking about the obvious bands like Oasis. You can hear that retro stuff in songs and guitar sounds. Young people dress like hippies. The 60s were a dividing line."

And what of those who sound like John Lennon? First of all, his son Julian. Dave Clark: "When I was making the album of *Time*, I was the first person to record Julian Lennon and it was weird because he is so much like his dad, both with his sense of humour and his performance. He's got more going for him in another way because he's got a deeper voice than John's. He's got a lot of talent and it's great that he's able to keep the family name alive."

Mike Batt: "The Liverpool accent and their vocal characteristics led to the Liverpool sound. The fact that Lennon, McCartney and Harrison all came from the same area helped to make them blend beautifully as singers. It's natural that Julian Lennon should sound similar. Funnily enough, I was brought up in that era and my phrasing is very similar. I usually tell singers, 'This is how I'd like it phrased', and then I demonstrate it. Julian slipped into it straight away when we were recording *The Hunting of the Snark*. He heard my demo, came in and sang it just right, the phrasing was perfect."

In 2010, James McCartney, Paul McCartney's son, released his first solo album and did a short UK tour. A little late in the day as he was thirty-two, but we will have to wait and see how this pans out. In 2014 he recorded 'Hello Goodbye' with the Cure for a tribute album to his dad, *The Art of McCartney*: nothing new, just a weak copy of the Beatles, so why do it?

V. Cover Versions

Note: In Beatle days, the phrase 'cover version' only referred to an alternative version of a new song, such as when the Beatles covered Arthur Alexander's 'Anna'. Now the phrase is used for the new recording of any song, even going back to Beatle times, so that Gareth Gates covered 'The Long and Winding Road'. We would, however, talk about a revival, not a cover, of a song from the so-called Great American Songbook for a pre-war success.

The Beatles started their career by performing covers and now virtually every band in virtually every style has performed a cover of a Beatles song at some stage in their careers. Some critics thought it was odd that Paul McCartney should perform live on the final for *The X Factor* in 2009, but it made sense. It was a way of saying thanks to Simon Cowell. *The X Factor, Pop Idol, American Idol* and other lesser reality shows constantly use the Beatles' songs for contestants, which must be highly lucrative.

The covers have come from all sorts of artists and it is interesting to see the Beatles' own heroes – Little Richard, Fats Domino, the Everly Brothers, Ray Charles – all recording Beatle songs. Ray Charles recorded successful soulful interpretations of their work and he was followed by Aretha Franklin and Wilson Pickett. Although a McCartney song rather than a Beatles' one, listen to Screamin' Jay Hawkins singing the hell out of Paul McCartney's 'Monkberry Moon Delight' (1979). It works, but as Nigel Kennedy says, "I love the Beatles but it's difficult to touch their songs without making them worse."

Among the many albums devoted to the Beatles' songwriting are:

Keely Smith Sings the Lennon-McCartney Songbook (1964)
The sleeve note says, "Keely Smith reveals the often surprising melodic richness and beauty to be found in the compositions of the Beatles." It took insight to recognise in 1964 that the Beatles were writing timeless standards. This imaginative album led to many of the great MOR singers following her lead. Come to think of it, Keely Smith already had a Beatle bob.

Count Basie – Basie's Beatle Bag (1966)
Big band jazz album, which was followed by *Basie on the Beatles* (1970) with Ringo Starr's sleeve notes. (Well, the other three were probably out of town.) I'm not saying that Basie was disinterested but he doesn't even mention the Beatles in his 400 page autobiography and it's clear from the cover that he regards it as a children's album.

Booker T & the MG's – McLemore Avenue (1970)
The soul band recorded a funky version of *Abbey Road* with the cover parodying their zebra crossing cover. Okay as background music, but resembles a funky night at the British Legion.

Revolver – Northern Songs (1979)
This Liverpool band concentrated on songs that Lennon and McCartney gave away, giving all of them an early Beatles flavour. 'Hello Little Girl' is far too fast, but 'Tip of My Tongue', again too fast, benefits from their harmonies. These are minor quibbles: this was a great idea.

Various Artists – Sgt. Pepper Knew My Father (1988)

An important stepping stone was the 1988 remake of *Sgt. Pepper's Lonely Hearts Club Band* by contemporary artists for the charity, Childline by the *NME*. It led the way for complete Beatles albums being reinterpreted by bunches of artists: current hitmakers, folkies or whatever. From 2006 to 2010, *Mojo* has worked its way through *Revolver, Sgt. Pepper, The White Album, Abbey Road* and *Let It Be*.

The Childline album led to a double-sided No.1 hit single for Wet Wet Wet and Billy Bragg. Billy Bragg: "It seemed to me that 'She's Leaving Home' was not only a track pertaining to Childline, which was a free phoneline for children who are victims of abuse, but also it was one of the few tracks on *Sgt. Pepper* that I could probably play. I was working with a keyboard player at the time, Cara Tivey, and she played the keyboards, did the backing vocals and then played the recorders and I just sang the vocal deadpan over the top. It is a great song and I like the fact that it mentions car salesmen. It's a good thing to have them in a song. I was really surprised when it got to No.1 but that's Wet Wet Wet for you."

Big Daddy – Sgt. Pepper's (1992)
The rock'n'roll group pretend that we are still in 1959 and here is a 50s reworking of the whole *Sgt. Pepper* album. The doo-wop arrangement of 'Good Morning Good Morning' is exceptionally good while 'Lucy in the Sky with Diamonds' is transformed by a Jerry Lee Lewis arrangement.

Original Soundtrack – I Am Sam (2001)
There have also been a number of one-off albums where contemporary artists have recorded Beatle songs, one of the most engaging being the soundtrack for *I Am Sam*, which starred Sean Penn and Michelle Pfeiffer. The artists included Sheryl Crow, the Stereophonics and Nick Cave, who made the utterly bizarre choice of 'Here Comes the Sun'.

The Persuasions Sing the Beatles (2002)
The Persuasions are more adventurous than most a cappella groups and have recorded tributes to Frank Zappa, the Grateful Dead and U2. This sublime and wonderfully inventive take on the Beatles' songwriting was recorded in St Peter's Church, Manhattan using a single microphone. The little squeals in 'Love Me Do' are irritating and the gospel group didn't grasp 'Imagine' as they fill it with references to "my Lord" and might have been more comfortable with 'My Sweet Lord', but it's a fantastic record.

Various Artists – Rubber Folk (2006)
BBC Radio 2 created a new version of *Rubber Soul,* now called *Rubber Folk,* performed with the cream of the UK's folk circuit. Not always successful but it does demonstrate that Lennon and McCartney have written the folk music of the future.

Barbara Dickson – Nothing's Gonna Change My World (2006)
So much thought has gone into the arrangements of this beautiful low-key album, which often takes the lesser-known songs.

Judy Collins Sings Lennon and McCartney (2007)
While they have so much in common, it's curious that there isn't a single song duplicated with the Barbara Dickson album. Also, they are nearly all McCartney songs. Being a folkie, there's no need to change the sex of the songs so casual listeners might think we have lesbian versions of 'And I Love Her', 'Norwegian Wood' and 'Good Day Sunshine'. Nevertheless, 'When I'm Sixty-Four' becomes 'When I'm Eighty-Four'.

Various Brazilian Artists – Beatles (2009)
The most ambitious project ever for recording the Beatles' songbook comes from the producer Marcelo Fróes, who has cut every one of their tracks with different Brazilian artists. There are two separate versions of *The White Album.* Some unexpected tracks too such as a version of the song Paul McCartney offered to Frank Sinatra, 'Suicide'. No wonder Frank thought he was taking the mick.

Various Artists – Lennon Bermuda (2012)
Double album set of Lennon covers, revised and reissued the following year. Largely put together to promote Lennon festivals in Bermuda. Some unexpected artists like Heather Nova, Judie Tzuke and from those Hamburg days, Roy Young.

Various Artists – Please Please Me (2013)
An intriguing BBC Radio 2 offering where the *Please Please Me* album was remade in a day. It included Squeeze with the title song and the Stereophonics with 'I Saw Her Standing There'. Non-original material included the Merseybeats and other contemporary Liverpool musicians with 'Boys' and a thrilling, gospel workout of 'Twist and Shout' from Beverley Knight.

Let Us In: Americana – The Music of Paul McCartney (2013)
Buddy Miller has great fun with 'Yellow Submarine', Steve Earle and Alison Moorer choose 'I Will' and Keith Secor of the Old Crow Medicine Show turns 'Give Ireland Back to the Irish' into a marching song.

Various Artists – The Art of McCartney (2014)
Two CDs and a DVD and a guest list to die for: Bob Dylan, Billy
Joel, Brian Wilson, Willie Nelson, Smokey Robinson, Dr John, B.B.
King, Yusuf (Cat Stevens) and Dion. Results are varied, but it's always
interesting. Alice Cooper singing 'Eleanor Rigby' anyone? Because
'Lady Madonna' sounds like a New Orleans song, it was a good idea to
pass it to Allen Toussaint.

There have been innumerable collections of covers of Beatle songs
and in 1976, the TV-advertised company Arcade issued a forty track
double-album, *Superstars Tribute to the Beatles*. This collection of
tracks from eleven different labels, a considerable achievement in the
mid-70s, included hits from Elton John and Joe Cocker as well as some
engaging oddities. K-Tel retaliated by releasing *With a Little Help from
My Friends*, which was then remarketed as *Forever*.

Since then, one collection has followed another, some of them
budget-priced and quite lame such as *All You Need Is Covers* (1999)
and *Help!* (2001), two fifty track collections from the Pye catalogue.
If you want Max Bygraves singing 'A Hard Day's Night' or Victor
Silvester's 'And I Love Her', this is the place for you, but somehow
Todd Rundgren is among this motley crew.

The best CD compilation is the thirty-six track, *And Your Bird Can
Sing* (1996) on Débutante, which included many of the hit recordings.
One of the oddest is *We Can Work It Out* (2005) on Harmless. The
first CD included some excellent covers from the likes of Al Green and
Ramsey Lewis, and the second CD reworked the tracks in a disco mix.

Bear Family has released CDs of cover versions of the Beatles songs
in French and German. If novelty is your thing, then go for the two
volumes of *The Exotica Beatles* on the Exotica label in 1993 and 1994.
Hear John Otway sing 'I Am the Walrus', Mae West with 'Day Tripper'
and Derek Enright MP, recite 'Eleanor Rigby' in Latin.

Then there's *Beatlemaniacs!!* a twenty-four track collection of
novelty singles issued by Ace in 2006. Some are daft novelties like
'I'll Let You Hold My Hand' from the Bootles and 'We Love You
Beatles' from the Vernons Girls. Nilsson's 'You Can't Do That', which
incorporates snatches of other Beatle songs, is sublime.

There are specialist collections. Trojan issued a 3CD box of
reggae artists singing the Beatles' songs, and there has also been *The
Lennon and McCartney Jazz Collection* (with Buddy Rich and the Jazz
Crusaders), *Glass Onion* (from Warner and Atlantic's jazz vaults with

Ella Fitzgerald and King Curtis), *Blue Note Plays the Beatles* (Bobby McFerrin, Dianne Reeves), *Motown Meets the Beatles* (Seems that the whole of Motown was told to cover the Beatles), *The Soul of Lennon and McCartney* (Aretha Franklin, Wilson Pickett), *The Fab Four Go Loungecore* (Cyril Stapleton, Sounds Orchestral) and *Nice'n'Easy* (Ronnie Aldrich, Frank Chacksfield).

The one that I like best though is *Come Together – Black America Sings The Beatles* (Ace, 2011). How John and Paul must have enjoyed the black artists they loved doing their songs and this superb twenty-four track collection includes Little Richard ('I Saw Her Standing There'), Fats Domino ('Everybody's Got Something to Hide Except for Me and My Monkey') and Roy Redmond's 'Good Day Sunshine'.

For what it's worth, these are cover versions that, I think, improve on the originals:

I Wanna Be Your Man – Rolling Stones (1963, UK No.12) Brian Jones slide guitar solo.

It's Only Love – Gary U.S. Bonds (1981) Perfunctory Beatles song turned into a cry of anguish by the 60s hit-maker with Bruce Springsteen's E Street Band

Octopus's Garden – The Persuasions (2002) Superb a cappella version of Ringo's song, and the so-called 'instrumental break' is whistled. Pity the Beatles themselves didn't record it like this.

Goodnight – Barbara Dickson (2006) First time I appreciated this charming lullaby.

Love You To – John Jorgenson (2009) Sensational 7 minute version by the guitar virtuoso: catch him in concert when it can be even longer. These are distinctively different:

A Hard Day's Night – Keely Smith (1964) Arranged like Peggy Lee's 'Fever'. Note the lyrical change: "When he comes home to me, Where he oughta be."

Eight Days A Week – Alma Cogan (1965) You'd think from the intro that Alma was about to launch into 'Unchained Melody': in fact, anything but 'Eight Days A Week'. The words and much of the melody are the same, but it sounds like a completely different song.

A Hard Day's Night – Peter Sellers (1965, UK No.14) Sellers as Olivier doing Richard III

Eleanor Rigby – Doodles Weaver (1966) Like Ronnie Barker with pismonunciation, Doodles stumbles over the lyric to good comic effect. I have mixed feelings about this record: sometimes it is in there with the best and other times with the worst – you have to be in the right mood to enjoy it.

Good Day Sunshine – Roy Raymond (1967) Whenever Macca is asked about cover versions, he praises this soul version of 'Good Day Sunshine'.

Ticket To Ride – Vanilla Fudge (1967) Get out the sledgehammers!

You Can't Do That – Nilsson (1967) Brilliant – Nilsson does all the voices and incorporates about forty titles in 2 minutes.

With A Little Help From My Friends – Joe Cocker (1968, UK No.1, US No.68 – yes, 68, what went wrong there?)

Hey Jude – Wilson Pickett (1969) (UK No.16, US No.23) The best screaming ever put on record and Duane Allman's guitar –what more do you want?

Revolution – Nina Simone (1969) So different that it is almost a different song.

Something – Isaac Hayes (1970) 12 minute slow burner.

I'm Lookin' Through You – Steve Earle (1995) Captures the angry spirit of the song.

I Feel Fine – Curtis Stigers (2003) The coolest of cool jazz interpretation, ending with scat.

Girl – John Tams (2006) Acting class: as though John is walking the street and musing on a relationship.

Blackbird – Julie Fowlis (2008) Enchanting Gaelic version

Eleanor Rigby – The Real Thing (2008) Top Liverpool acts were invited to record Liverpool No.1s from other performers. The Real Thing update 'Eleanor Rigby' to include the dispossessed in Iraq and Afghanistan. On paper, this might not have worked but it was perfect.

I Need You – The Webb Sisters (2012) Leonard Cohen's sirens with a George Harrison song.

Girl – Paul Carrack (2013) From the double CD, *Lennon Bermuda*. Paul Carrack could sing the entire Beatles songbook and not put a foot wrong.

Nowhere Man – Roy Young (2013) British rock'n'roller who was with Beatles in their Hamburg days. He was in his late 70s when he cut this but he sounds like Joe Cocker. Also from *Lennon Bermuda*.

I Want You (She's So Heavy) – PUTTINBEATLES (2014) Seventeen Russian bands sing the Beatles with varying results, but I love this one and I love the name. They say the name stands for 'Puttin' on the Beatles Style' and I hope the Kremlin feels the same way. Three accordionists and a guitar man and it's fantastic.

Run for Your Life – Cowboy Junkies (2014) Spaced-out, weird and totally compelling: if the Beatles had thought of it, they would have recorded the *Rubber Soul* song like this.

Blackbird – Joan Baez and David Crosby (2016) Two voices and Dirk Powell on guitar.

These are Grade A disasters:

When I'm Sixty-Four – Pinky and Perky (1968) The piglet puppets appeared on *The Ed Sullivan Show* before the Beatles and made five more appearances. Of course, no pig could possibly live to 64.

Lucy In The Sky With Diamonds – William Shatner (1968) To boldly go, indeed. From the spoken word album, *The Transformed Man.*

Give Peace A Chance – Louis Armstrong (1970) And all Louis is saying is "Give peace a chance".

Yellow Submarine – Lieutenant Pigeon (1973) Part of the *Mouldy Old Music* LP: instrumental version played fast on jangly piano with synth and heavy percussion.

Because – Alice Cooper (1978) Very bad, very spooky and produced by George Martin.

Being For The Benefit Of Mr. Kite – Frank Sidebottom (1988) I know Frank Sidebottom is an acquired taste, but do you know anyone who has acquired it?

A Hard Day's Night (All Day Night) – Sugar Minott (2001) "It's been a hard day's night and I've been thinking rub-a-dub."

Norwegian Wood – Waterson-Carthy (2006) Oh dear: this is the wrong song to turn into a sea shanty.

Things We Said Today – Bob Dylan (2014) This is a joke, right? Why does he continue?

VI. Liverpool

Just as Liverpool was known for its docks, Detroit was known for its car plants. In a recent TV documentary, Martha Reeves said how the car workers weren't impressed when Motown wanted to make a promotional film in a plant to promote her single with the Vandellas' 'Nowhere to Run'. Although Motown was good for Detroit's image, it was never pushed in the way that Liverpool was with the Beatles and so the benefits for the city and hence, tourism were marginal. Detroit is now a city in crisis and greatly in need of regeneration. Could tourism have saved it if given the chance?

Cavern City Tours has done much to bring visitors to Liverpool to show them the "places I remember" in the Beatles' life. Their Beatle Conventions every August Bank Holiday weekend gain popularity and attract star guests – Pete Best, Denny Laine, Tony Sheridan and a host of Mersey bands.

Rock photographer Mick Rock: "The Beatles transformed everything, including Liverpool. Liverpool might not have become the amazing modern city that it has become without them. I came here on tours in the 70s and the Liverpool was not a place where you went walking late at night. It was criminally infested and now there is something magical going on here. Carl Jung called it the Pool of Life and he was right."

The award-winning *The Beatles Story* at the Albert Dock is among Liverpool's top tourist attractions and although it is not feasible to have more than sixty visitors a day, John and Paul's childhood homes are 'must visits' for keen fans coming to Liverpool. Even if you are not into the Beatles, the homes are worth seeing as they reproduce a 50s home so well.

Come to Merseyside now and you can fly into Liverpool John Lennon Airport, which was opened by the Queen and Yoko Ono. How John would have laughed. Still, John did write "Above us only sky", while Paul wrote, "Man, I had a dreadful flight".

The Cavern is open to tourists during the day and has a programme of old and new music. Close to it is the Beatles Shop. Joe Elliott from Def Leppard: "I am a big fan of Ian Hunter's. I went to see him in Leeds and he was playing Liverpool the next day. I had never been to the Cavern. We got onto Beatle Street – it should be called that now – and we went to the shop and I bought myself an inflatable *Yellow Submarine* armchair and a few other bits and bobs. There's one born every minute! We had some food and a few pints and off we went to the gig. Ian and I are pretty tight and I got up and did 'All The Way from Memphis'. You're lucky to have the world's biggest piece of musical history on your doorstep."

The Hard Days Night hotel, which is also in the Cavern Quarter, has opened very successfully and it contains a very good souvenir shop where the products are surprisingly tasteful.

Even in 2015, you can hear old Merseybeat bands performing and both the Merseycats and the Lanky Cats have held charity evenings at the Cavern. Most engagingly, you can still hear the Quarrymen perform, admittedly without their most famous members.

VII. Legacy of the Beatles

Since the Beatles disbanded, journalists have been asking who will be the next Beatles. No one, not even Queen, Oasis or U2, has achieved that total breakthrough. Maybe the answer is the Beatles themselves as there have been a host of ingenious schemes to keep the band contemporary and appealing to the next generation.

Rick Wakeman: "Their story has a beginning, a middle and an end, and there are various periods – the pop period, the psychedelic period, the John and Yoko period, and so on. It's great for young musicians of today because they can see the complete works and the complete lifespan of the Beatles, which we could never do at the time. In the end, the media expected too much of them. The majority of performers would have been delighted with just one classic album, and the amount they turned out is astonishing. It got to the stage where everyone thought that everything would be a classic, and the pressure was too much for them. The Beatles will go down in history as the most influential musicians of the 20th century. The only sad thing for the kids of today and tomorrow is that the film clips on TV, and even the records, can't tell you what it was really like at the time because they can't ooze that atmosphere."

BBC DJ Alan Freeman: "The Beatles took note of the moral and social issues of the day and reflected upon them, and we are now in the midst of the revolution that the Beatles caused. They caused a lot of people to rethink their values. They freed me from middle-age. When the Beatles happened, there I was, heading for forty, and they made me feel terribly young again. It was great. They were sensational."

Justin Currie of Del Amitri: "I can't get beyond the 60s as when I have had too much wine or too much beer in the pub, I tend to go back to my vinyl and the best for me is still Jimi Hendrix, Bob Dylan and the Beatles. I am still obsessed by them all, for good or ill."

Neil Hannon of the Divine Comedy: "The Beatles had an influence on every succeeding band or artist that came afterwards. It may be a second or third generation influence, but it is still there. The Beatles changed everything and they are also the link between old-fashioned vaudeville, 20s flapper songs, Noël Coward and Cole Porter. Many of their records are not 4/4 rock'n'roll at all and are in that old tradition. Look at 'Eleanor Rigby', which was brilliantly arranged by George Martin. It was the second track on a No.1 album and a massive single at the time of a real rock explosion. It has a Bach like string arrangement and it is a remarkable track."

Singer/songwriter Jake Stigers: "Lennon and McCartney are like the Johann Sebastian Bach of Rock and almost everything has their influence. Their body of work is brilliant, there's song after song after song. Kids today can still relate to their songs because they know what they are about, and that doesn't happen to George Gershwin or Cole Porter. 'Jealous Guy' has a really basic lyric but it goes to show you can write a song with simple language and have it mean something really deep."

Author of *Beatles Gear* Andy Babiuk: "Lennon and McCartney wrote melodies and a lot of that is missing now. A lot of these heavy metal guys are noodling around as fast as they can on a guitar. It sounds like a blur and though technically it is impressive, there is no melody. Lennon and McCartney would use the instruments to complement their songs as opposed to writing great instrumental things."

Songwriter Frank Musker: "The Beatles can be enjoyed by many different generations. It is like Shakespeare. Babies enjoy the 'la la' melodies and serious analysts of society can listen to the words. All the tools that Lennon and McCartney were using have now been scooped up by the multinationals and are being used to sell trainers and everything else in our globalised culture."

For years, the Beatles, like Bob Dylan, did not allow their music to be used in advertising, even though this could be so lucrative. Nike used 'Revolution' for a TV ad in 1987 and now it is possible to use their music if your company has deep pockets. Rufus Wainwright did 'Across the Universe' for Canon digital cameras in 2004 and there was an incredibly annoying ad featuring 'All You Need Is Love' for mobile phones in cinemas.

The younger generation views music very differently from the 60s fans. Music now competes with other entertainment media and there are scores of radio stations that cater for particular tastes. You can hear most tracks you want for free with *Spotify*. Given a few more years, it seems unlikely that a musician will be able to make a living from his recordings alone and the money will come from touring. In the 60s we were at the mercy of what the local record store ordered and we didn't have enough to buy what we wanted. What were EPs but an opportunity to buy the best tracks from an LP for the financially stretched?

Scott Bennett from Brian Wilson's band: "It seems to me that nobody is promoting art anymore and I find that offensive. It is all, 'This person has sold the most records' or 'The Rolling Stones tour has grossed so many millions.' The big artists are caught up in this and they don't seem to be challenging other artists to do better."

As UK legislation took records that were over 50 years old out of copyright, most of the records that influenced the Beatles in their early years can now be released by anyone. However, the law was changed in 2012 so that the records that were issued in 1963 and beyond had a longer copyright term. 'Love Me Do' and 'P S I Love You' are out of copyright but all other Beatle tracks are protected. I suspect that much of this was down to skilful lobbying by Paul McCartney.

Mark Lewisohn: "The Beatles music will never, ever die, and people in the future will always be talking about how great it was. I do, however, feel that the phenomenon of the Beatles themselves will subside in, say, 10 years time. The reason you still find the Beatles all over the newspapers and the radio is because the people who run the media are the teenagers of the 60s. In 20 years time they will be the people who grew up in the 80s and they won't be so inclined to report on the activities of the Beatles."

To anyone under 50, the Beatles are history: okay, modern history, but still history. You would have to be 65 to have seen the Beatles at the Cavern.

Hunter Davies: "The thing about the Beatles is that the further we get away from them, the bigger they become: bigger in influence, bigger in that their souvenirs sell more and are more valuable: with the memorabilia and artefacts, more and more people are living off the Beatles. When Apple was at its height, no more than fifty people were employed by the Beatles. There are thousands of people in the world today living off the Beatles: the look-alike groups, the tours, the dealers, the writers, the university courses, it's amazing."

All the time these days we are celebrating anniversaries – there has been the 50th anniversary of John meeting Paul in 2007 (there were even postage stamps for this) and then we knock down 50th anniversaries for the next 10 years. In 2017, *Sgt. Pepper* and in 2020, the break-up, plus several others along the way. Shame I won't be around for the centenary.

What did Paul McCartney say? Ah yes, I believe in yesterday.

BIBLIOGRAPHY

As I've a library of around three hundred Beatle books, I suppose I have dipped into most of them while writing this. Here are some I've found useful and others are mentioned in the Contributors section.

Davies, Hunter – *The Beatles: The Authorised Biography* (Heinemann, 1968)
I bought the hardback when it came out and it cost me £1.10s. At the time, no one had written about popular musicians in such depth and for all its flaws (Davies accepted what the Beatles said at face value, and allowed Aunt Mimi to make amendments!), it is a tremendously good read that captures their individual personalities and contains an enlightening chapter on John and Paul writing a song. Oddly enough, the text has not so much been updated as had new sections tacked on. The latest, rather cumbersome version was published by Ebury in 2009.

Evans, Mike – *The Art of the Beatles* (Anthony Blond, 1984)
The Beatles' own art and cover designs as well as how others have viewed the band.

Lewisohn, Mark – *The Beatles Live!* (1986)
Brilliantly researched book about their live performances.

Aldridge, Alan (Ed) – *The Beatles Illustrated Lyrics* (Two volumes combined, Little, Brown, 1990)
Great to have all the Beatles' lyrics in one place and each one is lovingly illustrated by the leading artists of the period of the 60s. A constant delight.

Lewisohn, Mark – *The Complete Beatles Chronicle* (Pyramid, 1992)
What the Beatles did on a day to day basis. Very reliable.

Turner, Steve – *A Hard Day's Write* (Carlton, 1994)
A good analysis of each of the Beatles' songs including recording dates and personnel Here's an example: "Lennon later recalled 'Yes It Is' as a failed rewrite of 'This Boy'. Yet, while formally alike – both are in

12/8, employ an intricate three-part major seventh harmony, and use the standard four-chord doo-wop sequence – the two songs have little else in common." I'd have thought that was quite a lot, and both songs are about yearning for a past love too.

MacDonald, Ian – *Revolution in the Head* (Fourth Estate, 1994)
An even better analysis of each of the Beatles' songs.

Badman, Keith – *The Beatles Off the Record* (Omnibus, 2000)
Transcripts of their interviews, but 500 pages of solid type without an index means that the book is not as useful as it could be.

Babiuk, Andy – *Beatles Gear* (Backbeat, 2001)
An intricately researched book about every instrument played by a Beatle. Not nearly as dry as it sounds: wholly engrossing, in fact.

Kane, Larry – *Ticket to Ride* (Running Press, 2003)
The experiences of a TV reporter who toured with the Beatles. Comes with a CD of his interviews.

Pedler, Dominic – *The Songwriting Secrets of the Beatles* (Omnibus, 2003)
Thorough 800 page analysis of all the Beatles' songs. It's assumed that the reader can read music but even if he can't (like me), it is enthralling stuff. There are 11 pages on the links between Oasis and the Beatles. Asked to comment on the similarity between 'I'd Like to Teach the World to Sing' and 'Shakermaker', Noel Gallagher said, "It's fuck-all to do with the New Seekers. It's more a rip-off of 'Flying' by the Beatles."

Doggett, Peter – *You Never Give Me Your Money* (Bodley Head, 2009)
A detailed study of what went wrong for the Beatles. On nearly every page, you think, "Well, why didn't so-and-so do that?" but they never did. They had too much money and had forgotten what had made them famous in the first place.

Engelhardt, Kristofer – *Deeper Undercover* (Collector's Guide, 2010)
A well-researched book about the Beatles' guest appearances. Don't be put off by the horrendous cover or the author's tendency to include pictures of himself.

Since compiling this list in 2010, the first volume of Mark Lewisohn's trilogy about the Beatles has been published. It is called *Tune In* and is published by Little, Brown. If you can afford the time (it took me three weeks!), read the full 1,700 page version, but it ends in 1962 and so has little bearing on the text of this book which effectively starts with 'Love Me Do'.

CONTRIBUTORS

All of the contributors in this section come from my own interviews, mostly for BBC Radio Merseyside. This is a guide as to who they are. Thanks to all.

Tariq Ali was at the forefront of radical politics in the UK. His absorbing memoir of the 60s, *Street Fighting Years* (2005), is distinctly different from any other book on the period.

Frank Allen played bass for Cliff Bennett and the Rebel Rousers and joined the Searchers in 1964.

Before having hits with the Real Thing, **Eddie Amoo** was in the Liverpool group, the Chants.

Don Andrew played in the Remo Four, who were known as Liverpool's Fendermen, and he founded the Merseycats charity.

Rod Argent was, and still is, a member of the Zombies.

Peter Asher was half of Peter and Gordon and A&R manager at Apple Records.

Chet Atkins was a master guitarist and record producer in Nashville.

Comic actor **Rowan Atkinson** is Blackadder and Mr Bean.

Toni Avern managed the Barron Knights.

New Yorker **Andy Babiuk** plays with the Chesterfield Kings and wrote *Beatles Gear*.

Julia Baird is John Lennon's half-sister, the author of *Imagine This* (Hodder & Stoughton, 2007) and a director of Cavern City Tours.

Butch Baker was a Barron Knight, retiring in 2007.

Kenny Ball led his Jazzmen around the world for 50 years.

Dave Ballinger was the drummer for the Barron Knights.

Adrian Barber was a founder member of the Big Three and had success in New York producing the Allman Brothers and Vanilla Fudge. Now living in Hawaii.

Chris Barber has been leading his successful Jazz and Blues band since the early 50s.

As part of the Quiet Five, **Richard Barnes** made the Top 50 with a cover of 'Homeward Bound' in 1966, and had a solo hit with 'Take to the Mountains' in 1970.

Tony Barrow worked as a press officer for NEMS Enterprises from 1963 to 1968. He has written more LP sleeve notes than anyone in the UK and they include the Beatles' first three Parlophone albums, *Please Please Me*, *With the Beatles* and *A Hard Day's Night*. He wrote *John, Paul, George, Ringo, & Me* (which sounds like a Willy Russell play) for André Deutsch in 2005.

Lionel Bart wrote many early British rock'n'roll hits ('Rock with the Caveman', 'Living Doll') and the musical *Oliver!*

Mike Batt has written and produced numerous records including 'Bright Eyes', 'A Winter's Tale', 'I Feel Like Buddy Holly', all the Wombles' hits and three albums for Katie Melua. His musical adaptation of Lewis Carroll's *The Hunting of the Snark* was released in 1986.

A leading rock guitarist, **Jennifer Batten** was part of Michael Jackson's extravaganza.

Walter Becker is half of Steely Dan.

Maggie Bell sang with Stone The Crows and recorded the themes for *Hazell* and *Taggart*.

Brian Bennett played drums for the Shadows. I've seen them in two farewell tours – one with Cliff and one without. They may not return but I wouldn't put money on it.

Cliff Bennett led the London R&B band, the Rebel Rousers.

Scott Bennett was a key member of Brian Wilson's band.

Sid Bernstein was an American impresario who presented the Beatles at Carnegie Hall and Shea stadium. His memoir, *Not Just the Beatles*, was published by Jacques & Flusster in 2000.

Mike Berry recorded 'Tribute to Buddy Holly' (1961) and 'Don't You Think It's Time?' (1963) for Joe Meek. He played a shop assistant in the TV comedy series *Are You Being Served?* and returned to the charts with 'The Sunshine of Your Smile'.

Pete Best joined the Beatles as their drummer in August 1960 and was sacked two years later. He has written his autobiography, *Beatle!* (Plexus, 1985) and he performs in a 60s band with his brother, Roag. They're good, too.

Alf Bicknell was the Beatles' chauffeur from 1964–66 and his account of those years can be found in *Baby, You Can Drive My Car!* (Number 9 Books). In his foreword, George Harrison calls him an "uncorruptible friend".

Dr Ian Biddle is a lecturer in music at Newcastle University.

Once the drummer for the Kursaal Flyers and the Records, **Will Birch** has written a history of pub rock and a biography of Ian Dury. His songs include 'A-1 on the Jukebox' (Dave Edmunds) and 'Hearts in Her Eyes' (Searchers).

Did you know that **Cilla Black** was going to star in a film biography of Gracie Fields, but Gracie said, "No way"?

Stanley Black is a conductor and composer whose many credits include Cliff Richard's films, *The Young Ones* and *Summer Holiday.*

Billy Blackwood is part of the second generation Blackwood Brothers Quartet, a gospel group which influenced Elvis Presley.

Lionel Blair, actor, dancer and *Give Us a Clue* captain.

One of Britain's leading artists and now knighted, **Peter Blake** designed the *Sgt. Pepper* sleeve.

Film director and film historian, **Peter Bogdanovich** made *The Last Picture Show* and *What's Up, Doc?*

As leader of T.Rex, **Marc Bolan** had a long run of chart hits in the early 70s. He died in a car accident in 1977.

Now in his thirties, **Joe Bonamassa** is rated one of the world's leading blues guitarists.

Pat Boone had a long run of hits which ended in January 1963. There could be a cause and effect here.

Joey Bower was a member of the Fourmost.

Guitarist **Mick Box** is a founder member of Uriah Heep and still with the band.

Joe Boyd has produced Fairport Convention, Richard Thompson and Maria Muldaur and run his own label, Hannibal.

A regular on political talk shows, **Billy Bragg** is one of the UK's most passionate songwriters. He told me that songwriting is like having a crap: you never know what is going to come out.

Tony Bramwell was a factotum for the Beatles, which means that he saw almost everything. His 400 page memoir *Magical Mystery Tours* was published by Robson in 2005. In more recent times, he helped establish Eva Cassidy's music in the UK.

Joe Brown is a leading British entertainer, particularly with his brand of cheerful rock'n'roll. He was a neighbour and close friend of George Harrison.

London poet, **Pete Brown** was the lyricist for Cream and ran his own band, Piblokto!

Vicki Brown, a former member of the Vernons Girls, was married to Joe Brown.

When I met **Mike Brumm** at a party at the Casbah, he was playing with A Hard Day's Night, a tribute band to the Beatles from Ohio. Turned out they were really Ohio Express!

Bob Brunning a founder member of Fleetwood Mac, found success with Savoy Brown, became a headmaster and wrote *Blues - The British Connection* (Blandford, 1986).

Eric Burdon was the lead singer with the Animals.

Tito Burns managed Cliff Richard, the Searchers and the Zombies.

In pre-Beatle days, **Max Bygraves** was a chart regular - 'Gilly Gilly Ossenfeffer Katzenellen Bogen by the Sea', 'You Need Hands', 'Tulips from Amsterdam' and 'Fings Ain't What They Used to Be' were among the hits.

Sammy Cahn was a remarkable New York lyricist whose songs include 'High Hopes', 'It's Magic', 'All the Way' and 'The Second Time Around'. When he played Fred Astaire 'Call Me Irresponsible', Fred said, "Stop! That's the best song I've ever heard." Sammy Cahn said, "That's the best half song you've ever heard. May I continue?"

Dancer **Iris Caldwell** was Rory Storm's sister.

Ramsey Campbell has world acclaim as a writer of horror fantasy (*The Doll Who Ate His Mother, The Face that Must Die*) and is a highly regarded film critic.

Freddy Cannon had hits with 'Talahassee Lassie' (1959) and 'Way Down Yonder in New Orleans' (1960).

Patrick Cargill was a British comedy actor who appeared in *Help!*

Peter Carlin has written biographies of Brian Wilson (*Catch a Wave*, 2006) and Paul McCartney *(Paul McCartney; A Life,* 2009).

One of the most colourful characters in the business, **Hal Carter** was shepherding groups around the country and/or managing them for 40 years.

Rosanne Cash, the daughter of Johnny Cash, has scarcely put a foot wrong in her 35 year career of her own songs and albums.

Buzz Cason was a member of the Crickets and also wrote 'Soldier of Love' (recorded on *The Beatles at the BBC*) and 'Everlasting Love'

(Love Affair). He was also Alvin on the Chipmunks' records.

Beth Nielsen Chapman is one of America's best singer/ songwriters.

Stephen Citron is noted for his analytical studies of songwriters such as *Noël and Cole* and *The Wordsmiths*.

Dave Clark was the drummer and leader of the Dave Clark Five.

Allan Clarke was the lead singer for the Hollies.

An academic, **Martin Cloonan** wrote *Banned! Censorship of Popular Music in Britain: 1967–92* (Arena, 1996).

Melody Maker editor, **Ray Coleman** wrote biographies of John Lennon and Brian Epstein.

Judy Collins possessed one of the purest, loveliest voices of the 60s and she still sounds wonderful today.

Stuart Colman produced Shakin Stevens' 'Green Door', Little Richard's 'Lifetime Friend' and Cliff Richard and the Young Ones' 'Living Doll'.

Roger Cook is a prolific songwriter whose hits include 'You've Got Your Troubles', 'I'd Like to Teach the World to Sing' and 'Lovers of the World Unite'. Roger was in Blue Mink and half of David and Jonathan with his songwriting partner, Roger Greenaway.

Mike Cotton was swinging that hammer with his own, chart-making Trad band in the 60s and then playing trumpet for Acker Bilk.

Tony Crane, still fronting the Merseybeats after 50 years, made melodic beat group records in the 60s - 'It's Love that Really Counts', 'I Think of You' and 'Wishin' and Hopin''.

Strongly influenced by music of the 50s and 60s, **Marshall Crenshaw** became one of America's most idiosyncratic songwriters.

Bernard Cribbins made the comedy hits, 'Hole in the Ground' and 'Right, Said Fred', which were produced by George Martin.

Rodney Crowell brought a new level of literacy to country music songwriting.

Justin Currie is the leader of Del Amitri.

Chris Curtis was the drummer for the Searchers.

Sonny Curtis has been a member of the Crickets and is a superb country songwriter/ performer with 'Walk Right Back', 'More Than I Can Say' and 'I Fought the Law' to his credit.

Ivor Cutler was "very funny in a decidedly sinister way." (George Melly)

John Dankworth was a superbly talented jazz musician, whose film scores include *The Servant* and *Darling*. He was married to Cleo Laine and knighted for his services to music.

One of the UK's most prolific authors, **Hunter Davies** has written *The Beatles: The Authorised Biography* (Heinemann, 1968) and *The Quarrymen* (Omnibus, 2001). He has edited *The Beatles Book* (Ebury, 2016).

Paddy Delaney was the doorman at the Cavern.

Debby Delmore is the daughter of Alton Delmore of the Delmore Brothers, one of the first great country harmony acts. They made 'Blues Stay Away From Me'.

Jackie DeShannon was a lively singer/songwriter who recorded the original versions of 'Needles and Pins' (written by Jack Nitzsche and Sonny Bono) and 'When You Walk in the Room' (written by Jackie).

Bruce Dickinson is part of Iron Maiden.

Barbara Dickson was an established folk singer, who crossed over with *John, Paul, George and Ringo...and Bert* and became one of the UK's top stars.

The comic and observational style of **Richard Digance** has given him both a family audience and a cult following.

Never say the years immediately before the Beatles were bland. We had **Dion** who had hits with 'Runaround Sue' (1961) and 'The Wanderer' (1962).

Ken Dodd is Liverpool's greatest comic talent, but he is just as likely to be remembered for his long-running court case for tax evasion. A tireless worker for charity.

Tymon Dogg, a unique singer-songwriter from Formby, recorded for Pye, Apple and Threshold as Timon.

Peter Doggett was the editor of *Record Collector* for many years and has written extensively about the Beatles. *There's a Riot Going On* (Canongate, 2007) is a brilliant study of the 60s counter-culture.

Seen as Scotland's answer to Bob Dylan, **Donovan** developed his own style and his many successes include 'Catch the Wind', 'Colours' and 'Sunshine Superman'.

Val Doonican is an Irish balladeer whose hits include 'Walk Tall' and 'Elusive Butterfly'.

London singer/ songwriter, **Charlie Dore** is best known for her US hit, 'Pilot of the Airwaves'.

Craig Douglas had a run of hits ('Only Sixteen', 'A Hundred Pounds of Clay'), which ended in 1963. When the former milkman was on tour with the Rolling Stones, they put an empty milk bottle outside his door with the message, "Two pints please."

Dr. John is one of the mainstays of New Orleans music.

Chris Dreja is one of the Yardbirds.

Artist, musician and iconoclast, **Bill Drummond** had chart success as part of KLF.

Music writer **Paul Du Noyer** is the author of a history of Liverpool music, aptly called *Wondrous Place* (2002).

Singer/ songwriter **Steve Earle** brought left wing politics to American country music.

Duane Eddy, the man with the Twangy Guitar, had a string of instrumental hits ('Peter Gunn', 'Yep!', 'Because They're Young') and once released an album called *The Biggest Twang of Them All*.

John Einarson is a Canadian academic, writing books on the Byrds and various aspects of his country's music.

Joe Elliott is Def Leppard's lead vocalist.

Beat poet **Royston Ellis** wrote one of the first rock books, *The Big Beat Scene* (1961), which has just been republished by Music Mentor.

Ray Ennis led the Swinging Blue Jeans.

Clive Epstein was Brian's brother and a director of NEMS. As he died in 1988, I can't claim that all the interviews in this book are recent.

Former member of the Clayton Squares and Liverpool Scene, **Mike Evans** has written *The Art of the Beatles* and several other books.

Adam Faith, one of Britain's top pop stars in the early 60s ('What do you Want', 'Poor Me'), found acting success in the title role of *Budgie*.

The mystique of **Marianne Faithfull** increases with the years and the influence of French and German cabaret permeates her work.

Georgie Fame has had three No.1s - 'Yeh Yeh', 'Getaway', 'The Ballad of Bonnie and Clyde'. Now often plays with Bill Wyman's Rhythm Kings.

One of the UK's top R&B vocalists, **Chris Farlowe** also restored and sold antiques. He topped the charts with 'Out of Time' in 1966.

Horst Fascher was the tough-minded manager of the Star-Club in Hamburg.

Liverpool artist and club owner, **Yankel Feather** was openly gay in the 1950s.

Musician and film director, **Mike Figgis** is best known for the Oscar-winning *Leaving Las Vegas* (1995).

Singing in a mixture of Spanish and English, **José Feliciano** became one of the most intense performers of the 60s.

Wayne Fontana fronted one of Manchester's top groups, Wayne

Fontana and the Mindbenders.

The American record producer and performer **Kim Fowley** was known as much for his eccentricity as his talent. Best known for discovering the Runaways.

Working as a solo performer and conceptual artist, **John Foxx** was the original lead singer of Ultravox.

Pete Frame is famed for his *Rock Family Trees*.

Roddy Frame was the founder and lead singer of Aztec Camera.

Alan Freeman or 'Fluff' presented *Pick of the Pops* and many other BBC programmes.

Steven Gaines wrote *The Love You Make* (Macmillan, 1983) with Peter Brown and a no-holds-barred view of the Beach Boys, *Heroes and Villains* (Macmillan, 1986).

Benny Gallagher was half of Gallagher and Lyle and now performs both solo and with the Manfreds.

Rory Gallagher, the Irish guitar hero, formed Taste and then led his own band.

BBC presenter **Paul Gambaccini** has an extraordinary musical knowledge, both popular and classical. Mention an old single and he'll tell you the catalogue number and the B-side.

Snuff Garrett was a producer for Liberty Records, making many hits with Bobby Vee.

Freddie Garrity led Freddie and the Dreamers.

Record producer and producer **Bob Gaudio** was part of the Four Seasons.

Lorne Gibson fronted Britain's leading pop-country band of the 60s, the Lorne Gibson Trio.

Singer, songwriter and actress **Dana Gillespie** fronts her own blues band.

Broadcaster **Charlie Gillett** wrote a definitive book about American record labels of the 50s and 60s, *The Sound of the City* as well as being a champion of world music.

Joel Glazier, believe it or not, lectured on the 'Paul is Dead' theory. Well, he is American.

Drummer **Kevin Godley** was in 10cc and later made rock videos with Lol Creme.

Andrew Gold is best known for his 1978 hit, 'Never Let Her Slip Away'.

Ron Goodwin was a conductor and film composer, his scores including *Where Eagles Dare* and *Those Magnificent Men in their Flying Machines*.

Songwriter **Graham Gouldman** was part of 10cc.

During the 1960s, **Bobby Graham** was a much-employed session drummer, playing on scores of hits.

Specialising in world music long before it was fashionable, **Davey Graham** developed his own guitar style.

Michael Gray is the author of several authoritative books on Bob Dylan, especially *Song and Dance Man*.

Buddy Greco is a jazz singer and pianist, best known for his swinging interpretation of 'The Lady Is a Tramp' (1960).

Roger Greenaway, songwriter and former member of the Kestrels, taught the world to sing in perfect harmony. Formed David and Jonathan with Roger Cook and had hits with 'Michelle' and 'Lovers of the World Unite' in 1966.

Mike Gregory was part of the Liverpool beat group, the Escorts.

Sid Griffin of the Long Ryders and the Coal Porters is an American music writer and musician based in the UK.

Broadcasting pundit and sauce manufacturer, **Loyd Grossman** was once a punk rocker.

Mick Groves was the Spinner most interested in chart music.

Country music star, **George Hamilton IV** has had success with 'Abilene', 'Early Mornin' Rain' and 'Break My Mind'.

Johnnie Hamp was a leading producer for Granada TV. His autobiography, *It Beats Working for a Living*, was published in 2008.

Neil Hannon is the writer and lead singer for the Divine Comedy. Their biggest hit was 'National Express' (1999) but don't forget the theme for *Father Ted*!

Colin Hanton is the Quarry Men's drummer: he's also an upholsterer and made an excellent job of our lounge suite.

Emmylou Harris is an American country star and everybody's favourite harmony singer.

Michael Haslam was signed by Brian Epstein but one of his singles was unfortunately titled 'There Goes the Forgotten Man'.

Steve Harley was the front man for Cockney Rebel.

Those early **Rolf Harris** hits, 'Tie Me Kangaroo Down, Sport' and 'Sun Arise', were produced by George Martin.

Louise Harrison is George Harrison's sister.

Bill Harry was the editor of the *Mersey Beat* newspaper.

Bill Hatton is a founder member of the Fourmost.

Singer/ songwriter **Richie Havens** made his name at Woodstock.

Ronnie Hawkins is Canada's most successful rock'n'roll star.

Adrian Henri was a poet, painter and founder member of Liverpool Scene.

Mike Heron was part of the Incredible String Band.

In 1994 journalist **Mark Hertsgaard** broke the story that Paul, George and Ringo were working together. He wrote *A Day in the Life: The Music and Artistry of the Beatles* (Macmillan, 1995).

Paolo Hewitt is a music writer particularly known for his work on mod culture – from the Small Faces to Paul Weller.

Nick Heyward was a member of Haircut 100 before opting for a solo career.

Tony Hicks has been the Hollies' lead guitarist since 1962.

Chas Hodges was a member of Cliff Bennett's Rebel Rousers but made his name in Chas and Dave.

In the middle of all the beat group mayhem, **Engelbert Humperdinck** became one of the UK's biggest solo stars.

Ian Hunter is the front man of Mott The Hoople.

Johnny Hutchinson was the drummer with the Big Three.

In 1989, **Brian Hyland** was asked to ring a British newspaper because 'Sealed with a Kiss' was back in the charts. They forgot to say it wasn't his version.

Frank Ifield topped the charts with 'I Remember You' (1962), 'Lovesick Blues' (1962), 'The Wayward Wind' (1963) and 'Confessin'' (1963).

Neil Innes was part of the Bonzo Dog Band and had the John Lennon role in the Rutles. Catch his live shows: his introductions are superb.

Tony Jackson was in the Searchers until 1964.

"Don't call me a disc jockey" **David Jacobs** presented *Juke Box Jury*.

Tommy James led Tommy James and the Shondells and had a UK No.1 with 'Mony Mony' in 1968.

Liverpool country performer **Kenny Johnson** was Sonny Webb in Sonny Webb and the Cascades.

Actress **Sue Johnston** used to work for Brian Epstein in NEMS. Especially known for playing Sheila Grant in *Brookside*.

The late **Davy Jones** called his autobiography *They Made a Monkee out of Me*.

Hughie Jones was the Spinner most interested in songwriting. Still hosts a weekly folk club at the Everyman in Liverpool.

Paul Jones was the front man for Manfred Mann.

Music journalist **Norman Jopling** wrote for *Record Mirror*.

John Jorgenson was a member of the Hellecasters and the Desert

Rose Band and played in Elton John's band for six years. Now has the bluegrass band J2B2. Check out his Django-styled arrangement of 'Man of Mystery'.

Laurence Juber is a session guitarist and former member of Wings

Vic Juris is a noted American jazz guitarist.

Theatre director **Hereward K** was also in the Flying Pickets.

Larry Kane is the American news reporter who wrote of his experiences with the Beatles in *Ticket to Ride* and also wrote a book about John Lennon's childhood experiences.

Carol Kaye was a member of the Kaye Sisters.

Nigel Kennedy is one of the world's leading violinists.

Mark Kermode is known for his highly opinionated film reviews.

Songwriter **Richard Kerr** wrote 'Mandy'.

Barney Kessel was the world's foremost jazz guitarist. Innumerable guitarists cite him as an influence. He was also a superlative speaker, able to go for hours without saying 'you know' or 'I mean'.

B.B. King is the king of the blues guitar.

Ben E. King has had hits with the Drifters ('Save the Last Dance for Me') and as a solo artist ('Spanish Harlem', 'Stand by Me'). He wrote 'Stand by Me'.

Billy Kinsley is a member of the Merseybeats and Liverpool Express.

Graham Knight was part of a reasonably successful band, Dean Ford and the Gaylords. His manager was having breakfast and realised the band's new name was staring him in the face – Marmalade.

Liverpool singer **Billy J. Kramer** was backed by the Manchester group, the Dakotas.

Denny Laine is a former member of the Moody Blues and Wings. He wrote 'Mull of Kintyre' with Paul McCartney.

With his bellowing voices and songs like 'Jezebel' and 'I Believe', **Frankie Laine** was one of the 1950s biggest stars.

Judd Lander was with the Liverpool band, the Hideaways, and later played harmonica for Culture Club and the Spice Girls.

In the end, **Pete Langford** was the only original member left in the Barron Knights.

Syd Lawrence was an orchestra leader, primarily known for recreating Glenn Miller's sound.

Cynthia Lennon married John Lennon in August 1962 and was granted a divorce in November 1968.

Bunny Lewis wrote many 50s pop hits and managed Craig Douglas,

David Jacobs and Jimmy Savile.

Mark Lewisohn is the world's leading authority on the Beatles, except possibly Paul McCartney and Ringo Starr themselves.

Gordon Lightfoot is a Canadian singer/ songwriter best known for 'Sundown' and 'If You Could Read My Mind'.

Andy Linehan is Curator of Popular Music at the British Library Sound Archive on Euston Road.

Dennis Locorriere is the former lead singer of Dr. Hook.

Nils Lofgren is a singer/songwriter who has played in Bruce Springsteen's band.

Jackie Lomax, the lead singer of the Liverpool band the Undertakers, was signed to Apple as a solo performer.

Graham Lyle was part of Gallagher and Lyle. He won a Grammy for writing Tina Turner's hit, 'What's Love Got to Do with It?'

Kenny Lynch had several successful singles in the early 60s and toured with the Beatles.

Humphrey Lyttelton, trumpeter, broadcaster and host of *I'm Sorry I Haven't a Clue*.

Eamonn McCabe is an award winning sports photographer. Before he gave a lecture in Liverpool, I confronted him with the Beatles' album sleeves and said, 'What do you think of these photographs?' His answers, straight off the cuff, were fascinating.

Singer/ songwriter **Scott McCarl** has been in the Raspberries.

Paul's brother, **Mike McCartney** was a member of Scaffold.

Delbert McClinton played harmonica on 'Hey! Baby'.

Country Joe McDonald is famed for his Fish cheer at Woodstock.

Chas McDevitt had a skiffle hit with 'Freight Train' in 1957 and he is skiffling away to this day.

Mark McGann is one of four successful McGanns, the others being Paul, Joe and Stephen.

As a poet and member of Scaffold, **Roger McGough** has shown his remarkable wordplay.

Roger McGuinn was the leader of the Byrds.

Tom McKenzie was the compère for several of the Beatles' early appearances outside of Liverpool, particularly in Northwich.

Ian McLagen was from the Small Faces and latterly played with Billy Bragg's band.

Pete Maclaine was the Dakotas' lead singer before Billy J. Kramer.

Ian McNabb is a compelling stage performer, both on his own and with The Icicle Works.

John McNally was, still is and always will be a member of the Searchers.

Ralph McTell has written 'Streets of London' and many other poignant songs. He recorded 'Penny Lane' on his album, *At the End of a Perfect Day* (Telstar, 1985).

Ron Mael is the brother with the moustache in Sparks.

Rex Makin is a Liverpool solicitor who was a neighbour of the Epsteins.

Raul Malo led the Mavericks.

Colin Manley was a member of the Remo Four in the 60s and then toured with the Swinging Blue Jeans.

Fred Marsden was the drummer with Gerry and the Pacemakers.

The American rock journalist **Dave Marsh** wrote the highly opinionated *The Heart of Rock and Soul - The 1001 Greatest Singles Ever Made* (Penguin, 1989). The first entry for the Beatles was 'Ticket to Ride' at No.29.

Neville Marten, who tours with Marty Wilde, writes about guitars.

George Martin was the Beatles' record producer. His autobiography, *All You Need is Ears*, was published by Macmillan in 1979.

Barry Mason is a lyricist best known for 'The Last Waltz' and 'Delilah'.

Joe Massot directed *Wonderwall* (1968) and *The Song Remains The Same* (1976).

Dave Mattacks is a noted session drummer, best known for his time in Fairport Convention.

Brian Matthew presented *Saturday Club* in the 60s and *Sounds of the Sixties* today.

Huey P. Meaux produced the Big Bopper's 'Chantilly Lace', Johnny Preston's 'Running Bear' and many country hits for Freddy Fender.

Social commentator, jazz singer and proud Liverpudlian, **George Melly** wrote *Revolt into Style* (Penguin, 1970), one of the first books to analyse youth culture.

Drummer **Colin Middlebrough** was with the Jaywalkers and the Kansas City Five.

During the 60s, **Barry Miles** ran the trendy Indica bookshop in London, knew the Beatles well and has often written about his experiences. Recommended: *In the Sixties* (Jonathan Cape, 2002).

Gordon Millings worked for his father, Dougie, tailor to the stars.

Liverpool musician **Joey Molland** is a member of Badfinger.

Chris Montez took 'Let's Dance' to No.2 in 1962. He told me, "Elvis may have been the King of Rock'n'Roll, but Ritchie Valens was the hero on my block."

Paul Morley wrote cutting-edge journalism for the *NME* in the late 70s, promoted Frankie Goes To Hollywood and is now a media commentator.

Harry Moss was an EMI recording engineer.

As well as 'How Do You Do It', **Mitch Murray** wrote 'By the Way' (Big Three), 'I'm Telling You Now', 'You Were Made for Me' (both Freddie and the Dreamers), 'The Ballad of Bonnie and Clyde' (Georgie Fame) and 'Goodbye Sam, Hello Samantha' (Cliff Richard).

Frank Musker has written 'Too Much Love Will Kill You', 'Modern Girl' and 'Senza Una Donna'.

Graham Nash was in the Hollies and then Crosby, Stills and Nash.

Nasher or Brian Nash played guitar in Frankie Goes To Hollywood.

In 1972 **Bill Nelson** formed the prog rock band, Be-Bop Deluxe.

Naturally, I interviewed **Willie Nelson** on his bus. Does this man even have a home?

Cyril Neville is part of the Neville Brothers.

Once a pop star, **Paul Nicholas** appears in touring and West End musicals.

Simon Nicol has spent his adult life in Fairport Convention.

Film critic **Barry Norman** – and why not?

Geoff Nugent was with the Liverpool band, the Undertakers. Amazing that you can make a career from the phrase, "Mashed potato, yeah!"

Peter Noone aka Herman, led Manchester's Hermits to a succession of Top 10 hits in the 60s.

Film producer **Denis O'Dell** worked on *A Hard Day's Night*, *The Magic Christian* and the much maligned *Heaven's Gate*.

Brian O'Hara was lead singer with the Fourmost.

Sean O'Mahony, also known as Johnny Dean, was the founder of *Record Collector* and *The Beatles Book*.

Gilbert O'Sullivan had No.1 records with 'Clair' and 'Get Down', but 'Alone Again (Naturally)' is the hit we remember best.

Earl Okin is a singer, songwriter and comedian.

Although younger than the group (he was born in 1944), **Andrew Loog Oldham** managed the Rolling Stones.

Roy Orbison became Lefty Wilbury and joined George Harrison in the Traveling Wilburys.

Always a prolific writer, **Alun Owen** wrote the TV play *No Trams to*

Lime Street and the film script, *A Hard Day's Night*.

Tony Palmer is a filmmaker, often biographies of classical musicians, but he has also made *All My Loving* (1968), *200 Motels* (1971) and the TV series, *All You Need Is Love* (1977).

May Pang worked for John and Yoko and became his girlfriend in the mid-70s.

Alan Parsons, recording engineer with the Beatles, who formed the Alan Parsons Project.

Tom Paxton wrote 'The Last Thing on My Mind' and a perceptive song about John Lennon, 'Crazy John'.

George Peckham was a member of the Fourmost and became a cutting engineer. Porky's Prime Cuts, anyone?

Dave Pegg plays bass with Fairport Convention.

Carl Perkins was a rock'n'roll performer with Sun Records, noted for 'Blue Suede Shoes' and 'Matchbox'.

John Phillips was a member of the Mamas and the Papas and their chief songwriter.

The American star, **Gene Pitney** had his biggest hits during Beatlemania.

Ken Pitt managed Manfred Mann and the young David Bowie.

Brian Poole and the Tremeloes took 'Twist and Shout' to No.4 in 1963 and followed it with a No.1, 'Do You Love Me'.

Duffy Power is a much underrated Larry Parnes artist, but then Parnes never understood the blues.

Dory Previn is an American singer-songwriter, whose albums include *Mary C. Brown and the Hollywood Sign* and *Mythical Kings and Iguanas*. Many of her early film songs were written with her then husband, André Previn.

Alan Price used to be an Animal, but he seems very civilised now.

Filmmaker, author and researcher **Dominic Priore** specialises on 60s west coast sounds and wrote *Riot on Sunset Strip* (Jawbone, 2007).

P.J. Proby is an American performer who came to the UK for a TV special, *Around the Beatles*. He could have been as big as Tom Jones but the gremlins inside him messed it up.

Peter Prichard is a theatrical agent, long associated with the Royal Variety Performance. He took Mario Lanza out for a meal and Lanza ate seven whole chickens.

Full of integrity, **Bonnie Raitt** is a great blues rock guitarist and singer.

Mike Ramsden was part of Silkie, who recorded 'You've Got to Hide Your Love Away'.

Chris Rea is driving home for Christmas.

Pianist and composer **Les Reed** wrote many of his hit songs with Barry Mason including 'The Last Waltz' and 'Delilah'.

Shirley Alston Reeves was the lead singer of the Shirelles.

The 50s balladeer **Joan Regan** had hits with 'If I Give My Heart to You' and 'May You Always'.

Charlie Reid is one of the Proclaimers.

Robert Reynolds was one of the Mavericks and often plays with Kevin Montgomery.

Tim Rice has been knighted for his contribution to musical theatre.

Buddy Rich was noted as much for his forceful views as his drumming, so don't be dismayed Ringo, he's paying you a compliment.

Like George Martin, **Wally Ridley** was an EMI producer. Wally produced the Swinging Blue Jeans, Johnny Kidd and opera singers for HMV.

Jason Ringenberg is the leader of Jason and the Scorchers as well as the children's TV character, Farmer Jason.

Harry Robinson was Lord Rockingham.

Mick Rock is a rock photographer, noted for pictures of David Bowie, Queen and Pink Floyd.

Tommy Roe had hits with Sheila', 'The Folksinger' and 'Dizzy'.

Biographer **Johnny Rogan** had written about John Lennon, the Byrds and Morrissey. His book on rock managers *Starmakers and Svengalis* (Queen Anne Press, 1988) is both witty and highly informative.

Jeff Alan Ross is an American singer/ songwriter who now runs Peter Asher's touring band.

Norman Rossington was a Liverpool character who appeared as Cupcake in *The Army Game* and Norm in *A Hard Day's Night*.

Peter Rowan is an American bluegrass star.

Johnny Russell is a country music songwriter, who gave 'Act Naturally' to Buck Owens but also sang it himself.

Willy Russell is a Liverpool playwright, whose credits include *John, Paul, George, Ringo...and Bert*, *Educating Rita* and *Shirley Valentine*.

Chris Salewicz wrote *McCartney - The Biography* (Queen Anne Press, 1986).

The late **Mike Sammes** ran, would you believe, the Mike Sammes Singers. I met him at the time of his autobiography, *Backing into the Limelight* (Book Guild, 1994) and my abiding memory is that he had the biggest hands I had ever seen.

Ric Sanders plays violin for Fairport Convention.

Tony Sanders was in Billy J. Kramer's first group, the Coasters:

The highly perceptive music writer **Jon Savage** is best known for his study of punk, *England's Dreaming* (Faber and Faber, 1992).

Jimmy Savile presented *Top of the Pops* and ran the *Teen and Twenty Disc Club* on Radio Luxembourg and is now totally discredited.

Leo Sayer had a long run of hits in the 70s including 'You Make Me Feel like Dancing' and 'When I Need You'.

Alexei Sayle is a Liverpool-born comedian and novelist.

Want the Lowdown on **Boz Scaggs**? His UK Top 20 hits are 'What Can I Say' and 'Lido Shuffle'.

John Sebastian led the Lovin' Spoonful. His stoned ramblings at Woodstock are the highlight of the film.

Pete Seeger is the most legendary of all folk singers, the man who created 'Where Have All the Flowers Gone?', 'Guantanamera' and 'Turn! Turn! Turn!'

Ron Sexsmith is a Canadian singer/ songwriter with several albums to his name.

Del Shannon scored with forceful beat-ballads ('Runaway', 'Little Town Flirt', 'Keep Searchin'') between 1961 and 1965.

Helen Shapiro had her first hit, 'Don't Treat Me like a Child', in 1961 at the age of 14 and she followed it with two No.1's, 'You Don't Know' and 'Walkin' Back to Happiness'.

Stu Shea wrote and complied *Fab Four FAQ* (Hal Leonard, 2007) with Robert Rodriguez.

John Sheppard made the television documentary to celebrate the anniversary of *Sgt. Pepper; It Was 20 Years Ago Today*.

Tony Sheridan is an uninhibited, British rock'n'roller, who played with the Beatles in Hamburg.

Pete Shotton was John Lennon's childhood friend.

Stu Slater was the lead singer of the Mojos.

P F Sloan wrote 'Eve of Destruction', a 1965 hit for Barry McGuire.

Recording engineer **Mike Smith** made the worst business decision of all-time – he turned the Beatles down at Decca. Not to worry, he produced hits for Billy Fury, the Bachelors, the Tremeloes and Georgie Fame.

Another **Mike Smith** was the lead vocalist and keyboards for the Dave Clark Five.

EMI music historian and author, **Brian Southall** has written several books including *Northern Songs: The True Story of the Beatles Song Publishing Empire* (Omnibus, 2006) and, in 2015, the first biography of the Hollies.

A delight to meet, **Victor Spinetti** appeared in *A Hard Days Night*, *Help!* and *Magical Mystery Tour.*

Bob Spitz wrote *Dylan - A Biography* (Michael Joseph, 1988) and *The Beatles – A Biography* (Little, Brown, 2005).

Sam Spoons was in the Bonzo Dog Band.

Bob Stanley from Saint Etienne and music critic of *The Times*:

Viv Stanshall was the anarchist leader (if that's not a contradiction in terms) of the Bonzo Dog Band.

Alvin Stardust ('My Coo-Ca-Choo', 1973) was once Shane Fenton ('I'm a Moody Guy', 1961).

David Stark is the editor of *Songlink International*, a tip sheet for songwriters and music publishers.

After writing an excellent book about 60s television in America, *Glued to the Set*, **Steven Stark** wrote a study of gender issues in the Beatles' cultural history, *Meet the Beatles* (HarperCollins, 2005).

Freddie Starr sang with several Liverpool bands in the 60s including Howie Casey and the Seniors. He parodies many singers including Adam Faith, Ray Charles, Johnny Mathis and Elvis Presley ("When I was a lad, Old Shep was a frog").

Being a sculptor and a novelist, **Tommy Steele** is even more than an all-round entertainer.

David Stein is an American agent and manager, trained by Sid Bernstein and having success with the Bay City Rollers.

Eric Stewart was part of 10cc and also wrote songs with Paul McCartney.

John Stewart wrote 'Daydream Believer' and 'Gold'.

Now mostly a jazz performer, **Curtis Stigers** had his biggest hits in 1992 with 'I Wonder Why' and 'You're All That Matters To Me'. He said to me, "Spencer Leigh is a really cool name, you sound like a blues singer" so thanks to my parents for that.

Singer/ songwriter **Jake Stigers** is the brother of Curtis.

Alan Sytner was the original owner of the Cavern.

Sylvain Sylvain is a member of the New York Dolls.

Garry Tamlyn is an Australian academic specialising in drumming technique.

Alistair Taylor was first Brian Epstein's assistant and then General Manager of Apple. He was the Beatles' 'Mr. Fixit' and his memoirs,

Yesterday – The Beatles Remembered, was published by Sidgwick and Jackson in 1988

The dry humour of **Jake Thackray** is a feature of such skilfully crafted songs as 'Lah-Di-Dah' and 'Sister Josephine'.

Richard Thompson is a superlative singer, guitarist and songwriter, starting with Fairport Convention and then having an impressive career of his own.

Elizabeth Thomson is the co-editor of *The Lennon Companion* (Macmillan, 1987) and *The Dylan Companion* (Macmillan, 1990), both with David Gutman.

Without doubt **Billy Bob Thornton** is the coolest person I've met, although you could argue that a really cool guy wouldn't be talking to someone from local radio.

George Thorogood rocks with his bluesy band, the Destroyers.

Tony Thorpe has been a member of the Rubettes ('Sugar Baby Love') and the Firm ('Arthur Daley, 'E's Alright').

John Tobler is a noted British rock journalist. Pete Frame once wrote that he had three copies of every record released, two of them shrink-wrapped!

Peter Tork was a member of the Monkees.

Paul Trynka is a *Mojo* writer and editor of their lavish book on the Beatles.

Steve Turner is the author of several music books including *The Gospel According to the Beatles (Westminster John Knox, 2006).*

Jimmy Tushingham took Ringo Starr's place (and wore his suit!) in Rory Storm and the Hurricanes.

One of Liverpool's first pop stars, **Frankie Vaughan** is remembered for 'Tower of Strength', 'Green Door' and naturally, 'Give Me the Moonlight'.

Liverpool comic **Norman Vaughan** was one of the hosts for *Sunday Night at the London Palladium.*

It's a Wonderful Life for **Colin Vearncombe,** who is the lead singer of Black.

'Take Good Care of My Baby', the **Bobby Vee** hit from 1961, was often performed by the Beatles with George as vocalist.

One of the many Bobbys in the early 60s (BobbyVee, Bobby Rydell and Bobby Darin being among the others), **Bobby Vinton** had a UK No.2 with 'Blue Velvet' in 1990.

Jürgen Vollmer is a German photographer who met the Beatles in Hamburg.

Artist and bass player, **Klaus Voormann** designed the cover for *Revolver*.

Loudon Wainwright is a unique songwriter. Who else has a repertoire of songs about dead skunks, suicide, vampires, bees and doggy do?

Rick Wakeman is not as grumpy as his TV image would have you believe: he says Yes as much as no.

Gary Walker was one of the Walker Brothers.

Martyn Ware is a founder member of both Human League and Heaven 17.

Some claim that **Jimmy Webb** was the best songwriter of the 60s. Others think that 'MacArthur Park' was the worst song of the 60s.

Julian Lloyd Webber is a gifted cello player (*Variations*) and Andrew's brother.

Sonny West wrote 'Oh Boy!' and 'Rave On', both of which were recorded by Buddy Holly.

Jerry Wexler was a key producer for Atlantic Records.

Alan White was in the Plastic Ono Band but made his name in Yes.

Tony Joe White wrote 'Polk Salad Annie' and 'Rainy Night In Georgia'.

Marty Wilde, father of Kim, had UK successes with cover versions of 'Endless Sleep', 'Donna' and 'A Teenager in Love'. He wrote his 1959 hit, 'Bad Boy', himself, a rarity for that period. Still a great performer.

Aaron Williams was a member of the Merseybeats.

Edgar Winter is one of the best white blues musicians.

Mark Wirtz wrote and produced 'Excerpt from a Teenage Opera', a Top 10 hit for Keith West in 1967.

Johnny Worth wrote 'What Do You Want?' and 'Poor Me' (both Adam Faith) and 'Well I Ask You' (Eden Kane).

Formerly of Soft Machine, **Robert Wyatt** recorded the best political song since the heady days of Bob Dylan, 'Shipbuilding' in 1983.

John York was a member of the Byrds.

INDEX